VICTORIA HALE

The Girl in the Red Polka Dot Dress

authorHOUSE®

AuthorHouse™
1663 Liberty Drive
Bloomington, IN 47403
www.authorhouse.com
Phone: 1 (800) 839-8640

Published by AuthorHouse 03/30/2015

ISBN: 978-1-4969-7384-9 (sc)
ISBN: 978-1-4969-7383-2 (e)

Library of Congress Control Number: 2015903542

Print information available on the last page.

Contents

BOOK 3

BOOK 4

BOOK 5

Preface

A few years ago, I attended my high school reunion in Hawaii. I was amazed at the number of people in attendance, since my high school is located in Jamaica, West Indies. It was exhilarating to see the old familiar faces again, the faces that appear in my dreams from time to time, when I'm missing the carefree capriciousness of youth. I confess that I was taken aback that my contemporaries seemed as old as they did. I am surrounded by seniors, I thought wistfully. When I came home, I looked at the photographs we took and was surprised to see an old woman wearing the same dress that I wore, making the same expressions I made. She seemed to fit right in with that senior crowd, but she looked happy. Free. Despite the years I have lived, and the subsequent addition of wrinkles and grays, I am comfortable in the skin that I am in. I no longer fear the future, and more importantly, I've learned to forgive myself for the missteps I've made in the past.

Every now and then, I come face to face with the simple, undeniable fact that I have already lived the majority of my life. While I know that tomorrow is promised to no one, I am also acutely aware that I have fewer 'tomorrows' than 'yesterdays'. So I do not feed into the delusion of considering myself 'middle-aged'; how could I possibly be, since I am fairly certain I will not live to be one hundred and twenty years old? Even though that stark reality stares me in the face, day after day, I am not afraid. I tried to obliterate my tomorrows at one point, when my experiences in the wilderness became unbearable. To which God replied, "Not yet, my child; there's more work for you to do." And so I prevail. My regrets are many, but even so, the lessons and the rewards derived from my foibles helped to make me stronger in the end.

The most authentic thing about us, is our capacity to create, to overcome, to endure, to transform, to love and to be greater than our suffering…Ben Okri

BOOK 1

In The Beginning

CHAPTER 1

I stare dispassionately at my wrist, doing my best to ignore the pungent odor in the police van that threatens to make me gag. I try to cover my scars with the sleeves of my green sweatshirt, but my hand is cuffed to the inmate next to me. If only I could hold my breath for the next fifteen minutes, I think I'd be fine. Maybe I cannot blot out the noise around me, but I can certainly close my eyes and pretend that I am somewhere else, anywhere else.

The van jolts as it hits a pothole and we all sway in unison, as if our movements are choreographed. I keep my eyes tightly shut, resisting the impulse to look at anyone around me. Less than three months ago I was the vice-president of a major corporation, managing a team of almost fifty people. Today, my expensive St. John suit has been substituted for a pair of drab green denim slacks and a matching dingy sweatshirt...jail attire. I know for sure that my hair is completely grey; I have not been to the beauty parlor in months. How did I get here? *How did I get here?* I ask myself the same question, over and over. My mind supplies the county prosecutor's words in response. His voice rings endlessly in my ears, like a song you can't get out of your head. *Victoria Hale is formally charged with attempted murder, aggravated assault; possession of a weapon for an unlawful purpose; unlawful possession of a weapon; and two counts of burglary. Attempted murder...assault...burglary...attempted murder...*

And then, the refrain: *If found guilty, the penalty for all these charges could be more than forty years in prison.*

My story began in Jamaica, West Indies just over sixty years ago, I was born "under the clock" at Victoria Jubilee Hospital in the capital city of Kingston. My mother assured me that being born in Kingston was something significant. "You are a Kingstonian," she said, "and you should be very proud of that fact." In the 1960's, Kingstonians were reputedly more 'enlightened' than 'country' folks. Naturally, since I cannot recall the momentous occasion of my birth, I will attempt to relate my earliest memories.

I must have been about four years old, because my youngest sibling, Douglas, was still an infant. The memory is almost like a dream, but several things stand out in my mind. I saw a man we called Black Bwoy in the midst of a small gathering with one hand over his ear. There might have been blood on his hand – although I couldn't be sure – but I did hear someone in the crowd crying. Black Bwoy had inadvertently kicked dirt onto my brother's reusable cotton diapers that my mother had placed on a sheet of zinc to bleach white in the sun. When she discovered what he did, she grabbed a nearby scrubbing board and hit him over the head, knocking off his ear. Many years later, when I asked my mother about the incident, after voicing her disbelief that I could recall this 'minor' perturbation, she explained that she *may* have hit Black Bwoy, however, his ear was not completely severed.

To say that my mother was a colorful character is an understatement. I went through life with a love/hate relationship with her, mainly because of her drinking problem that escalated over the years. Not only did she drink heavily, she was a mean drunk, and I took on the brunt of her angst and anger. As I got older, the hate slowly dissipated and love blossomed – love that I hesitantly gave, mainly because she was my mother, but more so because she was my grandmother's daughter, and I loved my grandmother more than anything else in the world.

Admittedly, I also loved her because she had a good heart – when she was sober, of course. My mother is one of the most generous and enigmatic people I have ever known. She rarely places much value on material possessions for herself, but gives whatever she has to anyone in need. However, if you were unlucky enough to cross her when she was intoxicated, that same generosity went through the window, and one would be forced to return any and all gifts that were previously bestowed.

It took many years for me to admit to myself that I loved her, and that realization did not happen overnight; rather, it began to unfold when I was a teenager, and only when we connected in a way that neither of us could have imagined in a million years. But until then, we did not have a traditional mother/daughter relationship.

I had always lived with my maternal grandparents, Granny and Papa, and my first home was in a tenement yard. The yard, the people, and our home: those memories are indelibly etched in my mind.

"Remember this address, just in case you ever get lost," my grandmother constantly told me.

Each Saturday, our landlords, Mr. McGregor (or Mr. Mack, as we called him) and his wife, Miss Ruby, came by to collect their rent from all the tenants. It was not an unusual occurrence to see some of the tenants hiding from the landlords because they were not able to produce the rent money for that week. Mr. Mack was a big man. He seemed larger than life to me and one could sense his importance when he sauntered proudly around his property, always dressed in white from head to toe.

It was a large yard with several wooden structures that housed the tenants. The communal bathroom was a small lean-to shed with a shower, and there was also a scary outhouse in a small, dilapidated building nearby. For personal convenience each family owned a chamber pot, or 'chimmey', for nighttime use since there was no electricity in the outhouse. Some adults preferred to light their paths to the outhouse with a small aluminum lamp, fondly referred to as a 'kitchen bitch'. Our kitchen was a much larger shed where the women set up sections for their family's daily cooking. The stoves were coal pots that were placed on a large concrete slab next to a small basin for washing dishes. There were no refrigerators. There was a common stand-pipe in the middle of the yard for us to fetch water for cooking and laundry. The pipe always leaked. I remember that clearly, because one of our daily activities was to run around in the mud with our bare feet. Despite being very poor, our home and the surroundings were always clean. "Cleanliness is next to Godliness," was my grandmother's mantra. It was a good life, I felt, since at that time I knew of none other, and I was a reasonably happy child. My grandmother made sure that I was never hungry and that was pretty much what happiness meant to me.

My family consisted of the members from my mother's side only. I remember overhearing a family member remark one day that I was an 'orphant' (orphan). I did not know what that meant, but I knew instinctively that it was a bad thing. My mother also informed me at one point, "Yu no 'ave no fada,' and that made me sad even though I did not know why I needed one. I figured out eventually that there was a correlation between being an 'orphant' and not having a 'fada'. I did not like missing out on something that everyone else seemed to have, but I was comforted that I had Granny and Papa, my Uncles Bobby and Tony, and my Auntie Patsy and her family. Surprisingly, I did not think that I 'had' my mother because I was not quite sure of her role in the family, plus I was very scared of her. As a matter of fact, so was everyone else.

At some point I learned that the woman I was scared of, this Auntie Enid, was my mother. She was Auntie Enid to my older cousins, and since no one told me differently, that was what I called her, and still do to this day. Soon after the incident involving Black Bwoy, she and her husband, Mr. Milton moved away, and they took my sister, Sonia, who was two years old, and the infant, Douglas with them. I was left with Granny and Papa and the rest of the family.

One missing member of our clan was Auntie Yvonne, who was my mother's older sister. She went to Cuba in 1951 and eventually moved to the United States a few years later. Our family was very proud of her because she was living in the fairy tale land called America. From time to time we would overhear our elders reverently telling stories about her, and as a result, she became an iconic symbol of success in all the children's eyes. So much so, that every time we heard an airplane in the distance, we dropped everything, ran outside and tried to follow its path, yelling as loudly as we could, "Auntie Yvonne plane! Auntie Yvonne plane!" until it was out of sight. We truly believed our Auntie Yvonne owned all the planes in the sky.

Many years later I was tickled when my own nieces unwittingly followed that same tradition. Since I was the first in my immediate family to go to the United States, they too thought I owned the planes. They, along with their friends, followed each plane's path yelling, "Auntie Grace plane! Auntie Grace plane!" It was a source of pride for me when I heard that, because it brought back fond memories of my childhood.

In the late nineteen fifties, as was customary, my Auntie Yvonne 'sent for' Uncle Tony to join her in the United States. I remember seeing my Uncle Bobby unabashedly crying as he helped to take his brother's suitcases to the car. The entire family went to the airport that day except the younger kids and me. I found out that going to the airport was a major event for everyone; so of course I watched from the sideline as the grownups, dressed in their very best clothes – the men in suits and the women in colorful dresses, hats and gloves, prepared for the journey. I looked at them longingly as they piled in the few cars that were available. They all went to the airport, only to return later without the lucky person who had left the clan. It made no sense to me that everyone seemed happy whenever someone left, but they would spend the subsequent days and even weeks crying because that person was gone.

Even though I was not happy to see my uncle leave, I wished with all my heart that I could have gone go to this place called the 'airport', or even just go for a ride in a car. I did not want anyone to leave our family, but it seemed to be the only way I would ever get to ride in a car, and so I was willing to make the sacrifice. I knew also that I was too young at the time to occupy a valuable seat on that journey, so I waited patiently for the day to come when someone else was scheduled to leave. Hopefully I'd be old enough by then to warrant a seat. Since no one in our family owned a car, we did not have the luxury of simply going for rides whenever we wanted. Up to that point in my life, I had no recollection of ever being in a car.

My dream came to fruition just over a year later when my Aunt Yvonne finally 'sent for' Uncle Bobby. It took weeks of preparation for the family and me. Auntie Patsy made me a red and white taffeta, polka-dot dress with a crinoline attached, and my grandmother bought me a pair of white socks, black shoes, and an enormous red ribbon for my hair. It didn't matter to me at that point that my uncle was leaving, because all I wanted was the opportunity to wear my new clothes and ride in a car to the airport.

On the fateful day of my uncle's departure, after I got dressed, my grandmother applied the usual petroleum jelly to my arms and legs while I fidgeted impatiently. She then applied the usual Ponds body powder to my face. I couldn't wait to see myself in the 'looking glass'.

"You look like new money," my grandmother said proudly, and I was thrilled beyond belief.

I twirled around until I was dizzy, watching my dress fan out like the princess that I felt I was. Since we did not have a full length mirror, at every opportunity I'd look down at my dress marveling at how pretty I looked, ignoring my grandmother's fussing.

"Pickney, stop look down pon yuself," she scolded, but I couldn't stop because I wanted to remember that beautiful dress forever.

My entire family and a few of our closest friends crammed into the three or four cars that were available to us, and we finally made our way to Palisadoes International Airport. The ride seemed to take forever, even though it must have lasted just over half an hour. My cousins and I were ecstatic when we saw the beach for the first time as we drove down Windward Road toward the airport. I could hardly contain myself. When we arrived, I was even more fascinated by the unusual faces milling about. Some people were crying while others were welcoming friends or family; and of course, there were many tourists who had come to bask in the sunshine and lose themselves in the enchantment of our beautiful little island.

I followed everyone to the waving gallery upstairs, and looked in awe at the enormous planes with the BOAC and PANAM logos proudly displayed in bold letters. These planes could not possibly fly in the air, I thought, and furthermore, they could not be my Auntie Yvonne's tiny planes that we waved at in the sky. I had so many questions but I was too excited and overwhelmed to find the words to ask them. I suppose that was when the third wish surfaced in my mind: I wished I could go inside one of those planes. One day I will, I vowed, as I watched excitedly as the passengers began to board.

"Can you see him?"

"No, that's not him."

"Oh, there he is!" someone yelled, and we broke out in a loud cheer.

Like the other passengers, he turned and looked up at the waving gallery. We all waved frantically as we yelled our goodbyes. When he finally waved back at us we all cried with joy. At that point it finally made sense to me that even though I was the happiest I had ever been in my life, I was equally sad because my uncle was leaving. I looked back at my grandmother and saw her dabbing her eyes with her handkerchief, and so I walked over to her and held on to the side of her dress in a silent demonstration of comfort. She patted my head understandingly, and I stayed by her side until we were ready to leave. In my mind I thought we'd never see my Uncle Bobby again. After all, neither Auntie Yvonne nor Uncle Tony returned home. I felt a deeper sense of sadness then.

There were many firsts for me that day: the first time I rode in a car, the first time I saw my grandmother cry, the first time I saw a plane up close, and the first time I saw the beach; but best of all, it was my first time wearing the pretty red and white polka-dot dress. Although it was difficult saying goodbye to my uncle, life as we knew it continued when we got back home.

Auntie Patsy and her husband, Daddy Henry, moved away from the family yard soon after Uncle Bobby left. They had outgrown their tiny place because their fourth child had arrived. They rented a two-room mobile home with a large verandah about a mile away. There were fewer families living in their new yard, the rooms were much larger, and so they had more room to accommodate their growing family. Even though my brother and sister visited often, I felt very lonely because it seemed as though all my playmates had deserted me.

Not long after they moved, Granny, Papa, and I left Spanish Town Road as well, but for some reason we did not remain at any place for a very long time. I remember us moving four or five times in a very short period, but we stayed in the vicinity of our original home. It was only after my aunt and uncle purchased an enormous home on nearby Moore Street that we were able to settle for a while. My aunt rented each of the rooms to different families, while they continued to occupy the mobile home that they had moved over on a truck. I found it fascinating to watch the men load the house on a flatbed truck. I recall thinking that the house would fall and break into a million pieces, but it did not. After their sixth child arrived, they moved into two of the five rooms in the big house and rented their original place to two additional families. I was nine years old when we moved in with my aunt and uncle and stayed until I turned fourteen.

Early Lesson

CHAPTER 2

When I was around seven years old, the rose colored glasses with which I viewed the world began to taint. We had not yet moved to Moore Street, and I was beginning to realize how modest a lifestyle we had. In other words, I began to notice that some people had much more material things than others. We were the 'others' who had less, and even though I was not overly bothered by that fact, I wanted toys! I did not know then that my grandmother depended entirely on my grandfather's meager pension and a small monthly check that she received from my Uncle Tony for the family's support; but I knew that his familiar airmail envelope with the green ink was eagerly anticipated each month. At seven years old, there was a limit to the sacrifices I was willing to make. I wanted a doll! Not only did I want a doll more than anything in the world, I wanted a doll with real hair that I could comb. My grandmother was well aware of this, because I reminded her at every available opportunity. One day she surprised me by finally bringing home a doll, and I was ecstatic! Even though my doll did not have real hair, she was my first, and I loved her, despite her shortcomings--no hair. Polly was white, just like all dolls I had ever seen back then, but her 'hair' was made from hard plastic in the shape of a bun at the back of her head. Nevertheless, from the moment I received her, she was seldom far from my side.

A few weeks after the holidays, my cousin Lorna came to visit with her own doll in tow. Her doll had hair! She was beautiful, even more beautiful than Polly. I spent most of the afternoon combing and styling her hair while Polly lay nearby, all but forgotten. I was very disappointed when my cousin was ready to leave, but was overjoyed when she agreed to let me borrow her doll overnight. That afternoon I sat by my front gate singing to the doll and combing her hair for what might have been hours. Whenever passersby smiled at me and asked her name, I pretended that she was mine and made up a new name each time. I was very excited to show off 'my' new doll to an older girl who happened by. She might have been nine or ten years old but I knew that she was impressed. She told me that she had lots of dolls' clothes at her home and asked if I wanted to have some.

"Of course!" I replied happily, thinking how pleased my cousin would be when I showed her all the new clothes I got from this new friend.

When Jennifer informed me that she needed to take the doll home to make sure that the clothes fit, I was a bit reluctant. She saw my hesitation and immediately assured me that she only lived a few blocks away and she would return very soon. Although I was still apprehensive, I gave her the doll and told her I would wait by the gate for her to return. I could not accompany her home because I was not allowed to leave the front of my house. As she was leaving, she promised once more that she would be right back, and so I waited. All evening I waited, but Jennifer never returned.

Jennifer did not give me her address, but she told me that she lived next door to the clinic around the corner, and I knew the exact location of the clinic. After a while I got tired of waiting and toyed briefly with the idea of walking to her home, but common sense prevailed. Since I didn't want to get into more trouble, I stayed and waited some more. By dinnertime I was a wreck, I could barely eat a thing. I kept jumping up and peering toward the gate every time I thought I heard a voice.

"What's wrong with you?" my grandmother asked repeatedly. "Why are you jumping up and down like a jack-in-the-box?"

"I'm fine," I lied, trying not to burst into tears, but not daring to tell her what transpired earlier.

Eventually, I went to sleep that night with a cloud of doom hanging over my head. I slept fitfully, dreaming about dolls with and without hair - and clothes, lots of pretty doll's clothes. I arose early the following morning and after a quick breakfast resumed my vigil by the front gate. But by the afternoon when Lorna and her brother Glen came to get her doll, Jennifer still did not show up. I tried to sound cheerful while I explained that my friend was getting some new clothes for the doll, but my tone lacked conviction. Glen immediately deduced that I had been conned and suggested that I accompany him to the clinic around the corner so that we could find Jennifer's home.

With a deep sense of foreboding we walked the couple of blocks to Alexander Road, but to my horror there was a vast, empty lot on either side of the clinic. We went to several homes nearby and inquired about Jennifer but no one knew who she was. My bravado crumbled with each and every negative response we got, and finally the tears began to flow freely. I never imagined that anyone, more so my new friend, would steal my cousin's doll. Even when faced with the irrefutable evidence, I still expected Jennifer to return. Not only was I upset about losing my cousin's doll, but no one except my grandmother believed that the doll was actually stolen! I was accused of being jealous of my cousin and throwing her doll away. I was too young to make sense of all that happened over those two days; but my faith in humanity was nevertheless somewhat shaken.

Primary School Daze

CHAPTER 3

I suppose it was established from my birth that my grandmother would play a pivotal role in my life even by the name I was given. Like every young child, I knew my name and my address, or so I thought. It was not until my first day of elementary school, when I sat in Miss Christian's class proudly dressed in my blue and white overalls, that I had to unlearn a few of the early lessons. Sitting at the front of the class with my face, legs and arms glistening from petroleum jelly my grandmother had liberally applied, I was so excited that I could hardly sit still. At six years old I was finally in the 'big' school with the older children. My brand new exercise book and pencil were poised on the creaky desk in front of me. It was time for roll call. Miss Christian dutifully explained that when our name was called we should raise our hand and say, "Present, teacher." I already knew that routine because my cousins and I had rehearsed it many times before when we played 'school' together. This time it was for real and I was a bit nervous. I wanted very much for the teacher to like me and so it was imperative that I let her know from the beginning how smart I was. Everyone told me that I was smart and I believed them. After all, I could count up to one hundred and I knew lots of nursery rhymes. I could even recite all the books of the Bible, and knew each railway station from Kingston to Montego Bay in order. I was never quite sure why that was important for us to learn, but I was required to memorize it in pre-school.

I listened attentively as each name was called, and watched my classmates proudly raise their hands and repeat the required refrain, "Present, teacher." When she got to the name, Victoria Gregory, no one responded and since I was a very curious child, I looked around the classroom, wondering who it was that had the very same last name as mine.

Miss Christian repeated more sternly, "Victoria Gregory!" And still there was no response.

She squinted her eyes and looked around at our eager smiling faces; and just as I turned once more to see who the offender was, I heard a stern voice ask, "Child, don't you know your name?" I wanted to snicker, but I held my composure. This time I almost rose from the bench because my curiosity had gotten the better of me.

"You! Rubberneck! I am talking to you!" I looked back at her and saw that she was looking in my direction.

"Me?" I mouthed pointing to my chest.

"Yes, you! Stand up child! Don't you know your name?" There must be some terrible mistake I thought, mortified.

"Stand up!" she repeated. Again I pointed to my chest, looked behind me once again just to be sure, but by then I was certain that she was talking to me.

"What is your name child?"

"Grace Gregory." I replied - more a question than a statement because I was confused.

"That is not your name," she responded crossly, "Your name is Victoria Gregory."

She replaced her glasses and looked down at her book signaling that I was dismissed. That was not a good beginning for my first day at the 'big' school. The other students were glancing at me with pity in their eyes and I knew that I could not afford to cry because after all, I was now a big girl. I couldn't wait to get home to tell my grandmother about this colossal blunder. I knew that she would fix it and my teacher would realize that I was indeed very smart and that my name was Grace Gregory. Thankfully, my day improved, and I soon forgot the early misunderstanding. But as soon as I got home that afternoon I ran to Granny and told her about my first day in school.

"The teacher thinks that my name is not Grace," I complained, not remembering the strange name she had been calling me all day.

To my disappointment, Granny laughed and confirmed nonchalantly that my name was Victoria Gregory.

"How come no one told me that before?" I questioned.

I can't recall if she responded, but since it was not unusual for a grownup to ignore a child's question, I was forced to accept the fact that our conversation was over.

My mother explained it best some time later. When I was born my grandmother wanted her to name me Grace, but she had read a poem entitled, 'Victoria, Bride of the Sea,' and thought that was a prettier name for me. Since she was only sixteen years old when I was born, she dared not openly defy her mother, so she secretly registered me with the name she preferred. No one knew of the deception until my new school requested a copy of my birth certificate in order to enroll me. But by then I was known as Grace to all the family. Upon realizing that her duplicity would be uncovered, she confessed to her mother what she had done but she failed to inform me of the facts. To this date, I am still called Grace by most of my family members.

In spite of my almost disastrous first day in school, I soon became a teacher's favorite because I was a diligent student. I was eager to please authority figures and reveled in the praises I got in school. At home, I began to be more aware that I was lacking an important component in my life – the man who was supposed to be my father. Since no one in school knew my secret, I pretended that I was just like everyone else. But I began a secret campaign to find the man who I heard was a police officer. Ironically, this knowledge made me deathly afraid of the police, which made finding him seem absolutely impossible. I was aware on some level that this fear was irrational, but that made it no less real.

I was jealous of my siblings and cousins who had real-live fathers. My new friends in school constantly talked about their mothers and their fathers as well, and so I created stories of what I wanted my ideal family to look like. My mother was still not around very much, but she had begun to gain a reputation for her hot temper and the fact that she 'liked' to drink. My father, on the other hand, remained an enigma that was only real in my mind, and so I had an uphill battle to climb.

It wasn't until late 1959, just days before my sixth birthday that I realized just how much I was affected by the fact that my father was missing from my life. One of Jamaica's sons, Collie Smith, a famous cricketer, had died in England from injuries he sustained from a tragic car accident. The entire island was in mourning and his body was flown home to be interred at the May Pen cemetery in Kingston. My mother insisted, against my grandmother's wishes, that I accompany her to the funeral. I was petrified! Not only did I not want to go to a funeral because I was afraid of duppies (ghosts), but I did not want to go anywhere with my mother because I was also afraid of her. Naturally, my mother won, and so off we went. I had never seen so many people in my life. She and I, and everyone else in the whole world, it seemed, were in attendance at the cemetery. She introduced me to everyone she knew as her "big dawta" and they all expressed surprise, since many of them seemed not to know that she had a child as old as I was.

It was almost impossible to keep up with her and pretty soon my worst fear was realized when I lost track of her in the vast crowd. There were gravestones and fresh grave mounds everywhere. People meandered around, many crying, but most seemed to be partying while I alternately walked and ran around, looking up frantically at all the strange faces of mourners and revelers, trying to locate my mother. I saw several police officers attempting to maintain order in the crowd, but my unrealistic fear that one of them could be Philip Gregory, my father, terrified me even more.

I tried to hide whenever one of them came near me because I could not and would not make myself speak to an officer. After a while, I began to cry, not knowing what else to do. Eventually, someone noticed that I was wandering around aimlessly by myself and asked why I was crying. I couldn't maintain my bravado any longer and confessed that I had lost my mother. To my horror they summoned an officer and I was forced speak to him. He eventually convinced me to give him my mother's name and my address, and I waited for the best or the worst to happen. Soon other officers joined us and in my childish mind I was certain that my father was among them, but unfortunately that was not the case.

I did not find my father that day, but somehow they were able to locate my mother when the crowd thinned. At first, she was very upset with me when I explained that I was afraid to speak to a police officer. She did not understand my irrational fear and I was utterly unable to understand or communicate my feelings to her. However, she seemed visibly relieved that she did not have to tell my grandmother that she had lost me at the cemetery. We went on very few outings after that incident, but not even my grandparents could allay my fears pertaining to the police after that day. No one mentioned my father after that, but I continued to look for him, albeit from a safe distance. I was told that he looked like me, and that was the only other information I had up to that point.

I continued to do well in school. I had begun to carve out an identity for myself, and soon I was able to pretend that I was confident and self-assured, and everyone believed that lie. I managed to fit in comfortably, and maintained as normal a life as I could muster. We still had very little money, but few families did. I was adored by my grandparents and that made me content.

Since there was never much money to spare, and even though I hated it, I had to enroll in a subsidized lunch program in school. I remember the hot lunch we fondly referred to as Bollo Slush (a bowl of slush). It was actually very tasty, but back then, I would never have admitted it. I would have preferred to purchase junk food from the many vendors who paraded their limited display by the school gate. The hot lunch menu, though not much of a selection, consisted of rice and a variety of stews with peas and pork or salted cod fish. Each meal included a large dumpling made from flour and cornmeal. Hands down, my favorite was the stewed peas and rice! Back then, the more discriminating kids, like me, pretended not to like Bollo Slush and pretended that we ate it only at our parents' insistence.

I ate Bollo Slush from Monday through Thursday, but splurged on junk food each Friday. Mr. Joe was the only officially approved vendor at our school. His specialties were beef patties, coco bread, grater cake and sugar buns. His snow cones were always a crowd pleaser, since the temperature in Kingston fluctuated from ninety to ninety-five degrees year round. There was a never ending supply of fruits from other local vendors. Each one had pretty much the same stock: bananas, star apples, mangoes, naseberries, otaheite apples, june plums and guineps. We made our selection based on our relationship with the various vendors.

It was commonplace and accepted to nickname folks based on their physical appearance or disability, and that practice was applied to our vendors as well. One of the more colorful vendors was Deaffie, so named because she was extremely hard of hearing. She was a mean soul, but we supported her because she was very eccentric and made us laugh. She would not allow us to 'feel up' her fruits and not make a purchase. If we did not make a purchase, we knew that we would be cussed out in her high pitched unintelligible voice, and sometimes she'd throw a fruit at us if she was angry enough.

I would be remiss if I didn't mention the fruit called Tinking (stinking) Toe. It was delicious! It was also called Locust, which sounds equally as abhorrent. Not surprisingly, its smell is far from inviting, but after cracking the hard shell, usually with a rock, and ignoring the foul odor, you would be rewarded with a very tasty, powdery, greenish yellow treat. The fruit would usually stick to your teeth, so while enjoying your delicious Tinking Toe, smiling was not recommended, at least not until you thoroughly rinsed your mouth. Like Bollo Slush, Tinking Toe was a very guilty pleasure. The more chic among us pretended not to like or eat the fruit, so it had to be purchased in secret, taken home, and eaten behind closed doors. I felt it was worth the risk of discovery, and so I confess that I was among the guilty chic.

I participated in many after school activities. I briefly enjoyed the camaraderie of the 4H club, but I wasn't fond of livestock and so that zeal quickly dissipated. I was good at track and field events, though not competent enough to be a star. Nevertheless, I stayed on the track team and competed in any event for which I qualified. My true passion was my many accomplishments in the Brownies. I always had a fondness for clothes and fashion, so I spent many hours making sure my uniform was neat and crisp and my badge was one of the shiniest in the troupe. I loved it when we were required to wear our Brownies' uniform to school or any Brownie related activity. My former Brown Owl would be proud to know that I can still tie the many knots she taught, like the reef knot and the round turn with two half hitches. I still remember the semaphore signs she grilled us on, although I never once had occasion to use any of those skills.

Corporal Punishment

CHAPTER 4

Once upon a time there was a little girl whose behavior was abominable. Her mother chose not to discipline her because she thought that everything her daughter did was cute. Furthermore, she loved her child too much to hurt her, she thought. Everyone complained about this little girl, but to no avail. Mom held firm to her convictions. So the little girl was raised lacking any sense of right or wrong and inevitably ran afoul of the law as an adult. Her mother was devastated, and couldn't believe this had happened to her only child. One day, during one of the mother's regular visits to the prison, her daughter sat across from her quietly ruminating on the things that led to her incarceration. She eventually raised her head and beckoned to her mother to come closer.

"I have something to tell you," she whispered.

Mom eagerly leaned forward with a sad smile on her face. The young woman held her mother's face in both her hands and moved over as though to whisper something in her ear. She then grabbed her mother's ear lobe between her teeth and bit into it as hard as she could. The old woman screamed in agony.

"Why did you do that?" she shrieked, as she looked at her daughter in total disbelief.

"I did that because you failed to discipline me as a child and that's why I ended up here."

That story, or a similar version, was told to children all over the West Indies. It gave license to every parent to exercise corporal punishment.

"Mi naw meck yu bite off mi aise (ears) when you get old," was the common refrain used by parents to justify a good whipping.

Corporal punishment was indelibly etched in the framework of family life. Time-outs were unheard of. As a matter of fact, I did not know that time-outs were a form of punishment until many years later when my youngest child was a toddler. I must confess that although I used that method a few times, I never failed to remind my child that were we living in Jamaica, the consequences for bad behavior would have been much more severe. To my horror, I actually repeated the story of the incorrigible little girl from time to time. Each time, my children would look at me as though I had lost my mind.

Whippings or beatings were not contained within the four walls of our homes. Teachers were also encouraged to dole out discipline whenever they felt it was necessary, and they did – gladly, it seemed. Rarely would a child complain to a parent or guardian that they got a beating in school. There was absolutely no up-side to that complaint; as a matter of fact, the downside was that you were exposed to a second beating at home, because you embarrassed the family by earning the penalty in the first place.

Punishment in school was not limited to beatings; thus, mild forms of torture were eagerly administered at the teacher's discretion. Younger children were made to kneel on the concrete floor in the classroom for as long as the infraction warranted. Another teachers' favorite for older children was to have the child stand on one leg, hold the other leg behind him/her with the opposite hand, while simultaneously holding on to the opposite ear lobe with the other free hand. Usually, the child would end up hopping around the classroom trying his best to keep his balance, while the other children giggled nervously – secretly thanking God that someone else was being humiliated.

One instrument of torture was the strap (an eighth of an inch thick by about two inches wide). But the truly dreaded one, the infamous cane, was introduced during the pre-teen years. This flexible bamboo rod was liberally utilized not only as a consequence for bad behavior, but also as an encouragement to get to school on time, to complete assignments, or even to remember pertinent facts in the various subjects we were taught. I had the displeasure of being the recipient of a few canings, not because of bad grades, because I was consistently among the top three in my class. My canings occurred because I was a chatterbox in class, and because in one instance, I actually engaged in a fisticuff with my best friend.

If the teacher chose your back or legs as the target for these blows, there was very little you could do but try to dance around in an undignified manner to avoid the blows. However, if the teacher requested that you hold out your palm to receive the blows – which was the preferred stance, the trick was to time the delivery perfectly, and then lower your palm just before the blow connected. This caused the blow to lose some of its velocity. Unfortunately, in doing that, sometimes the cane missed the target completely and more often than not it ended up hitting the teacher's leg. If and when that happened, you would have succeeded in incurring more of the teacher's wrath. All hell then broke loose, the usual propriety would be dismissed, and the back and legs became the targets.

There was a rumor circulating throughout our school that corporal punishment was illegal in the United States, but of course no one ever believed it to be true. Our young minds could not conceive of an organization such as The Division of Youth and Family Services and its regulations to protect children's rights. We had no rights! It was even more inconceivable that neither parents nor guardians were encouraged or allowed to beat their children. Had we been able to confirm the story as factual, we would certainly have had some form of civil disobedience or an outright revolution. We would perhaps have arranged for a mass scale hijacking of airlines and sought political asylum in America. But that rumor was never substantiated, and in spite of the aforementioned troubles, we took everything in stride and made the best of what we felt was a horrifying situation. Today, I look back almost fondly on those days, and from time to time I swap stories with my peers about the times we outwitted our taskmasters. Astonishingly, the general consensus was that teachers we admired the most, the ones who were the most positive influences in our lives during our elementary school days, were the strictest. Topping the list was the infamous Mrs. Thompson, who, armed with her well-used-cane, put the fear of God in us. She believed the biblical mandate that sparing the rod spoiled the child.

Mrs. Thompson was my homeroom teacher for most of my primary school years and she was relentless! In addition to private evening lessons that she gave to students who needed additional help, a select group of students were required to do Lunch Time Work! Parents paid a very nominal fee for her time for the after-school classes, and even though my grandmother could not afford to pay her, she allowed me to take the classes free of charge. Her favorite saying was that if we were awakened in the middle of the night and asked to give an answer to any mathematical problem, we should, without hesitation, be able to give the correct answer without thinking about it. I took that very seriously and became an 'A' student in mathematics. Mrs. Thompson became one of my favorite teachers over the years and on several occasions she stepped away from her role as teacher and became more of a mentor to me.

Her kindness was partly attributed to the fact that her husband was my grandfather's nephew. The family tie was discovered accidentally when I would either complain or brag about her to my family at home. My Aunt Patsy investigated and confirmed that she was our Uncle Willie's wife. Once the family relationship was revealed to her, I became her special project -perhaps because she was aware of my mother's drinking, and also that my father was absent. I confess that many times I was not happy to be the recipient of all that attention because she expected much more from me than she did the other children. One day when I was being particularly belligerent, Mrs. Thompson called me to her desk, scolded me, and then informed me, "The problem with you, Victoria Gregory, is that you do not have any ambition." I was deeply hurt even though I did not know what it meant at the time. But later when I discovered what she meant, I became adamant to prove to her that I did have ambition. I was determined to show her that I would make something of myself and that was exactly what she wanted me to do.

One summer, the Thompson's invited me to spend a few weeks at their home. It was the most thrilling, yet frightening, experience of my young life. They lived in a very nice section of town far away from my neighborhood. The streets were lined with beautiful trees and there were actually manicured lawns in front of these homes. What was more amazing to me was that each home housed only one family! The Thompsons' home had several rooms that I learned had different functions. The spacious drawing room was furnished with beautiful couches, a couple of decorative tables with lamps, and exquisite paintings all over the walls. Astonishingly enough, no one slept in that room! There was actually a room just for eating and no one slept there either. It was called a dining room, and more notably, the kitchen and bathrooms were indoors! It was similar to the homes I saw in the movies. Up until this point, I truly believed my uncle and aunt were very rich.

The bedrooms were decorated with matching sheets, pillowcases and fancy bedspreads. How I would have loved to bring Granny and Papa here, even for one night! My eyes were opened to a whole new way of living, and I realized that was the 'ambition' Mrs. Thompson wanted me to have. She wanted me to strive for better than I had and it helped that I was able to see firsthand that it was possible.

Disaster struck one day when she asked me to set the table for dinner. I had absolutely no idea what she meant for me to do, but was too embarrassed to ask for help, so I did the next best thing. I told her that I didn't know how many people I should set the table for. She immediately realized my discomfort and asked her daughter to help me. I watched her place the knife on the right, fork on the left with the plate in the middle, and a pretty flowered glass next to the knife and serviette. Although it was a modest table setting by most standards, the picture was blazed in my young mind for a very long time. At first it was awkward and seemed senseless to struggle with a knife and fork when one could easily use a spoon, but I acquiesced to their custom, and soon became accomplished at using the utensils. I volunteered to set the table every day for the next two weeks that I was there.

That experience with my teacher's family was life-changing for me. However, like the saying goes, "Be it ever so humble, there is no place like home." Actually, there was no place like home for me, because the people I loved the most in my life were at home. In my undeveloped mind, I wished with all my heart that we could have had just a fraction of what the Thompsons had. My grandparents were old, and I wanted for them the best that life could offer; and the best was what I saw at the Thompsons' home. I no longer wanted my grandmother to cook outdoors, and more than ever, I wanted her to have a beautiful coffee pot like the Thompsons'. I hated the old 'beat up' pot that she used to make her coffee each morning. I told my grandparents everything that I learned from the weeks I was away, and I promised them that when I grew up, I would get them a house just like the Thompsons'. They too would have beautiful things, I promised. At no time did it ever occur to me that my grandparents would not live forever, so my dream for them became a driving force in my life. I did discover ambition after all.

Sex Education

CHAPTER 5

Like many children, I learned about sex from my friends. The misinformation was widespread, but we would NEVER dare ask for clarification from our parents or guardians. We knew instinctively that the subject was taboo, and so we educated ourselves with whatever could be gleaned by eavesdropping or from the exaggerated tales from older kids. Because we lived in such close proximity to each other - often a whole family sharing a single room, kids tended to learn about sex at an early age. Not so in my household, even though we too shared only a single room, Papa and Granny slept in separate beds. I gathered tidbits about the sexual act but promptly dismissed those stories as mere fiction because I was absolutely certain that my grandparents NEVER indulged. For one thing, they were much too old, in my opinion. Additionally, I could never, not in my wildest dreams, imagine my grandparents engaging in such despicable acts.

However, by the age of eight, we discovered that one day we would eventually grow breasts like grown-up women, and it was just about that age that we became preoccupied with that fact. My friends and I used to place rolled up handkerchiefs or tissue paper under our dresses to simulate breasts. We were certain that we had everyone fooled.

At that age, we were not particularly fond of boys either, but we managed to spend an inordinate amount of time making fun of them. Personally, I found boys to be particularly disgusting mainly because I had to assist my grandfather from time to time with his personal hygiene. My grandmother tried to shield me from that chore as much as she could, but it was virtually impossible since he was totally dependent on us for his daily care and routine. So, for many years I was actually revolted by the male anatomy and by conversations about the sex act. I had no real name for it back then. It was called 'de ting' which was the generic name given to all uncomfortable topics…sex, menstruation etc. It was something you did not discuss openly, even though it was the proverbial 'elephant in the room'.

To the best of our knowledge, there may have been a connection between 'sex' and the 'Black Heart Man' whom we were cautioned about as children. We must stay away from this man at all costs, we were told, but we were never told how we could identify him. I suppose grown-ups felt that because they imparted that information to us, and also warned us that we should not take candy from strangers in the street, we were sufficiently prepared. This bogeyman was a faceless stranger with a black heart, walking around tempting children with candy. Hence, when Mr. Buck arrived on the scene, he slipped completely below our radar.

Mr. Buck was a family friend. He was a traveling barber, and so he stopped by our place once or twice per month to cut my grandfather's hair. He also had a few of the tenants as customers and so he was trusted and accepted by all the families. The children liked Mr. Buck. He made us feel special. Unlike many of the adults we were accustomed to, he spent an inordinate amount of time talking to us and listening to our childish banter so obviously it was no surprise that he gained our confidence and became a friend pretty quickly. There were times when we felt uncomfortable, though, like when he tried to tickle us or when he became overly friendly, but we ignored the signs. After all, he was just a funny little man who loved children. We did notice, however, that whenever other adults were around, he became aloof and ignored us. Adults tended to act strangely at times, so in our innocence we accepted that as the norm.

As predators are wont to do, Mr. Buck slowly began to act more aggressively. He smiled more, touched more, and tickled more. One day he brought us candy, and that sent alarm bells going off in my head. He gave us all a generous amount, and then called my friend Patti over to him, while the rest of us ran off with our bounty. After a few minutes, I returned to the room just in time to see my friend squirming and on the verge of tears while she sat on his lap. I sensed that something was terribly wrong, but I did not know what to do. Fortunately, Pat's mom walked in behind me, immediately realized what was happening and demanded that he let her go. There was quite a bit of shouting after that and soon other neighbors became involved in the foray. Of course, Mr. Buck denied any wrongdoing, but he quickly disappeared when someone threatened to summon my mother.

Both Pat and I were very shaken up, and felt that we must have done something wrong. No clear explanation was forthcoming about what could have happened to her and to the rest of us. We never saw Mr. Buck again, and somehow we knew that we never would. Whether it was the fear of dealing with my mother or the fact that he was caught just at the point where he was being inappropriate, we never knew. The explanation we got from Pat's mother, after she ascertained that her daughter was not harmed, was short, succinct and to the point. "No meck no man touch yu no way. If dem try, just scream an tell yu mada or fada." Obviously, that was not very clear to eight-year-olds. We were more confused after the incident, but as was the custom, we did not ask questions and no additional explanation was volunteered.

As the years rolled by, I began to learn more and more about the human body and sex. My most trusted teacher was an older cousin, Lynn, who lived in the country and spent the summers with Granny, Papa and me. By the time I was ten years old, I got first-hand information about menstruation, 'de ting'. The information was not disseminated with any subtlety or finesse, and so for the next couple of years I was in fear for my life. Frankly, other than growing breasts, there appeared to be very few things that seemed palatable about growing up. I grew up with an unhealthy fear of relationships and something tantamount to disgust about the human body. My friends in school, who had older siblings, reported their findings and we all compared notes, most of the time staring open-mouthed at each other in disbelief.

By the age of eleven, in spite of my fears and insecurities I began to discover that some boys were really cute. They were dangerous, but cute; and my friends and I admired them from a distance. I also discovered that I was considered a 'nice looking black girl'. James Brown had not yet released his mega hit, "Say it Loud, I'm Black and I'm Proud", therefore, I had not yet gotten permission to embrace my 'blackness'. So, on an island where more than ninety percent of its population was black, I felt insecure because I was 'too' black. I learned to live with compliments like, "She is nice looking, BUT she is black."

'De ting' arrived with gusto when I was a gawky, insecure twelve-year-old. Many of my friends had already started menstruating, but I was still scared and embarrassed to tell my grandmother. She had not had the 'talk' with me. One of my friends was in possession of her older sister's well used copy of Ellen G. White's *'On Becoming A Woman'*, but it was in such great demand that I never got to borrow it. It was clandestinely passed around from one child to the next. We were sure that if we were discovered with this contraband we would have been severely punished. I was very grateful that I had learned about de ting from my cousin, and so I knew that I was not bleeding to death. Eventually, I mustered the courage to whisper to my grandmother that, 'de ting come'. It was not lost on me that she looked like she would have preferred to have had any other conversation rather than the one at hand. Frankly, I felt the same. Before she could begin her version of 'What Every Young Girl Should Know', I quickly told her that Lynn had explained everything to me two summers before. She relaxed gratefully when she realized that she did not have to reiterate this painful message that she may or may not have imparted to her daughters many years before.

Unfortunately, I was not yet out of the woods. A few months later, my mom stopped by for a visit, and as usual I tried to stay out of her way. But, on that fateful day, she called me over and began, "Grace, one day yu goin to see a ting." Oh no, I thought, not sure which of us was more embarrassed. I nodded and kept my eyes averted, but not before I noticed Granny smiling sheepishly in the corner… "An so when it come, yu mus tell me or Mama," she continued.

"Mm hmm," I nodded, knowing that I would never in a million years tell her that de ting had already come. When she felt satisfied that she had sufficiently informed me and had now fulfilled her motherly obligation, she hugged me. She then looked at me expectantly as though she wanted me to say something. I couldn't wait to leave her presence, and hoped that she wouldn't complete the discourse with the 'Where Babies Came From and How' conversation.

I was grateful that she was too embarrassed to continue and we were both spared the torture. I discovered later, however, that I did not know as much as I thought. I had begun to learn the art of flirting, and so when Mr. Tom, another 'family friend', asked me to show him my breasts, I did. He was a disgusting looking old man; but I liked the attention he showed me. Fortunately for me, he never went to the next step. Perhaps it was because he too was afraid that I would tell someone and that my mother would find out, and so I was saved from any further harm or indignities.

Sonia & Douglas

CHAPTER 6

My brother and sister moved back and forth from their paternal grandparents' home to my home with Granny and Papa. Their dad and my mother had an on-again, off-again marriage. They never divorced, but when their relationship became too chaotic, they would go their separate ways for months or even years at a time. Being the free spirit that my mother was, she was never pinned down with either of her three children or her husband. To me, she was this elusive entity that floated in and out of our lives, at times with disastrous outcomes when she was not sober. Her husband, on the other hand, was always a stabling influence in their lives and I liked him a lot. At times I pretended that he was my dad as well, but even though he was kind and pleasant toward me, I was never invited to stay at his parents' home with my siblings. Nevertheless, in my mind, he, Papa, and Philip (my biological father) were three fathers who loved me.

My youngest sibling, Douglas, was an amazing dancer and when he turned seven years old, my cousins and I decided to take his show on the road. He was our version of Michael Jackson. We nicknamed him Stagger Lee from the then popular rock and roll hit by Lloyd Price. We took him to local bars and restaurants to perform. We waited outside until we were able to attract the attention of some of the patrons and then we prompted him to dance while we sang. He did not need much encouragement to begin his act. His repertoire included the 'Shake a Leg' and the 'Twist'. At the end of his performance, adults cheered and gave him loose change. As his managers, we collected all the loot and promptly went off to the ice cream parlor nearby and treated ourselves to sugar buns and ice cream - goodies that we could never have afforded otherwise. Our profitable enterprise was soon discovered and we were forced into a premature retirement from our show business career.

My sister, Sonia, suffered from a severe asthmatic condition and so she was referred to as the delicate one. Douglas and I became her protectors. We had not yet discovered that she also suffered from sickle cell disease, but whenever she was bullied, it was our responsibility to fight her battles for her. On one of those occasions I was involved in an altercation with one of my friends, Megan Brookdale. She made a disparaging comment about my sister and I decided to end our friendship when she refused to apologize. As was the custom in our circle, one evening after school was dismissed, our friends decided to take matters in their hands and force us to end our on-going feud. When all attempts to reason with us failed, they opted to push us toward each other so that we could hug, apologize, and eventually make up. Unfortunately, that did not work either because I felt that the egregious comment that was made could not be rectified with a hug. As a result, when the peacemakers pushed us together, we began to hit each other. As soon as they realized that their new effort failed, they pulled us back for another strategy session.

In the midst of the pow-wow, I saw my sister crying and I immediately realized that she must have heard what Megan said and she was very upset. It was now up to me to defend her honor. By then, Megan must have sensed my resolve, so she and her friends tried to escape to the nearest bus stop, hoping that I would retreat. My friends and I pursued them; I wanted to make sure that it was clearly understood that no one could get away with making fun of my family. Megan broke from the crowd when she realized that we were closing in. She stopped, bent over and picked up a small rock, aimed, and fired it directly at me. I stood motionless with one hand on my hip, while my heart was pulsating at a death defying rate, wishing that I could retreat. To my relief and even though we were only a few yards apart, the rock sailed easily over my head. I hesitated for a few seconds, wondering whether it was wise to attack now or back off and still save face.

Megan gained more momentum from my hesitation and immediately picked up another rock, locked into my line of vision, aimed, and fired once again. Like the boy David, when he fired at Goliath, her blow connected with the target. For a split second I actually saw stars in front of my eyes and immediately realized that I was hit. I raised my hand to the offending spot on my forehead and felt a lump the size of a large marble. My assailant and her group, sensing victory, raced to the bus that had just pulled up and got in. By the time my friends and I regrouped and made another feeble attempt to chase them, the bus drove off. My rag tag band of losers and I had no choice but to limp back to my home, while I nursed the throbbing and burgeoning lump on my forehead.

Sadly, the appendage showed no sign of disappearing and so I had no choice but to report to school the next day with the very visible sign of my defeat. I walked through the halls at school with my head hanging, but I could not drown out the snickering behind my back. For the next few days, there were some not too subtle references of 'sergeant major' because it appeared as though I was saluting when I tried to cover the lump with my right hand. The kids were merciless, and I was ashamed and embarrassed. The valuable lesson I learned that day was that words were a lot more effective than the fist. Had I not pursued Megan with my friends but opted to open a dialogue with her, I would not have been in the predicament I was facing. Not only did I have to deal with the immense shame and obvious evidence of my defeat, but both Megan and I were severely reprimanded by our teacher. Her words and her cane hurt much more than the physical pain that the rock inflicted.

Douglas, Sonia, and I continued to be a close-knit family even though we lived apart most of the time. Even after I moved to the United States, we kept in touch through letters and my frequent visits to Jamaica. Our times together were filled with laughter at ourselves, our circumstances, and more often than not, our Auntie Enid stories. Although many of the stories were incredibly sad, we learned to laugh through our tears when we compared notes about our early years.

Papa & Granny

CHAPTER 7

Like many families in our community, we were not inclined to go to the doctor on a regular basis. As a matter of fact, I cannot remember ever seeing a doctor when I was a child. There was always a lay person around who had the ability to diagnose any ailment that arose and there was usually some form of home remedy that was used for the cure. Papa had 'nerves', which meant his nerves were bad, or so everyone said. As far back as I can recall, he was bedridden. From the 'bed to the chair' was my grandmother's terse description of his condition. He had a hearty appetite and he slept well, and since there was no doctor around to refute that diagnosis, we felt that we were doing the best we could for him.

Looking back at his symptoms, I believe my grandfather suffered from an advanced case of Parkinson's disease. His hands shook most of the time, he had trouble standing, walking and talking, and he needed assistance in doing the most basic things for himself. My grandmother and I cared for his needs, daily. We made sure he was comfortable and that he was not in pain. We loved him and did what many families did back then – we cared for our elderly and sick at home with whatever simple means we had at our disposal. I learned at a very early age to help my grandmother with papa's daily routine. He slept on the 'little bed' while Granny and I slept on the 'big bed'. Instead of a box spring on his bed, we placed one-by-six planks across the bed frame to support the thin mattress. According to my grandmother, this provided much better support for his back.

Each morning before school, I helped to get him ready for the day by assisting him from the bed to his rocking chair. The ritual was to lift his legs, then gently place them on the floor and then lift his shoulders to help him up to a sitting position. I would hold on to both of his hands and then pull him with all my strength to get him to stand. That routine was very difficult for me in the beginning, but as I got older and stronger, I became more adept at it. Once he was steady on his feet, I led him slowly to his rocking chair, carefully holding on to one arm to prevent him from sitting too heavily or hurting himself. Either Granny or I then assisted him with his morning ablutions before one of us would spoon-feed him his breakfast, much as we would a small child.

After Mr. Buck was fired from his position, I became Papa's unofficial barber. I became very skilled at cutting his hair with the only pair of scissors we owned, since we could never afford to purchase clippers. Regretfully, there were times that I chose to play with my friends and ignored my grandfather's calls for help. But as I grew older, I began to cherish the times we shared. Although Papa wasn't much of a talker, most times only communicating his needs, when he was in the mood he was an extraordinary raconteur. His face was never very expressive; possibly a symptom of Parkinson's disease, but his eyes spoke volumes. After a particularly bad day in school, the look in Papa's eyes made me feel like I was safe and cherished, and that memory stayed with me all my life.

He held my attention for hours at times, recounting tales of the years he and Granny spent in Cuba. My favorite story, by far, was his well-loved 'snake tale'. With as much animation as he could muster, he spun the fascinating yarn about the day he arrived home from work and found my grandmother screaming frantically. A snake had completely wrapped itself around their infant daughter, Yvonne. He said that he immediately summoned the neighborhood snake charmer who rushed to the scene with his "pungi" – a type of flute. The charmer played a haunting melody while the petrified audience watched as the snake slowly uncoiled itself from around the infant, and eventually slinked away into the woods. During the whole dramatization, Papa had a mischievous gleam in his eyes, which made me wonder whether or not he was pulling my leg. Stories like that tended to pique my insatiable curiosity about other islands but left me feeling decidedly equivocal about foreign lands. I was grateful that Granny and Papa moved back to Jamaica because I was never a nature lover.

Frankly, I had enough problems dealing with the lizards and chameleons that scurried about our own yard.

I especially loved Papa's low belly laugh whenever I related funny stories about my school activities each day. He would look at me with expressive eyes, and every now and then, his whole body shook when he laughed at the antics I performed for him. At times he did not make a sound, but I knew he was laughing because his whole frame shook. He was a very good listener, and so we spent a lot of time together – sometimes just sitting in silence with my head on his knee.

One Sunday afternoon, I was sitting on our verandah chatting with Papa about nothing in particular, when I heard a rustling sound in a nearby tree. I ran quickly out to the yard and peered up in the tree to investigate the cause of the disturbance. To my horror I spotted two lizards fighting and darting from limb to limb. Because I was deathly afraid of lizards, I ran off screaming in fright, but obviously not fast enough. Before I could move from their dangerous path, one or both of them fell on my head. I let out a blood curdling scream and must have jumped a death defying ten feet in the air. Once I hit the ground, I performed an exaggerated version of the St. Vitus dance. I proceeded to beat myself almost senseless on the head trying to rid myself of the creatures. Each time I touched a braid on my head, it felt as though the lizard(s) still clung to me. The phrase 'my skin crawled' felt all too literal during those brief moments.

In my frenzy I did the only thing I could, I ripped off all my clothes, not for a second caring about the spectacle I was creating. I eventually calmed down – mostly because I was out of breath – and only when I heard another alien sound. I looked around wild-eyed toward its direction and saw my grandfather laughing so hard that there were tears streaming down his face. I grabbed my clothes and bolted toward the house, humiliated and crying, still taking a swipe at my braids every few seconds to make sure that there was nothing on my head. After I dressed and composed myself somewhat, I went back outside and glared at him. He held out his shaky arms, still laughing at me, and at that point I realized how ridiculous I must have looked. We both laughed together until our sides ached. Whenever I thought he wasn't looking at me, I'd take a swipe at my head again, just for added assurance that there was nothing hiding in my hair. In retrospect, that was one of the funniest moments I shared with Papa.

Papa always encouraged me to save my pennies; and I tried to do so even though I never had much money at any given time. One day Granny rewarded me with a small wooden box with a slot at the top in which to slide coins. After a few months it began to get pretty heavy with my ha'pennies, pennies and thro-pences (three pence coin). Every now and then I shook it just to listen to the coins clinking inside; afterward I would slide it back under the bed in its safe hiding place.

One day my mother stopped by on one of her usual unannounced visits. I was always very uncomfortable when she stopped by, and as usual, I tried to stay out of her way as much as I could. Since my grandmother was at the store, my mother asked me if I had any money. I briefly considered lying but I was too afraid that she could see through me, and so I reluctantly retrieved my prized box and gave it to her. Unbeknownst to us, Papa was lying in bed listening to our conversation. It did not matter if he heard what was going on; both my mother and I knew that he was unable to defend me against her. But we were wrong, at least on that day!

When he heard the coins rattling, he began calling for my grandmother, "Edith! Edith!"

My mother went to him and asked impatiently if she could help, but Papa replied emphatically, "Mi no want you; mi want Edith."

She then told him that Granny had gone to the store. Unperturbed, Papa continued to call out his wife's name, more loudly each time. My mother now seemed like a kid caught with her hand in the cookie jar, and so she tried to make a break for it before my grandmother returned. Unfortunately she was too late; Granny rushed in the room unexpectedly, and hastened to her husband's side because she had heard the urgency in his voice. In the meantime I was hiding in a corner, scared to death, watching the drama unfold in front of me. My grandparents were probably the only ones who stood up to my mother; everyone else feared her wrath. But sadly, many times I became the pawn in the game, and they were all aware of that fact. At times when they did not give in to my mother's demands for money, she insisted that I pack my things, and announced that she was "taking me back". During those times I felt more like an object than a person. I remember on one occasion my grandmother actually called her bluff and refused to budge and I was forced to pack all my things, all the while weeping and hoping that someone would tell me that it was a joke. My grandmother eventually gave in to my mother's demand for money just before she dragged me away. My mother then whispered to me that everything was fine; I didn't have to leave my grandparents after all. She left immediately afterward, never once realizing the damage that was being done to me.

"Enid tek de pickney saving box and tek out all ar money", my grandfather responded breathlessly to his wife's inquiry.

My grandmother became furious. She looked over at my mother accusingly, while I continued to stand nearby, not even daring to breathe.

Rather than being contrite, my mother lashed out at her father. She began to scream at him in anger, "Yu too nosy, yu on yu deathbed but yu still a spy pon mi. Why yu no mind yu own business?"

She continued her tirade at Papa, as she headed toward the door, still trying to escape with the change she had managed to extract before Granny got home. My grandmother stood her ground, and demanded that she return the money while I still cowered nearby, hoping that this time I would not have to pack. My mother threw the change at her and left in a huff. When we felt that she was out of earshot, we looked at each other for a while, and burst out laughing. I was very happy that my grandparents won that battle, not so much because of the money, but the fact that they stood up to my mother and won! That incident eventually became a family joke. My grandmother remained indignant for a long time and wasted no time in telling my Aunt Patsy what had transpired. That story spread like wildfire and became fodder for the family gossips. I can still remember hearing my Aunt Patsy telling and retelling the story about her sister getting busted by the old man. I watched as tears streamed down her face and then I too would laugh. I was very proud of my formidable team.

———————

When I turned ten years old, Papa took a turn for the worse; he was in his mid- seventies by then. He began to get even more feeble and listless than he usually was, and each day he grew increasingly lethargic. He preferred to stay in bed most of the time. My grandmother was concerned, and I noticed that she spent more time by his bedside seeing to his comfort.

She eventually notified my aunts and uncles of his failing health, and very soon after that we pretty much kept vigil by his bedside trying to anticipate his needs. Friends and neighbors stopped by with home remedies almost every day and I believe my grandmother faithfully tried each and every one.

One Friday morning just before I left for school, my grandmother and I noticed that Papa was not breathing normally, but appeared to be gasping for air. Maybe it was a premonition, but she kept me home from school that day, because she felt that one of us needed to be with him at all times. The following day there was no change in him and it became increasingly obvious that he was seriously ill. I tried to listen to the grown-ups as they whispered among themselves, oblivious of the scared children hanging on to their every word. Since my grandmother seemed very worried and preoccupied, I took my cue from her. I thought my Papa was going to die and so I prayed that he would get better: "God, please help Granny and Papa, and make Papa better."

Aunt Patsy made her solemn diagnosis later that morning.

"He is traveling."

The look on her face confirmed my suspicions as to her meaning. By then I didn't dare leave his bedside because I firmly believed that my presence somehow would give him the strength to get better. After a few minutes, I noticed that he began to stiffen his legs and arms as he lay on the bed. His face as usual showed no emotion and he appeared to be at peace and in no pain. Very soon after that, there was no visible heartbeat, just a slight pulsing of a nerve in his neck. The rest of the family joined us, and we continued to watch his inert body until a neighbor stopped in and placed a small mirror under his nose for a few seconds. She then looked at the mirror and shook her head; there was no evidence of breath.

"Papa is gone," she said simply, as though it was the most natural thing in the world.

I kept hearing that phrase in my head over and over. It just was not possible that my papa was gone. I refused to think of the word 'death' because even though that was my first time dealing with it, the feeling of loss and despair overwhelmed me. I knew that I would mourn him for the rest of my life. What would Granny and I do without him? Why did

God not answer my prayers? I wanted to hide in a corner forever and grieve because the pain felt too much for me to bear.

Word spread through the community rather quickly that Papa was gone, and over the next few days, many of our neighbors and friends stopped by to pay their respects. I did not see my grandmother or aunt cry, which surprised me, but then again adults rarely cried. They seemed to take everything in stride, no matter how solemn or sad. It was particularly hard on me because I did not have another father figure. Papa had been the closest male influence in my life. All the children walked around like zombies while the adults went through their rituals. There were no doctors or ambulance or police; everyone seemed to know instinctively what to do. I grieved a long time for the man who was my grandfather – the old man who was deeply loved by his five children and adored by his many grandchildren.

On the day of his death everyone waited with bated breath for the other shoe to drop: my mother had to be told. We expected the drama to begin when she arrived and we were not disappointed. Somehow, the news got to her a lot sooner than we expected and she showed up later in the afternoon.

From somewhere in the distance toward the end of our block, we heard a gut wrenching wail, "Lawd, mi puppa dead; oh, mi puppa dead!"

That was repeated several times until my mother made it to the house. She covered her face and wept openly and unapologetically. She then lay on Papa's bed next to him; hugged and kissed him while we all stood around watching her.

No one said a word as she continued to wail loudly, "Mi puppa dead!.. Aright, mi naw bawl no more."

But she continued her gut wrenching cry on and off for several hours. Mournful as we were, my cousins and I couldn't help but snicker behind her back. We knew that she was very upset but her antics and theatrics on that day were hilarious.

In the next few days, one of my grandmother's chores was to collect Papa's life insurance benefit from his lodge for his burial. To her dismay, she was informed that he was 'non-financial' - the policy had lapsed because the premium was not paid for several months. Granny had faithfully paid Papa's insurance for more than thirty years, (three shillings per month), but unfortunately, she was unable to make a payment for a few months. I watched her cry for the first time since Papa's death. She was a very proud woman and it hurt her deeply that she would now have to look to others to assist her with the final expenses for her husband. The lodge held firm to their decision even after my mother tried her own approach to remedy the situation. They would not accept payment for the past due premium, nor did they buckle under her attempts at embarrassing them. Despite the financial disappointment to the family, the now infamous lodge had a huge presence at the funeral. As was their custom, their members dressed in full uniform and paraded through the streets with the usual pomp and pageantry.

If a person's life is measured by the size of his funeral, Papa was a very successful man. People came from all over the island to say goodbye. They stopped by our home day and night for nine consecutive days to sit with the family and swap stories about my grandfather. The next major event after the burial was on the actual ninth night after his death, or as we called it, the 'Ni Night' celebration. This is much like a wake; but the ritual stemmed from more of an African tradition. It is believed that this was the time that the spirit of the deceased passed through to say goodbye to the living before going to his or her final resting place. The celebration was open to everyone, and because there was usually a generous supply of alcohol available, Ni Nights were regular haunts for heavy drinkers.

My mother was in her element. Every known 'drinker' in the community showed up. The most memorable was her close friend, Miss Armstrong, who as I understood, was a regular Ni Night participant. The menu for the night included a generous supply of Appleton 'Over-proofed' White Rum, whole fried fish and bammy or bami, which is a traditional Jamaican cassava flatbread. It was a true celebration. They sang hymns, danced and told stories until the wee hours of the morning. It was not unusual for the more belligerent to get involved in fights and other disturbances throughout the evening as they became more and more intoxicated. Since many of the attendees could not read or may not have known the words to the hymn selections, there was one person designated to read the lines from a weather-beaten hymnal. The crowd tuned in, singing loudly and off-key but with much sincerity. There was one little ditty that was a favorite, entitled 'Gimme De Fry Fish an Bammy or Mi wi Mash up de Ni Night an Go 'Way'. Actually, there wasn't much more to the song – they just repeated that phrase over and over.

At midnight someone from the crowd picked up an unopened bottle of rum and led the singing group to the nearest crossroad. Everyone, including the children marched behind him singing a liturgical hymn. Not knowing what to expect since it was my first Ni Night, I followed very closely behind my grandmother. I refused to stay at home with the younger children because I was terrified of the duppies that were believed to be in attendance. Once the crowd reached the crossroads, the leader selected a large rock on which he broke the bottle of rum in a ritual similar to the christening of a ship. The crowd applauded, sang another hymn, and then they slowly walked back to our home still singing. It was believed that my grandfather's spirit followed the crowd to the crossroad, and remained at the spot where the rum was spilled. Even though I loved my grandfather dearly, I avoided that particular intersection for a long time. I told my grandmother that I thought it absurd that they believed Papa would be tempted to follow the crowd brandishing a bottle of rum, since he never drank alcohol. I did not get a response that night, perhaps because she did not know the answer herself.

The celebration continued in full force after the breaking of the bottle, but not without incident. Our very near casualty of the evening was Miss Armstrong whom we discovered passed out, with an empty bottle of bay rum by her side. Apparently, before the last stragglers left, very soon after all the alcohol was consumed, we believed that she imbibed the entire contents of the bottle. We feared for her life, because not only was the substance made from almost 60 percent grain alcohol, but it was meant for external use only. Bay Rum was primarily used as a rub for the neck, back and head to help to reduce fever. To the family's relief she survived, but left us with yet another funny tale to add to our ever-growing list of 'You'd Never Believe It' stories. "Rememba de night when Miss Armstrong drank de Bay Rum and nearly died?" And so, the story would begin about my grandfather's Ni Night celebration...

Bible & Key

CHAPTER 8

Nadia was one of the many kids who crossed our path when we lived on Moore Street. Her Aunt Annie was almost like a member of the family because she was one of our long term tenants. Nadia was a couple of years older than my cousins and me, but she was what the adults referred to as a bad seed. We were never sure why the grownups labeled her as such, but we were warned to stay away from her. My grandmother and aunt never failed to remind us of the saying, "Show me your company and I will tell you who you are." Nevertheless, my cousins and I did what many kids do: we ignored our parent's requests whenever we felt we could get away with it. This practice, however, came to a crashing halt when she crossed a very important line.

It was about the time when my grandmother had begun to panic. Each day she watched the mailman ride by without stopping. There was no familiar airmail envelope with the neat green handwriting forthcoming. It was drawing close to the end of the month and we needed to get groceries and prepare to pay our rent soon. We no longer received my grandfather's monthly pension checks because he had passed away, and so we relied solely on the checks from my uncle. The handkerchief that Granny kept in her bosom with her money wrapped in it, had shrunk, and from time to time I heard her ask my aunt for suggestions about what to do next. It was a very scary time for us. "De letta no come," was her refrain each day when the mailman rode by on his bicycle.

One day one of the kids found a crumpled envelope addressed to my grandmother discarded in the back of the yard. He immediately brought it to Granny's attention and we realized that our letter had been stolen. Upon further investigation, my uncle's money order was also discovered. It was crumpled and endorsed with a childlike scrawl. The bank advised my grandmother that it was not negotiable in its condition and suggested that she should get a replacement. My grandmother had me write a letter to my uncle explaining what happened and we included the damaged money order as further proof.

With the business of the replacement check handled, my Aunt Patsy immediately sprang into action to find the culprit responsible. She requested a Bible, a door key, and a piece of string. She placed the bottom section of the key in the Bible at a specific passage in the Psalms, and then tied the Bible securely with the string, carefully leaving the circle at the top of the key visible. The keys we used back then were large – almost four inches long with a large circle at the top. The circle was meant for hanging the key on a hook since those keys were not designed to be carried around on a key chain. Once the key was secured in the Bible, my aunt and a friend sat across from each other, and each of them balanced the key (with the bible tied securely to it) on their index fingers. We all sat in a circle, eyes transfixed as they began to chant, "By St. Peter, by St. Paul, by the true and living God, [insert name] stole the letter." They repeated the chant, each time adding a new name until Nadia was the only one left. Finally, when they inserted her name, the key slid from their fingers and the Bible crashed to the floor. We were all pretty certain even before this ritual that she was the culprit, and so it was not a surprise to anyone when the Bible fell. Because hers was the last name called, that was further proof to me that everyone thought she was guilty.

When the bible fell, everyone's eyes were rooted to it lying on the floor, as though it was alive. No judge or jury was necessary; this questionable method was conclusive proof of her guilt. Even at that age, I saw the inherent flaw in this ritual, but I was outnumbered. Nadia, the accused, upon noticing that all eyes eventually turned to her direction, tearfully confessed and begged for mercy. The whole scene was very disturbing, but the guilty party was duly chastised and sent back to her mother in the country. I was still not convinced that this mock trial made any sense nor did I believe it was logical, but it seemed to work. Everyone was satisfied that justice was served and eventually my uncle replaced the money order and the incident was forgotten.

Several months later, the opportunity to put the Bible and key to the test reared its ugly head once more. This time, my aunt was missing thirty shillings that she said had been placed in her sewing machine drawer. Apparently, when she went to retrieve the money the following day, it had mysteriously disappeared. This time I was the likely suspect, being the only other outsider, and since Nadia was no longer in town. Once again, everyone gathered on the verandah and the now familiar ceremony commenced. I watched and listened as each person's name was called. As anticipated, the Bible did not fall. My name was noticeably left for last, which convinced me that I was assumed guilty. I wanted to be wrong about that mock trial, and hoped that when they called my name, the Bible would not fall. I was innocent and seething inside because they dared to suspect me, but there was nothing I could do, I had no way of proving my innocence. I watched closely along with everyone else, and listened.

"By St. Peter, by St. Paul, by the true and living God, Grace took the money," and as I feared, the key 'mysteriously' slid off their index fingers and the Bible fell to the floor. I was outraged when that happened! Not only did it prove conclusively to me that the practice was flawed, but I felt even more helpless. Everyone turned toward me expectantly, waiting for a confession or perhaps tears, but none was forthcoming. I suppose they were all disappointed when I placed my hands on my hips and proceed to tell off each of them. I held my tears until later when I was alone. I felt lonely and even more victimized than ever, even more so than when my cousin's doll was stolen.

I was very grateful that my grandmother believed me and did everything she could to comfort me. Today, some fifty years later, I still wonder if everyone believed that I was a thief. Back then and even now, I did not believe that anyone stole the money. I did not believe that any of my cousins would steal from their mother, but neither would I. I believe that the money was simply misplaced and later found, but my aunt was too embarrassed to apologize for wrongfully accusing me. I sulked for a long time after that incident, and, to my family's embarrassment, I still mention it once in a while, hoping for the apology that I never received.

Things That Go Bump In The Dark

CHAPTER 9

Superstition ran rampant in Jamaica when I was a child. The 'Bible and Key' incident was not the only one that defied logic and common sense. Duppies were believed to roam at will just about everywhere but only a select few of the population could see them. I was grateful that I was not one of the lucky ones born with 'the gift'. I was quite satisfied to live in my own private world without bumping into them. There were reported instances when these restless souls got violent and inflicted bodily harm on the living. Their preferred method of attack was a slap or 'box' to the face of innocent bystanders. Again, I never had first-hand knowledge of these events, but I took every precaution to protect myself, just in case. I would never point my finger toward the cemetery because I was told that it would fall off. The only known remedy to counteract the spell was to immediately bite on each finger. I even tried to avoid going outside alone after dark, because duppies were known to wander around after six o'clock. I lived with an imminent and unhealthy fear that one day I might have a face-to-face confrontation with one of them, but I never did. However, my story would be incomplete without a real-life duppy experience that hit very close to home.

The saga of Mr. Basil and his wife, made me very adamant about moving to America. I was told that there were no duppies there because it was much too noisy. It was a very scary time back then, and I had no logical explanation for the surreal events that occurred over the next few months. The young couple and their infant daughter were new tenants in our yard when the hauntings began. We gleaned that there was some discontent surrounding their marriage and since I had developed quite a skill at eavesdropping, I stayed on top of the latest gossip in the yard. The rumor was that 'another woman' wanted to steal Mr. Basil away from his wife. After exhausting every traditional method to accomplish this task, the other woman resorted to Obeah.

Obeah is powerful and dangerous stuff, much like witchcraft, and with the aid of an obeah man or woman, one could inflict harm on anyone perceived to be an enemy. There were many local obeah practitioners on the island; however, in order to get the most favorable results, one must seek the assistance of the top dog in the business, L.W. de Laurence. This champion of the occult was born in the United States in 1868 and had published widely on the occult. Even though he died in 1936, his faithful followers continued to supply believers in Jamaica with magical and occult goods by way of mail order - a practice now banned by the Jamaican Customs. Back then in the 1960's, his organization wielded more power than any of our local sorcerers and no one could counteract his spells. If you were unfortunate enough to have someone consult with them about you, you were in serious peril.

Rumor now had it that de Laurence was believed to be the source of the incidents surrounding my neighbors. Miss Rosie was in for the fight of her young life. In fact, several threatening messages were surreptitiously delivered to their room, warning her to leave her husband. At first she ignored them, but soon unidentified objects began to appear in the meals that she prepared for her family. Because the kitchen was a separate building away from the main house, I felt that anyone could have been the culprit, but neighbors claimed that duppies were responsible for these acts of aggression.

In order to counteract the spells, and because the couple was afraid that their food would eventually be poisoned, they consulted with local obeah men for assistance, but to their dismay, the mysterious hauntings only escalated. The situation had become so perilous that one evening the couple's bed inexplicably caught on fire while their child was sleeping in it. Fortunately, a neighbor smelled the smoke, peeked through the window to investigate, and was able to save the baby's life by extinguishing the flames.

During those weeks of turmoil, everyone was terrified, and so most evening activities were curtailed. I remained skeptical about the source of these hauntings, but decided to stay close to my cousins in case everyone else was right. If they were, that meant we were powerless against an unknown and unseen entity, and therefore completely helpless.

I recall a tenant saying that an eerie darkness had covered the backyard by the couple's room, but I chose not to confirm it. I was so fearful that at one point I tried to convince my grandmother to move, but she resisted all my efforts. After the travesty of the Bible and Key incident, my logical mind still did not want to believe that duppies really existed. I believed that there had to be a reasonable explanation for all this, but deep down there was that nagging fear that they just might be real.

One night, a very ominous message was scribbled on a piece of furniture in the couple's room. It threatened, "Rosie, you shall die tonight!" By that point, our fear led my cousins and me to begin to travel in packs. We were separated only when we went to sleep, and that was only at the grown-ups' insistence. I recall that later that evening we all sat on the verandah discussing the latest ghoulish happenings. After a while, Miss Rosie approached the gate with a bag of groceries. She was wearing a knee length black 'hobble' skirt (similar to today's pencil skirt). As she came closer, we noticed that her eyes seemed strangely vacant and she appeared to be confused or perhaps lost in thought. After a tense moment of silence we watched as she suddenly dropped her bag to the ground, pull her skirt up above her knees, and darted down the street. We looked at each other in bewilderment at her strange behavior and for a few moments we were riveted to the spot. My oldest cousin jumped up and we all followed him as he ran to the gate. We looked in the direction where she had fled, but she was nowhere in sight. We then raced over to a group of men nearby and frantically explained what had just happened. They immediately ran out to the street and looked around in each direction, but she was gone. The consensus was that she had taken a side road that led to a narrow ledge across the gully. Several search parties were dispatched while we all tried to ignore the creeping sense of impending doom.

After several hours, when no one returned, we became even more concerned for our neighbor's safety. We took turns comforting her baby while her husband paced restlessly, completely distraught over his wife's fate and unknown whereabouts. Then just after midnight several of the men returned with her. They had both her arms pinned by her side, but she was cursing, kicking and screaming at them, demanding that they let her go. At times she appeared to be conversing with an invisible person or persons, and from time to time she would laugh eerily. Her rants were incoherent, but every now and then, she became calm and requested that some unseen entity should wait for her. It took quite some time for her to eventually calm down and we were happy she did not die that night as the note stated. In the days ahead, she slowly seemed to revert to her normal self, except for the vacant look that would appear in her eyes now and then. We were all curious and desperately wanted to ask her what had transpired the night that she ran off, but we were cautioned by our relatives not to do so.

Unsurprisingly, the couple moved away a few weeks later, leaving us with no real answers to the strange events that occurred during the months that they lived among us. There was a rumor that the night she disappeared, Miss Rosie was found wandering aimlessly in the cemetery. As far-fetched as that explanation may seem, at ten, eleven, twelve years old, respectively, we believed them to be true, and even to this day I am still baffled by what I witnessed.

The Canadian Invasion

CHAPTER 10

By the age of twelve, elementary school students were required to sit the Common Entrance examination in order to gain acceptance to the high school of their choice. Along with many of my friends, I chose to apply to the high school I thought would be the most fun. Unfortunately, this plan was thwarted by Mrs. Thompson, who strongly suggested that I select a more prestigious school – one known for its academic acuity. Since I knew that the decision was out of my hands, I reluctantly agreed to follow her advice. There was much eagerness in the air as the senior class studied and crammed for this life changing experience. The post examination excitement was even more intoxicating, and I was in a daze during the long wait for the pass/fail results. If I failed the examination, I would be denied a scholarship to high school. The alternative was that my grandmother would have had to pay an exorbitant fee for my continuing education, an option that was out of the question because we had very little money. The weeks dragged by and the excitement continued to build while parents, students and teachers alike all waited for the results to be announced in the local papers.

Finally, the Saturday morning arrived when twelve-year-olds around the island waited impatiently at every newspaper outlet for the Daily Gleaner, the local paper in which the results would appear. I was among the frantic, frazzled group, but as I nervously scanned the names listed under St. Andrew High, my heart sank. Victoria Gregory was nowhere in sight. I looked at the names listed under my second choice, Wolmers High, and my name was conspicuously missing there as well. I was devastated!

How could I possibly go home and report to my grandmother that I had failed when everyone, including my teachers, had such high hopes for me? Just on a whim, I decided to see which of my friends opted to go to Willoughby Township High School and that's when I noticed that my name was listed there. I had PASSED! My emotion did a complete turnaround. I giggled stupidly with relief and ran all the way home, not caring how or where my name was displayed.

It was only then that it dawned on me that I never chose that school, and so I wondered if there was an error in the placements. I managed to put it aside temporarily. The only thing that mattered there and then was that I was successful. My family was overjoyed! I had never seen my grandmother more animated, and from time to time she looked at me with a big smile on her face. My journey toward success had begun. I did have ambition after all. Later that afternoon, my mother stopped by waving a copy of the newspaper and sporting the biggest grin, "Mi big dawta pass scholarship," she repeated, ad nauseam, and this time I did not mind the fuss.

On Monday morning, it was still a mystery as to why the students from Willoughby Township Primary school were denied admittance to the school of our choice. When we complained to our teacher on Monday morning, we were informed unceremoniously that it was not an error and that the principal would be meeting with our parents individually to explain why such a decision was made by the Ministry of Education. Later that week, Dr. Gale, our high school principal, came to our modest home to meet with my grandmother. She was so nervous that I was sure she understood very little of what he said. He explained that the students who were successful in passing the common entrance examination were the best and the brightest at Willoughby Township Primary. Since none of us chose to attend the high school, but instead, opted to go to other high schools, Willoughby Township Comprehensive was left with only the 'average and below average' performing students. The objective of the decision makers was to cultivate an environment of success, and so they needed high performing students to help them achieve that goal. Additionally, they were offering parents a small stipend each semester to assist with uniforms and books for students who agreed to stay at the high school.

The fact that I would receive financial aid only if I opted to go to Willoughby Township High was the deciding factor. So, at the beginning of the semester, with my disappointment in not going to St. Andrew High almost forgotten, I entered the gates of Willoughby Township Comprehensive High School. Like all the girls in the seventh through tenth grades, I wore a pleated brown jumper over a brown and white plaid shirt, and brown shoes and socks. The eleventh grade girls wore pleated skirts instead of jumpers. All boys wore khaki shirts and pants, and a necktie. Any deviation from this uniform resulted in a detention.

Since my grandmother could afford only two jumpers and two blouses each school year, I was very fastidious in maintaining an impeccable look each day. Not only was my attire important to me, but I was committed to playing a role I'd scripted for myself to the T. My aspirations were simple. I didn't want to change the world, nor did I want to discover a cure for cancer; I wanted to be a teacher. My teachers were great role models and many of them not only taught me – they inspired me.

My first high school teacher was fierce and had the reputation as a no-nonsense educator. I was a very quiet and well-behaved student, and so to the chagrin of many of my classmates, she appointed me as the form captain by the second week of school. They felt that they were denied the privilege of voting for their favorites for this enviable position. I was just as surprised at this appointment as they were, but no one dared question Miss Moncrieffe's decision. So, here I was, thrust into a position I had not sought, and rebuffed by many of my classmates. There were times that I wished to be free to act the fool like my friends, but I was bound by the weight of the title. My math teacher, Mr. Conville, once cautioned me, "Uneasy lies the head that wears a crown," and I found that proverb to be true in many respects.

By the end of the seventh grade, I was one of the popular girls in school. I had a robust group of friends and I continued to maintain good grades. I always had a best friend throughout high school. There was Maureen at one time, then Marva and then Ruth. I also had a few boyfriends along the way: Orville (Ollie) who sported a real mustache even in the eighth grade; Luke, who was tall, proud, and smart; and later, Harper to whom I was introduced by a mutual friend. He was a student at one of the more prestigious high schools and the one I planned to marry someday. In my fourteen year old mind, he possessed all or most of the salient attributes I felt I needed in a husband: he was drop dead gorgeous, smart, 'high yellow' and had 'good' hair. More importantly, he professed his undying love for me, so how could I not love him back? By the age of fourteen, I had already decided that my children needed to have a light complexion so that they would not experience the prejudices and pain that I did because I was too black.

The Canadian invasion occurred in 1966 when Warren and Elspeth Pardmore, along with their six-year-old daughter Katie, took Willoughby Township by storm. They were affiliated with Canadian University Service Overseas organization (CUSO), an organization made up of people of all ages who collaborate with local groups on projects in the Caribbean. These volunteers share their expertise in a variety of disciplines with their host countries, and CUSO is one of North America's largest non-profit groups that promote long-term development through its volunteers.

The Pardmores were the only whites and non-Jamaicans who taught at Willoughby Township High School during my tenure, and their very presence was a stark contrast to the extreme poverty of the area. First and foremost, they looked 'different': they were white; and they talked 'funny': they had a Canadian accent. It was interesting to note the difference in their teaching styles in comparison to my other teachers: I felt that they were not as focused on discipline and they were more interested in me as a person, not just a student. They asked for my opinion on matters we discussed rather than tell me how and what to think. As a result, I felt valued as an individual, and that endeared me to them even more.

Just before completing their two-year volunteer program in Jamaica, they were able to convince my grandmother and my mother to allow me to return to Canada with them at the completion of ninth grade. The plan was to complete my high school career in Canada, thus ensuring me the opportunity for higher education. So, two years after the Pardmores landed at Willoughby Township, I was on an airplane for the first time in my life, on my way to Toronto, Canada. The dream of the little girl in the red polka dress was finally being realized. I was very grateful for the opportunity that the Pardmores afforded me; but unhappy to leave my grandmother and everything that was familiar.

Warren taught English and Elspeth taught music, and I excelled in both subjects. I did not understand why they got such a kick out of our spoken language and accent, since I thought their accent was strange. We made fun of each other constantly because of the expressions we used and our pronunciation of certain words. Warren would frequently point to his palm and ask, "What's this?"

My response would simply be, "Hand middle."

He would then point to the sole of his foot and I'd shrug, offering "Foot bottom." The fact that he and Elspeth found that to be funny totally escaped me back then. One of my all-time favorites was their pronunciation of the word 'cucumber'. To me, the word was ku-kum-ba (with short "u's") while Elspeth delicately and incorrectly pronounced it as, 'kyoo-kumber'. We did, however, manage to live with each other's shortcomings, and as a result, we learned a lot from each other.

I learned more about my island home from these Canadians than I ever knew before. On regular occasions they took small groups of girls with them to explore the island. Prior to meeting them, I had never set foot outside of Kingston, the capital. I discovered not only the beauty of the white sandy beaches in Negril, but also the wonder of Fern Gully with its winding scenic stretch of road, and wide variety of ferns towering above us as we drove under its shaded tunnel of lush greenery on our way to Ocho Rios. These were places I had seen only through the eyes of photographers in travel magazines. The five or six girls and I who were lucky enough to go snorkeling in the warm Caribbean waters or climb Dunns River Falls owe so very much to the Pardmores. They opened up a whole new world to us - *our* world that we had not yet discovered.

The Best Of Times, The Worst Of Times

CHAPTER 11

In the summer of 1968, while my grandmother and I began to gather my belongings for my life-changing trip to Canada, I was trying desperately to hide a very big secret: I suspected that I was pregnant, and I was not yet fifteen years old! For the past three months I had moved zombie-like in total denial of the events that were beginning to unfold. They were just too irrational and cruel to be real. I had a boyfriend, Harper, and although we felt that we were in love, we were never allowed to date. On the occasions he visited with me and my cousins at my home we were never alone at any time, neither were we sexually active, having made the decision to remain pure until we got married. So how could I possibly be pregnant? My fears re-surfaced each time I recalled my gruesome experience months before, when our teachers took us on an outing to Gun Boat Beach, located on the outskirts of Kingston.

I woke up that morning very excited because I had grown to love the beach. I still could not swim without the aid of flippers, but it didn't bother me much because I preferred to walk the beach and enjoy the view and the feel of the sand between my toes. While most of the students were frolicking in the water, several of us went off to collect seashells. After a while, we separated but I continued to enjoy the stroll. Pretty soon, I heard raucous laughter behind me and realized I had company. I spotted some older boys carousing nearby and I noticed they were not from my school because they were wearing street clothes. Boys from my school would have been wearing the required uniform or swim trunks. Although I immediately had a sense of foreboding, I tried to ignore them, certain that my other friends were nearby. Instinctively I knew that these boys were up to no good. I also noticed that the pack was coming directly towards me, and so I walked faster and eventually began to run. Looking around I realized I had wandered too far away from the group and had become confused. I lost my bearings and was unsure in which direction to run.

The sand was wet and heavy, and there was no traction for me to run fast enough to get away from them. Eventually I heard heavy breathing and laughter directly behind me, and then someone grabbed my arm. I was being attacked by two of the boys, and there was no one in sight to help me!

I remember the feeling of hands everywhere, clawing at my swim suit, while dirty hands covered my face trying to prevent me from screaming. I couldn't fight them both, and eventually fell face down in the sand still struggling; unable to defend myself against two boys who were older, bigger, and stronger than I was. There was sand in my hair, my eyes, my nose...everywhere.

Suddenly, over my whimpering and pleading, I heard someone else shouting and I felt myself being released. I looked behind me and recognized a boy from my school running toward us. When he got to where I was seated, he knelt over and told me that the boys had run off. He attempted to hold me, but still in a panic I fought him as well. I was still traumatized and afraid that the boys would return. I desperately wanted to get back to the safety of the group.

I eventually calmed down, even though I was still trembling. I remember feeling very cold all of a sudden, and then I realized that my protector, this boy, was getting more intimate. I thought I was finally safe; but I was wrong. Before I knew what was happening he began attacking me as well. To my horror, he pinned me down while he too, tried to undo my swimsuit. I finally lay limp, crying silently, knowing that my life was over; I had no more fight left in me.

Afterward, I sat on the hot sand, curled in a ball covering my face and my body, and whimpering. He didn't go away then; he stayed with me and began to speak nervously. He told me that he always watched me in school and that he liked me. He said that I appeared never to notice him, even though he had tried to get my attention. I continued to cover my face because I hurt everywhere and I sat quietly, tending to my own thoughts and despair, knowing that at any moment I was going to be sick all over myself.

"Don't touch me," I sobbed, eventually getting up. "I am going to tell the teacher what you did to me." I ran, not knowing where I was going at first, but I had to get away as fast as I could. Pretty soon I began to panic again because I was afraid that I would run into the other boys. How does one will oneself to die? I asked myself. Fear and helplessness held my whole being in a tight grip. I looked around frantically, and then I spotted a small mound where the sand had drifted. Once I got there, I was able to see a group of my friends playing and splashing in the water. I felt a bit safer then as I ran toward the group, but stopped short as I got closer. Once more I looked around to see if I was being followed but none of my attackers were in sight. Instead of running to the teacher, I ran straight to the water keeping a safe distance from the crowd. I stepped in and waded up to the point where the water was just about at my waist. I looked at my friends having fun and I looked at the teachers standing nearby, but just could not muster the courage to tell anyone what had just happened to me. I felt dirty and ashamed, and I felt violated. I stood there for a long time, allowing the water to cleanse me.

For the rest of the day I stayed close to everyone, but was very quiet and withdrawn. Every now and then, one of the teachers would look at me, and I felt certain she could tell what had happened by just looking at my face. Eventually she asked if I was ill and I almost blurted out the whole story, but did not. I just shook my head and whispered, "No." For a second she seemed to doubt me, but quickly became distracted when someone called for her attention, and I was immediately forgotten.

I looked over at the boy who sat nervously nearby, and knew that he was wondering if I was going to tell the teacher what happened. At no point did I make a conscious decision not to tell, but felt that if I did tell the teacher, everyone would find out, and I knew that would have been too much for me to bear. I suspected that the boy might have guessed that I felt that way also, because he disappeared and was no longer hovering nearby. Before we left the beach that day, I went in the water once again hoping to erase the memory from my body and my mind. Although I had gotten rid of most of the sand that clung to me, the memory of being violated never left me.

I did not see the boy in school the day after the attack, but it was too much for me to handle alone, I had to tell someone, so I confided in my best friend. She tried to convince me to tell our teacher, and I told her that I would – but I couldn't. I still felt dirty just talking about it, and I prayed that the feeling would go away. Even though the memory did not go away, it intensified each time I saw the boy in school over the next few weeks. I still felt that it was better to protect my reputation than to expose the wrong that was done to me and so I held my head high and tried to pretend that it never happened.

Perhaps a month or so later, I realized that my period was late. I didn't really know for sure because I was irregular most of the time anyway, and so I chose to ignore that as well. I reasoned that since I was an unwilling participant in the act, and since it was the very first time I had been with a boy, it was virtually impossible for me to be pregnant. I had also heard that an orgasm was necessary for pregnancy to occur, and I knew that I certainly did not have an orgasm even though I was still a bit unclear about what an orgasm was. I muddled through my daily activities as usual, until several weeks went by and I could no longer avoid the signs. I still did not get my period and by then I began to notice tenderness in my breasts. I decided then to do the next best thing – I began to worry…and pray.

Who can I talk to, I wondered? What do I tell my boyfriend, Harper? I finally approached the one other person who knew exactly what happened on that day.

Although I felt embarrassed and angry in doing so, I went to the boy and spoke to him quietly, "I heard that in order for a girl to get pregnant, a boy had to do something." I was referring to ejaculation, but I couldn't bring myself to say the word. "Did you do it?"

He looked at me as though I had two heads; I guessed he was surprised that I spoke to him after all that time had elapsed.

He looked away embarrassed, and asked, "Are you pregnant?" When I did not respond, he continued, "My aunt warned me to keep away from Willoughby Township girls." At first I was puzzled by his comment and then I realized that he did not answer my question.

"He said Willoughby Township girls," I thought stupidly, "What does that mean?" This was just too surreal. It could not be happening. The derogatory manner in which he spoke made me feel even more upset, and so I walked away and began to pray earnestly. I knew for certain that I could not afford to have a baby at that time in my life.

During the next few days that followed, I vowed never to speak to him again and I didn't until many years later when I received a call from him. He had heard from the friend I had confided in, that I had a son, and he wanted to meet him and be a part of his life. I refused, turning him away.

The weeks crept by slowly. My period did not come, and I never stopped praying. For added insurance, I began to act like the consummate tomboy. I climbed trees and jumped from the highest branches, almost breaking my neck at times. I ran, jumped, skipped and did just about every physical activity I could, but nothing changed. There was never a waking moment that I did not worry about my pregnancy, my family, and my impending Canadian trip, but I did not say a word to anyone. I suffered in silence.

One day, my Aunt Patsy approached me and asked if something was wrong. She noticed that I was unusually quiet and kept to myself. I was so grateful, so tired of hiding my secret that I blurted out the whole incident. She asked who the boy was, and I lied that I did not know him, but I told her the truth about the rape. I begged her not to tell anyone and she promised she would not. The next day she took me to a local drugstore, Hyatt's, and told me to wait while she spoke to the druggist. As I sat in a nearby chair, I couldn't hear all their conversation but I overheard the woman say that she was sorry, but she could not help. As we left the pharmacy, my heart sank, and as we made our way back home, my head in a whirl and I was afraid to ask what would happen next. I kept on praying, even though my faith was weakening daily.

All too soon, my departure date arrived. We were going to Canada! I was more than three months pregnant by then and had done everything I could to hide the fact that I was sick all the time. I pretty much starved myself because I was unable to keep any food down. I stayed awake at nights thinking and planning – for what, I did not know. When the thoughts became too overwhelming, I would close my eyes tightly, hoping to blot out the craziness around me. At my grandmother's insistence, I went to my mother's home and said goodbye to her the day before my flight. How I wished that I could have told her what was troubling me, but at that point in my life I was sure that I hated her and never wanted to see her again. My family accompanied us to the airport and I sat and joked with everyone, all the time feeling like this was an out of body experience.

On our way to Ottawa, we had a few hours layover at JFK International airport in New York, and we were met there by my Aunt Yvonne. I had only met her twice before when she visited us in Jamaica, and she looked beautiful and sophisticated. She walked over to me, hugged me tightly and said she was happy that I was going to Canada. I introduced her to my new family and they shook hands vigorously. She told me that she needed to speak privately with the Pardmores. They moved away out of earshot while Katie and I continued to gawk at the unfamiliar surroundings. While they talked, I noticed that they were giving me furtive looks, and judging from their somber demeanor, I guessed that Aunt Patsy must have told Aunt Yvonne about my predicament, and she was now telling Warren and Elspeth. I must have appeared frightened because Katie kept asking if I were alright and I nodded my head absently.

After their conversation ended, Aunt Yvonne walked over and hugged me again, then said simply, "Victoria, this is not the end of the world." I don't remember much more of our conversation because I expected to be put on the next plane back to Jamaica. My Aunt eventually left and Warren and Elspeth were amazingly sympathetic. They comforted me and assured me that we would work it out even though they must have been in shock at hearing the news. They made me promise never to keep secrets from them in the future, and I promised. Every now and then, a feeling of relief would surface because the burden was no longer just my own to bear. Nevertheless, the thought of telling my grandmother about this, did nothing but exacerbate the pain and guilt. "It would break her heart," I murmured, and so they too promised not to tell her.

We went on to Ottawa and had a wonderful time with Elspeth's parents. We also stayed in Quebec for a few days before we went to the idyllic Prince Edward Island to see Warren's parents. I enjoyed traveling with the Pardmores and lost myself totally in the beauty and majesty of this foreign land. I was now exposed to people and cultures that I'd only read about in books or seen in the movies. Only occasionally would I allow myself to think about my pregnancy. I fell in love with Margo, a blue-eyed little girl with blond ringlets cascading down her back. I thought that she was the most beautiful child I had ever seen. Every now and then she would rub on my arms to see if the "chocolate" came off, she explained. I soon became her chocolate friend and she was the closest thing I had seen that resembled the princesses portrayed in my story books.

When the vacation was finally over, we settled in Don Mills, a suburb of Toronto. This was the place where we would make our home. It was beautiful! I even had my own bedroom! But something had yet to be done about my condition. Eventually, Warren, Elspeth, and I sat down and discussed my future with them. They kept their promise and did not reveal my condition to my mother or my grandmother. I did not hear from either of my aunts and so it was still a mystery to me what they thought or how they felt the matter would be handled. When Warren asked if I had any relatives outside of Kingston, where I lived, I quickly told him that my cousin Lynn lived in St. Theresa, about forty miles away from Kingston. We decided to write to her and ask if I could stay with her until my baby was born. The Pardmores explained that not being a Canadian citizen, it was virtually impossible to put my black baby up for adoption in Toronto in 1968. Our plan was that I would put the child up for adoption in Jamaica as soon as it was born and then return to Canada. In my letter to my cousin, I told her that no one else in Jamaica knew of my plans and begged her to keep my secret. She responded immediately, agreeing for me to come and stay with her and her infant daughter, and so at the end of August, 1968, I returned to Jamaica. My new home would be in the community of Bloomfield in the rural parish of St. Theresa.

Michael

CHAPTER 12

Although I had never been to St. Theresa before, I knew that living in the country was going to be a unique adventure. This was going to be my home until my baby was born. My cousin, Lynn, may have been in her late teens or early twenties at that time. Once I arrived at her home, I was certain that I would never get used to living in the country; it was beyond rustic and as close to nature as one gets.

Bloomfield and the surrounding towns were quiet and serene with very few distractions from the natural beauty of God's creation. There were no high risers, hardly any traffic at all and just a few homes dotting the beautiful countryside. There were the occasional sounds from the chickens and goats and other livestock that were raised for food. The country folk were uncomplicated, 'salt of the earth' type of people. There were no credit card problems here, no worries or rumors of wars, at home or overseas. Life was about the here and the now. It was about family, friends, and neighbors. There was very little crime and only a very privileged few owned television sets that brought the ills of the world to their living rooms. This tranquil little village had even fewer telephones, and the radio was still their main lifeline to the outside world. Everyone knew everyone else and whenever a stranger came to town, the word spread like wildfire.

Entertainment was scarce except for a movie each Friday night at the local school room in the neighboring Harris Store – so named because Mr. Harris once had a store there. Of course, one could choose to go to the movies in the larger adjoining towns of Gatewood or Green Bay, if one owned or had access to a car. There were no trains and there was only one bus in the morning and another in the evening. A few local entrepreneurs converted their family car into taxicabs to earn additional income, but there was no guarantee if or when they would show up. Because of the scarcity of house phones, you learned to wait, and things got done eventually – "no worries mon, Jamaica, no problem!"

There was no indoor plumbing and no running water in my new home, unless one considered the Wag Water River, a few miles away; or a few tributaries nearby that fed into the Wag, as the river was affectionately called. There were two huge drums that sat on stilts outside our home to catch rain water from the roof. I shuddered when I saw mosquitoes swimming in the water that we used as our only supply for drinking, cooking, and 'tidying up' at night. During extended dry spells, we had to trudge to the stream for water. Many people walked barefoot over rocks and uneven surfaces with containers to fetch the water. It was truly amazing to watch women and children alike carry these containers filled with water on their heads over the very rough terrain. The secret was to roll a piece of fabric in a circle (called a cotta), place it securely on your head, and then set the heavy water container on top of the cotta. I was even more intrigued and impressed when I thought of models attempting to walk while carrying a book on their heads. A trip to Bloomfield and the grueling chore of fetching water would have done wonders for their posture. I soon became eager to try my hand or, more accurately, my head at this task, but unfortunately, I became the laughingstock of the group when the container immediately fell, soaking me from head to toe. At times I even tried holding on to the container with both hands, but would still get soaking wet when I arrived home and often had little or no water left. Lynn was truly gifted and a master at this. She was able to carry a container full of water on her head and simultaneously fetch two buckets of water (one in each hand) without spilling a drop.

I did not realize how poor my family was until my early teen years, but we had running water and a functional bathhouse – no more outhouses – even though it was a communal bathroom. My short visit to Canada further confirmed that we lacked some very basic necessities of life, but Bloomfield, in 1968, felt like I had somehow reverted to the nineteenth century.

The nearby town of Harris Store housed a small post office and two scantily stocked shops. In order to get there from Bloomfield, one must descend 'suicide hill'. I named it thus because it was incredibly steep, and there was nothing but shrubs along the side of the unpaved road to prevent one from careening down the hill. I never managed to conquer that hill, even though no one else had a problem ascending or descending, and so whenever possible I avoided going to Harris Store. I envisioned myself rolling downhill, and landing curled up in a ball at the bottom.

At least every other week we all walked approximately six miles by the side of the dangerous, winding Junction Road to the Wag to bathe and do our laundry, because our water supply was precious and usually scarce. Children and adults frolicked naked in the river, ignoring the traffic rambling nearby over the single lane bridge. Sometimes the tourists driving by would stop to watch us (the natives) as we bathed. A few would sometimes pull over to take photographs – for *National Geographic*, I suppose. I could never partake of that frivolity. Like Adam and Eve after they fell from the Garden of Eden, I too realized that we were naked, and was definitely ashamed. As a matter of fact, I was quite comfortable being different, and so I wore a swimsuit and absolutely refused to pose for the cameras. I was never bothered by the fact that that made me different from the group.

In spite of the rustic lifestyle and the lack of almost everything, I enjoyed living with my cousin and meeting her friends. I also appreciated that she shared her modest home with me. This is only temporary though, I kept reminding myself, because I knew that I would be returning to Canada soon; and so I made myself comfortable in the small two-room frame house. I shared one room with Lynn and her infant daughter Angie, while a woman named Pearl and her two children shared the other room. Each of the two rooms was similarly furnished with a full-sized bed, a table and chair, and a bureau for storing clothes. There was also a hanging shelf over the bed where we hung our 'good' clothes. There was an enclosed shack next to the house that served as a kitchen, and of course an outhouse was erected away from the house toward the back of the yard. I suppose the reason that I never liked camping, even as an adult, was because I felt that I had my fill of the outdoor rustic living. I 'lived' camping, I explained to my children much later in my life. I hated it then, and I would much rather not do it now.

Warren and Elspeth had given me enough money to take care of my needs while I was in St. Theresa. They made me promise to contribute weekly to the household rather than taking over purchasing groceries altogether. Of course, I did exactly what I promised not to do. The need was so great that I could not hold on to the money when the cupboards were bare, as they so often were. I could not cook, nor did I desire to learn, and so I purchased whatever I wanted to eat – mostly cakes and deserts from the local store. In no time at all, I ran out of money and was afraid to ask for more, but the Pardmores were very faithful and continued to send me money on a regular basis. As far as my relatives in Kingston were concerned, I was still living in Canada. All my mail was routed through Canada. Letters that came to me from Kingston were, of course, sent to Canada, and the Pardmores would then mail them to me in St. Theresa. My responses were sent to Canada to the Pardmores and they would return them back to Kingston to my family. Everything was going according to plan.

One afternoon, Lynn announced that we were invited to a party hosted by a family in Harris Store, and that meant we had to descend suicide hill to get there. I was close to six months pregnant by then and was even more afraid of the hill. My cousin accused me of being lazy, and I suppose I was, but I did not care. My pregnancy did not change the fact that I was still a fifteen year old child. Because of the remoteness of the town and the fact that entertainment was very limited, I actually began to consider attending the party, but two very compelling reasons made me hesitate – my growing bulk and my enemy, the hill. I eventually acquiesced and down the hill Lynn and I trekked, while I held on to every branch that grew by the side of the road, making a silent plea to God to prevent me from falling.

We eventually made it to the party, but throughout the trip I endured my cousin's eye rolling and disdainful looks as she waited for me to catch up to her. I promised her then that I would buy her a house at the bottom of the hill when I became rich, and I meant every word of it then. The party was hokey, I thought, but the people were friendly and very kind to me. After all, I was Lynn's pregnant cousin from Canada. I recognized some of the younger crowd, and so eventually I began to feel more relaxed as the night progressed.

As happens in my favorite romance novels, suddenly across the crowded room, I spotted the most handsome man I had ever seen in my life. He was very tall – over six feet, I imagined. Our eyes met and held as the DJ began to play Neil Diamond's *Red, Red Wine*. He walked slowly toward me with a gentle smile as he held out his hand to me. I felt very fat and ugly, and in those few seconds, I considered refusing, but I found myself being guided to the crowded dance floor. That was singly the best experience of my life up to that point. After a while, I closed my eyes, rested my head on his shoulder, and allowed myself to be transported to another time, another place. I fell in love with Michael Matthison by the end of that evening, and in less than six months, we became man and wife.

BOOK 2

I Is A Married Woman Now

CHAPTER 13

Michael was Prince Charming. He courted me like a proper gentleman, and very soon he became my everything. He was twenty years old and lived with his parents in Harris Store. He also owned a car, which was a rarity in the village, and we went sight-seeing almost every evening after he came home from work. I discovered from my cousin that he was considered one of the most eligible bachelors in town and I felt very lucky to have caught him. He worked as a printing and photographic technician at the University of the West Indies in Kingston, which made me even more convinced that he was a man of the world. We casually discussed my plans for the baby and also talked about my impending return to Canada. I ignored his suggestion of not returning, but promised to make a decision about our future after my baby was born. Our relationship was beginning to get more complicated than I envisioned, and while I looked forward to the time we would be together, I chose not to think beyond the present moment. Up to that point I had not yet investigated any adoption plans for my child and secretly hoped that I could leave him with my cousin until I completed school in Canada. Because legal adoptions were very uncommon at that time, I did not know where or how to begin the daunting task of exploring my options. Instead, I chose to wait for life to unfold and for new revelations to come to me on a daily basis.

One day, I made the decidedly scary trip down suicide hill to go shopping in Harris Store. It was a beautiful day, and as I stopped to talk to some of my newfound friends, I noticed a well-dressed woman walking across the street toward me. She stood out because of her stylish attire and her purposeful stride. It was obvious she was not a local, and I gave her the obligatory smile. As she came closer, I realized that she was a longtime friend of my mother's. Norma had immigrated to England a few years before and I knew that she had lost touch with my family during that time. Nevertheless, panic set in as she stood directly in front of me. We hugged stiffly, both pretending that this was just a casual happenstance. No mention was made of the fact that I was in St. Theresa, and neither was any mention made of my obvious pregnancy. We exchanged a few pleasantries and I accepted her invitation to meet for dinner sometime in the next few days, knowing full well that I would never show up. She told me that she was returning to England soon, and I vowed silently never to set foot in Harris Store until I knew that she was gone. The chance meeting bothered me for a while, but over the next few days I had no choice but to dismiss it from my mind.

Time continued to drag by slowly and I was engrossed in my comfortable relationship with Michael. One day, as I sat on the small verandah of our home reading the latest book that he bought me, I heard the sound of a car engine as it slowly struggled up the hill. As usual, whenever we heard the rare sound of a vehicle, we stopped whatever we were doing to see who the visitor was. It was a yellow cab. I squinted in order to get a better look at the lone passenger sitting in the back seat, and my heart suddenly began to pound at a very rapid rate. Although the person's face was indistinguishable, I knew that it was a woman. I watched closely as the cab slowly drove by. Then took a deep breath, and slowly exhaled, but just as I began to relax, the cab stopped, and slowly reversed. I stood mesmerized, planted where I stood as the door creaked open, and my mother slowly emerged from the back seat. We stared at each other for what seemed like forever. At first, she did not move and neither did I. When I saw the tears slide down her cheeks and her arms finally outstretch toward me, a new connection was made between us - mother and daughter. It was a connection like we never had before. I knew intuitively that in her mind she had traveled back in time, to more than fifteen years before when she was in the same predicament that I now found myself. She too, had been a scared, pregnant teenager.

We hugged and cried for a long time before I could bring myself to tell her the whole story that began seven months before. She listened, never once interrupting me. She said nothing until it was clear to her that I had finished my story. "My grandchild will never be put up for adoption," she said simply. "I will take it. Your mother is here now and you don't have to be afraid anymore." Later that evening she met Michael and his parents, and that too was love at the first sight for them. I received nothing but love and comfort from my grandmother when I finally had to face her, and it was then that I recalled my Aunt Yvonne's prophetic words, "It is not the end of the world." I believed it then, more than ever before.

When Michael asked me to marry him, I accepted immediately and completely. My family was not as enthusiastic, but in time they too joined in and decided to help with the wedding celebration. My son, Martin Anthony, was born on Christmas day, 1968, at Green Bay Hospital in St. Theresa. It didn't take long for me to adapt to my new role as mother. And a mere four weeks later I stepped into another role: the wife of Michael Hubert Matthison. I did not have much time to celebrate or to regret my decision, because two weeks later, I said goodbye to my family, my new husband, and my newborn baby, and I headed back to Canada for the second time.

This time the Pardmores met me at the airport. I was overjoyed to see them, but felt a small pain tugging at my heartstrings because I wanted to be with my child and my new husband. I had also broken my promise to my benefactors and had yet another secret that I kept from them, and I was restless. I could not sleep and I felt guilty. Finally, I sat down with them a few days later and confessed that I had gotten married. I told them about Michael and I also told them that my family knew that I had the baby and that he was never put up for adoption.

"Do you want to go back to Jamaica?" they asked me, and I nodded affirmatively. They respected my decision and I immediately wrote to everyone telling them that I would be returning home. There was still a seed of doubt in my mind as to whether or not I was doing the right thing. I loved this new adopted family who showed me nothing but unconditional love and tolerance at all times. They embraced me when I left Toronto International Airport and we promised to always stay in touch.

My new husband greeted me with open arms at the airport. I was so happy to be home again that I did not give much thought to where we would live permanently. I assumed that at some point, we would move to

Kingston, because after all, Michael worked in Kingston. Living in Harris Store was…well, at the risk of insulting its residents back in 1969, I will say it was a tad mundane, especially to a poor fifteen-year-old city kid. Reality hit pretty hard when I realized that not only would we live with his parents, but Michael had designs of building a house for us next to his parents. Since I was still on a high and very much in love, I tried to look on the positive side of this situation.

The Matthisons' large holding consisted of several acres of raw farmland with every imaginable variety of fruit trees growing wild, as far as the eye could see. There was even a brisk running stream bordering the northern section of the property. From time to time, Michael and I would take our laundry there for a thorough wash and then bathed in the clear fresh water. Still, I secretly thought that this lifestyle made for much better romantic reading than for actual living. It was difficult, and I was not prepared, nor was I ready, to accept it. My stark reality was that my young family was now sharing the senior Matthisons' residence with them, four additional grandchildren ranging from five to ten years old and a dotty old lady… Aunt Dore (my husband's paternal grandmother).

Aunt Dore was a character. Her bedroom was in the rear of the home next to the kitchen. She never came into the main house because my mother-in law would never permit her to do so. She was old -too old, I thought. Frankly, she gave me the willies even though she was very small in stature – probably less than five feet tall, but that was because she was hunched over. She was stone deaf and had a big wart on the side of her nose, and so she reminded me of a storybook witch. In retrospect, she was actually a sweet old lady and had a ready smile whenever she saw me. From time to time, I would see her wandering around the property with her ever-present cane. She moved with surprising speed, despite her age and frailty, and that was a bit unsettling to me. I shuddered at times when Aunt Dore would suddenly approach me from behind, and requested that I come to her cluttered tiny bedroom. She would smile, grip my hand with her bony fingers, and show me old faded photographs of people long gone, but who were obviously dear to her. She proudly displayed trinkets that she stored in her trunk, and told me stories about them. Although I did not understand most of what she said, it was much easier to nod and smile. I learned that that was easier than asking her to repeat herself. After a while, I began to feel closer to her and would sit in her musty little room and listen to her ramble on about anything her heart desired at that moment.

My mother-in-law often complained that the old woman was cunning and deceitful and rarely spoke to her, even though she never failed to have Aunt Dore's meals set aside each day. I often wondered what could possibly have happened between these two women to create such derision on the part of my mother-in-law. No one was willing to tell the story if they knew, and I learned to live with the silent feud. Both women eventually passed on…first the older and then the younger, and sadly, to the best of my knowledge, there was never any reconciliation between them.

In spite of this failing that I saw in my mother-in-law, she was otherwise a lovely woman. She had long, bone-straight, steel-gray hair that was always braided in one plait and rolled in a bun in the back of her head. Both she and her husband were very light complexioned. I discovered later that both of my in-laws had a white grandparent. My mother-in-law was a true beauty when she was young and she usually had a kind word for everyone, except of course, Aunt Dore. I admired the way she cared for her garden. She loved plants and flowers and had a profusion of rare plants in her garden surrounding the sagging front porch. I loved to watch her prune and water her plants each day. Everyone commented on the vibrant colors – reds, greens, and yellows – that welcomed them to the Matthisons' residence.

Working Girl

CHAPTER 14

Michael and I continued to be blissfully happy in those days. We went for walks almost daily through the rugged property, and it was during those walks that I confirmed that I was more of a city girl and Michael was a confirmed country boy at heart. We spent a lot of time learning about each other's dreams and aspirations – something we glossed over during our whirlwind romance. He planned on modernizing his parents' home, he said, and he wanted my opinion about where on the property we would build our own home. Decisions of that magnitude were way out of my league. It was difficult to acknowledge that only a year ago my biggest concerns were maintaining good grades in school, and imagining what it would be like to kiss my boyfriend for the first time. Now, I was trying to make grown-up decisions about a newborn baby, a career, a husband, and a home. I hoped with all my heart that my husband was not serious about staying in St. Theresa permanently, but would consider relocating to Kingston.

I was eventually able to persuade him to take me to Kingston with him so that I could begin job hunting. We decided that I would ride in with him a couple of days each week so that I could look around for work and also spend some time with my family. On the first day, we dropped Martin off at my grandmother's and I began my job search. At first I went to major department stores and inquired about positions as a sales clerk. I did not have a high school diploma and was pretty much unqualified for any position. I was not yet sixteen years old and not exactly what employers were seeking, but I would not be deterred. As a last resort I finally decided to research the classified ads on the weekend.

The following Sunday I purchased a newspaper and began the tedious task of circling the few positions that I wanted to apply for that week. There was one ad that I found particularly interesting. It was from one of the largest banks on the island, Broadmoor Bank, and it stated that there were several positions available. I thought back to the times when I was little girl and accompanied my grandmother to the Government Savings Bank, and how much I admired the elegant and sophisticated looking bankers. I told my grandmother on one occasion that one day I would get a job there. So as not to disappoint me, she cautioned me that all of the employees were of Asian or Caucasian descent or what we termed as Brown (light-skinned blacks). I knew that my grandmother loved me dearly and she believed me to be smart, but she was afraid that I would be hurt if I dared to dream too big. Neither of us had ever seen a banker that looked like me, and so she believed that my black skin would prevent me from acquiring certain positions, and that was just the way things were.

With that memory still nagging me, I went to the bank on Monday morning feeling less confident than I did over the weekend. I was very excited when I spotted a well-dressed, young, black man right there among the other bankers. His skin was as dark as mine and I immediately felt that I had found an ally. The fact that he did not acknowledge my smile did not dampen my enthusiasm in the least, because I had bigger hurdles to navigate. In a matter of a few hours I was lucky enough to get an interview and was surprised that I was not required to produce a high school diploma, which I stated that I had. I was also not required to show any proof of my age, which I documented as eighteen. I breezed through a series of math and basic grammar questions, and was hired on the spot. I wanted to be a teller because I felt that that was the 'face' of the bank, but instead I got a position in the current accounts department, behind the scenes. My grandmother was shocked when I told her that I had gotten a job at Broadmoor Bank, and told everyone who would listen that her granddaughter was now a banker.

I grew up at that job, even though I only worked there for just over a year. It was in that position that I experienced the upheaval when Jamaica converted their currency from sterling to dollars and cents. It was a difficult transition, especially for us in the banking industry, as many of our customers felt that they were being gypped because our dollar was valued more than the American dollar. It was there that I met Venus, Susan and Joan, who became lifetime friends. Joan told us many stories of her kooky room-mate, Amanda. I would never have guessed then that Amanda and I were destined to walk side by side in a beautiful friendship – from our teen years in Jamaica to our eventual move to the United States. We experienced much laughter and tears; through marriages, divorces and childbirth, and as we matured, so did our walk with the Lord.

Within a few short weeks at the bank, I discovered that I was pregnant with our second child. Shelby arrived on January 9, 1970, just thirteen months after her older brother, Martin. This job was also where I learned to speak my truth with kindness and empathy. That lesson, though painful, became a benchmark for many uncomfortable confrontations that I would encounter in my life.

The incident occurred when I was still a fairly new employee at the bank. My husband and I had very little money at the time, because I had just started working and we had an infant to care for. Luckily for me, we were required to wear uniforms to work, and so I did not have the added clothing expenses. Having spent most of our ready cash on these uniforms, I had to delay getting new shoes immediately. Admittedly, my shoes were not exactly new nor were they attractive, but I hoped that they would go unnoticed until I was able to purchase new ones. One day, a fellow employee, an older woman, approached me and told me that she needed to talk to me privately. Once we were out of earshot, she proceeded to tell me that she owned several pairs of 'old broken down' shoes, and while they were very comfortable, she would never dream of wearing them to work. She further advised me to do the same, not knowing that for me, those shoes were not a choice but they were all I had. I thanked her for sharing her story, but in my mind I wished that I could immediately die from abject embarrassment. I felt back then that her talk was more of an indictment than a show of kindness. It was even more painful because I was still forced to wear my 'old broken down' shoes in shame, until I was able to purchase new ones with my next paycheck.

Michael and I eventually rented a small studio apartment in Kingston after Shelby was born. It was very convenient to my job in the Cross Roads section of Kingston. I grew more and more accomplished as a machine operator at the bank, and while there were few career development courses available at the clerical level, I tried to get as much information as I could about continuing education. I tried to transform myself from a fifteen-year-old high school drop-out, to what I thought was a sophisticated woman. In just over a year, I used the experience I garnered to get a new position in the accounts department of a large retail store downtown. Although the move netted me a much higher salary, in retrospect it was an ill-advised move. I was fired after a few weeks because I was unfamiliar with the machines they used in their accounting programs. My trainer, a young woman just a few years my senior, had me sit next to her while she operated her machine at breakneck speed and seldom allowed me to actually get any hands-on experience. By the time I was let go, I was about ready to leave anyway because I missed the camaraderie I had at my previous job.

My mother babysat Martin during the week while my in-laws babysat Shelby, and on weekends we picked up both children and we were a family. It was a cumbersome arrangement, but we were able to save the money we would have spent on a babysitter, and we also felt comfortable that our children were well cared for by their respective grandparents. I, on the other hand, was doing the best I could to adapt to married life, but was failing miserably. I hated most things about being married. I was still a rotten cook and I hated to do laundry because everything had to be washed by hand. I enjoyed caring for the children and I also enjoyed caring for our home. Cleaning and decorating were all I wanted to do.

All too soon, my Prince Charming began to turn into a frog, once we moved away from his parents' home. He was very demonstrative regarding his feelings about the meals I tried to prepare. If the meal was not to his liking, he would undo his belt and beat me as though I was an errant child. I was miserable and did not know how to get him to stop, plus I was too embarrassed to tell anyone. He then developed the habit of staying away from home until the wee hours of the morning. That behavior escalated and pretty soon he began to come home intoxicated several nights per week. Some nights he did not bother to come home. As a result, he lost his job at the university when he refused to go to work, due to his hangovers. I watched my once handsome and attentive prince deteriorate before my eyes. He became sullen, ill-tempered, and moody most of the time. I tried to ignore the problem, hoping that he would come to his senses sooner rather than later, but I saw my husband become my mother when the alcohol controlled him. I did not understand this insidious disease of alcoholism.

My mother made my childhood very miserable and now, unwittingly, I chose a husband who appeared to have a similar problem as she did. We did not classify the problem as alcoholism; back then, it was not considered a disease. If you drank too much, you were considered a drunkard and not a fit member of society. In my naiveté, I felt that both he and my mother's problems stemmed from the fact that they liked to drink and that they could stop whenever they wanted to, but they just did not care enough to do so.

I did not consider leaving Michael then, even though I was desperately unhappy. The feelings of hate and shame that I felt for my mother were now being transferred to my husband. The physical abuse caused the love I felt earlier in our relationship to be replaced by fear and shame. In addition to the physical and emotional abuse, I felt that he was having an affair or affairs, but I had no proof. He was unemployed more often than not, so there was always a shortage of money. I merely existed those days. I was ill equipped to handle our various problems but I tried to survive. When I thought of leaving, I knew that he would never allow me to take our daughter from his parents. Since Martin was not his biological child, I knew that he could not prevent me from taking him. I waited and hoped for a change, because deep down I was terrified to make a move. I was trapped.

So here I was at sixteen with high school friends long forgotten, friends at work who were going to nightclubs, dating, and having a good time. I, on the other hand, was living with an abusive man who rarely worked. My teen years were almost over and I never had a chance to enjoy them.

I clearly remember the day that I knew for sure that I was going to leave my husband. We went to the country on a Friday evening to spend the weekend with his parents and I was relieved that I could get away from cooking, if only for the weekend. As usual, he went off alone on Friday night and did not show up until late Saturday morning. His parents and

I were appalled when he returned looking green and disheveled. He then proceeded to throw up in the middle of his parents' living room floor. I looked at him in total disgust, picked up my purse, and walked to the nearest bus stop, which was almost six miles away.

I wanted to go home to my grandmother, and I did just that. I tearfully told her how miserable I had been, and she was very surprised since I had never told her about the problems we were having. She may have wanted to encourage me to leave my husband, but he showed up a few hours later and apologized to us and promised that he would be a better husband. At that point, she felt she had no option but to encourage me to go back to him. Although he was never physically abusive after that, his drinking continued to get worse. I slowly began to formulate plans to leave and waited until I felt that the time was right.

In the meantime, I began to learn to cook, even though I still did not enjoy it. My friend, Judy, was a wonderful and patient teacher, and although things did not get any better at home, I slowly began to feel better about myself. I wrote to one of my cousins in New York asking for assistance in securing a visa but I never got a response back and so I waited for another opportunity. By that time I had a position as a teller in a small bank downtown Kingston, and I was very happy, though not for long. That job proved to be more dangerous than I anticipated.

The first time I came face to face with danger occurred on a normal weekday morning when things were pretty slow at the bank. It changed dramatically as the day progressed when a man approached my window and slid a checking account withdrawal slip toward me. I glanced briefly at him and asked what type of account he had. He responded that he had a savings account, and so I slid the form back to him, pointed to the kiosk behind him and informed him that he could get the correct slip from one of the slots. He hesitantly retrieved the form and I proceeded to serve the customer behind him.

Within a few minutes, the man approached my window again and slid the same form toward me. I glanced at it and was surprised that he still did not have the correct form. I looked up at him a bit annoyed and began to explain patiently that the correct forms were behind him. As I looked a bit closer at the form I noticed that he had bold writing all over it and I guessed that he was probably unable to read or write well.

"THIS IS A HOLD-UP. HAND OVER THE TENS AND TWENTIES" was written in bold ink.

I looked up alarmed, and noticed that he had his right hand hidden in his jacket and there was a suspicious bulge that he was moving up and down. Again I looked directly in his eyes with skepticism, while in my peripheral vision I saw the teller next to me looking over at us with obvious interest. She immediately closed her drawer and performed the worst acting job of pretending to casually walk over to our supervisor's desk. When I noticed my customer fidgeting, I quickly stuffed the bills from my drawer in the brown paper bag he provided. I also tried to include a stack of 'decoy' fifty cent notes that we kept in our drawer for just this occasion. When he saw those notes he gestured "NO" to me with a tilt of his head. I quickly put the decoy notes back. As soon as the bag was sufficiently full, he grabbed it from my hand and walked briskly out the door. The teller and our supervisor immediately walked over to me and led me to a room in the rear of the bank. She had noticed that I was being robbed because she had a similar experience some months before.

The police were called in, but reported that the robber had escaped on a motorcycle going the opposite direction on the one way street in front of the bank. I might have appeared to be in shock because one of the officers put his hand gently on my shoulder and asked my name. I heard him clearly, but I could not mouth the words to respond. I was so nervous that I began to shake from head to toe. Someone handed me a glass of water and had me sit for a while to compose myself before giving my statement to the police. The robber was never apprehended, and for weeks my heart lurched whenever someone pushed a form toward me. The bank was robbed again several months later, and so I decided that being a teller was a bit too dangerous for my liking, and began to seriously consider leaving the position. Even though I got a better look at the robber the second time and was able to describe him to the authorities, he too was never caught. As a matter of fact, we felt that it might have been the same robber each time because he had been lucky enough to elude capture each time.

Pygmalion

CHAPTER 15

Not only did my home life continue to deteriorate, but my health was also being affected as well. I was nervous most of the time. It seemed that everything around me was falling apart and even my job was no longer satisfying. Since I was the only one with a steady income, whenever necessary I would come in to work early and stay late. I wanted to be a model employee because I could not afford to get fired. As one of only three tellers in this small bank, I knew most of the customers well. At times, some of the male customers flirted innocently with me. There was one customer in particular who managed to have a kind word and a smile for me whenever he came in to do his banking. David Simmons was the president of a successful business enterprise and he kept several of his accounts at our bank. On occasion, he invited me out to lunch, but I politely refused because I felt he was just being kind. We both knew that the other was married and so the invitations became a standard joke between us. Never-the-less, when he persisted, I was flattered by the attention.

One afternoon we met accidentally as he was finishing his meal at a restaurant near my office. I accepted his invitation to join him at his table and we shared a pleasant lunch. However, I did refuse his offer to pay for my lunch because, as I joked to him, I did not consider it a date. He walked me back to my office afterward and suggested that we have lunch again at some point in the future, and I promised that we would. He added that the next time it would be a date, to which I responded coyly, "Maybe". I knew that it was highly improper to go out with him, but I gave myself every excuse I could think of. My frustration about my job and my crumbling marriage were at the top of the list. David and I lunched together regularly for about a month and he eventually became my confidant. While he gave no advice about whether to stay or leave, he made it very clear that he would help me financially should I choose the latter. The prospect of leaving my marriage was still very daunting, so I thanked him for his offer, but politely refused.

When my husband did not show up for three nights in a row and finally stumbled home drunk, I called David and told him that I was ready to leave. He promised to speak to a friend about an apartment and get back to me. The next day he took me to Havendale, a very exclusive neighborhood, and showed me a furnished apartment that he thought would be perfect for me. We signed a one year lease and he paid whatever rent and security deposit was due, and then he gave me the key. The following day I packed all my clothes and my children's clothes, and hired a cab to take me to my new home. I did not speak to Michael, but I wrote a letter to his parents informing them that I had left their son.

Over the next few weeks I was very nervous that Michael would come looking for me, but he never did, and so I began to feel safe. I was very excited about with my new place; it was beautifully furnished but I had to share the kitchen with the landlord. Since I had no intention of cooking, that was never a problem for me. The warning, 'look before you leap' kept ringing in my ears, but I chose to ignore it. David was very wealthy and more than twice my age, plus he was a married man and I knew that I was flirting with danger. He was well over six feet tall and not particularly handsome, but his face had character. He was also a fine man; I thought and felt that he was committed to helping me because he knew I was in a desperate situation. In the beginning we went shopping for the groceries and toiletries that I needed and I felt happy and free. My mother totally supported my move but by then my grandmother had moved to the United States and lived with my Aunt Yvonne. I chose not to tell my mother about my benefactor and so she continued to babysit my son during the week. I did not see my daughter for several weeks because I was afraid to go to the country to see her. Michael's parents informed me that he had moved back home with them and I felt it was wise to stay away for a while.

On my first dinner date with David, I dressed in what I considered a sophisticated grown-up dress and waited expectantly for him to arrive. When he looked at me appreciatively, I felt that I had succeeded in dressing the part. He opened the car door for me and fussed at me throughout the evening to make sure I was comfortable, something my husband had long ceased to do. I was still not yet seventeen and I had never tasted alcohol before, but I decided that it was time for me to try. I wanted to appear sophisticated, so I told my server that I would like a glass of "Harvey's Bristol Cool Sherry." I thought I heard a friend order that drink at one time. He smiled at me and brought us our drinks a few minutes later. I took only a few sips that evening because I was unaccustomed to the taste, but I felt that I was playing my part well. I was mortified when I learned later that the drink was Bristol "cream" and not Bristol "cool" like I ordered. That's when I realized why both David and the server seemed amused most of the evening. I was very happy that I nursed that one drink all night, through dinner, and did not have to repeat my order – so much for sophistication.

As our relationship progressed, David elicited the aid of one of his friends to take me shopping for clothes that were appropriate for the functions that we attended. I listened closely to her advice. I copied her speech patterns and tried to mimic the way she walked and even the way she sat because I thought she was one of the most glamorous women I had ever known. David and I went to the finest places on the island, or so it appeared to me at the time. My most memorable experience was going to the very formal Governor General's Ball with him and actually meeting and shaking hands with Sir Clifford Campbell, the Governor General himself! I was living a fairy tale lifestyle and it was intoxicating. My naiveté was a thing of the past. I became a quick study and I knew he was proud of me. He was my Henry Higgins and I was Eliza Doolittle. What more could I ask from life? I was the envy of my friends. David's friends also became my friends even though they were closer in age to him than to me. I knew that they looked up to him and also that they accepted me, naturally, because I was with him.

Although David did not forbid me to see my friends, I knew that he preferred that I did not. I would never have stood up to him nor would I have done anything to upset him. He owned the new me but all too soon

I felt I was beginning to suffocate. I wanted to rebel but I liked my new lifestyle. I was again at another crossroads in my life and did not know what was best for me.

One day, I noticed a well-dressed woman who stopped in the bank to speak with the manager. My friend Kay, who was also a teller at the bank, handed me a note informing me that she was Mrs. David Simmons. I was terrified that she had found out about David and me and was there to confront me. I immediately placed a "next teller please" sign in my window and quickly left the office in case a precipitous retreat was in order. Luckily, she wasn't there to see me, but I was nervous for the rest of the day. That night, I told David that I met his wife, but he spent a long time trying to convince me that he and his wife had an 'understanding' and that she knew about me and that I had nothing to worry about. Eventually, I calmed down, but things never returned to what he considered as normal. I wondered if at any point he would divorce his wife and marry me, but I also was unsure if that was what I really wanted.

A few months after my relationship with David began, my friend Kay and I noticed a very handsome young man who stopped in the bank to open an account. We both mouthed, "WOW!" as we helped our respective customers. For the next few weeks, Brad became a regular visitor to the bank, and sometimes he flirted openly with Kay and me. One afternoon, he invited us both to a concert at the National Arena. He also promised to bring a friend and so Kay and I eagerly agreed to go. Of course, my immediate problem was David: how would I get his approval to attend the concert? Even more importantly, did Brad like Kay, or did he like me? Of course, Kay gently reminded me that I already 'had' David, so I should back off. I rejoined that I did not 'have' David, his wife did. In fact, every now and then when I thought of his wife, I began to feel ashamed. I was still riddled with guilt, no matter how much David tried to convince me otherwise. The life I was leading was quickly losing its shine and I knew that I had to end the relationship. I desperately wanted to go out with friends my own age and was actually tired of only associating with people twenty to thirty years my senior. I was once again, caught up in a relationship that was too much for me to handle – my marriage had been too much of a bad thing, while this new relationship was possibly too much of a good thing.

On date night, Brad and his friend, Jim, picked me up first. I sat in the back seat of the two-door sedan while we drove the few blocks to pick up my friend. When we got to her place, she was already waiting for us. She joined me in the back seat and we looked at each other questioningly and shrugged. We both agreed that although Brad's friend, Jim was a good looking young man, we both preferred Brad. The concert was exciting but there was still no clear indication by intermission who had won Brad's heart. The balance of power shifted back and forth throughout the evening because both men appeared to give equal attention to Kay and me. She and I decided that the ride home would be the deciding factor. The winner would be whoever was taken home last. When the concert ended, we knew that the moment of truth was fast approaching. Brad informed us that he was taking Jim home first since he lived closer and so Jim sat next to him in the front. I, however, made a tactical error; I sat directly behind Brad, thereby giving Kay the advantage of moving to the front seat when we dropped Jim off. She must have been thinking the same thing, because as soon as Jim said his goodbyes and left, she was out of the car in a shot and promptly sat in the coveted seat next to Brad. I had never seen anyone work with such speed and agility. We said our "we had a good time" mumblings, "we'll do this again soon," and then we were off. I silently mouthed to Kay "I'll get you for this" and began formulating plans to kill her and get rid of the body.

In about twenty minutes or so, we rolled to a stop…at Kay's place. It was now her turn to shoot me death glares. I, in turn, grinned and waved goodbye from my new position in the front seat. Brad and I drove the couple of minutes to my home in silence, and once we arrived, I told him about my relationship with David. He was not impressed. Rather, he did his best to convince me that I needed to end the relationship immediately – something I was afraid to do. Even though Brad was a great guy, my track record to that point was far from stellar. I felt that I could no longer trust my judgment regarding relationships anymore, so I listened more than I talked. He promised to call me the following week and I promised to consider going out with him once again. This time it would be just the two of us. By the end of the week, I was pretty anxious to see him again. Kay had gotten over her jealousy but wasn't at all sure what to advise me about David. She was not much older than I was, and she too was dazzled by David's affluence. By the end of the week, I found myself agreeing to go out on another date with Brad.

Since I did not end the relationship with David, we decided to go out on Friday night instead of Saturday because I knew that David was usually unavailable most Fridays. We decided not to take any chances, so Brad drove me home from work and I quickly grabbed the clothes I needed for our date. As I walked out the door, I looked furtively up and down the block before I got in his car to make sure that David was not around. We went to Brad's parents' home, where I proceeded to shower and dress for the evening. His mother was very cordial, I thought, despite the fact that I, a strange woman, was showering and getting dressed in her home.

By the time we got to the trendy night spot, I was bursting with excitement. I was unfamiliar with the latest dances and some of the more popular music but I was a quick study and in no time I fit right in with the boisterous crowd. We met some of his friends at the club and I felt very comfortable with their conversation, when we could hear ourselves over the music. I never wanted the night to end, but inevitably it did, and finally Brad drove me home. Interspersed with the fun I had that night was the strange sensation that I was not being my true self. This girl that Brad seemed to care for was someone manufactured by another man; she was not real. I continued to play the part, however, and was grateful that I was so lucky.

Again, as a precautionary measure, I did not invite Brad in when we got back to my place, and we parked just down the block like we did the weekend before. Our conversation was also reminiscent of the week before. He urged me to end my relationship with David and I promised that I would. We eventually said goodnight and I walked back to my place, smiling. My head was truly in the clouds because I fell asleep almost immediately, not thinking of any possible consequences for my actions.

I awoke with a start around ten o'clock the following morning when I thought I heard a loud banging at my door. As I walked over to let them in, I wondered if my husband, Michael, had finally decided to make a scene. It wasn't Michael, but Daphne, one of David's friends. She appeared very nervous and ill at ease as she stepped into my living room.

"Where were you last night?" she whispered accusingly. "David is livid!"

Before I could respond or even think of an adequate response, she continued, "He is waiting outside in my car. Be careful."

I won't deny that I was scared, but I mustered up as much bravado as I could and told her that I would be out in a minute. I dressed quickly, trying to think of a plausible story to tell, all too aware that this would not be the appropriate time to end our relationship. When I got to the car, I noticed that David was sitting in the back seat. He motioned me to sit next to him while Daphne got in the driver's seat and slowly pulled away from the curb.

"Where were you last night?" he asked quietly, looking straight ahead.

"My husband found out where I lived and he came by. So, I decided to leave with him, in case you came by unexpectedly."

My explanation sounded rather hollow, even to me. I was trying to think rationally, but was failing miserably. I noticed that Daphne's shoulders tensed as I spoke. We sat in silence for what seemed like forever. He turned to look at me, and then he picked something up from the seat next to him and pointed it at my head. I stared at him in disbelief, terrified, and I suppose I must have started to cry. The gun that was now pointed at my head was bigger than anything else around me. I heard his voice speaking to me in a tone I had never heard before. I could also smell something quite unpleasant – was it fear or metal or possibly a combination of both?

"What are you trying to do to me? You little tramp. I picked you up out of the gutter and made something of you. I know you are lying. I am going to blow your brains out!" He continued like this until Daphne urged him to stop, pulling over to stop the car.

"*What is wrong with you?*" she screamed. "You are scaring the poor girl to death!"

After a few moments, David moved the gun away from my temple, dropped his arm onto the seat, and stared up in the ceiling. I continued to cower in my seat with my hands covering my face, too afraid to move a muscle. Daphne slowly drove to her home, to my chagrin; all I wanted was to get back underneath my covers. When we arrived at her house, David and I sat in the living room while she went into the kitchen and began to putter around, probably almost as nervous as I was.

"Can you get me a drink?" David requested politely, as if the events of the past hour had not happened.

Without hesitating, I went to the bar and poured just a drop of scotch and then I filled the glass to the top with soda. The last thing I needed was for him to get intoxicated. He was never a heavy drinker, at least not around me, but I did not want to take any chances. After the first sip, he looked at me over the edge of the glass and smiled sheepishly.

"Get me a real drink," he said softly, waving the glass toward me.

There were a few other friends in the home at the time, and I was extremely uncomfortable because I didn't know how much they knew. I obeyed and we sat in silence, waiting for our nerves to settle. I glanced furtively at David from time to time and noticed that he was staring moodily outside from the other end of the room. It was more apparent to me then that the stilts on which I had been trying to build this so called charmed life were wobbling badly. This was the time to find my true reality, whatever that may be.

We were both still in a somber mood when we left Daphne's that afternoon. He did not ask me again about the night before and I did not volunteer any information. I suppose we both knew that whatever name we gave our relationship would be redefined as of that day. We were now officially exes. When he pulled up to my place, he reached out for my hand and held it for a moment. He opened his mouth to say something but I shook my head and told him that we would talk later. I walked to my apartment, never looking back. He sat there for a while after I went inside. Then eventually I heard his car drive away. I had never felt quite so alone.

"What is wrong with me?" I thought. All I wanted, all I craved, was to get away from the life I had while growing up. I wanted to prove to myself and others that in spite of the fact that I had a baby at fifteen, I was still viable. I never forgave myself for being in the wrong place at the wrong time, and, unfortunately, in life, there was no opportunity for a do-over. David's loving me, teaching me, and taking care of me made me feel like I was relevant. Indeed, he did pick me up out of the gutter – the gutter in my mind, that is. I had yet to believe that I was good enough. I did not understand that I could be strong on my own, that I didn't need a Henry Higgins to make me feel worthwhile.

The following day, when I recounted the intense events to my friend, Kay, all she could say was, "Oh my God!" repeatedly. When I was finally finished, she asked what I intended to do. The only thing I could say was,

"I'm done." I didn't tell Brad everything that happened, but he knew that David and I were over. However, I had become a different person after that day, and any long-term prospects between Brad and me were doomed. I concentrated on my job and my children, and pretty soon I reunited with my friends, Joan and Amanda, and began learning, a bit late, how to be a 'normal' teenager.

BOOK 3

Coming To America

CHAPTER 16

Slowly, I began to try to re-invent myself. Although I made a conscious decision to take control of my life, there was no script to follow and the only thing I could do was to try to live each day as it came, doing my best not to repeat the errors of my past. Now, at almost eighteen, I was pretty resilient and I began to do the things that I considered normal for my age. David had helped me to get my driver's license a while back – he knew someone at the Division of Motor Vehicles, and that opened up a whole new world for me. My friend Amanda was also a brand new driver, and whenever we could, we pooled our funds and rented a car. I was finally somewhat free to be free. Freedom meant that during the week, I had few 'real' responsibilities.

Amanda got her license a few months before I did, and I felt that she was the better driver, so it often became her responsibility to do the driving. She was also the most out-going and adventurous of our group (which consisted of Joan, Amanda, and me) and was pretty comfortable in taking on the leadership role. But we had a problem: most of the cars had a manual transmission, and we found that balancing the clutch and gas pedals in order to facilitate a smooth start was more challenging than expected. Manipulating the clutch to move from an intersection was particularly nerve-wracking, especially when the road had an incline. Not to be deterred, Amanda generally waited for the driver behind her to come around, because she knew that our car would most likely roll back a few feet, or stall before we could hiccup reluctantly forward. From time to time we encountered obstinate motorists who refused to come around, so her ace in the hole for those occasions was to actually get out of the car and pop the hood. The driver behind us, thinking that there was a problem with the vehicle, would eventually take off in a huff. She would then return to her post behind the wheel amid our knee-slapping, thunderous laughter. She had her pride, after all, and refused to let the world know that she was an inexperienced driver.

One day, Amanda promised to meet me for lunch because she planned on renting a car. By twelve thirty when she did not show up, I figured that she was somehow delayed and opted to grab a sandwich instead. Since we had no cell phone or even a house phone back then, I had no choice but to wait until after work to find out what had happened. On my way home, I stopped by Amanda's place to find out what happened, but as soon as she opened the door and saw me, she began to laugh hysterically. She told me that she arrived at my job just before noon and rode around the block a couple of times looking for a parking space. Eventually, she spotted a small space less than a block away from my office and proceeded to maneuver the car into the spot. After she parked, she got out of the car and began to walk away, but when she looked back she saw that the car was yards away from the curb. She got back in, pulled out, and tried to back in once more but did not get much closer. After four or five unsuccessful attempts, she said she knew that people were beginning to stare. Finally she became so embarrassed that she pulled out for the last time, kept going, and did not stop until she got home. I looked at her incredulously, because I could actually see her doing just that. At first I smiled good-naturedly, and eventually I couldn't help but to join in her laughter, vowing to myself, "No more lunch dates if Amanda was driving."

It was around that time that Amanda came up with the brilliant idea that we should go to the United States for a vacation. I had considered it before, but I was apprehensive about traveling alone and so I put it on the back burner. Joan had dismissed the idea because she had an infant daughter at the time, and no trusted babysitter, so it would have been impossible for her to travel. Since Amanda had a knack for making every adventure seem easy, I began to warm to the idea again. She had close friends living in the Bronx, and coincidentally, many of my relatives, including my grandmother, were now living there also. We wrote letters to our respective contacts, and within weeks the matter was settled. My aunt and Amanda's friends agreed to have us share their homes for the three weeks we planned to vacation in the United States. We immediately applied for our visas and were successful. We were given three month clearances. Ideally, we would have liked to obtain work visas and move there permanently, but we discovered that it was virtually impossible to do so because we were not employed in fields that were in demand overseas. We decided that once we arrived in America, we would figure out a way to stay there.

Before we left, we hosted the biggest going away party the neighborhood had ever seen. Apparently, David heard about the party through the grapevine and decided that that was the perfect opportunity to mend fences. We had not communicated since that disastrous morning, but he had continued to pay my rent until I moved out a couple of months later. When I was summoned to the front door and saw him standing there, I was surprised but extremely hesitant to let him in. He smiled and asked me to walk with him to his car so we could talk. The memory of that frightful morning immediately came rushing back and I hesitated, unwilling to make the same mistake. I looked back at Amanda and she nodded in my direction, assuring me that she would be watching.

We left the group and walked to his car, talking about what was and what might have been. David and I made our peace that night and I was relieved. He apologized repeatedly for his behavior, but stopped short of apologizing for our relationship. He said that he had never done that before or since, and he hoped that I did not hate him. I told him that I did not.

"At least, not anymore," I quipped.

I asked about his wife but he did not want to discuss her, and truthfully, I did not want to hear either. I did not know what else to say.

"If you ever need anything…" he began uncertainly, and I nodded and smiled. We finally said our goodbyes, and he left. I did call on him many years later, when my brother needed a job, and he was kind enough to employ him at one of his companies. We never saw each other again.

Despite our party being a huge success, I spent the majority of the night wondering why we threw this elaborate soirée. While we were hoping to extend our visas when we got to the United States, there were no guarantees that we could do so. Should we be unsuccessful, we would be right back in Jamaica in three months. I did my best to ignore my worries and enjoy the party, determined to hope for the best.

During the three weeks it took to shop and prepare, Amanda and I talked non-stop about our plans. We saw ourselves playing a big role in the Black Power and Civil Rights movements that were unfolding throughout the United States. I had a poster of Huey P. Newton prominently hung on the wall in my bedroom, and we frequently marveled over Amanda's uncanny resemblance to Angela Davis – afro and all. We both read Eldridge Cleaver's *Soul on Ice* and Alex Haley's *Auto-biography of Malcolm X* to further prepare for the 'struggle' ahead. I researched Dr. King and decided that my new heroes were the Black Panthers. Frankly, we were very idealistic teens who boldly proclaimed that we could and would change the world.

What a sight we must have been as we boarded our flight to JFK, dressed in blue jeans and matching red, white, and blue t-shirts! The memories of my trips to Canada were still pretty fresh in my mind, but this trip was different. I was officially emancipated! If things worked out the way we hoped, Amanda and I would be able to secure permanent visas and make the United States our home. Upon our arrival at JFK, we meandered through the airport, listening to the unfamiliar accents and different languages. We gazed at the oversized billboards promising beauty, fun, and riches beyond our limited imaginations. The people appeared sophisticated and fashionable but they seemed to walk much too fast. We moved along with the crowd and the confusing signs as we sailed through immigration and then on to baggage claim. Once we retrieved our meager luggage, we soon found our relatives and made introductions, eager to see our respective homes for the duration of our stay. The $50 tucked securely in my purse seemed woefully inadequate, but that was the maximum amount we were allowed to legally take out of Jamaica at the time. It would simply have to suffice until I could find a way to make some more money.

My cousins were as excited to see me as I was them. I couldn't help but gaze in awe out of the windows of the car, amazed at how busy the roads and highways were, despite it being late at night. I watched and listened eagerly as my cousins pointed out various landmarks and told funny stories about their lives in the Bronx thus far. As we drew closer to our destination, the streets became narrower and more congested and I noticed that there were still many people milling around. The buildings appeared dark and foreboding and there were fewer and fewer trees. It will look much better in the morning, I consoled myself, but I wasn't truly concerned, still too excited to have anything dampen my spirit. I was a bit bewildered when we entered our building and began to climb several flights of stairs to the apartment. By the time we got to the third floor, I could barely gasp out a bewildered "How much farther?" through all of my huffing and puffing. When I heard we had to continue to climb until we reached the fifth floor, I asked in alarm why we could not have just used the elevator. My innocence was met with hearty laughter. I was not accustomed to high rise apartment dwellings, because most of the apartments back home were one-level garden apartments. New York was a strange, yet wonderful place so far.

The following day, while I still hadn't completely adjusted to the stairs or the gloomy-looking building, I adapted quickly enough. My major problem, however, was the weather. Although it was mid-June and the temperature was in the sixties and seventies, I was ill-prepared. Frankly, I could not understand why people kept talking about how 'beautiful' it was! Why were these people so obsessed with the weather? It didn't take very long for me to experience what truly cold weather was like, and I too became weather-obsessed. Our first order of business when Amanda and I eventually met up with each other was to purchase coats - not for the winter, but for everyday living. While everyone else continued to praise the 'gorgeous' weather, we were actually shivering.

My younger cousin, Susan, considered it her duty to keep me abreast of the latest fashion and dance moves. The show 'Soul Train' became a requirement for me to watch. But as I watched the dancers gyrating and twirling around the floor, I was certain that I would never be able to mimic their moves. Susan's critical review of my dance moves when I did my best to dance to 'Yankee' music in our overcrowded living room was a resounding 'thumbs down'. I will stick to my familiar reggae moves, I promised myself.

A few days after my arrival, we took a trip into the city. The trip to Manhattan was an unbelievable: I felt like a newborn just opening her eyes to discover the world as I stared at the enormous buildings that towered above us. In Harlem, I was transported back to the early 1960's, listening to Ben E. King crooning *The Rose in Spanish Harlem.* I truly loved New York!

After two weeks of drinking in the sights and sounds of the Big Apple, Amanda and I had to make a decision about our legal status in the country. We did not want to return to Jamaica, that was a given. So now we needed to explore the various options open to us for permanent visas. My aunt suggested that I meet with her attorney, while Amanda's friends helped her to secure a student visa by providing her with an affidavit of support. She immediately enrolled in school and was fortunate enough to get a job soon after, so things were going well for her. Since I was unable to obtain an affidavit of support, I had no other option but to extend my vacation visa for an additional three months. I eventually got a clerical position at an insurance company, but was perpetually nervous that I would be discovered and deported to Jamaica. I worked hard to stay under the radar in case the immigration department got wind of the fact that I was working. Now that we were both gainfully employed, long forgotten were our dreams of teaming up with the Freedom Fighters and joining the Black Power Movement. We had sold out to the Establishment! We had quickly learned that food was more important than ideals.

My salary was a whopping $90 per week and things couldn't have been better. I was in seventh heaven. Against the advice of wiser family members, we decided to rent our own apartment. There were some basic things that we wanted and needed, and we felt that living on our own would help us achieve these goals. Dating was one of our aspirations, of course, and additionally, I still hated the fact that there was no elevator in my aunt's building. We found an apartment in a beautifully kept building near the Fordham section of the Bronx. Although it was only a one-bedroom apartment, it had almost everything else we were looking for – location, charm, and AN ELEVATOR, but it had very little privacy. Obviously, we did not give much thought to furnishings, because for the first few weeks, we had absolutely no couches, chairs, tables, utensils, or even a bed - just our clothes and toiletries. Even the lack of these things became an adventure. We slept on the floor of the living room, using newspapers and our clothes as mattresses.

Our first purchases within the next few weeks were twin beds and linen. Someone gifted us with a television set and eventually we purchased some much-needed kitchen supplies. Once our kitchen was ready, we ate grilled cheese sandwiches with boiled eggs much of the time, and when we could afford it, Hamburger Helper. We became experts in adding spices to make it more flavorful. Obviously, our budget was very tight and so we watched every penny. Amanda and I were less than thrilled when her boyfriend, Doug, went grocery shopping for us one Saturday and returned with various types of cheeses and breads. We looked in dismay at the fare that he spread out on the table.

"What are we going to do with all of this cheese?" we demanded.

We were expecting groceries for the week! I could not understand a need for various types of cheese, as at that time, I only ate cheese with a spiced bun during our Easter season celebration, as per the Jamaican custom. Obviously, Doug was never asked to shop for us again.

Eventually, Amanda and I settled into a routine and things were going relatively well for us. We were both dating, we went to parties regularly, and we were slowly adapting to the fashion of the day, although our mode of dress tended to be more formal than that of our American counterparts. Our rent was late, more often than not, and of course, our diet was abysmal. One evening when I arrived home from work, I realized that I lost my wallet, and even though I had very little money at any time, losing cash was a severe hardship. None of these things put a damper on our newly found freedom. Amanda continued to attend classes several nights per week and I fell in love with Shirley Temple and *The Burns and Allen Show* on weekends.

One downside to my new life was my job. To me, it was extremely boring. This was probably because I wasn't totally sure of exactly what I was expected to do. I vaguely remember verifying dates and cities on insurance claim forms, but I did not expend much brain energy on these tasks. Even now, I wonder how I could have fumbled through the few months that I worked for the company. The job was so mundane that at times I went to the ladies' room, locked myself in a stall, and took a nap. I am not sure if I was ever missed, but I felt that was at least preferable to sleeping at my desk. One morning, after taking one of my power naps, I woke up after what I felt was a few minutes. I splashed water on my face, cleared my throat, and walked out, hoping that the rest of the day would go by quickly. To my amazement, all of the desks in front of mine - maybe twenty or thirty or a hundred (never mattered much) were all empty. I panicked! How long had I actually been asleep? I looked at my watch and saw that it was still within the normal working hours. Warning bells were now pealing in my ears. I ran to my desk and sure enough, my department was just as empty!

Where the heck was everyone? Did the rapture occur and I got left behind? I looked out through the large picture window to see if the streets were also deserted, but there appeared to be hundreds of people standing under the eaves of the building across the street and spilling over to the end of the block. Bewildered, I noticed some people from the crowd looking up at me and beckoning for me to leave the building. I ran to the stairwell and descended three steps at a time. I froze just before I got to the first floor because I was now hit with a new emotion – embarrassment! How in the world was I going to face all those people? They were all going to be wondering what I was doing in the building all by myself. How long had they been standing outside? I briefly considered merely hiding in the building and facing the consequences later, rather than facing the crowd. Deciding that would only make things worse, I forged ahead, walking through the double glass doors to a burst of cheering from the crowd.

I desperately wanted to be just about anywhere else in the world at that moment. I laughed nervously, waving to the crowd and hoping that I looked more at ease than I felt. I mumbled something about not feeling well and staying in the ladies room until I felt better. I immediately asked what was going on and why was everyone standing outside. They informed me that there was a bomb scare and everyone was ordered to evacuate the building. What puzzled me was why no one checked the bathrooms, but I didn't dare ask. We were all allowed back into the building after the police and the bomb squad deemed it safe, and I remember thinking as I rode home that evening, that it was one of the longest days of my life.

Inevitably, my six months came to an end and I still had no immediate prospects of extending my Visa. My attorney told me that it was almost impossible to get another extension and suggested that I should return to Jamaica or apply for a student visa. Since I could not get an affidavit of support from my family, and I did not want to return to Jamaica right away, I decided to continue working.

One day, I got a frantic call at work from Amanda informing me that a stranger rang the doorbell and asked for me. She said that they mentioned something about a social security card. I immediately panicked, thinking that it must be someone from the Immigration and Naturalization Services. I deduced that since they came looking for me at home, it would not be long before they came to my job inquiring about me. My only solution to this problem was to quit my job immediately and move into a new apartment. I called my friend Susan, who was living in Brooklyn at the time, and told her about my predicament. Without hesitation, she suggested that I move in with her immediately and figure something out. I tendered my resignation that same day, telling my employer that there was an illness in my family in Jamaica and I had to return home immediately. If INS checked, they would believe that I returned home, I thought. Amanda helped me to pack my things and I moved to Brooklyn that night. Much later, I realized that the stranger who came looking for me was a Good Samaritan who had found my wallet with my Social Security Card inside and was trying to return it to me.

On The Lam

CHAPTER 17

Now I am unemployed and sharing a small apartment with my friend and her young daughter in Brooklyn. Susan was an amazing woman; we met each other back in Jamaica when we both worked at Broadmoor Bank. She and her family had moved to the United States a couple of years before and she was now a single parent. She was an exceptional cook and she went out of her way to make me feel welcome, but after a couple of weeks of not being able to find a new job, I began to get discouraged. Amanda was also affected by my move because she could not afford to maintain the apartment on her own and so she was forced to move back to her friend's place. We were both miserable.

Each morning I rode in to Manhattan, handed out my resume, filled out job applications and waited to be called, but nothing happened. I did manage to get a few interviews, but whenever I was asked to show my Green Card, I made an excuse and left. Returning home to Jamaica was beginning to appear to be my only prospect by then, but Susan encouraged me to keep trying. Late one afternoon, as I was about to drag myself to the subway by 59th Street and Lexington Avenue, I decided to stop by a nearby bank and submit one last application before I got on the train. The bank's security guard showed me up to the personnel department on the second floor where I completed an application. There again was the dreaded question about my status in the country. I checked the box indicating that I was a legal resident but left the space blank where it asked for my Alien Registration number. I was about to leave, dejected once more, but I was asked to wait while they reviewed my application. I sat obediently, knowing that I was wasting my time. The interviewer perused the form and then asked me if I would mind answering a few more questions, to which I answered, "No." She handed me another clipboard and showed me to a small office where I completed a personality profile and a few math questions. I handed her the paperwork a few minutes later and waited for the dreaded question about my status, but all she did was look over my profile and my math answers. Afterward, she consulted with her supervisor and finally invited me to take the seat across from her desk.

"Upon reviewing your test scores," she began, "I would like to recommend a position in our Financial Accounting Department. You've done exceptionally well on the math portion of the application, and as it turns out, we do have an opening."

She then informed me that the position paid one hundred dollars per week, while the position of teller paid ninety-five dollars per week.

I was ecstatic! I was hired on the spot and stayed a few more minutes to complete more paperwork, singing to myself the whole time because I had finally found a job. We agreed that I would start at eight forty-five on Monday morning. I thanked her profusely. We shook hands and I headed for the elevator but as soon as I pressed the button, I heard her call my name. I paused and the now familiar dread filled my heart.

"If you could, I'd like you to bring your Alien Registration Card with you when you come in on Monday."

"I will," I croaked as I stepped in the elevator, knowing that I was not going to be back on Monday.

I walked slowly to the train in a daze. When I arrived at Susan's, I told her everything. At first she was excited until I got to the end of my story.

"What are you going to do?" she asked.

I just shook my head because I didn't know what to say. Over the next couple of days, I thought of nothing but how I could get this job. I needed the money and I was very close to packing my things and returning home. I had no immediate answers and by Monday morning my head ached from lack of sleep the night before. I was now operating on auto-pilot; I showered and dressed and I knew that Susan was wondering what my plan was.

Suddenly, I had a thought, "May I borrow your daughter's Green Card?" I asked.

She looked at me with a puzzled expression on her face.

"What are you going to do with it?" After all, her daughter was only about five or six years old and her photograph was clearly visible on the card.

"I dunno," I said in desperation. "I just want to try something."

The ride to Fifty-Ninth Street and Lexington Avenue was over all too soon. Upon arriving at the bank, I was again directed to the second floor where I met Jane. I gave her a sincere compliment and waited for her to take the lead. I was given more instructions about my new position and told who my supervisor was and where my department was located.

"Mr. Jackson is expecting you," she said. "And by the way, did you remember to bring in your Alien Registration Card?"

The moment of truth had arrived, "Yes, I did," I said all too quickly, and reached into my purse, and pulled out the Green Card that I placed in my purse that morning. I then looked up at her sheepishly and said, "I am so sorry, I was so nervous this morning when I was getting ready to leave, that I picked up my friend's Green Card instead of my own, I am so sorry," I repeated.

"Oh, never mind," she said nonchalantly, "Whenever you remember, just stop by so that I can make a copy of it for your file, OK?"

"Thank you," I grinned.

If I could have, I would have done cart wheels right then and there, but instead I walked briskly to the elevator, and once the door closed, I screamed wordlessly and said a quick prayer of thanks. For the next three years I avoided Jane because I did not "remember" to bring in my Green Card. I became very skilled at avoiding her because she had to pass through the accounting department to get to the lunchroom on the third floor. At her designated lunch time I would either be in the lunchroom with my co-workers, or I'd be engrossed in some project until she walked by. That was my pattern each and every day and I became a master at stealth.

Unlike my old job at the insurance company, this job was terrific! I made many friends. One of the saddest experiences that occurred at this job affected my then best friend, Clarence. He stopped by my desk one morning and complained that he had a "strange" feeling all morning that he couldn't shake. When I asked him to define "strange" he said he wasn't sure how to explain it, it was more like an uneasy feeling; it was almost visceral, and he felt it meant that bad news was imminent. I brushed it off and started to hum the theme song from the popular television show *Twilight Zone.* That response got a chuckle from him and I promptly forgot about it and continued on with my day. Later, as I passed by his desk, he looked up and told me that the feeling was gone. He smiled and said he felt fine and I began to hum the *Twilight Zone* theme song again, as I walked away.

A few minutes later the phone rang at my desk, and at first, it was difficult to understand what the caller was saying. After she repeated her name a couple of times, I realized that it was Clarence's mother. I thought it very strange that she would be calling me at my office or even calling me at all. I had met her on a few occasions when she visited from North Carolina but we were never friends. I told her that she must have been transferred to my extension in error but she quickly interrupted and said that she desperately needed to speak to me.

"It's really nice hearing from you, Mrs. Sullivan. How are you?" I asked politely, still a bit surprised.

As I listened to her, the blood must have drained from my face because a couple of my co-workers began to look at me anxiously.

She told me that Clarence's wife, Mona, who was almost eight months pregnant at the time, was involved in an automobile accident. She was on her way to her doctor's appointment when she was hit. Sadly, Mona did not survive the accident but the doctors tried feverishly to save the babies. We all thought she was having twins, but they discovered that she was having triplets, instead. Two of her babies were born dead but a little girl who they later named Victoria, lived for an hour, then she too passed.

Somewhere in a distance, I heard Mrs. Sullivan repeating, "Hello, hello," because I was speechless throughout the entire conversation. I was finally able to respond to her and asked if she had spoken to her son.

"No," she said, "I did not want to give him this information over the phone."

With blinding tears streaming down my face, I finally realized that Mrs. Sullivan wanted me to break the news to him.

"Oh no, Mrs. Sullivan, I can't tell him that. Please, do not ask me to."

I could hear her sobbing in the background, as she told me that she was still at the hospital. I somehow collected myself enough to get all the pertinent names and telephone numbers for my friend to call, and promised to get back to her later, after I broke this incredibly sad news to him.

I couldn't do it alone and so I elicited help from another close friend, Naomi. I gave her all the information I had and we both approached Clarence's desk together. The minute he saw us approaching his desk, he covered his ears with both hands, shook his head, and repeated several times, "I don't want to hear it." Then he walked briskly to the men's room. We followed him into the men's room and begged him to listen to what we had to say. He looked at me with the saddest eyes, and repeated that he knew he was going to get some bad news today. All I kept thinking was, you cannot imagine how bad this news really is. The horrible news spread around the office like wildfire and we all grieved with the Sullivan family for a very long time. It took many years before the spark returned to my friend's eyes again.

Legit

Chapter 18

After working at the bank for a while, I was eventually able to get my own place. I rented a tiny studio apartment in the Bronx, not far from my Aunt's place. My friend, Doug (who had bought cheese with our grocery money) kept trying to set me up with a friend of his who was his basketball partner. At first I refused to be set up because I heard horror stories about blind dates. He knew that I did not date much, and so he decided to take the bull by the horns and stop by my place with his friend after they were done playing ball one Saturday afternoon. Matthew was six feet, two inches tall, with full lips and great eyes; he also had the best legs I had seen on any man and I thought he looked really good in shorts. In addition, he had a great sense of humor and I found myself agreeing to dinner and a movie the following weekend. On Friday night, Matthew arrived with a bottle of wine and we both had a glass before leaving on our date. Dinner was great and the movie, *Blazing Saddles,* was hysterical. We hit it off that evening, and even though we did not have a lot in common then, we began to date each other exclusively in a matter of weeks.

Matthew David Benjamin, III was from an upper middle-class family. He and his family lived in one of the more exclusive buildings on the Grand Concourse near the old Yankee Stadium. I never felt quite comfortable around the Benjamins, and neither did I feel that they were comfortable around me. I thought that my being West Indian might have been the reason. His father, I felt, was extremely reticent and lacked warmth, while his son was the characterization of a really "nice" guy. A few months after we began dating, Matthew convinced me to get married. He knew that I did not have a Green Card and wanted more than anything else to have my children with me. Because he was a US citizen, I would be able to get the coveted Green Card soon after we married. There were no stars and no fireworks, but I really liked him as a person, and after all, I was not sure that I even understood what romantic "love" was. The only marriages I had been close to were far from demonstrative about love. Is it possible that the love and happily after theory we see in the movies and books, was only a fairy tale? In any event, I was now older and wiser, and hoped that I would meet a great guy and we could provide a decent home for my children.

We both announced to his family that we planned on getting married and they seemed genuinely happy for us. At some point, a decision was made that since Matthew's younger sister and her fiancée were dating for many years, it would be a good idea for us to have a double wedding. The argument was that it would defray the cost for all involved, since the Benjamins would be inviting the same people to both weddings. So, our plans for a small wedding flew out the window and we all began planning a major event with the family. Since I was still very concerned about my legal status, and was very anxious to have my kids join me here, Matthew and I got married secretly at City Hall. I immediately began the arduous process of filing my paperwork with the INS, while we went ahead with the big wedding plans to please his family. Like most young women, I soon got swept away in the planning, and the wedding turned out to be a spectacular event. Both my sister-in-law and I were beautiful brides. My Maid of Honor was my friend, Amanda, while Matthew's youngest sister was the Maid of Honor for her older sibling.

Our wedding day, Sunday, October 26, 1975, was the last day of Daylight Savings Time. All clocks were scheduled to be turned back an hour. Luckily, our groomsmen did not realize this, and so when they all raced in the church red-eyed and hung over after a night of celebrating, they were half an hour early, rather than half an hour late, like they thought. That confession was made after the wedding because I had warned everyone about the importance of being on time since our wedding was performed at high mass on a Sunday morning.

Matthew and I moved to an attractive apartment in the Briarwood section of Queens. We made friends with several young couples in our building and we entertained often. I was still uncomfortable around my in-laws because I knew that my husband never told them that I was married before, nor did he disclose the fact that I had two children. I told him that I felt we should do it soon because I planned to bring my children here as soon as possible, but he kept changing the subject. I think that we had waited so long that he was afraid of how they might react. Within months of the wedding, his sister announced that she was pregnant, and I took that opportunity to mention how I felt when I was pregnant with my first child. You could have heard a pin drop in the living room. I must confess that everyone quickly regained their composure and the conversation resumed. Inevitably, we arrived home to an impatiently ringing telephone. We both guessed who the caller was, and so I gave my husband the privacy he needed to speak to his mother. We managed to get through this very difficult situation after I had a heart-to-heart talk with her. She was very understanding but voiced her disappointment that she was not informed of the situation before hand. We made our peace and began to look forward to the arrival of my children.

Finally, the paperwork was approved for my status change and I was required to return to Jamaica to present my documentation to the American Embassy there. I told Matthew that I would prefer to go alone since I would more than likely be running back and forth, rather than enjoying a relaxing vacation; and he reluctantly agreed. I arrived at JFK International Airport with my suitcases bursting at the seams. The airline representative was very lenient and did not charge me for my overweight luggage. I returned to Jamaica feeling both ebullient and terrified. I was worried that something could go wrong and my Visa would be denied. Plus, I was very anxious to be reunited with my children again. I could hardly sit still throughout the three and a half hour flight. Finally, the only message I allowed my senses to send to my brain was one of unequivocal satisfaction. My children and I are finally on our way to become legal residents of the United States. This was nearly five years after Amanda and I arrived in the United States; two years after my marriage to Matthew and I was finally on my way home. Will my children remember me? Did I purchase enough gifts for the family? And on and on my thoughts rambled...

The flight was uneventful, but as we landed at Palisades International Airport, tears began to flow. I am home! It felt good. As I deplaned, a wave of heat engulfed my body. I closed my eyes and whispered, "Home sweet home." Then for a few moments, I felt another pang of uncertainty. Why did I leave this island paradise to live in the United States? It was certainly not 85 degrees when I left JFK Airport this morning! In spite of these thoughts, I regrouped and kept up with the crowd so that I could take care of the business at hand.

My plan was to see my son as soon as possible because I had heard rumors that my mother was a less than capable guardian, and he was left alone on many occasions when she was on a binge. I expected him to be at my Mom's and so I wanted to surprise them. My next stop was scheduled to be at my brother's and sister's place before my final stop for the evening at my friend, Venus's place. Shelby was at her grandmother's in St. Theresa and so I planned to rent a car the next day and drive to St. Theresa to see her. I prayed very hard that I could tackle the dreaded Junction Road, and I was very nervous about seeing my ex-husband for the first time after all these years.

I sailed through customs, grabbed my luggage, and stepped briskly through the double doors and headed towards the first cab on line.

"Where to?" the smiling driver asked.

I gave him the address from memory and waited for him to assist me with my luggage.

There was a very distinct change in his demeanor as he said, "No sista, mi naw go a Jungle."

For a minute I was perplexed, and then I recalled that my mom's neighborhood was now referred to as "The Jungle." This "Jungle" was where I went to school – Willoughby Township, was now an area that was crime infested and extremely dangerous.

I began to rethink my resolve to go to my Mom's place first, after the third cab driver politely refused to take me to the "Jungle." I took a deep breath and decided that I had traveled too far and waited too long to make this trip, and nothing would discourage me now. I formulated a new plan of attack.

I strode over to the next cab in line and asked affably, "Do you know Pegasus?"

I knew that my mother's nickname was Pegasus, and I also knew that she was very widely known in Kingston because of her political involvement.

"Everybody know Pegasus," he responded. "How you know her?" he asked, looking up at me.

"Never mind that," I responded. "I'd like you to take me to her." I read the address once more and quickly added, "I'll pay double the fare." He smiled slyly and appeared to ponder my offer.

"Please," I said coquettishly. He continued to smile and finally conceded.

"Okay, lady, get in, and I will get your bags."

"Mi name Junior," he said and shook my hand.

"I am Grace," I responded, giving him the name my family called me.

As he sped down Windward Road, Junior lowered the volume on the radio, scratched his head, and asked again, "Ow come a nice lady like you known Pegasus?"

"She is my mother," I replied politely.

Even before my mom became "Pegasus", I had been asked that question all my life. Junior threw his head back and laughed out loud, slapping his thigh. He then raised the volume on his radio and we both listened to the reggae beat vibrating from his car radio, both of us deep in thought, while I peered out the window at the familiar sights. The pace was dramatically slower than New York. People seemed to meander slowly as though they had no particular destination in mind. The houses and the businesses were painted with bright vivid colors. I saw splashes of reds, yellows, blacks and greens, everywhere. I remembered the scenery; I even remembered the people. Nothing had changed in the five years I was gone. It was as though time, as I knew it, had stopped since June 23, 1972. Someone had pressed the pause button on the remote control, and today, the day of my return, they just hit the "play" button and I was watching it all in slow motion. I was home!

Once we reached Willoughby Township, instead of taking me to the address I gave him, Junior pulled up at a bar sporting a large billboard advertising Red Stripe beer. He really does know Pegasus, I thought.

He tapped his horn twice and addressed a woman who poked her head around the billboard, "Yu see Pegasus?"

109

"She was 'ere dis morning," responded the woman. "Check the bar down de street."

And so, the investigative work began. We must have stopped at four or five neighborhood bars. Each one told us that she was there earlier and suggested that we go on to the next. I interjected that we should try her home; I did not think it would be so farfetched that she would be home, but before I could continue my discourse, I heard loud voices approaching. Junior pulled over to watch the procession heading our way, and I looked closely at the group of people approaching us. I squinted when a saw the woman leading the group, visibly intoxicated, because of her gait. She had a wide grin on her face as she tried to run toward the cab. In the blink of an eye, the smile became a frown and then she began to cry. Sure enough, the leader of the pack was Enid, AKA Pegasus, my mother. We hugged.

She kissed me several times and grasped my face in her palms, Grace, Grace, yu come."

I understood the emotion she felt at that moment. The joy I felt seeing my mother and my familiar surroundings far outweighed the pain I felt when I saw that she was still drinking. Even though it was embarrassing to continue our conversation in front of the crowd that was getting alarmingly larger by the minute, I followed her cue and began to cry. Junior, my driver, seemed very comfortable as he too exchanged pleasantries with my mother.

With much difficulty, I was able to ascertain that Martin was at my sister's but I'd have to wait until she was good and ready before I could leave for the second leg of my trip. My mother and I, followed by the well-wishers and Junior, slowly made our way through the Jungle, as she introduced me to everyone who stopped to look at our procession. I whispered to God with a smile permanently etched on my face, "Are you seeing this, Lord? I know that you have a special blessing for me." In between introductions, I inserted my obligatory scolding about her drinking. She promised me that she had cut back significantly. She said that today had been an exception. Maybe she had one or two drinks, she said, when she heard that a woman from foreign was looking for her. She claimed that she knew that it had to be her daughter.

"I believe you," I lied, as I indicated to the driver that we would be leaving soon.

We eventually made it to Boston Road to my sister's home where I was finally reunited with my son. It was a joyous reunion despite the fact that he was barefoot and his clothes were dirty. Actually, he looked pretty much like all the other kids around. But somehow, that did not make me feel any better. He stood close to me and held my hand when I spoke to him, while the other kids gathered around teasing him. "Martin, yu mother come from foreign." He grinned with his fingers covering his mouth shyly. He and I talked about everything. He later told me that he'd watch out for Grandma when she came home drunk and I discovered that he did not attend school regularly. I decided then, that I needed to act immediately to make some changes for my son. It broke my heart that he had become a statistic.

The next leg of my trip was to visit Shelby in St. Theresa. My brother, Douglas and I left Kingston fairly early the next day. He was very excited about the trip, and enthusiastically sat next to me in the passenger seat. I didn't have the heart to tell him that I'd never driven on the Junction Road before, and I was actually nervous driving on the left hand side of the road. I started out pretty confidently and immediately asked Douglas to turn off the radio. I found it distracting and very difficult to concentrate with the radio on. As we climbed the mountain at the beginning of the journey, I looked toward the road ahead and my eyes darted to the perilous drop to the right. The only protection for motorists was an ineffective guardrail. We meandered through the dangerous hairpin turns on this two-lane death trap hugging the yellow line to my right as judiciously as possible. I tried not to slow down too much because the cars behind me kept tooting their horns impatiently. The approaching traffic whizzed by with ease while I sat straight up holding on to the wheel for dear life.

We were five miles from Kingston when I noticed that my passenger was also sitting bolt upright in his seat. His eyes were like saucers while he kept them riveted on the road. I took a minute to tease him about being nervous driving with me.

"No, mon, mi good mon he responded in a high pitched voice. Since I too, was nervous, I could not laugh at him but I promised to let it out once I'd "conquered" the Junction Road. An acquaintance of mine once said that in order for a new driver to get their license, the examiner should let him loose at the start of the Junction Road, and if he made it to the end, he would have earned his license, hands down.

We made it safely to the Matthisons' home in Harris Store and my brother emitted an involuntary deep breath and relaxed when I parked. I could be wrong but it appeared that he held his breath for the entire thirty-mile trip that took well over an hour. My former In-laws were warm and welcoming as always and when I saw Shelby approaching, I couldn't believe how tall and graceful she was. Just like with Martin, we hugged and kissed and spent a long time talking. She too, was shy at the beginning, but as we talked, she began to be more comfortable with me. When I reminded her that pretty soon she'd come to America to live with me and her brother, I could see the apprehension in her face. Her mood mirrored mine when I too, faced the prospect of leaving my grandparents. Next, Shelby, Douglas, and I visited my cousin Lynn who had moved from the house I stayed at nine years ago in Bloomfield. It was tough to say goodbye to Shelby yet again, but I knew she was in good hands and so it was easier for me to leave. Douglas and I braved the Junction Road once more, heading for Kingston, but I was a bit more comfortable on the return trip. I even turned the radio on, though the volume was low.

I eventually made it back to my friend's home, and on Monday morning she drove me to my appointment with the Immigration Department. The line was several blocks long and I thought I would never get to see an official that day. It was almost like waiting in line for a popular rock concert but with added trepidation. Similar to other occasions, the anticipation was far more stressful than the actual event, but I did manage to see several officials that day, and thankfully I was very well prepared. All of my documents were in order and by early afternoon I had my Visa secured in my purse. I accomplished a lot that week in Jamaica but now I needed to get back home to the United States so that I could begin the process for my son and daughter to join me. My goodbyes were even harder than five years before because I knew that this wasn't a three-week vacation. It would be several months before I'd be back for my children.

Once I returned to the United States, I felt more relaxed than I'd ever been since I arrived in 1972. I was now a legal resident; happily married and I had a great job that I liked. I had even gotten a promotion to Supervisor in the Financial Accounting Department. I did have some unfinished business I needed to tend to – Jane, from the Personnel Department. I actually approached her early in the week, beaming, and offering a cheery, "Hello!" I never forgot that four years earlier, I promised her that I'd bring in my Alien Registration Card to prove my legal status in the country, and now I was finally able to do so. Obviously, Jane did not remember that promise, but I did. I stood there with a stupid grin on my face when she told me that whenever she passed by my department, I seemed always busy at work.

"Keep up the good job," she praised, and I responded with a rousing "Thank you!"

Jane did not know that, for four years, I made sure I saw her before she saw me and had mastered the art of hiding from her or shrinking into the background. "No more," I whispered to myself as I returned to my desk, – "I am finally legit."

I made a conscious decision to get my son here first for several reasons; my daughter was pretty comfortable in St. Theresa with my ex-husband and his parents. Martin's situation on the other hand, was very precarious. My mother continued to be unstable and her drinking had continued. Even though I moved Martin away to live at a boarding school while I was in Jamaica, I needed to get him here, and settled as soon as possible.

———

My husband and I decided to purchase a home for our ready-made family and so we began to save our money toward that end. I enjoyed living in Queens, but we wanted to move to a more suburban area on Long Island where we felt it would be better for the kids. I certainly would not miss the hustle and bustle of the E and F trains I took to get to the office each day. It was very challenging in the mornings to get to work because most times, by the time the train arrived at the Hillside and Jamaica Avenue Station, it was jam packed and extremely difficult to force one's way onto the train. At times, two or three trains would go by before I could safely position myself on the platform to board.

One morning as I was boarding the overcrowded train, the car was bursting at the seams even more so than usual. I was running late and so I was determined to make it on board. Sure enough, I as well as all the commuters on the platform held our collective breaths and moved as one unit through the door before it closed. The conductor made several attempts to close the door and we all knew the routine; do not exhale until the doors closed behind you! As soon as the doors closed, I managed to squirm a bit, and finally was able to try to put my right foot on the floor, since I was propelled in the car, sliding in on one foot. The minute I set my foot down, I realized that my bare foot hit the ground. It was shoeless! My immediate feeling meter hit a few notches way above the embarrassment scale. I began to panic and tried to look down to locate my shoe, but no one moved because they couldn't. Luckily, the doors rolled open once more and all I could do was yell. "'scuse me, 'scuse me" and barreled through the door, leaving a few disgruntled passengers behind, glaring at me. The train doors closed behind me while I stood lopsided on the platform watching the train slowly disappear from sight.

I kicked off the other shoe to get my balance and then looked around on the platform, hoping to get an answer, any answer, to my dilemma. I spotted a lone woman who had gotten off the train, walking toward the steps leading to the exit. I looked down at the tracks. I'm not sure why I did, but I was looking for answers anywhere. To my amazement, I spotted my beautiful grey pump lying forlornly amid the garbage on the tracks. I want my shoe back! I looked back toward the stranger once more and saw that she was beginning to ascend the steps.

"Scuse me!" I yelled, as loudly as I could.

She stopped and looked back at me. I tried to look as sane as I could, knowing that I needed help from above to accomplish that task. After all, I am standing on a train platform, barefoot, holding one shoe, and looking a tad disheveled.

"My other shoe fell on the tracks," I explained, pointing downward, showing its mate to confirm my sanity.

The stranger began to walk hesitantly toward me. "I want to go down there to get my shoe. Can you help me back up on the platform?" I asked.

I know now that I did not think that scenario through. I really loved those shoes and I was at that really confident stage in my life where I felt I could do anything. The woman nodded, and so I quickly sat on the platform and slid down on the tracks, knowing that I needed to hurry before the next train pulled in. "Oh no!" I thought, "This is a lot deeper than it looks from up there." But, I was focused. I grabbed the offending shoe, threw it on the platform and looked expectantly for my angel of mercy to help me up. But I was eerily alone; my angel had disappeared from sight. I believe I spotted the soles of her shoes as she fled, once more toward the steps, taking her to freedom from me – the crazy lady on the train tracks.

I am not dying here, I thought to myself, and so I grappled the edge of the platform with my elbows and utilized the skills I learned from my childhood days. With the aid of the adrenaline pumping throughout my body, I swung first my right leg up on the platform and then I slid my body up while my stylish red suit was almost sticking to the black, grimy edge of the platform. I eventually gained the leverage I needed to get back on the platform. As soon as I stood upright I saw the new crowd that had gathered, waiting for the next train. They were all gaping at me in in shock. A few seconds later I heard the horn of an oncoming train. I did not look anyone in the eye. I picked up my purse and my shoes and focused only on running up the stairs behind the devil that'd left me to die. All I wanted to do was hit her with my shoe. Common sense prevailed though, perhaps a bit late, but I had to get away from the crowd. I waited until the train left and then I went back down to the platform, looking like a chimney sweep. I ignored the stares of my fellow passengers and went straight to my office. I was mad! In retrospect, I am not sure why I was, or more importantly, who I was mad at, but I was late, dirty, and maybe a tad crazy. Needless to say, when I got to my office, my co-workers stared at my bedraggled look. Some even dared to ask what happened, but stopped short when they saw the murderous look on my face. I wanted to laugh because I had accomplished a death-defying daredevil feat, but I kept my cool. Later that morning I went out and purchased a new dress for the rest of the day. I wasn't brave enough to tell the story to my friends and co-workers until the following day, and when I did, even I was amazed at my stupidity, and still am – to today.

Papa Was A Rollin' Stone

CHAPTER 19

Six months after my initial trip, I returned to Jamaica for the second time, focused on remedying my son's living situation. I was still waiting for his approval papers from the INS, but he needed immediate help. My mother took him and refused to return him to the boarding school where I had placed him. It was extremely troubling to me, and I needed to find more secure living arrangements for him as soon as possible. I had to find a place where he would be safe from her. I was still terribly upset with her because I thought she could, at the very least, have done for my son what she did not do for me. I realized that I still harbored anger and a deep-seated bitterness toward her. From time to time when it reared its ugly head I would lash out at her, and predictably, after I calmed down, the guilt ripped through me, almost immobilizing me. There seemed to be no relief in sight. The bitterness I felt for years did not dissipate; rather, it mushroomed into something that was destroying me. I had no doubt that she loved Martin, and in her moments of sobriety she wanted to do the best for him. But in that fog in which she existed, my mother believed that it was in Martin's best interest that he stayed with her.

I met with Mrs. Thompson, my former teacher, and asked her to recommend someone trustworthy to care for Martin temporarily until I was able to get his paperwork processed. She suggested another teacher we both knew, Mrs. Brown, and I made an appointment to meet with her at her home the following day. I arrived at the Browns' residence just after noon, as promised, and when I explained my predicament, she agreed immediately to have Martin stay in her home for an agreed upon fee. I had a good feeling about her because she had raised a family of her own, and she and her husband lived in a modest home that felt very warm and welcoming. Since I had already purchased new clothes for Martin, all we needed were a few incidentals and he would be ready to settle into his new temporary residence. My mother, of course, was not happy with my decision, especially since I refused to tell her where Martin would be staying. I knew beyond a shadow of a doubt that if she found out, as soon as I boarded the plane to return home, she would fetch him again and no one would dare stop her.

"Martin a mi handbag," she moaned, "Mi carry im wid mi everywhere mi go."

I ignored her arguments and prepared for my flight back to the US in the next couple of days. The day before my departure when I took Martin to the Browns, he was very tearful. He was loyal to his grandmother and I knew he would miss her terribly.

Just before I left for the airport I dutifully stopped by my Mom's to say goodbye. I was happy that she was sober and so there was no acrimony on our last day together. After some stilted small talk, we eventually said our goodbyes and headed to the main road to get a cab – this time, without the usual procession of her friends. She surprised me by asking if I would like to meet my paternal grandmother, something she had never brought up in the past. I agreed without hesitation, even though I dared not feel hopeful that I would finally get information about my father's whereabouts.

I walked with her to the old lady's home, surprised at how close she lived to my mother. Why had she never introduced us before? We found her sitting outside her gate, talking to the neighbors as they walked by. She looked like a typical grandmotherly type, much like a character in a "Come back to Jamaica" television ad. She was genuinely happy to see my mother, and after the introduction, she held on to my hands and couldn't stop smiling up at me. I felt a pang of regret that I had never met her before; she reminded me of my Granny whom I had loved all my life. She asked me about my life and I volunteered as much information as I could about my new husband and my children. After a few moments of polite conversation, I couldn't help but blurt out the question that had plagued me for as long as I could remember.

"Do you know where my father lives?"

I had heard a while back that he had moved to the United States, but I had no more information on his exact location. She confirmed that he had relocated, and added that he lived in New York.

"Yu want im address?" she asked.

"Yes!" I exclaimed.

She left us at the gate, and returned a few moments later with a piece of paper with an address in Queens, NY scribbled on it. Goose pimples rose on the back of my neck and arms when I read the address. My father lived less than twenty minutes from my home!

I thanked her profusely, and promised to stay in touch. All I wanted to do at that moment was to find my father. I was no longer a little girl lost in a cemetery. I was ready!

That evening at the airport, my mind was fixed on the possibility that I may have finally found my father. Once I arrived at JFK International Airport I couldn't wait to share my good news with Matthew. He was as excited as I was when I told him that I planned to visit my father the following day. He offered to accompany me, but I was so nervous about the reception I would receive that I told him that I preferred to go alone. My mind was consumed with the impending meeting. Every now and then, a voice in my head tried to convince me that it was much too late to try to forge a relationship with the man who had been a phantom all my life.

On Saturday morning I woke up around 5 am and waited impatiently for a decent hour to meet my father for the first time at the age of twenty-four. All my years of anticipation rode on this one morning. I wanted to make the best impression I possibly could. I wanted to be at my absolute best for my father. My father! The words slid off my tongue over and over.

I had several outfits laid out in my living room because I could not decide what to wear. Poor Matthew had to contend with a barrage of my never-ending questions: "What do you think of this dress? How about slacks? Do you think a casual look would be better? No, no, jeans – yes, that's it, I want to look as though I am just casually dropping by." On and on I deliberated, never satisfied with a decision for more than five minutes. To be honest, although I asked for Matthew's opinion, I was barely listening to his responses. He eventually turned his back to me and refused to offer any more of his input.

"You are absolutely no help," I pouted as I stormed off to take my shower.

My 'leisurely' shower took all of two minutes. My makeup took much longer; I didn't walk away from my vanity until I felt satisfied completely with the result. I settled on the smartest outfit in my closet: a beige and brown silk dress I had just purchased, with matching shoes and handbag. My shoulder length hair was perfectly coifed the day before by Eric, my faithful hairstylist. Eric and the all the other stylists at *Soul Scissors Salon* promised to root for me after I told them about my upcoming adventure, and only *after* I was finally satisfied with my new haircut.

"Are you planning on leaving sometime this morning?" Matthew teased, watching me pace meaninglessly, fully dressed, throughout the apartment. It was time. It was now, or never. I assured him once more that it was wiser for me to take this trip alone, and then gave him a quick hug, praying, as I walked out the door, that my deodorant would not fail me.

As I made my way slowly to Cambria Heights, a fantasy image of my father began to form in my mind. He'd be a handsome man, I thought; maybe about 6 feet tall and dark skinned. I imagined that he would resemble one of my favorite actors back then, Sir Sidney Poitier. I rehearsed the old speech I had made up for exactly this occasion, with a few changes since I was now an adult and the mother of two – his grandchildren.

The house was very easy to locate. I drove past it three times, looking around at the surrounding homes. There were a few neighbors mowing their lawns, but there was no one outside of his house, and so I pulled up slowly in front of the neat Cape Cod style home, verifying the number that my grandmother had given to me. At this point my heart was pounding – audibly, I felt. I took one last look at my face in the rearview mirror, smiled, and checked my teeth for lipstick. I was good to go. I took a deep breath, slid from behind the wheel and walked up to the front door on shaky legs.

Ding, dong, and I waited. I wasn't sure that my heart was even still beating at that point. The moment stretched on into infinity as I waited. Just as I was about to ring the bell again, I heard footsteps approaching, then a woman's voice said, "Just a minute." When the door opened, a woman about my mother's age stood there and smiling politely she asked if she could help me.

"Good morning, Is Mr. Gregory home?" I asked breathlessly.

"I'm sorry; he's not home right now. Can I help you? I'm Jane Gregory."

I hesitated a moment, my heart sinking.

"When do you expect him home?"

The change in her demeanor was almost imperceptible, but I continued quickly, "My name is Victoria Benjamin." She looked at me expectantly, waiting for more information.

"I am Enid's daughter," I responded, not knowing what else to say. I was certain that she was Jamaican because of her accent, and gambled that she would recognize my mother's name and put two and two together. Frankly, I wasn't sure if I was doing the right thing, but I had failed to make a Plan B – I hadn't even considered the possibility that he might not be home.

To my relief she responded, "*You* are Enid's daughter?" I nodded, tears welling up in my eyes.

"Come in, come in," she gushed, stepping aside and waving me in. We sat in the beautifully decorated living room facing each other, unsure of how to continue after that bombshell of an introduction. She broke the silence by telling me that she knew my mother well. I nodded, thinking that she must be aware then that I was her husband's daughter.

"I knew that Philip, I mean Enid, had a daughter…"

I relaxed and smiled, but couldn't help glancing around, wondering where he was. As though she could read my mind, she gently let me know that he had left for Jamaica yesterday.

"*Yesterday?*" I parroted in disbelief. I didn't know why, but I felt a momentary relief, followed closely by a deep disappointment.

"He's due back on Friday," she continued, sensing my dismay. I guessed that she would be an ally, and I was right. I took another deep breath and confided that I had never met him before, and that I had gotten his address from his mother (my grandmother) in Jamaica. I also volunteered that I had just returned from Jamaica the day before. We looked at each other uncertainly before bursting into bitter laughter at this unhappy coincidence.

Her eyes gleaming with mischief, she whispered that I should return the following Saturday and pretend that I had never been to the home before. The element of surprise was extremely important, she stressed, and this plan must be flawlessly executed. We chatted for a few more minutes before promising to see each other in a week. We hugged and I left, wondering just how I would survive the next seven days.

Inevitably, Saturday arrived once again. I showered and applied my makeup with much less fanfare than the previous week. To my dismay, I had to settle for my second best dress - this time I wore red. Making a good impression was still of paramount importance in my mind.

This time, Jane was waiting for me when I arrived. I thought it was impossible to surpass last Saturday's attack of nerves, but I was wrong. When I entered the front door she informed me *sotto voce* that Philip was in the shower. I took my now familiar seat in the living room and waited, crossing and uncrossing my legs, unsure which position made me appear more sophisticated and at ease. When the bathroom door opened, I looked up surreptitiously, using a copy of *Essence magazine* to partially cover my face. Did he look like Sidney Poitier? Or more importantly, did I look like him? I couldn't decide in that split second, because my eyes blurred and my focus was off. My insides were like jelly, but by God I was calm and poised on the outside. Or so I hoped.

"I'll be with you in a moment," he said.

I opened my mouth to respond, but emitted a croaking sound instead. I cleared my throat, aware that every muscle in my body was taut. My aim was to be pretty, sociable, and engaging.

Lean back Victoria, relax; cross your legs at your ankles just so. Think back to an evening many years ago. You may have been around nine or ten years old. Your mother took you to a bar on Maxfield Avenue, gave you a bottle of Pepsi Cola, and introduced you to four men sitting at a bar.

"This is my big dawta," she had boasted proudly. You gave the obligatory smile, merely glancing in their direction, but you focused more on the treat she had just given to you. As you sat by the door and sipped on the ice cold soda, it was so refreshing that you continued to ignore the grownups talking animatedly behind you. After they concluded their conversation, your mother signaled to you that it was time to go. You waved goodbye and stepped outside. She held your hand as you both headed toward home.

She then asked a few minutes later, "Yu see di man in de blue shirt?"

"Mm-hm." you lied because you barely noticed any of them.

"Dat's yu fada."

"De man in de blue shirt???" I couldn't remember him! Why didn't I feel something when I looked at him? I should have known it. I should have felt it. Why did she wait until now to tell me?

"I'm sorry to keep you waiting," came a deep voice, interrupting my reverie and making me jump. I cleared my throat, trying to ignore the nerves that threatened to overtake me.

"That's quite okay," I replied softly in a trembling voice. I couldn't stop staring at him, drinking in his appearance. He shifted unsteadily under my gaze.

"What can I do for you, Miss…?" At his questioning look, the speech that I been preparing for years, that I had just minutes ago practiced in the car, completely flew out of my head.

"My name is Victoria," I began, and paused, unsure as to whether the name would sound familiar to him. Not even a flicker of recognition crossed his face. I was about to add, "Gregory," but I decided to attempt the same approach that I had used with his wife the week before. As a matter of fact, I could see her from the corner of my eye, pretending to do something nearby so as not to miss the show.

"My mother is Enid." He blinked. *Now I have your attention, buddy.* He squinted and looked a bit closer at my face as though he was searching for something to jog his memory. Perhaps something he would recognize that connected me to him. Maybe if he ever thought of me, he would have a picture in his mind to match my dream of him looking like Sidney Poitier. I watched him sitting across from me, willing him to say something, anything.

Breathlessly, I continued, "All my life I've wanted to meet you." Silence reigned. No hug or tears on meeting this long lost daughter were forthcoming. This was certainly not the kind of emotional reunion that I had seen in movies. As tears began to well up in my eyes, I clenched my jaw, vowing not to break down and cry.

"Weren't you ever curious about me?" I couldn't help asking. "Ever? Were you completely heartless?"

My incendiary remark was permitted to pass unchallenged. I looked more closely at him, trying to read his expression. Eventually, he opened up about my grandfather threatening him when my mother's pregnancy was discovered. He was scared, he admitted. My mother was ashamed, very ashamed, and she too was scared. After all, she was only sixteen years old and he was seventeen. He talked about the progression of her drinking later on. I nodded, trying again to picture my mother, pregnant at sixteen, and remembering my own shame – pregnant at fourteen. Nonetheless, I still could not let him off the hook. Twenty four years had elapsed since a sixteen year old girl became pregnant by a seventeen year old boy. The baby that resulted spent her life searching for that father who would make her demons disappear - a father to love her and make her life complete. Or so she had felt.

We talked for a long time that morning, but I didn't reveal everything to him. Eventually, we became friends. I called him Philip; never 'Dad'. And, as it turned out, I was wrong about one important fact about my father; he did not look like Sir Sydney. He was dark skinned like me - handsome, but in a different way than Sir Sydney, and was about six feet tall. He had an amazing sense of humor and I often wondered what it would be like if I had grown up with him in my life. Later, whenever my children referred to him as grandpa, I felt proud.

I also acquired four new relationships: dear Jane, his wife, and my three half-sisters, Samantha, the eldest, quiet, unassuming and warm; Yandi, the lovable rebel with a quick smile and an equally quick wit; and sensitive Latoya, who remembers to call me every year on my birthday, despite the fact that I usually forgot hers.

Meeting my father did not bury all my demons as I had hoped, but I made a solemn promise to myself that my children would never be without a father figure if I could help it. They would have the 'family' that I did not have. I also vowed then to reveal to my son who his real father was when the time was right, as well as the circumstances surrounding his conception and birth. I vowed to tell him that despite those circumstances, I loved him with all my heart. I would instill in him the importance of having respect for women and the value of fatherhood and family.

My mother was living with me when I invited my father to dinner for the first time. I was surprised at how nervous she was. I watched the woman who had put the fear of God in so many, smile nervously as she let him in. Even though she was a bundle of nerves, there was a look of victory in her eyes as she watched him sitting in my living room. A look that I imagined said to him, "I did something right after all, you bum".

BOOK 4

On The Road Again

CHAPTER 20

Following my third trip to Jamaica, I was finally able to take my son back to the United States with me. My mother had somehow discovered that he was with the Browns and had taken him back to live with her. Martin, now ten years old, was a big hit with the flight attendants on the plane back to New York. I remembered my fascination when I left the island for the first time: the sights, smells, sounds, and the people, and so I tried to be the very best tour guide for him. He stayed awake for the whole trip and so I was happy that he was able to get a window seat. Even though we experienced a bit of turbulence he did not seem to mind; as a matter of fact, he seemed disappointed when the time came to disembark at JFK International.

I was convinced that things would only get better for Martin now that he was here with me in New York. From time to time, I would watch him playing with his new toys in our living room and my heart would ache with joy. His curiosity was limitless. I will never forget the look on his face when he saw a picture of Stevie Wonder on an album cover and blurted out in surprise, "I didn't know that Stevie Wonder was blind!" He was in awe of everything. I loved to introduce him to new sites around the city and watch his face light up. I saw him slowly discover and learn to appreciate everything this new world offered. Even though he was quiet and reserved at first, mostly due to the language barrier, he made new friends easily and soon adjusted to his new lifestyle.

Math and English continued to be his most difficult subjects in school for a long time, and so I spent most evenings working with him to help him improve. Matthew began to work with him also, but I tried to dissuade him from doing so. I felt that he was too impatient with him. Martin seemed terrified, at times, because Matthew's method was to have a belt in one hand and a book in the other. Because I grew up in a similar environment back home, where corporal punishment was the answer for every infraction, I did everything in my power to be the one to work with him on his assignments. I also served as peacekeeper, while simultaneously trying not to alienate my husband. There were many times when Martin and I studied together because I was preparing to take my General Education Diploma (GED) examination at that time as well. It was my dream to go to college, and since one of the perks of my job was full college tuition reimbursement, I was anxious to take advantage of this great opportunity.

Matthew and I began to argue with increasing frequency, as his treatment of Martin grew steadily worse. At times I thought him cruel, and my child actually seemed to be regressing and becoming more introverted. I felt that during the year that Martin was living with us, Matthew had begun to have second thoughts about being a father. If that were the case, I knew that I needed to get my son away from that environment as soon as possible. He had been through too much disruption in his young life, and all I truly desired for him now was stability.

One evening I came home from work and found Matthew holding Martin upside down by the ankles, beating him with a belt. Horror-struck, I demanded that he put him down immediately, and warned him never to put his hands on my son again. Right then and there I realized he did not fit the role of the father I desired for my children and immediately began to make plans to leave him.

Martin was a 'latch key kid' back then. After school he let himself into the apartment, and stayed by himself for about two hours until we returned home from work. Matthew usually got home an hour or so before I did, but if he was running late, Martin stayed with our friend in the building who also had a son his age. We were a tight-knit group in the building and watched out for all of the children, so there was never any concern about his safety. Leaving Matthew was not going to be easy because I had my son's welfare to consider. I needed to be in an environment where he would be safe, especially since I would now be a single mother.

A few days after my argument with Matthew, I came home from work just in time to see two men leaving the building with a television set and a stereo. I stepped aside and held the door open for them and they smiled, nodded and thanked me. I noticed that there was a red stain on top of the television set, similar to the one on mine where I had inadvertently spilled nail polish a while back. I watched as they loaded everything in a black van and eventually drove off. This was a quiet and safe neighborhood, I thought, and so I ignored the nagging thought that it could be mine, shook my head, and proceeded upstairs.

The first thing I noticed when I got upstairs was that my front door was ajar. I immediately made a mental note to remind Martin to lock up before he went out to play. When I entered my bedroom, I was greeted by total chaos. Our television set and stereo were gone, of course. Drawers were opened or on the floor; clothes and jewelry were strewn all over the floor as well. Imagining the worst, I ran throughout the house yelling for Martin. When I did not find him, I ran downstairs without waiting for the elevator and was overjoyed when I spotted him coming in from the playground. I was so glad that he was safe and unharmed that I hugged him tight to my bosom. Matthew came home very soon after that and we called the police and reported the burglary. Naively, I expected them to come to our home immediately and do what I knew the police did, based on my 'extensive knowledge' of crime solving, but all they did was take my statement over the phone. To my shock, the officer merely laughed at me when I asked him when he planned to show up and dust for prints. He casually accused me of watching too much television, wished me a good evening, and hung up!

That was all the motivation I needed to move immediately. Once again, I called my friend Susan. This time I needed a place for me and my son. Without hesitating, she agreed for us to move in with her. The following day, with the assistance of a couple of my friends, I took our clothes and my bedroom set and we moved to her place while Matthew was at work. He was very distraught, of course, but under no circumstances would I watch him repeatedly abuse my child, and neither did I feel that my son was safe when I was away. I felt that it was better for us to leave now rather than wait until I brought my daughter to New York.

I had a pretty secure job, so all I needed was a place to stay temporarily until I could find us an apartment. It didn't take long for me to find a beautiful townhouse on Staten Island. I wanted to get as far away from the Benjamins as I could and so when my friends suggested that I look for an apartment there, I jumped at the opportunity to do so. Furthermore, through some research I discovered that the school district where we would be living was one of the best in the borough.

Just before Martin and I moved, I called Amanda, with whom I had recently reconnected. She had moved to New Jersey a few years back. She was very upset when I told her what happened between Matthew and I, but understood that I needed to keep my son safe. When I told her that I was looking for an insurance agent to redo my automobile insurance portfolio, she recommended a friend who worked with her at the insurance company. She told me that he was one of the top sales agents there and he would more than likely meet with me in New York to get all the paperwork done.

I called Charles Hale a few days later and, told him Amanda had recommended him, and explained what I needed. We made an appointment to meet at Susan's place on the weekend. Charles and I had met briefly once before and so I felt comfortable working with him. He came by to see me the following Saturday afternoon and we were able to get all my insurance needs handled. Just before he left he asked my permission to refresh his drink. I nodded and told him to help himself while I continued reviewing the documents in front of me. I was still engrossed in the paperwork when I felt a light touch on the back of my head. I whirled around to find Charles standing directly behind me, caressing the back of my head. He was actually *leering* at me, and I was so shocked that I did a double take. I blinked a few times, surprised, not believing what was happening. I was very disturbed and uncomfortable at how unprofessional his behavior was, not to mention the fact that he was married. He immediately sensed my discomfort at the unsolicited caress and apologized profusely. We were just about at the end of our business meeting and I could not wait to usher him out the door and be done with him. I debated whether or not to tell Amanda what he had done, but decided against it. I knew she would be embarrassed, having recommended him, and so I casually mentioned that I did not like him without giving her an explanation.

My new home in Staten Island was beautiful, and I slowly began to add the furnishings we needed to make it comfortable. The only pieces of furniture we had in the beginning were our bedroom sets. I finally had everything I wanted here: an excellent school system and a safe suburban neighborhood where I felt I could comfortably raise my children. The only major drawback was my daily work commute, which was more than two hours each way. I drove a half hour to the ferry (which did not include the mad search for parking) and then rode the ferry for twenty minutes to Battery Park. The final leg was three separate trains that finally deposited me at the Fifty Ninth Street and Lexington Avenue station. Exhausting was not the word.

By mid-winter, I realized that the commute would not be my only issue. I was living in an all-electric apartment, and for the very first time since moving to the United States, I had control of the thermostat, because I was renting from a private homeowner. I became accustomed to the electric stove pretty quickly, but heating the home was a bit of a challenge. As soon as the first cold spell of the season hit, I turned the temperature up to eighty degrees and opened my bedroom window just a bit so that I could still enjoy the fresh air. Yes, it was the best of both worlds...until I got my utility bill, which was almost as much as my rent! It took a few months and more than a few conversations with the electric company before I finally got current with my bill. I learned to manage the financial aspect of my life very quickly but the commute to work remained a daily source of stress.

Amanda and I had been estranged for a while, but now that I was living in Staten Island, which was much closer to New Jersey, we re-ignited our friendship. She was recently divorced and so we spent a lot of time talking about our future and our current love interests. Amanda's latest was Wade, who lived in Los Angeles. They were introduced by a mutual friend and although they had never met, they quickly developed a friendship over a matter of weeks. It was during one of their phone calls that Wade described himself as a Richard Roundtree look-alike (the actor who played 'Shaft' in the early 1970's) and we felt that she had hit the jackpot since Roundtree was very handsome.

"Wade has everything," Amanda reported proudly. "He's a great conversationalist and he's good looking."

Finally, after months of phone conversations, he decided that it was time that they met. Although he had relatives in Brooklyn, he wanted Amanda to pick him up from the airport because he was very anxious to meet her. Amanda and I were very excited as well, but I chose not to accompany her to the airport - I figured they did not need a third wheel when they met for the first time. We agreed, however, that she should bring him to my place as a precautionary measure rather than take him to her apartment immediately. I must admit, I was also curious to meet this great guy as soon as possible.

Later on in the evening when my doorbell rang I rushed to my front door and flung it open. Amanda said very little - the look on her face spoke volumes. I looked up at the man standing behind her smiling from ear to ear, and thought that there was nothing about him that remotely reminded me of Richard Roundtree. He was tall and that was it! As soon as we were able to get away, Amanda and I went into the bedroom and tried to smother our laughter because we did not want to embarrass our guest. We eventually regained our composure and joined Wade in the living room where he was patiently watching television. Later, I felt badly about laughing, because Wade was really a nice guy and it was very obvious that he was smitten with Amanda. Perhaps the outcome would have been different had he not raised her expectations about his appearance. Anyway, the relationship was doomed the moment they met, but Wade never gave up hope.

A couple of months after he returned to California, his mother called Amanda and tearfully told her that Wade had died. He was at a party at the home of a popular actor who played on a current sitcom. Apparently, the actor had hosted a barbeque for his friends, and somehow Wade, a non-swimmer, fell in the pool and drowned. Amanda was expected to attend the funeral because his mother was under the assumption that she was his girlfriend. Amanda begged me to accompany her to the funeral and I agreed, knowing she did not want to be surrounded by people she did not know. The funeral was to be held in Brooklyn. Neither of us knew Brooklyn very well, even though I had lived there for a few months. We resolved to go and get it over with, knowing it was the right thing to do.

We dressed in our requisite black and headed to Brooklyn the following Saturday. We were met with hugs and handshakes from the immediate family. They seated us in the second pew at the church, next to the actor, and we watched as family and friends grieved over the young man who had lost his life so tragically. Amanda played her part well: she managed to dab her eyes and sniffle a few times, earning sympathetic glances every so often from members of the congregation.

As soon as the service was over, we walked over to the family to say our goodbyes. Before we could make our getaway, however, they made it clear that we were expected to accompany them to the cemetery. I did everything I could not to roll my eyes because even though I felt sad for the family, I had only met Wade once, and for only a couple of hours. Furthermore, I needed to get back to Staten Island to get my son from the babysitter's. Amanda looked at me with pleading eyes and so I relented, leading the way to my car and pulling into the traffic behind the procession that was heading to the cemetery. By the time we got to the third or fourth intersection, I noticed that the car I was following was heading in a different direction from everyone else. I realized then that we had lost the procession. Panicked, we began to frantically look around, but it was almost impossible to spot the family because the roads were pretty congested on that busy Saturday morning.

Finally, we spotted a car that looked familiar, and since the headlights were on, we assumed that it was heading for the cemetery. Relieved, I quickly re-joined the procession and we continued on our journey. After pulling over to park, we walked over to join the other mourners who were already standing around the gravesite. I watched Amanda while she once again assumed her role, sniffing and dabbing her eyes with all the grace of Mary Magdalene. When she grew bored with her routine, Amanda turned to me and whispered, "Do you recognize anyone here?"

"They're your family," I retorted sarcastically, but not before quickly scanning the crowd.

She's right, I realized. This was a much older crowd than the one we had left, and furthermore, neither the actor nor Wade's mother were there. Simultaneously, we looked at each other in quiet horror. We were at the wrong funeral! As though our movements were scripted, we both began to back away slowly, and once we deemed it safe, walked briskly toward my car. Once we were inside, we held our heads down and burst into hysterics for what seemed like hours before making our way back to Staten Island. Naturally, the return trip took twice as long because we got hopelessly lost in Brooklyn before we spotted a familiar landmark that led us home.

The Good Life

CHAPTER 21

From time to time a few of my coworkers and I would visit a quaint French restaurant in mid-town Manhattan for dinner and drinks. Patrick, the bartender, was generous with his drink and food portions. I truly enjoyed these times, as the fare was always enjoyable, our conversations were scintillating, and it was our chance to unwind before the exhausting trip home.

One evening, while we sat at the bar, discussing the issues of financial disparity in the workplace, an older woman sitting by herself at the end of the bar joined in our conversation. She was not at all shy in voicing her opinion on the topic. She spoke eloquently and passionately, and pretty soon we had a rousing discussion going. She introduced herself as Miranda Pryde, President and CEO of JOVELLE Magazine. She pulled a couple of media kits from her oversized purse and handed one to me when I told her that I worked in the accounting department at a bank. She asked me several questions about my job, and at the end of the evening she invited me to meet her for lunch at her private club in Midtown the following day. I was sure she was only being courteous, but accepted her invitation nonetheless, expecting her to forget about our date the following day.

We all shared a cab and dropped her off at her Upper East Side apartment later that night. Naturally, she became the main topic of conversation in the car as soon as we said goodbye. She had made a huge impact on us - not only because of her conversation, but the way she dressed. She was probably a hair over five feet, dressed in white stiletto heels, white pencil slacks and a white oversized blouse with splashes of bright colors on the front. Her nails were long and painted shockingly pink. She had very long eyelashes and huge platinum blond hair. Miranda seemed ageless; she never told her age, and I am pretty sure she did not remember it herself. It was hard to believe that she was the president of a seemingly conservative company, but when we looked at the magazine she gave us, her picture was prominently displayed inside.

The following morning, when my friends asked if I planned on meeting with her for lunch, I reiterated that she probably forgot about it. Frankly, I was a bit intimidated by her and had decided overnight that I was not going to show up. I was surprised when I received a call from her late that afternoon and asked unceremoniously why I 'stood her up'. Nervously, I sputtered an excuse and apologized. She chuckled and made me promise to meet with her the following day, and I did.

I arrived at her club fifteen minutes early to make up for the day before. A pretty receptionist welcomed me, assured me that I was indeed expected, and showed me to a private dining room to wait for Miranda. A server came in and took my drink order, then informed me that Miss Pryde would join me shortly; she was running a bit late. (I learned later that Miss Pryde always ran late for her appointments.) The club was so elegant that you could almost smell money wafting through the interior; the carpet was plush and the walls were covered with what appeared to my untrained eye to be very expensive paintings. I sipped my club soda and tried not to keep looking at my watch. I had only an hour for lunch.

Eventually, I heard Miranda's deep voice inquiring if I had arrived, followed by the clanging of her bracelets which signaled her approach – another Miranda trademark. We shook hands and she asked what I was drinking.

"Just a club soda," I replied meekly. She nodded to the server to refresh my drink and bring her 'the usual'. He seemed to know exactly what she wanted and how she wanted it.

"So you stood me up yesterday," she began, but her eyes betrayed her mirth. Relieved that she didn't appear to be angry, I tried to apologize once more, but she brushed me off.

"Tell me about your job again," she demanded. I told her that I had been there for more than five years and explained some of my responsibilities. She seemed very interested and nodded as I spoke, appearing to be deep in thought but never interrupting. The server magically reappeared each time her glass was empty and replaced it with another drink. She must have noticed that I began to fidget, so she immediately placed our order.

"How much do you make at the bank?" she asked bluntly. I told her my salary, slightly embarrassed because it seemed very low in this setting. I quickly added that I had several benefits: a pension plan, medical insurance, tuition reimbursement, et cetera.

She smiled knowingly, but graciously didn't comment. She began to tell me more about JOVELLE, her company. I worried about the time, since Miranda apparently seemed to think I was able to enjoy a leisurely lunch and did not have to report to a supervisor, but I threw caution to the wind, sat back, and listened attentively.

"...and so I decided to purchase my partner's share in the business, and now I need to hire someone with a financial background to be my new controller," she concluded, shooting me a knowing glance. I put my fork down, sat up straighter, and tried to put on my best poker face. Did she say 'financial controller'? My job title?

"So what do you think, Victoria?"

"Well, Miss Pryde..."

"Miranda," she interrupted.

"Miranda," I amended sheepishly, "I wasn't considering a job change at this time since I am currently in school and..." I trailed off, totally dumbfounded and unsure of how to voice my bewilderment at this unexpected offer.

"Look, I will pay you enough so that you can pay your own tuition, and pretty soon my company will provide health insurance benefits to employees. What else is preventing you from coming on board?"

"I'll have to think about it," I conceded. Despite my admiration for her and her apparent wealth, I was very unsure. As a now single parent, I could not afford to take foolish risks with my career. However, Miranda understood my reluctance and made me an offer that, as they say, I simply could not refuse. It was done. We shook on it, and I told her I would tender my resignation immediately.

Miranda, of course, was a very skilled and shrewd negotiator and I was putty in her hands. She told me, later, that she had not originally planned to double my salary, but when I told her about my benefits and my recent promotion, she realized that I was on a fast track at work and decided to dangle that carrot in front of me. The result, it turned out, was definitely a benefit for the both of us.

I made the short journey back to my office in complete shock. Had I really just accepted a brand new job? What would this mean for me, for Martin? I tried to sneak back into the office quietly, not wanting to call attention to my having taken an almost two hour lunch.

"So? What happened?" one of my coworker asked when he saw me return.

"I'll tell you later," I whispered, quickly getting right back into my work.

It wasn't very long until everyone was congratulating me on my new position. For the next two weeks I did my best not to second-guess my decision, and simply enjoy the attention I was getting and the promise of a much higher salary.

After saying my goodbyes at the bank, I excitedly began my new job at JOVELLE. I was surprised to see that there were only two other full time employees, in comparison to my old job, which had several offices throughout New York staffed by hundreds of employees. In my opinion, there was a certain sense of security in numbers. I began to wonder, once again, if I had just made a terrible mistake.

Walking A Tightrope

Chapter 22

My new office was tiny, but it boasted a prestigious Fifth Avenue address. As Miranda had explained, it was important that our national magazine feature a prominent New York address. Somehow I did not expect Miranda to be in the office early, and I was right. The two staff members welcomed me warmly and showed me around, which did not take much time. There was a small section of the room that was designated as the editorial area, and at the other end of the room, a desk was set up for me. Behind my desk were Miranda's semicircular glass table and an enormous green chair that would better be described as a throne. Hurricane Miranda, dressed again in all white, breezed into the office around eleven with bracelets jangling, as usual. She gave me a half an hour overview of my job and was gone again, headed to the beauty parlor. For the next few hours, I learned about my boss' many idiosyncrasies and habits from my bemused coworkers. Despite her many eccentricities, I quickly learned that she was a brilliant woman, and I was grateful that she took me under her wing and became my mentor.

My job required me to accompany her to major Fortune 500 companies to promote partnerships with our elite membership of executive women. I also occasionally traveled out of state for some of these meetings. She had an amazing memory and thus wrote nothing down; it was our responsibility to take notes for her. She worked from home most of the time, and since there were no cell phones back then, we kept a note pad with all her messages. She demanded that we keep all her messages on an 8 ½ by 11 note pad; absolutely no slips of paper! I believe she may have had her own personal phone at her hairdressers', because if we could not reach her at home, chances were we would be able to reach her there, at least three to four times per week.

During my second holiday season with JOVELLE, Miranda decided that the staff bonuses should be something personal instead of the customary cash. The company had grown significantly by then, and our profit had grown likewise. Miranda took our magazine editor, our network director, and me downtown to her furrier and bought us all the fur coat of our choice. My choice was a full-length beaver, and I was completely enamored. I would not hear a word against Miranda Pryde, the best boss I had ever had!

We hosted several successful national conventions during my tenure there. The more memorable keynote speakers were Barbara Walters and Dr. Ruth Westheimer, a controversial radio sex therapist. During the eight years I was with JOVELLE, we outgrew our space numerous times and had to relocate to larger premises. When I left after the birth of my third child in 1988, the company had grown tremendously: we had fifteen full time staff members in addition to several freelance writers and artists.

My life, at that time, revolved around my son and my work. With my significant salary increase, I was now able to afford a beautiful townhome in Avon, New Jersey, closer to my friend Amanda. Although she later moved to Maryland, I still had a few friends that I continued to meet with occasionally at our French Bistro in Manhattan. I rarely dated, but I was content and confident about my bright and promising future.

One Saturday morning my doorbell rang. To my surprise, it was Charles Hale, stopping by to invite my son to accompany him and his son to the park. His son, Christian, was two years younger than Martin. I had no intention of allowing my son to go with him, even though he had called and apologized for his offensive behavior on several occasions. Although he seemed sincere, I was not swayed, and still felt that he had crossed a line from which there was no turning back. Still, I invited him in, but politely refused to allow Martin to go with him, explaining that we had made plans for the day. He said he understood and was soon on his way. I did not expect to see him again.

I was wrong. Charles returned a few weeks later, this time claiming that he was just in the neighborhood and stopped by to say hi. He had brought his son with him again and the two boys chatted for a while. I quickly learned that he was persistent. He would drop by on occasion, although I still refused to allow Martin to go to the park with him. After a while, my opinion of him slowly began to change. He claimed to be a nature lover and often extolled the virtues of allowing our boys to have the freedom to explore and play outside.

His persistence eventually did the trick, and I soon relented and allowed Martin to go with him and Christian to the park on a few Saturdays. Toward the end of the year, we became friends, and he invited my friend, Sylvia, and me to a New Year's Eve party that some friends of his were hosting. I gave him an ambiguous response even though neither Sylvia nor I were dating anyone seriously at the time, and I probably would have readily accepted the same invitation from someone other than Charles. I had confided in her about the incident in Brooklyn months before. She seemed put off, but his behavior in the recent months seemed promising. We eventually decided to accept his invitation and agreed to meet him at the party in Parkington.

A couple of days before the party, Sylvia called and told me that she was badly ill with the flu, and apologized for not being able to attend the party. She felt badly that we were both going to spend New Year's Eve at home because she knew that I would not go to the party alone. Even though I had lived in New Jersey for more than a year, I was still a New Yorker at heart. I did not take the time to learn much about my town; rather, on weekends Martin and I would return to New York for our entertainment. I told her I did not feel strongly one way or the other, and as a matter of fact I was very comfortable watching the festivities on television from the comfort of my warm bed.

When Charles called the following day to confirm that we were going to meet him at the party, I made my apologies and thanked him for his invitation. Again, he did not give up in trying to wrestle a 'yes' from me, and when that didn't work, he offered to pick me up instead. I thanked him again and declined his offer; going to the party alone with him was not an option I would consider. He was a friend, and I thought he was a very intelligent man; he had a very strong personality at times, but he also seemed ill at ease. I caught myself dissecting his image as we spoke: his face was not unattractive, but he had a very large nose and his head seemed a bit too big for his body. His nervous laugh at times was followed by a loud intake of breath that I found unappealing. Definitely not my type, I concluded, plus the fact that he was married further convinced me that going to a party alone with him on New Year's Eve was a very bad idea.

Despite my many misgivings, I again succumbed to his pleas. I reasoned with myself that we truly had become friends, and I, like most people, tend to overlook shortcomings in others that seem overpowering before you get to know them better. He said he would pick me up at ten o'clock and we would go to the party together. His friends were very decent people, he assured me, and promised that if at any time I felt uncomfortable, he would take me home immediately. It was only one evening, I thought, and so I called Sylvia and told her it was her fault that I was stuck going out with this guy on New Year's Eve. We both laughed. She told me to try to have a good time and I promised to call her in the morning.

He looked very handsome when he picked me up that night. He complimented my dress and said all the right things to make me relax. I kept thinking as he drove to the party that this certainly felt like a date, and I began to regret saying yes. Charles picked up on my uneasiness and was the perfect gentleman. He introduced me to the host and hostess, who were very charming. The food was wonderful, as was the conversation. After midnight, they began to play some of my favorites: Percy Sledge's greatest hits like "When a Man Loves a Woman" and "Warm and Tender Love", among others. Charles and I danced together for the first time and he was a surprisingly good dancer.

By the time we were ready to leave the party, I told Charles that I was glad that we came out after all, and that I had a very good time. We had a great conversation on the way home and he opened up to me about his personal life, something he had never done before. Once we got back to my place, we stayed in the car while he talked freely about his marriage. For all intents and purposes, it had been over for years, he revealed. He and his wife pretty much did whatever they wanted. He said that he was in the home only because of his children, and then he reminded me about the relationship that was beginning to form with my son. The hair-caressing incident suddenly became all too easy to forget. I began to feel sorry for this man who seemed so loving, and I wondered why his wife did not appreciate him.

We spent the rest of the evening together, him pouring out his soul to me about his life, his goals and his vision for the future. I was the kind of woman he always wanted by his side, he whispered. I was smart, I had a career, and I was everything his wife wasn't. He told me that he married her only because they had a child together, and he had hoped that eventually he could overlook her shortcomings and be able to build a life with her. Unfortunately, she did not want what he wanted, and was satisfied only to stay at home in front of the television set all day, while he single-handedly supported the family and their lifestyle. He confessed that she was addicted to prescription medication and he was afraid that she also had a drinking problem. My heart went out to him while he spoke. I was very flattered when he then confessed that he had cared for me from a distance for a long time and that he always knew that we would end up together.

We saw each several evenings in a row after that evening, and I began to grow more and more comfortable with him. I began to ask more about his children. He obviously loved them, because he said he stayed in a failed marriage only because of them. He confessed that he was a very lonely man and thanked God for bringing me into his life. It was very easy for me to ignore the warning bells that were ringing in my head. Once again, I was getting involved with a married man, something I had not done since my relationship with David ended disastrously when I was seventeen years old.

However, my situation was different this time, and I had to think carefully about what I was doing. It was no longer only myself getting involved, but also my son. After a few days of introspection, I decided to end whatever it was that had started. While I liked Charles very much, I was not in love with him. He knew that children were very important to me. I told him that I had grown up without a father, and he was aware of the effect it had on me. I trusted that I was making the right decision, and that Charles would understand.

The next day I sat him down and told him that I did not want to see him anymore. It did not matter to me that he was in a bad marriage, I would never be the other woman, and I encouraged him to try for the sake of his children to make his marriage work. He then said the words that many married men say to the women with whom they are having affairs: "I am going to leave my wife." I knew that most married men never leave their families for the other woman and so I brushed it aside. Frankly, I was not even sure I wanted a relationship even if he left. My track record with relationships was not great at this point: two failed marriages by the age of 26!

The next day, Charles came by my apartment with two suitcases filled with his clothes.

"I want you," he said simply, "and I told you that."

I was impressed that he did what he said he would do, but I was nervous that I allowed this man to move into my home within a week of the first time we dated. It was still the first week of January! I felt sad for his children because I knew what it was like to grow up in a broken home. He reminded me over and over that I did not break up a marriage; it was broken a long time ago. As far as his children were concerned, he would always be a good father and provide for them as he should. And indeed he did. He visited the children two to three times each week. At times, I thought that he might move back home because of how clearly he missed them.

I was curious about his wife and asked him about her reaction whenever he visited his children. In response, he handed me a cassette tape that he said he made during his last visit home. My heart broke for him again as I listened to his wife screaming and berating him while he quietly and repeatedly asked her to calm down. It did not occur to me at the time that he was not likely to respond to her in kind if he was the one recording the conversation. I could not understand much of what she said because she was extremely emotional, and at times seemed to be crying. But I heard her say very clearly, "I want to meet that woman you have, to tell her the kind of man you are." Again I ignored the warning bells ringing in my ears. After all, he told me that his wife did not want him.

Within a week of his moving in, I went out to my car one morning and found the four tires slashed and my car sitting on the rims. Charles confronted his wife, and she denied any wrong-doing.

"You see," he reminded me. "She is crazy!"

I purchased new tires, and had no direct confrontation with her. Within weeks, he began to bring both of his children to our home. His daughter, Sadie, who was a few years older than Christian, was very quiet and withdrawn; but because I had met his son several times before, it was easier to talk to him. From that point, it seemed that things began to escalate with increasing speed. Charles told me one day that his children had called him at work and said that they wanted to move in with us. I was very shocked, but I told him that I was thrilled because I had grown very fond of them.

"How does your wife feel about the children coming to live with us?" I asked.

He said she told him that he could have the children if he gave her the house. I was taken aback that any woman could cold-heartedly bargain her children away for real estate.

We had a two bedroom apartment, but there was also a finished basement which I felt would be quite suitable for the two boys. We then moved Sadie into the second bedroom. I anticipated getting a larger apartment by the time my daughter, Shelby, came to the United States, but for now we could make do. I welcomed them with open arms, especially because I was told that their mother did not want them. I wanted to give these children all the love that they needed.

Looking back to January 1st, 1981, I cannot believe that in a matter of only a couple of months, I had a new man in my bed and his two children living in my home.

Cracks In The Foundation

CHAPTER 23

It was very difficult to keep up with the twists and turns my life was taking. I was now balancing a household with three children—two of whom I was just getting to know—a new man in my life, and a very demanding career. At first, Charles and I never argued. It was uncanny; this man was a saint! I took it upon myself to be the fixer in the home whenever disagreements arose among the children, and he good-naturedly allowed me full reign.

It was abundantly clear to me very early that he was not a slave to fashion, and I found it quite endearing as I considered myself a stylish dresser, though perhaps slightly more conservative than average. I also discovered that Charles' fashion sense (or lack thereof) was generally kept under wraps, and so, fortunately, I was able to nip it in the bud before he made his debut to my friends and family.

The day Charles moved in, I watched him pull something bright green from his suitcase.

"What is that?" I breathed, horrified. He proudly responded that he had purchased it at a flea market. 'It' was a leafy green seersucker suit. He then produced its twin, in bright yellow, and proudly hung both in the closet space I had provided for him.

"Why?" I wondered aloud, dumbfounded. He seemed genuinely hurt that I did not like his suits. He explained that he planned on wearing them to parties.

Not with me, I barely managed not to say out loud, not wanting to shame him any further than I already had. I could not believe he was serious. When he realized that I was genuine in my dismay at his sartorial differences, he generously offered to donate them to my brother in Jamaica. I graciously declined his offer, all the while imagining my brother's face if he thought I sent him those suits. I was able to convince Charles to donate the suits and other equally 'edgy' outfits to Goodwill. From that day on, it became my responsibility to shop with and for him, even though I eventually tired of the responsibility. But I had seen the damage that he was capable of when he went shopping on his own, and so in the pursuit of a simpler life, I accepted the task and managed to make it work.

I would be remiss if I did not reveal my own wardrobe faux pas that Charles brought to my attention. He was a bit more subtle than I was as he opened my closet door and asked me pointedly to tell him what was wrong inside.

"Nothing," I replied, straining to see what he could be referring to.

"Look at the lack of colors," he prompted. That was when I realized that all of my clothes were varying shades of brown and beige. I had no idea how boring and unimaginative my color selections were, and have since brightened my wardrobe quite a bit with more bold and vibrant colors.

With our three children, Charles and I were now a family. They had begun to settle into their new life and I wanted to be a good stepmother, despite all of the fairy tales to the contrary. Christian was the more outgoing and extroverted of Charles' two children. Not only was he his older sister's protector and confidant, he became the spokesperson for his siblings as they got older.

From the moment I met her, Sadie was a quiet child, and she remained aloof longer than I had hoped. She was, frankly, perfect: she never disobeyed, always did as she was told, and never made waves. To be honest, I was worried about her, because I felt this behavior was somewhat abnormal for an eleven year old girl, having watched other kids of the same age interact with their parents. She rarely smiled and seemed most comfortable disappearing into the background. One day, I decided to write her a letter in which I tried to say things that from a preteen's perspective might have been uncomfortable in a face-to-face conversation. I wrote mainly about life, relationships, and the family dynamics; and most importantly I told her that she was a beautiful young girl. To my surprise, in response to my letter, she thoughtfully articulated her fears and insecurities about her physical appearance and low self-esteem.

I began to understand a bit more about some of her fears and concerns, and so I formulated a plan to help bring out the beautiful girl I knew was buried deep inside. Firstly, we went shopping. Among the things I purchased was a beautiful red and white dress with matching shoes, reminiscent of the dress I so loved when I was a little girl. I styled her hair over the weekend and watched her smile as she looked at her reflection in the mirror.

On Monday morning, as she left for school in her new red and white outfit fresh hair-do, she walked with a confidence I had not seen before. My friend Sylvia called a few minutes later to ask if that was indeed Sadie she saw strutting down the street. I was proud to say it was. Sadie and I formed a special bond from that day. We had an open line of communication via our letters, and I knew it would only be a matter of time before she would feel confident enough to verbalize her feelings instead of just putting them in writing.

I began to learn more about the dynamics of the Hale's family life as time progressed. I discovered that Christian was closer to his mom while Sadie was closer to her dad. To my surprise, when her father discovered that Sadie and I had begun to get close, he strongly suggested to her that we curtail our letter writing activity. Our relationship suffered a bit, since she preferred to communicate through writing. Charles was never forthcoming about his reason for thwarting my attempt to develop a relationship with her, so I assumed that he wanted her close to him because the family had just experienced a traumatic upheaval.

Charles and I did not go out alone very often during those early days. Our hands were full with trying to blend our household, but we did manage to eat out as a family on a regular basis. We all enjoyed dining out, and although I would have liked to see a movie every now and then with the family, we were never able to do so because he did not like the movies. We were learning each other's likes and dislikes as we went along, and while they differed vastly, we certainly had the love of our children in common. I loved Charles' hands-on approach with the children. He was beginning to look more and more like the father I would have wanted in my life, and therefore he seemed to fit the role of attentive and caring husband and father. I had finally hit the jackpot! Although I missed my occasional dinner and drinks with my friends in the city, my life was full of caring for, and being with my new family.

A few months after Charles and I got together, I called from work to tell him that I would be about an hour late in getting home. He expressed surprise when I told him that I planned on meeting with friends in the city for dinner. He informed me matter-of-factly that there was absolutely no reason for me to be with my friends when I had my family at home. Our conversation quickly grew heated as he began to make me feel that I was an unfit mother for even thinking of being away from the family for any other reason except working. A co-worker standing next to me overheard my end of the conversation and raised her eyebrows when she heard me canceling with my friends. I, on the other hand, felt that it was more important keep my family happy than to argue about an occasional dinner out. My friends tried to warn me that he was too controlling, but feeling they did not understand my need to keep my new family intact, I ignored them.

Some months later, I decided that it would be a good idea to invite Charles yet again to come into the city for dinner with my friends. It was my friend Martha's birthday and I thought it would be a perfect time for him to get to know the people who were a part of my life before I met him. I wanted them to meet him as well, to dispel their feelings that he was eccentric. I was overjoyed when Charles agreed to join us. I had hoped that by getting to know them, he would be more at ease and less antagonistic in the future if I wanted to have an occasional evening out in the city.

The evening went well, I thought. Although Charles seemed ill at ease at first, as the evening wore on he seemed to finally relax and joined easily in conversations. The next day, Martha and one of the women who had dined with us the previous night asked me to meet them for lunch. I agreed because I was anxious to hear what they thought about him. When I arrived at the restaurant I immediately noticed that they seemed uncomfortable. I was perplexed, since we had been friends for years and could talk to each other about pretty much anything. My initial feeling was that they did not like Charles. I eventually asked what the problem was, and they dropped a bombshell that I could not believe.

Martha told me that during dinner, my boyfriend kept touching her inappropriately under the table when he thought no one was looking. At first she thought it was a mistake, but when he looked her in the eye, leered at her and did it again, she knew that it was intentional. She immediately slapped his hand, and wanted to tell me right there and then, but not wanting to embarrass me, decided to talk to me privately. She confided in another friend and sought her counsel, and they both agreed to tell me the following day. I was dumbfounded! I did not want to believe them, but could not understand why they would lie. The rest of my day went by in a daze because I was trying to figure how I could confront Charles with such a shocking accusation.

As soon as I got home, he immediately sensed that I was upset and wanted to know what was wrong. I was certain he would deny the accusation and I knew then that I had to make a choice between my old friends and my new man, and hands down, he would win. I was also afraid to tell him what they said because I knew he would somehow use this incident to support his argument that I should limit the amount of time I spent away from the family.

I blurted out to him what I was told, and my chest constricted when he hung his head in silence. At that point I could not bring myself to finish my story. He began to cry, held my hand, and apologized profusely.

He claimed that he had had too much to drink and therefore lost his head. He continued to make excuses, but they were so nonsensical that I could barely understand what he was saying. I couldn't see how he could possibly have drunk so much since he seemed fine to me on the way home. I had heard enough.

Without another word, I walked into the bathroom and shut the door before becoming violently sick. My heart was broken and I felt like a fool. Yet another relationship was going down the drain. How was I going to break this to the children? Not only was I going to end my relationship with him, but I was breaking up with Christian and Sadie as well. There was no way in the world that I could accept this behavior, and so all his apologies fell on deaf ears.

Later that evening, I went downstairs when he and the children had just finished having dinner. They sensed that there was a problem but were afraid to ask what had happened.

It was when I looked into their nervous faces—Martin, Christian, and Sadie—that I began doubting how I reacted in my previous relationships.

Was I too hasty in ending them at the first sign of trouble? Was I too intolerant? After all, no one is perfect and neither was I. Still, I couldn't shake the terrible sense of betrayal and shame that engulfed me.

I decided that I would have a frank talk with Charles that night and then decide if he should leave or stay. We spent hours discussing what happened, how and if we could move forward, and the impact a separation would have on our family. After much soul searching and tears, I decided to stay with him, but only if he apologized to my friend. He wrote a very contrite letter to Martha apologizing to her for his behavior, and even though I still felt like a fool, I decided to take it to her the very next day.

I prayed that my friends would not tell anyone else what happened, and I was grateful that they did not. Even though I had made the decision to stay with Charles, I was still unsure if I had done the right thing. I believed by then that I truly loved him, and I knew for certain that I had fallen deeply in love with his children.

We did not speak much over the next few days. Truthfully, I still cringed whenever I thought about the incident. Martha had been gracious when he called and apologized, but I knew that she and our friend, Rose, had expected me to throw him out. I decided that I could not trust him around my friends just yet. He needed to prove himself, but I was not sure how he could. Until then, I felt that the best course of action was to stay away from my friends. This was not very difficult, as I felt that they might have lost respect for me because I stayed with him.

Clearly, our relationship was tenuous at best for the weeks that followed. I knew that infidelity was not an uncommon practice in relationships. After all, at the tender age of seventeen, I entered a relationship with a man I knew was married. How could I have allowed myself to make the same mistake? I deeply regretted my involvement with Charles, and began to suspect that his betrayal was my retribution for repeating the mistake I made almost ten years prior.

Every day became a struggle. My conscience was screaming for me to go one way; my heart, however, was stubborn. Each night at the dinner table I looked at our children and their smiling faces melted my heart. Charles was on his absolute best behavior; he bought me spontaneous gifts and treated me even better than he had before. What I did not know at the time was that this pattern of behavior was common practice for the man with whom I was getting deeper and deeper involved

When I explained my regret about how our relationship began, he reminded me that his wife had moved on. He also reiterated that his marriage was over long before he met me, and furthermore, our new family was now intact. While I still found what he did impossible to forget, with time I found it easier to forgive. I did not want to hold him hostage forever and so I committed to trying to put the pieces of our relationship back together again. Eventually, life continued normally, and though at times I looked at him and wondered how and why that could have happened, I consoled myself with the fact that he was a good father. In my mind, the children's happiness and well-being was paramount.

Some time later, Charles suggested that I trade in my four year old Chevrolet Camaro for a newer car. He reasoned that after three or four years, cars tended to break down frequently and we should be proactive in making our next move. Since I had no previous problems with my car, I was reluctant to trade it, but I soon realized that what Charles wanted, Charles got. He researched the trade-in value and decided that we would do much better if we sold the car privately. I looked at the difference between the trade-in value and a private sale and agreed with his decision. We placed an ad in the local papers and soon had buyers stopping by to test drive my car. We finally sold it for a very good price, but I could not deny the feeling of loss as the buyer drove my car away. The following Saturday, I was ready to go car shopping, but Charles had other plans. I had no reason to believe that he had no intention of helping me to get a new car, but since he was always available to transport me back and forth to the train station daily, I eventually gave up nagging him about it. Because there was no public transportation in our neighborhood, not having a car was a huge inconvenience, but Charles made sure that he was available as much as he could. As a result, we did everything together: shopping, doctor's appointments, and miscellaneous errands. After a while, it just became another aspect of my new life to get used to.

Charles began meeting regularly with a colleague who was a general agent for several insurance companies. One day, he suggested that we both meet with Philip and his wife, Cathy, so that I could learn more about their business. He wanted us to start a business together and he felt that we could glean a lot from them. We met with them in their home and they showed us around and explained that they were doing quite well together. So well, in fact, that Cathy did not have to work outside the home. I was skeptical, but thought that maybe this would be a good thing for our family. Charles and I had been at odds with each other on the few occasions that I had to go out of town on business. He once claimed that he called my hotel room and was upset that I was not there to take his call. He knew he was jealous, he explained, but it was because he was so much in love with me and did not want to share me with anyone else. I patiently explained that he had no reason to be jealous because I was totally committed to him and to our family. That seemed to appease him for a while.

There were many days that I sped wildly through Penn Station, praying that I would not miss the 5:40pm New Brunswick local. Charles was always very upset if I missed that train home or if I had to work late for any reason. Our disagreements had gotten so bad that he even threatened to call my boss to confirm that I was indeed at the office whenever I told him that I had to work a few minutes late. He backed down when I threatened to end our relationship if he did. His jealousy was quickly becoming unbearable, and it was for this reason that I reasoned his idea for us to work together might be better for the family. At his suggestion, I enrolled in school and acquired my Life and Health insurance license.

When I told Miranda of our plans, she was adamant that I should not leave my job. She tried to explain that Charles was manipulating me and I needed to open my eyes and see what was happening, but I was too deeply entrenched in the relationship by that point. She reluctantly gave me her blessings after I promised to stay in touch and even consider returning to the company if our plans did not succeed.

Charles and I had been together for almost two years by then. Even though he was now teaching at a high school, he had been a successful insurance agent previously. He began to teach me everything he knew about insurance sales, and I began the laborious task of calling my friends, hoping for the opportunity to review their insurance portfolio and sell them one of the products we carried. I was not good at it. My heart was not in it and it quickly became apparent to me that I had made a big mistake.

During that time Philip and Cathy remained our mentors. They helped us to connect with several companies with whom we could do business, and we valiantly tried to make a go of our new enterprise. I stayed at home and made calls all day while Charles taught high school, and then we went out on appointments together in the evenings and on weekends.

One evening he invited Philip to our home to consult with him about a client we had acquired. After the meeting was over, we both walked him to the door to say goodbye. They shook hands, and then Philip hugged me and congratulated me on the job I was doing thus far. Charles was livid! He accused Philip of acting inappropriately toward me and threw him out of our home. Philip stood on our porch looking dumbfounded, while all I could do was look at him in shock. Needless to say, we lost Philip and Cathy's friendship after that bizarre confrontation.

In the days that followed I began to slip into a depression. Business was slow, almost non-existent. I was beginning to fall behind in my bills. Charles had brought a lot of bills of his own; he owned two rental properties with first and second mortgages, in addition to two mortgages on the home his wife occupied. His teacher's salary was insufficient to cover them, and to the best of my knowledge, she was still unemployed and so we were responsible for paying those mortgages as well. I recall sitting in my living room crying my heart out when it finally dawned on me that I had no job, no car, and I had turned into the woman that Charles had walked away from. He had told me that his former wife was not ambitious because she sat at home daily and did not want or seek gainful employment; her whole life revolved around soap operas. The problems in our relationship began to weigh heavily on me and I did not like the person I was becoming. I was completely dependent on Charles.

I finally began to rebel. I wanted a car and needed a job. Frankly, I did not care what kind of job, because I knew that I could not continue to sit at home with no means of transportation. Charles came home one afternoon and announced that he found a car for me. I eagerly went to the dealership with him, but later limped home in my very used Volkswagen Rabbit with over eighty thousand miles on the odometer. It was all we could afford at the time.

I asked myself over and over how on earth I allowed myself to get into this predicament. My only consolation now was that I had begun to slowly regain my independence. I started a frantic job hunt and quickly found a position with a small metallurgical laboratory in Leesville, just a few blocks away from Charles's school. My salary was a fraction of what I made in New York, but I was desperate. Charles was not happy. Whether it was because of the salary or my new job, I wasn't sure, but I think he realized that he had pushed me too far. He was also faced with the stark reality that he was not financially able to single-handedly support the family.

After a few months on the job, Charles began to make cracks about my boss, who happened to be an elderly gentleman from Jamaica. He did not trust him, or me, and alluded to an affair between us. I soon learned to ignore his jealous rampages altogether, but still tried to do everything I could to allay his fears and jealousy. At times he appeared fine, but the times that he became unreasonable drained me and took its toll on our relationship.

In 1984, just over two years after we got together, I decided to give Charles a surprise birthday party. I thought that would further convince him of my commitment to him and our family. I invited family members, neighbors, and our few remaining acquaintances and made plans for the party on a Friday night after he left work. Fridays were his late nights because he was now teaching night school to supplement our income. He was genuinely surprised when he finally arrived home to a houseful. Throughout the evening, everyone catered to him and I felt that the party was a smashing success. When the last guests finally left, we collapsed onto the couch, exhausted. It had been a very long day for us both. As we sat together in silence, hands entwined, I patiently waited for him to confirm how surprised he was and possibly thank me for making his day special.

Instead, he looked me in the eyes and stated seriously, "If you could pull this off behind my back, I wonder what else you could be doing that I am not aware of."

I was so surprised and hurt that I could only gape at him with my mouth wide open. Words had failed me. He must have immediately grasped what he had implied and how much he had hurt me, because he quickly apologized, but the damage was done. I realized, at that moment, that there was simply no pleasing this man, and felt a deep sense of foreboding for our future.

Still, like many relationships facing serious challenges, we moved forward. Charles continued to be the 'good' father and I was committed to make this relationship work, because I was, as always, determined to keep the family together. I hoped that eventually he would begin to trust me and our relationship would thrive.

When the small company that I worked for began to experience financial difficulties, I was forced to begin seeking employment elsewhere. Charles' jealousy never abated, and I felt that any move would be a blessing in disguise. One day, Charles claimed that he called my office and was told that I was in the boss' office with the door closed. He wondered why I felt that level of privacy was necessary. I thought the accusation to be so preposterous that I responded that since I was the bookkeeper, secretary and payroll clerk there were many occasions that I was in the boss' office alone with him. I reiterated that my boss was a happily married man with a family and was almost seventy years old. This logic did little to allay his suspicions.

Although it was becoming more and more difficult to live with these accusations, I chose to ignore them whenever I could. I was always grateful for his moments of clarity when his reasonable side compensated for his frequent insecurities. All I needed to do was to show him, daily, how much I was committed to him and our family, and eventually he'd be more secure in our relationship. I began to dress the way he wanted me to, I walked and talked the way he wanted, and I waited for our life together to settle down.

Charles was not as committed to this vision of domestic harmony. He would pick the most inopportune times to ask me completely random questions, trying to trap me into saying something to confirm his wild suspicions. I decided that it was better if I chose to get another job quickly; maybe he would be appeased. Providence stepped in just in time, and I received a call from my former boss, Miranda Pryde. She told me that she had just terminated the young man hired to replace me, and she wanted me to come back to JOVELLE. She knew that nothing ever came of our grandiose plans to build an insurance business because she and I spoke occasionally. I immediately agreed to go back to New York and told Charles of my decision a couple of days later. Of course he was terribly upset, but I would not be deterred. I went back to New York to work with Miranda and was rewarded with a sizable salary increase.

Our children helped to keep me sane during these precarious times. I was a voracious reader in the past, and reading became my solace once again when I felt trapped in the crazy world in which I now found myself. Friendships outside the home were not encouraged, therefore my life revolved around my family. During my train ride to and from work I managed to get a lot of reading done.

One evening, as I was on my way home from the train station, the cab driver opted to take the other passengers to their destination first. I didn't mind because I was deeply engrossed in the book I was currently reading. I vaguely noticed when the driver dropped off the female passenger first, then made his way slowly through the meandering streets to take the other passenger, a young man, to his destination. The young man sat in the passenger seat next to the driver and directed him to pull over. I looked up as he got out and told the driver that he was going into his house to get the fare. The driver nodded, and rather than entering the house, the young man immediately jumped over the fence and disappeared from our sight.

The driver cursed loudly. "He's running away with my fare!" Shoving his door open, he immediately took off running in the direction of the fleeing man.

Oh well, I thought to myself, and looked down at my book to resume reading.

Suddenly, I had the sensation that something strange was happening. I glanced over to my right and saw the trees moving forward and the houses following suit. I realized that the cab was moving backwards. I looked to my left and saw the driver standing two houses away, screaming at the long gone passenger. I was alone in the backseat of a moving car!

The driver looked behind him, spotted his moving cab, and immediately changed his focus and began to scream frantically in my direction. "She is stealing my cab!"

He was obviously referring to me, but I didn't have time to protest. Apparently, in his haste to get the fleeing passenger, he neglected to put the car in park, and since the road was on a downhill slope the car was moving backward and I was trapped in the back seat. I quickly tried to come up with a plan of action. Do I try to jump in the front seat and press the brake? No, I wasn't sure I could make that move work in time. I opened the door and tried to step out, but the car was moving much too quickly. To make things worse, it was heading toward a busy intersection. I surveyed the situation once more and threw caution to the wind. I opened the door and jumped out of the moving car.

I somersaulted across the asphalt quite ungracefully, scratching my elbows and knees. Staggering to my feet, I quickly looked around to see if any of the neighbors had seen my death-defying escape, trying not to make it too apparent that I was dying of embarrassment. I looked back at the cab as it weaved on to a neighbor's lawn, hit a tree then finally came to a stop. Seconds later, the driver sprinted past me towards the vehicle on the lawn. He got in and drove over to where I was standing, stunned, in the middle of the road. I quickly got in, still hoping that there were no other witnesses. I sat bolt upright for the rest of the trip, my once-engaging book long forgotten.

As soon as I stepped through the door, Charles looked at me with alarm and asked what happened. I told him about the incident and he immediately took me back to the station to speak to the dispatcher. Upon our arrival, we were informed that the driver had just gotten back, quit his job, and left immediately. I was still shaken but was not seriously hurt, and all I wanted to do was take a warm bath and get into bed. Charles encouraged me to file a lawsuit against the cab company but I refused. I knew that my pride had suffered much more than my body, and I was not prepared to relive that horrifying experience in a courtroom. Shaken as I was, my story of the worst cab ride ever served as a hilarious story to tell for years to come.

Chapter 24

Shelby was still in Jamaica with her grandparents, and I was missing her terribly. We decided that it was time for us to get a bigger place because I was expecting her visa application to be approved soon. Charles and I decided that rather than renting a bigger place, we should try to purchase a home. I had secretly stashed some money away from my earnings when I returned to work in New York, but we had no other savings to fall back on. Still, we decided to look around because Charles was confident that there were some creative financing strategies available to us.

Luckily, at that time, prices were very low, which I learned was considered 'a buyer's market'. House hunting became our family weekend activity. Each Saturday, we drove around looking at various neighborhoods, researching schools and commuting options. On Sundays we went to open houses. We had a wonderful time. The children and I, of course, loved the houses that we could not afford, but Charles was more practical and realistic. Eventually, we hired a local realtor and began focusing on the Parkington and Ellwood areas. I had inherited a pool table when I rented my apartment in Avon and we had all become serious pool players, so finding a home with a finished basement to accommodate our pool table was of utmost importance. Many of the homes we could afford were bi-levels or raised ranches, and therefore too small for our growing family, not to mention the pool table. We were disappointed again and again, but remained committed to our search until we found the perfect home.

Finally, our realtor called and told us that she had found the perfect house for us. She stressed that it was a 'hot' listing, meaning there were already many offers on the property, so if we liked it we would have to make an offer immediately. We loaded up the car and rushed over to Parkington to see this amazing house.

It was certainly large, I thought. It had five levels, including a finished basement for our pool table, four bedrooms, two full baths, an oversized family room and an attached garage. But I was not impressed. The entire house smelled awful and did not show well. We learned that the previous owner had moved out, and her son now occupied the property with several of their cats.

For Charles, on the other hand, it was love at first sight. It was a fixer-upper, he conceded, but the property was enormous, almost two acres. I was also outnumbered when the children saw the in-ground pool in the back yard. We made an offer immediately, although the question remained as to where we would get all the money needed for the down-payment and closing cost. I finally confessed to Charles about the money I had saved, and with a small loan from a friend, we were able to close on the property in two months.

Not long after we moved into our new home at 328 Westminster Close, Charles and I went to Jamaica and brought Shelby back with us. Our family was now complete. According to our friends, we were the modern day Brady Bunch. From the outside, we were the perfect family. No one had any idea of what went on behind closed doors. Despite our troubles, Charles desperately wanted another child. I argued that our family was complete; I had my hands full with four children, a very high maintenance husband, and a full time job in another state. I hoped that eventually he would agree with me and put the matter to rest, and he did for a while.

We all loved our new home. On hot summer days, friends and family joined us for pool parties and backyard barbeques. I felt that my dream of true happiness was finally just around the corner. Charles still ruled the roost with an iron fist, but I felt that it was a good balance since I was naturally the more permissive parent. I continued to work in New York and was required to make dinner every night for the family. It was also mandatory that we all ate together at the dinner table. We went camping together during the summers, even though I hated it, and we also took vacations together regularly. It was becoming easier for me to ignore Charles's bouts of jealousy, he was being faithful, to the best of my knowledge, and the children were happy, or so I deluded myself.

Charles was an avid but unsuccessful entrepreneur who got involved in just about every multi-level opportunity that came his way. We had many heated discussions whenever I refused to call my friends and family members to encourage them to joint venture one business endeavor or another. We sold insurance and investments products, vitamins and beauty aids, water purifiers, jewelry, paintings, and a host of other products, all in the hopes of accruing the great wealth these businesses promised. Alas, that promise was never realized. Each business enterprise lasted for a few months or even weeks before the ideas were discarded for something more promising. He often admitted that he was not a finisher, and he was right. Dabbling halfheartedly in these businesses caused not only frustration, but also a severe drain on our finances. It was also a source of embarrassment for me when friends joked good-naturedly about all the businesses we promoted.

Our initial arrangement was that I would turn my checks over to him, he managed our finances, and I was given a weekly allowance. When I discovered that our bills were being left unpaid in order to finance other business ventures, we argued incessantly and eventually agreed on a new arrangement. Now, Charles would be responsible for paying the mortgage and I would manage all other household expenses, including food and clothing for the family. As soon as we were back on track with our bills, he wanted to revert to the original arrangement, but I staunchly refused. I was accused of usurping his position as head of household.

The two multifamily homes that Charles owned were also a drain on our budget, because more often than not, they were unoccupied. Because he taught school full time during the day, he spent many evenings and nights fixing plumbing or electrical issues that cropped up with his less than desirable tenants. I admired his dedication back then; it seemed that there was nothing he could not repair.

Even though we saved quite a bit of money by not hiring contractors, we were never able to maintain any substantial savings. To make matters even more complicated, his profession as a public school teacher gave him the option of either having his annual salary spread over the ten months that teachers generally worked, or spread over the entire year. The latter would allow him to get a salary during the summer months when school was out. Charles, of course, opted for the former. He claimed that he would get a job during the summer months because he wanted to get the higher monthly checks. That plan worked for only one year: he did get a short-term summer job and we managed to make do, but were very happy to see his first real paycheck in the middle of September. When the lack of summer income became an issue in later years, Charles' solution was to refinance our home almost annually. So much so, that eventually I would not agree to be a co-borrower and he did the refinancing on his own. At the height of his refinancing in the 1990's, our home was mortgaged at over half a million dollars. We had purchased it for just under one hundred thousand dollars in 1984.

He eventually sold one rental property and the home he shared with his ex-wife, but there was very little profit left over after he paid off the mortgages. A year later, one of his tenants accidentally burnt down the other property. Thankfully, no one was hurt, so eventually we were relieved of those monthly payments.

We began attending a local church in Parkington. When the pastor discovered that Charles and I were not married, he gently suggested that we do so, for the sake of the children. I was reluctant at first, because I did not believe that Charles could be a faithful husband. I was also tired of his insecurities and his controlling attitude and was desperately afraid of another failed marriage. I was worried that he would be unfaithful again, but I was still not prepared to split up our family because our children had already experienced so much turmoil in their lives. So, although I was conflicted, I eventually agreed to get married again, although I strongly suspected that we would not have a 'till death do us part' marriage.

To the world, I might have appeared to be a forward thinking woman who was in control, but I was in many ways still a little girl desperately yearning for a family. I was determined to keep us together at almost any cost. I could take whatever Charles dished out, or so I thought. Were he physically abusive, I never would have stayed in the relationship. At the time, I never dreamed that the scars from mental and emotional abuse could be equally or even more devastating. In any event, I reasoned that all of our children would be emancipated in just over four years, so the question was whether or not I could hang on until then. I convinced myself that I could, by repeating the iconic phrase from Helen Reddy to strengthen my resolve: "I am strong, I am invincible, *I am woman!*" So in June of 1985 I married Charles Hale.

When the next year rolled around, I had a feeling of dread. Charles seemed more distracted than usual, and he was always busy with a new business venture. It was in the spring of 1986 that he introduced me to one of his co-workers, a Swedish woman named Ursula. She was extremely friendly, and paid the family many unannounced visits, which made me pretty uncomfortable. Although I liked her, I still felt she was more Charles's friend than mine. What surprised me was that he actually had a friend, and even more astonishing, a female one. Neither Charles nor I encouraged close friendships back then; I felt it easier to have acquaintances. Whenever I got close to anyone, they would eventually drift away, and it was years later that I discovered that my husband had been making inappropriate advances to my friends, which had caused them to stay away.

Charles confided in me one day that Ursula was planning on leaving her husband and suggested that she move in with us until she was able to get a place of her own. I told him that I did not want to do that because I did not know her well enough to have her living in our home indefinitely. Furthermore, I did not want to disrupt the children's lives so that a stranger could move in. I knew he was surprised at my stance, since our home was always a haven for friends or family who needed a place to stay. This was one of the few times that I got my way, and we did not speak about her moving in anymore, although she continued to visit often.

In the beginning of September, just before he was ready to start school, Charles woke me up late one night and told me he had something very important to discuss with me. I was very concerned and immediately thought that perhaps he was going to break the news of some terrible illness. I sat bolt upright in bed, terrified when I saw the somber look on his face. I listened as my husband confessed to me that he and Ursula had been having an affair in our home during the summer, in our marital bed, with our children nearby, while I was at work in New York each day. I desperately wanted it to all be a joke, but I knew it wasn't.

Ursula called me the next day and admitted to the affair. She told me that Charles had promised her that they would move away to Florida together. There was no mention of the children, and so I thought that he planned on leaving them with me, which I was grateful for, at least. He confessed the infidelity only because Ursula had finally given him an ultimatum: leave me or she would tell me what was going on. Obviously, at that point I felt that our marriage was over. His pleas fell on deaf ears this time. I wanted him out of the house, but he refused to leave, and so I moved downstairs to the family room because I needed time to sort things out. It took several weeks before I could look at him; the children were miserable and our home was in turmoil. The tears stopped eventually and I moved back to our bedroom only after purchasing a new bed.

After the revelation of the latest affair, Charles re-discovered religion and we began to go to church every Sunday. He demanded a new reverence for God and I fell in behind him, thinking maybe this was what we needed as a family in order to survive. I was also traveling out of state for my job three or four times per year, and so his insecurities kicked in once again and the bickering continued. Life in the Hale household took a different turn. I was now not 'religious' enough for him, and he proclaimed that his relationship with God would be the answer to his issues. He chastised me for being the reason that we were 'unequally yoked', to which I responded, "I was not the one to break our marriage covenant." Even though the mistakes of my past reverberated in my head, I was a different person. That person was always a step behind Charles because I was not as obedient or submissive to him as he wanted me to be.

We eventually went to counseling, at my request, but when it became too painful Charles was hesitant to continue. During the therapy sessions, he spoke freely about the reasons for his infidelity, and I listened carefully because I desperately needed to understand him. But when I spoke about what he had done and how it was affecting our family, he decided that therapy was not the answer. God was the answer. Charles knew the Bible inside out because he was practically raised in the church during his childhood in South Africa. I allowed him to be our spiritual leader while I prayed every day for the ability to forgive and to submit, because I felt that was the right thing to do.

Deep down, I knew that this life I was living was a lie, but I felt conflicted, and thus paralyzed. I was still dealing with the issues of abandonment in my past, my two failed marriages, an unfaithful and controlling spouse, and the vows to which I recommitted when I became a Christian. Divorce was no longer an option.

We changed churches multiple times as Charles became increasingly fanatical about religion. He complained that the churches we attended were either too liberal or the pastors' messages were flawed. Our household structure became even more rigid, as though we had to pay penance for the sins he committed. I thought that my husband was very hypocritical, but I felt the need for us to maintain a united front for the sake of the kids. Nothing was real anymore; we were all living a gigantic lie. We did what was necessary to survive. Even though the love was all but gone, if Charles's new persona meant that he would be a faithful husband, then I would continue to muddle through at least until the children were emancipated.

Sadly, I found out later that the children I was trying so desperately to protect were also miserable. This was a particularly bad time in our marriage; forgiveness did not come as easily as before and our intimacy suffered as a result. I would not and could not rebound as easily as my husband wanted, and he could not understand why it was becoming increasingly difficult for me to submit to his leadership, although he was a cruel and ineffective head of household. He threatened to leave and I told him to go. I suppose even after everything we had experienced, I did not think he would, but there was a big surprise ahead for me.

———— ⁓⁓⁓⁓⁓ ————

One Sunday afternoon, my Aunt Yvonne stopped by and introduced us to a new multi-level business in which she was involved. Charles was immediately interested and we agreed to pursue a new career selling jewelry. We did pretty well for a while and recruited quite a few people in our organization. Although I did not enjoy attending all of the required meetings, I truly loved the jewelry.

Sometime later I received a call from a friend who asked me if we had a family member in a hospital nearby. I told her that I did not think so and inquired why she had asked. She told me that she saw Charles at the hospital a few times, visiting a woman who was a patient there. When Charles got home later that night I asked him about it, and he told me that Gladys, a former co-worker and one of the women he had recruited in the business, had undergone surgery recently. He went on to explain that he visited her once in a show of friendship. He volunteered no further information, and so I assumed that the subject was closed.

My friend called again the following day to tell me that Charles was at the hospital again. I explained that the woman was a family friend and that Charles was just being helpful. There was complete silence on the line for a minute, and then my friend hesitantly continued that it appeared that our 'family friend' was being discharged, because Charles was packing her things and they seemed very cozy. I pretended that I knew that he would be there with Gladys, but after hanging up the telephone I decided to drive to her home to find out what was going on. There were no cars in the driveway, so I waited. I wanted to find out if Charles was lying to me when he tried to assure me that there was nothing going on between him and 'that woman', as he referred to her.

In less than fifteen minutes his car pulled in the driveway. I watched, fuming, as he got out of the car, opened the door on the passenger side and helped her out of the vehicle. I stalked over and demanded an explanation of what was going on, and sarcastically added that I just wanted to help. He simply looked at me, clearly humiliated, while Gladys refused to look me in the eye. Livid was not the word for how I felt in that moment. I pushed her out of the way and yanked his glasses off his face because I knew he could not see well without them. I threw them on the ground, stomped on them until they were in pieces, and stormed off.

He came home a couple of hours later, packed his clothes, and ordered his children to pack their clothes as well. The children were in tears. They looked at me, wondering what was going on, but had no choice but to do as their father commanded. Within the hour, they were gone. I had no idea where they went that evening, but I figured he would come crawling back later that night or the following day begging for my forgiveness. The next day, our son Christian called me, crying, and told me that their father had moved them in with Gladys and her son.

Am I finally free? I asked myself. I felt none of the triumph I thought I would have... My feelings fluctuated from relief to devastation to betrayal. I felt like a fool. My family was broken, I was broken, and I had nothing left to give. Charles had finally left and I was ill-prepared. The friends who tried to warn me that Charles was no good for me were right, but I had kept holding on to my fantasy of an ideal family, looking at my world through rose colored glasses. Now I was finally paying the price. Rather than celebrate my freedom, I became more and more depressed.

I thought of the silly little things I could now do that I could not have done before: I could finally use my dishwasher! I walked into the kitchen and loaded it with the few dishes that were in the sink. Charles was no longer around to chastise me for wasting water. Encouraged by this small act of defiance, I went through each room, turned the lights on, opened all the blinds and allowed the natural daylight to flood the rooms. I felt energy suffuse my veins with each step I took. My neighbor used to tease me that it seemed we were having a séance in our home because Charles demanded that we kept the drapes drawn if the temperature dropped below fifty degrees. Slowly, I began to feel that I was finally free. I made a mental note to call my friend Simone. Now, with him gone, I would be able to speak to her and any other friend I wanted to, without being told that I was on the phone too long (and always loud enough for the other party on the line to hear).

I could now eat my food in whatever order I chose: rice and salad first and meat last, and it did not have to make sense to anyone but me. I opened the cabinet below the sink, pulled out a saucepan, placed it in the refrigerator and closed the door. In my head I heard Charles screaming at me, berating me, for leaving a pot of leftovers in the refrigerator. The never-ending list of "don'ts" reverberated in my head, and my body sagged in blessed relief at the thought of having my days free of nagging or bickering! Most importantly, I would not be made to feel like a slut for any obscure, random reason that came to his mind.

Was I unhappy now? Did I love Charles or was I addicted to him? Did I even love myself? Perhaps I was suffering from a psychological phenomenon somewhat like Stockholm syndrome, because I began to identify with hostages who have empathy, even sympathy, toward their captors. The truth was, I began to miss Charles.

Days later, after my euphoria had passed, I walked through the house in a daze, hearing the children's laughter echo in the walls. I looked back at the times when we all sprawled out on the couches on Christmas mornings amid brightly colored wrapping paper and gift boxes everywhere. We were usually dressed in some of the brand new clothing we received as gifts. Our beautifully decorated tree stood regally in front of the large picture window, the smell of savory garlic pork permeating the house. I remembered Shelby's beaming face when she opened one of her gifts and found the "Epilady" that she had begged me for, and then her anguished screams when she tested it, brutally yanking the hair from her legs. Our laughter, eventually joined by hers, had filled the room for a very long time. There was usually Jamaican fruit cake that I stayed up until dawn baking the night before, sitting prominently on the coffee table. Everyone ate and drank eggnog in whatever amounts and whenever they wanted. Charles and I would be dressed in our robes, and I would run up and down the stairs to check on the garlic pork throughout the lazy morning. Much of it would end up being burnt to a crisp, but we didn't care. Our Christmas movie playing in the background was usually either *Pocket Full of Miracle*, or *It's a Wonderful Life*. We laughed or cried in unison at the familiar scenes, no matter how many times we'd seen them before.

I looked outside through the square panes of our large picture window, wincing yet again at the one pane that was slightly clearer than the others. It was recently replaced after Charles threw the VCR out the window when he found our teenage kids and me watching the movie *Alien*.

"It is filth," he had proclaimed, and accused me of being an unfit parent because I had allowed such a movie in our home.

Somehow, these awful memories made me as lonesome as the happy ones, and I spent most of my days in tears, completely lost in my own head.

Martin and Shelby were my pillars of strength during those times. They watched over me, crying when I cried, but secretly happy that their stepfather was gone. They did miss their brother and sister, but not Dad. Christian called me every day in tears, wanting to make sure I was alright. Shelby never called. I went to several therapy sessions, hoping to find some outside relief that I could not find within myself. I was prescribed an anti-depressant, which only made me even more depressed. I looked at my two children and felt that I had disappointed them yet again. I could not keep another marriage together, and for that, I felt that I was a failure.

Two weeks later, I bought a bottle of over-the-counter pills, parked in a lot at a medical school nearby, and swallowed a handful. Deep down, I did not want to die, but I did not want to live either. I immediately became afraid and went in to the receptionist and told her that I had taken some pills and I was deeply depressed. They took me to the hospital and kept me overnight for observation. After I was discharged, I went to speak with a pastor that Charles and I knew, because I knew I needed guidance. I had to learn how to live with myself and still be a good mother to my children. The coping strategies I adopted in order to survive with Charles now needed to be adjusted to a new life without him. After our conversation, the pastor requested a meeting with us both. Because he was aware of Charles' history with his ex-wife, he chastised Charles and told him that his pattern of behavior was wrong. He told Charles that he needed to recognize the example he was setting for his children, and then charged him to honor the vows he made before God and the church. Charles was very repentant and moved back home a few days later. He had been gone for almost two months.

Gladys was devastated and called our home repeatedly. Her father also called and asked Charles to return to her, but he did not. Then one day she called to apologize and tell me that there was a very important matter she needed to discuss with me. She told me that Charles had confided in her that he suspected that I was having improper relations with his fifteen-year-old son. I could not believe what I was hearing. She told me that upon her insistence, they took Christian aside and asked him if it really happened. The boy was so upset at the absurd accusation that he attacked his father, trying to hurt him. Charles tried to apologize, but his son was inconsolable. She said I needed to know this because she wanted me to know the moral fiber of the man I was fighting for. I imagine she knew that I would be devastated upon hearing this and possibly throw Charles out of the house. I suppose that would have been her revenge on him for having left her so abruptly.

I confronted Charles as soon as I got off the phone and he denied that it ever happened. He told me she was lying because she was hurt. According to him, he told her he was returning home because he knew he had made a mistake in leaving. I did not know who to believe, and although I was embarrassed to ask our son if this had really happened, I needed to know the truth. I wanted to know if Charles was capable of lying about something as vile and contemptible as that accusation was. A year passed before I could muster the nerve to ask Christian about it. He confirmed that Gladys was telling the truth, and his father had lied to me. By that point, I had to simply live with this despicable lie, as no good would come of confronting Charles about it all over again.

It was at this point that I came to the realization that some people have character flaws, but the man I had married had a flawed character. The betrayal I felt was so deep that I did not even consider the legal ramifications that such an accusation could have had on me. Had Gladys gone to the authorities with the story that Charles concocted, my life and the lives of our children could have been severely disrupted.

Our 'normal' routine eventually continued. Forgiveness of the wrongs inflicted was mandatory, but forgetting was not nearly as easy, despite Charles' frequent reminders that I should.

One day I overheard the children having a very heated discussion in the family room and approached them slowly, intent on mediating whatever argument I had stumbled upon.

I stopped in my tracks when I heard someone yell, "You can take Dad, and I will take Mom".

Another voice responded vehemently, "No! I want Mom; YOU should take Dad!"

"Why are you divvying up me and your father?" I interrupted curiously. None of the children seemed particularly ashamed at my sudden presence.

"We are deciding who will take you and Dad when you get old, but nobody wants to take Dad."

I half-heartedly chastised them for being mean, and made them promise not to let Dad catch wind of this conversation. Deep down, I felt validated that they recognized and appreciated my devotion to them. Perhaps I was wrong about the way I felt, but at that time, I needed validation from someone, anyone, who understood my plight.

Truth be told, I adored my children and relished their presence. They often sat with me in our dining room while I prepared our evening meal. These were the times that we talked about their experiences in school and the challenges they faced as teenagers. Usually, as soon as they heard their father's car enter the driveway, they would scatter to their respective bedrooms or to the family room. They knew from past experience that Charles did not approve of any closeness between them and me when he was absent. He felt that I coddled them too much and should maintain a certain emotional distance from them.

I had stopped taking the pill after Charles moved out, and at his suggestion, I did not continue when he returned. He believed that this was the ideal time to have another child and to solidify our commitment to each other. Inevitably, I got pregnant within six months after he returned home. Again, I was faced with my longstanding conflict: the vow that I had made to myself years ago, that I would leave Charles after the kids were out of the house. The day my pregnancy was confirmed, I stood on my front porch and realized that I would be stuck with him for another eighteen years. I was still living in a fool's paradise, believing that I was invincible, that I could survive that long with him as my partner. I did the only thing that I could, and prayed fervently to God for strength.

Second Chances

CHAPTER 25

It was around that time that we met a wonderful couple, Dave and Judy, who led a marriage workshop in our church. I spoke with Judy at length and confided some of my experiences in my marriage. She and Dave began to counsel us on a weekly basis in their home, and that was when Charles made the revelation that he was addicted to sex. He confessed to the many affairs he had in his first marriage and during his marriage to me. The life that he led before he met me was fraught with infidelity and betrayal, but Dave and Judy comforted me that it was possible that a man can change. Charles certainly appeared as though he truly wanted to change. Over the next two years, we went on couples' retreats regularly, continued counseling with our friends, and our marriage steadily improved. David was very patient with Charles and was somehow able to communicate that being a man did not mean he had to control my every action. He tried to explain what true love, agape love, and romantic love meant. We both learned a lot from our friends and we saw them display in their marriage—a model of what ours could be, I hoped.

I did not return to New York to work after Chelsea, our youngest, was born. This time, I was a stay-at-home mom until she was potty-trained. I purchased a sewing machine and taught myself to sew by making dresses for her. Later on, with the help of some simple dress patterns, I made dresses for myself as well and soon began to make clothes for my friends. I was learning the pleasure of creating things with my hands and being paid for my handiwork. However, because the process was so tedious and labor intensive, I was not able to earn a decent living from sewing alone.

Charles was very complimentary; he encouraged me to continue to sew and he too began to try his hand at the craft. Ultimately, I decided to give it up, as it was not truly my passion; it was more a hobby for me. He was very disappointed when I decided to go back to work outside the home.

When Chelsea turned two years old, we enrolled her in a Christian school nearby and I went back to work part-time with the same metallurgical laboratory I worked at previously. Their business had improved and they had moved to a new place in Ellwood. I was once again the secretary, bookkeeper and all around 'Girl Friday'. This was where I met Howie, who was also working there on a part-time basis. He told me that he had a small business in the garment industry in New York. After hearing more about his business, we decided to become partners in selling women's clothing. I went to New York with him and met with some of his wholesalers. I started out by purchasing a few items of clothing, wholesale, and sold them from my home to friends and family. It was very exciting venture for me, as I had always loved fashion and shopping. It seemed to be the perfect fit for me. Very soon, I had a thriving home-based business going.

Meanwhile, Charles and I were enjoying the bliss of new parenthood. Chelsea was an amazing child and we were enjoying our small family; the older kids were away at college or pursuing a career.

One day, when Chelsea was about five years old, I came home from work and saw her playing on her bed. She called me over to her, smiled, hugged me, gave me a big kiss on my cheek, and then fell back on her bed. She then looked up at me seriously and asked, "Mommy, did we just fall in love?" As the tears welled up in my eyes, I knew that I would always remember that precious and beautiful moment we shared. I thanked God that I did take Charles back, because we were blessed with our beautiful and loving daughter.

Dave and Judy moved away some time later, and we began attending a different church in Mayfair. Things were going very well for us during that period, and I was content. I started to believe that my husband was a new man. I was now very familiar with his idiosyncrasies and we lived almost completely by his rules. His jealousy was still a bit unnerving, but I felt I could live with it if my family stayed intact.

One day, as I was heading home from work, I noticed that there was a store for rent. I decided to stop in to see if I could convert it to a clothing store. The rent was affordable and it certainly had possibilities. I told Charles of my plans and he tried to discourage me from such a huge undertaking. I was determined, so I went ahead anyway. I purchased stock from a store in North Jersey that was going out of business and the rest I purchased from New York. Each day I stopped by my store and single-handedly painted, decorated, and stocked it, and within a month *Le Victoria Boutique* had its grand opening. I hired two part-time college students as sales clerks while I was at work and prayed for business to pick up.

Even though my merchandise was a bit upscale for the neighborhood, it was the image I wanted. Eventually I attracted some steady customers and business began to pick up even though there was not much profit to speak of. About six months after my grand opening, I was alerted that there was a fire in the beauty salon upstairs. I was forced to evacuate when the fire department showed up, and watched from across the street as they began to use their powerful hoses to extinguish the flames. Unfortunately, my store was in the 'line of fire', and my merchandise sustained extensive water damage. To my dismay, I was forced to close down for renovations. In the end, I had a fire sale and opted to move the balance of the stock to my home and not re-open the store.

I continued working at my part-time job but decided to pursue a career in real estate. Charles and I did some research and we found a school in South Jersey just off the Garden State Parkway and I went to classes each Saturday. I was very excited about my decision and settled in quickly with thirty other bright-eyed real estate candidates. I met a young man in class who was particularly enthusiastic about the business. Or perhaps he stood out to me simply because he was also from Jamaica. We spoke a few times after class and he told me that he and his family lived in a nearby town. One day, after class, he told me that his car was in the shop and his wife had dropped him off earlier that morning. He asked if I could help him out by dropping him off at a gas station at an exit on the expressway. Since it was on my way home and I willingly agreed to help. Both he and his wife were very grateful, and we promised to stay in touch. Of course we never did; and after we completed our required hours in school, we wished each other good luck and went our separate ways.

About a year later, Charles and I attended an overnight marriage seminar at a hotel in South Jersey. On day two of the seminar we went down to the cafeteria for breakfast and while standing in line I realized that someone was tapping me on the shoulder. I looked around and there was the Jamaican gentleman whom I had met in my real estate class. Trevor beamed at me and asked if we were enjoying the sessions. It was pretty obvious that neither one of us remembered the other's name, and so he quickly re-introduced himself, and I did as well. I quickly introduced him to Charles, who by this time had backed away from the cashier. I explained to him that we had met at the real estate class that we both took some months before. They shook hands and mumbled polite greetings to each other.

"How's the real estate business?" Trevor asked.

"Not that great," I confessed. "I'm doing it part-time for now."

"Well, I'm not setting the world on fire yet, but I'm not giving up."

"Good luck! Maybe I'll sell one of your listings."

Trevor walked away after waving goodbye and I turned my attention back to Charles. While we were still at the counter, Charles realized that he left his wallet back in our room and he asked me to wait while he went to fetch it. While I waited for him at the counter, I noticed that Trevor and his wife were getting ready to leave. They walked over to me again and his wife and I shook hands and exchanged a few pleasantries. I explained to them that my husband had gone back to our room because he had forgotten his wallet. Trevor generously offered to pay for our breakfast. I protested that it would not be necessary, but he insisted. He explained that one good turn deserved another, and told the cashier that he would take care of our small tab. I eventually thanked them both, we waved goodbye, and they left.

When Charles returned a few minutes later, I told him that Trevor and his wife paid for our breakfast to show their appreciation. I explained that had I given Trevor a ride once when his car was in the shop. What happened next was hard to believe—or maybe it wasn't. Charles was livid, to put it plainly. He accused me of planning this liaison with Trevor, and berated me for my underhanded behavior.

"How long has this 'thing' been going on?" he demanded.

Just like I did in times like these, I accused him of being crazy. I reminded him that he was the one who had suggested that we come to this seminar, and asked him why he thought I would invite someone to meet me here if I was indeed carrying on a secret affair. It was very frustrating dealing with his irrational jealousy and rage, and I was beginning to be weary of attempting to defend myself. I suggested that we try to find Trevor and his wife so that he could confront them directly.

He never did, which meant that I had to live with months of accusations and disparaging remarks about my alleged affair. At one point, after Charles and I had yet another disagreement, he told his brother about the incident in an effort to explain how deceitful I was. While I listened to his story, I wished that I knew Trevor's last name so that I could call him and have him explain to reasonable people what had happened that morning.

After that embarrassing incident, I decided to change real estate offices and pursue a full-time career as a realtor. I secretly hoped I would run into Trevor again so I could have him speak to Charles about the accusation he had made, but we never saw each other after that morning. I worked at a small franchise office in East Byfield, the next town over from Parkington. The prospect of finally selling homes was fascinating, but I soon learned that it was not as easy as I thought. I wanted the fancy cars that realtors drove and the lifestyle that I thought realtors had, but was not prepared to do the work that needed to be done to achieve it. Yes, I was a realtor and had business cards to prove it, but I was not making any money.

One Sunday afternoon, my friend Emily and I were returning home from church. We spotted a FSBO (For Sale by Owner) sign on the way and I convinced her to accompany me to preview the house. After all, I was a realtor and that was what realtors did. We pulled off the main road and drove down the narrow side street, looking for the house. About two blocks down, we saw the sign indicating that the home was being held open. We parked, walked up to the door and rang the bell. The home was tiny, but it had great curb appeal. The lawn was nicely manicured and the front entrance was very inviting. A well-dressed woman answered and I immediately handed her my business card. She invited us in, probably assuming that my friend Emily was a client. She was very pregnant and there was a small child strapped in a highchair at the dining table.

"My name is Carolyn and this is my husband Steve," she introduced, as she showed us around their home. It was tastefully decorated and it was evident that they had done their homework on how to host an open house. I was impressed, and they were visibly pleased. We walked through the home and listened to them pointing out its best features, while I nodded and complimented them on their attention to the tiniest detail of the home. After exchanging a few final pleasantries, I thanked them for their time and we left.

About a week later, I happened to be in my office when I received a call from Steve. He told me that they were no longer interested in trying to sell the home on their own and wanted to hire me as their agent. I was dumbfounded! I asked if I could put him on hold for a minute, ran to my manager, and quickly explained what was happening. Even though I had completed my training, I was still ill-prepared to work with a real live client. My manager was able to calm me down and told me to get the pertinent information and the time they wanted to meet with me. I went back to the phone and made the necessary inquiries, hoping that my voice relayed cool confidence and professionalism. A few days later, I met with them and received my very first listing. I made several blunders during the transaction, but managed to sell the property very quickly and at a very reasonable price.

Because that was my first listing, I did everything possible to make it a success. My clients were happy and I was even happier to get my first check just two days after Christmas, and approximately five months after I had become a realtor. That was when I got bitten by the 'bug', and so for the next ten years I was the most committed sales associate I could be. I was very successful in my new career and fought many battles, both at home and in the field. Things were going splendidly at work, but at home, rather than an "atta girl" congratulatory slap on the back, my success was met with the now all-too familiar disdain.

My Uncle Tony died in 1992 and left me a sizable inheritance. I couldn't believe it; I was an heiress! Charles and I decided to invest half of the money and then make some major and much needed improvements to our home with the other half. We planned to hire a general contractor to oversee the work that had to be done. The house needed a new roof, and we wanted to expand our master bedroom and add a skylight. We also wanted to remodel and expand our master bathroom and install a hot tub. Our second bathroom needed to be remodeled and we wanted to add a half bath on the lower level by our family room. That was our wish list. We knew that we could not get everything done with the money we planned to spend, but we decided to look at proposals from contractors.

I suggested to Charles that since I knew reputable contractors who had worked with our clients, we should meet with a couple of them, give them our wish list, and listen to their proposals.

We made an appointment with the first contractor and he met with us over the weekend. He showed up on time, listened to what we wanted done, and asked us several questions—most of which I was not able to answer, so I allowed Charles to take the lead. Within an hour, I knew that the interview was not going well, and I began to wish that I had not made that recommendation. The contractor's fatal mistake was in looking directly at me when he spoke. I suppose he did that simply because he knew me, but Charles was growing more and more antagonistic as the meeting progressed. Unfortunately, the contractor could not have known the criteria by which he was being judged, and I had failed to warn him.

After the interview, I prepared myself for the onslaught, and I was not disappointed. The accusation was made that I was 'probably' having an affair with this man. Sure enough, the contractor's tendency to look at me while he talked was Charles' 'confirmation', and as usual, he could not be reasoned with. After days of trying to convince him that it was all in his head, I told him that he could pick whomever he wanted to do the work; I no longer wanted to be involved in the decision.

He chose Cecil, a contractor he had recently met. Cecil promised to do everything we wanted for the unbelievable price of sixty thousand dollars. He brought pictures of other jobs he claimed that he had done, none of which were overly impressive, in my opinion. But the clincher for Charles was when Cecil claimed to be a Christian. That won him the contract, hands down. Because of my experience with many self-proclaimed 'Christians', including my husband, I was very skeptical. I felt that he made the profession of faith simply because of the way Charles spoke and thus he guessed (rightfully) that it would help him to get the job.

Since the money was left to me and not Charles, I voiced my opinion on this new contractor and there was the usual argument. Charles was the expert. He was an expert and should be trusted on matters such as this. I was accused of wanting to control every situation in our marriage, and that was the reason, he continued, that we were having serious problems. I was very accustomed to this rhetoric. Whenever I tried to make recommendations on any matter, it was the tactic he used to shut me down. Colossians 3:18

may as well have been woven into a quilt and displayed on the wall in every room of our home because it was also my husband's mantra: *Wives, submit yourselves unto your own husbands, as it is fit in the Lord.* When that failed to get the results he wanted, he would remind me of 1 Corinthians 6:14: *Be ye not unequally yoked together with unbelievers: for what fellowship hath righteousness with unrighteousness? And what communion hath light with darkness?* I could fight with him, but how did I fight with God? Charles knew the Bible inside and out and could quote passages verbatim to suit his every whim. I backed off once again, hoping that he was right about Cecil. The objective was to get the job done, get it done in a timely manner, and for a reasonable amount of money.

One third of the cost up front, the second third when the job was half finished, and the final payment at the end: that was the agreement that we made, and we all signed a contract. Charles handled everything and we were overjoyed when the work began with gusto a week later. Within three weeks, however, our house was in complete disarray. Our bedroom was a disaster, the family room was a disaster, and one worker actually fell through the sheetrock from the bedroom down to the living room. Very soon, the work that had begun with such passion began to slow down drastically less than half way through. We lived in this state of confusion for weeks, and I was beside myself.

"You have to talk to Cecil," I pleaded. "I don't think he's planning on finishing the job."

We had a big blue tarp thrown over our roof to cover the hole where the skylight should be, and two enormous dumpsters in our driveway. It was an eyesore in our beautiful neighborhood. I realized then that my husband epitomized the definition of a bully. He was extremely domineering, controlling, and overbearing toward me, however; he was deathly afraid to confront the contractor to find out what was going on with our home. In retrospect, my eyes were opened to many of his personality traits and his reasons for doing the things that he did. Even the profession he chose helped to prove a deep seated weakness in his character. He was able to dominate and control kids, which is why he chose the teaching profession. I do not believe that all teachers have a controlling attitude, but that it is likely for someone with that particular weakness to choose that profession, as it may help to feed that particular flaw.

He continued to shy away from confronting the contractor, and I was miserable. I finally called Cecil one morning and complained about the lack of progress on our home. He told me that the money he received up front was not enough to purchase the material needed to complete the project. He also confessed that he had underestimated costs and so he needed additional money in order to continue. This was not at all what we bargained for but we could not leave the home in that condition indefinitely. We were trapped. Under pressure, Charles finally spoke to the contractor and we agreed to advance him another twenty thousand dollars. The work resumed, but again, after two more weeks and very little progress, we were at another standstill. Yet another check was paid out, and after he cashed it, he never returned. We had invested tens of thousands of dollars, including most of the money slated for savings, and our home was still far from finished. Charles eventually completed most of the work himself, often cutting corners because we ran out of money. It took him well over a year to get the work done, but our beautiful home had now become, in my opinion, somewhat of a 'handyman special'.

It was more apparent to me, because as a real estate professional, I had seen many homeowners fall into that very same trap. I did the best I could with the aid of creative decorating to cover the glaring flaws. I appreciated that Charles was able to get as much done as he did, and never failed to compliment him on his ability as a 'Jack of all trades'.

"We will have the home we want," he often promised, and I agreed, because I planned on hiring the next contractor myself. I consulted an attorney about suing Cecil, but I discovered that he had no assets, and furthermore, that he had many homeowners waiting in line to sue him as well. We decided to cut our losses and we moved on.

Charles, Chelsea and I had settled in at yet another church home. We taught Sunday school and began to make friends. I was thrilled that Charles now had positive male influences in his life. I thought that this would make him understand more about how a loving relationship between a man and wife should be. I wanted him to see that his philandering ways were harmful to our family, and I especially wanted him to see that there could be trust between a husband and wife. I began to grow as a Christian as well, and became very involved in several ministries in the church. A few years after we became members, our pastor and the church leadership selected several men to become deacons in the church. To Charles' disappointment, he was not one of the men selected. He complained bitterly every week before we went to church and accused the pastor of favoritism. He was especially upset because a friend of ours who he claimed had only been a Christian for a few years was selected. He whined that his only stumbling block was the scripture in 1Timothy 3:12, that said, *let the deacons be the husband of one wife, ruling their children and their own houses.* His prior marriage and subsequent divorce must have caused the leadership to disqualify him from the coveted position, he believed. Even though his first wife had died by then, he believed that the leadership might have frowned on the fact that she had divorced him and he was not a widower when we married.

He decided to start on a campaign to distort the facts. At every opportunity he could, he mentioned that he was once a widower. He then asked for a meeting with the pastor and apparently was able to convince him that he was right for the position. Charles was ordained as a deacon in the church a few months later. I knew about the deception, but I did not reveal it to anyone. I did not know if his divorce was ever truly a factor in him not being selected originally. Charles was content, and I believed then that he genuinely loved the Lord and was ready to become a servant in the church.

The Beginning Of The End

CHAPTER 26

My real estate career blossomed and I was ranked among the top performers in my office. Each year I competed against myself to become more successful. It was, of course, financially rewarding, and that added bonus massaged my perpetually bruised ego. My young daughter had become the joy of my life, but I continued to walk on eggshells at home. I was constantly in a state of awareness and was never disappointed when the proverbial 'other shoe' dropped. Peace never lasted long in our household. As time went by, I began to suspect that something might have been clinically wrong with Charles.

Sure enough, he told me that he felt depressed most of the time. I thought that his sadness and depression stemmed from external sources and since his constant anger and frustrations were usually directed at me, that it must have been my fault. I tried even harder to please him. He was happy for short periods before the unexplained sadness emerged for no known reason to him or anyone else around him. He constantly complained that he could not sleep at nights and that too took its toll. My sleep was usually troubled as well, because more often than not, he would wake me up, complaining that I moved around too much in my sleep. He said it disturbed him and caused him to be irritable for the rest of the night, and thus the cycle of unhappiness would continue into the following day.

I had a very close friend who moved from New York to Parkington. Simone and her family lived a few blocks away from us, for which I was very thankful: her friendship often kept me from going over the edge. I had hoped that Charles would become friends with her husband, but sadly, he still did not know how to cultivate friendships. He told me a while back that he and I could live on a deserted island alone together and that would make him happy. At first I thought it was very romantic, but as time went by, I realized that Charles wanted to own me, much like an inanimate object. He desperately wanted me to ignore all outside relationships, just as he preferred to do himself. At times I would observe my friend Simone and her husband together and desperately wish that Charles and I could enjoy similar camaraderie. They loved, trusted, and respected each other. They could tease and laugh easily at, and with each other, and that made an enormous difference in their relationship. I could not dream of doing any of these things with Charles.

Simone became my confidant and she tried to befriend Charles as well. The few friends I had before were mostly long gone. We rarely entertained, and when we did, Charles would at times get bored, claim he was tired, and insist that it was time for me to go to bed; much like one treated a small child. At those times, in order to keep the peace, I would obediently bid our friends goodnight, whether or not I wanted the visit to be over, and usher them to the door. My friends were always sympathetic when Charles constantly belittled and berated me for my personality quirks, like enjoying watching television. But Simone understood that Charles was 'different', and so I did not have to be embarrassed around her when Charles was being Charles. Very few people understood why I allowed him to get away with this behavior, and at times, neither did I. I suppose I felt guilty because he constantly reminded me that we were "unequally yoked" and I wanted to prove that I could be the good wife, the good mother, and the good provider whenever he dropped the ball.

Because I did not want another divorce, I almost paid the ultimate price for the ideal family that I craved. My outer shell was beginning to crack and I knew it. I was very brittle on the inside also, but to the outside world, and for appearance's sake, it was imperative that I appear to be in control.

The day arrived when my lifeline, Simone, and her family relocated to Atlanta. My daughter, Chelsea and her best friend, Cassandra (Simone's daughter) clung to each other and cried on that very last day. Simone and I watched them with our own eyes brimming with tears. I felt a deep sense of loss because I had no one to turn to when Charles became Charles. My daughter has lost her best friend and she would be stuck with us and our constant bickering and my unceasing tears. I didn't leave Charles when the older children left, but then again, had I left, I would not have had Chelsea. I dared not harbor regrets, although at times like these, it was difficult. I tried to continue living as though we were the model family. I tried to live by the rules, even though by now I was well aware that the rules tended to change unexpectedly in the middle of the game.

"Some man called the house looking for you and he didn't sound like a client." Another day, another accusatory message from Charles left on my cell phone.

Not again, I thought with despair. All of my clients had my office and cell phone numbers from my business card, but there were a few clients to whom I would give my home number, depending on how critical their transaction was at the moment.

"Did he leave a name or number?" I queried, but I was firmly told that 'he' did not.

The days following that call were torture. He tried to get me to confess to this affair that I was having with someone I did not even know. I recall the first time that I stopped at a liquor store on my way home. I purchased a bottle of vodka and had a drink when I got home. It helped greatly because I fell asleep right in the middle of his tirade. I liked it! It was an excellent way to avoid arguments and also have a good night's sleep. So every now and again when things got out of hand, I would self-medicate, instantly blocking the insanity that had become my life at home.

When I didn't want to drink, I discovered another means of escape from my torture: driving. I discovered the most scenic views in my surrounding neighborhoods, the Watchung Mountains, the beautiful subdivisions in Alpine and Bernardsville and the beaches by the Jersey Shore, — just about everywhere my car would take me. By the time I got home, I was calm. Nothing bothered me.

After one particularly bad episode that lasted for days, I went driving each evening to clear my head before I got home. I was still very upset when I decided to go home, so I purchased a half pint of vodka and pulled into a rest area on the Garden State Parkway. I must have consumed half of the bottle. When I got back on the road I felt fine but I began to get sleepy as I drove. All I wanted was to get home and get in my bed, so I persisted. Just before I pulled off the exit, I saw flashing lights in my rear view mirror and pulled over quickly. That night I was arrested for DWI and taken to the state police headquarters somewhere in Toms River, an hour away from home.

I was humiliated! I was also scared, because I did not realize how intoxicated I was until I got out of the car. I called my friend Emily, and was not sure how much information beyond the fact that I was in jail was given to her. An officer gave her directions and I waited for what felt like hours. While I waited, I cried and begged the officers to let me out of the cell because I was claustrophobic. They were very kind to me and allowed me to sit just outside the cell, but I remained handcuffed to a wall.

When Emily arrived, she signed some papers and I was released. Unfortunately, my car had been impounded at a garage in another town. We did not say much to each other on the way home, but I knew she was disappointed in me. Years later, Emily explained that she kept quiet because she knew I had beaten up myself enough. She didn't need to add to that. All she wanted to do was get us home safely. She was indeed disappointed, because she had frequently tried to convince me to get away from Charles' torture rather than bury my sorrows in a bottle. I spent the rest of the night in my family room crying and reliving the events of the past evening, wondering how I had gotten to that point. I thanked God that I did not kill anyone while I was trying to get home. I don't know if I could have lived with myself if anyone was hurt because of something I did.

The next day she drove me to get my car. Once again, silence reigned while she drove. Another very dear friend who is an attorney represented me in court a few months later and my license was suspended for three months. Although it was extremely inconvenient and financially damaging, I was still grateful because the outcome could have been much worse. I never told Charles about the incident; the only people who knew were my two friends who had helped me. I was able to keep this secret from Charles because I made the decision then that our life together was over. At night I slept in the family room, and avoided him as much as I could during the daytime. I worked from home most days, and if I needed to go to the office I would take a cab or ask for a ride from one of my friends. The few clients I had were turned over to other agents because I was not able to drive. He noticed the drastic change in me and again began a campaign to win me over. I considered telling him my secret, but I couldn't. I suffered in silence. The days, weeks, and months dragged, and eventually the suspension was lifted and my license was again valid. I went to a few therapy sessions because I knew I needed to regain control of my life. I had ignored all recommendations to get out of a bad situation before it was too late, but I continued to lie to myself that I could handle it. This was the beginning of the end for me.

I was never going to change Charles, and if I wanted to stay sane, I had three options. The first: I could ask Charles to leave, which I did, but he staunchly refused. I knew that was not his style; he would leave only if he found a woman with a place for him to go to. He would never go out and get a place of his own; his addiction to sex forced him to always have a woman with him at all times, no matter who got hurt in the process. The second option was to leave with our daughter, which I considered to be the most viable. However, I knew that Chelsea loved her father, and I felt that breaking up the family might not be in her best interest. I also knew that it would be a bitter fight between Charles and me, because I had no doubt that he loved her and would not let her go without a fight.

The third option was to change me. Whenever Charles did anything that was a bit odd, friends or family members usually shrugged and said matter-of-factly, "You know Charles, that's just the way he is," as if that could explain away everything. But I did know Charles. He would probably never change, but ultimately, I was learning, whether he did or not was clearly beyond my control. This meant that I needed to change myself. I was the only person in control of my own behavior and reactions to whatever he said and did. So I chose option number three. I changed.

In 2005, I was finally successful in helping my mom, my brother, my sister, and her family to come to the United States, and they lived with us until they were able to get out on their own. By then, I was pretty good at ignoring my husband's erratic behavior. I was also very grateful to him for agreeing to have them stay with us, and was especially happy that my mother and I bonded as well as we did. They all catered to his every whim and he continued to rule the household with an iron fist. He was still a deacon at our church and he reveled in his prominent position. Still, accusations continued to rear its ugly head from time to time, but I was better able to handle it. Whenever he accused me of infidelity with any church member, I'd simply say, "Yes, you got me. I'm having an affair with (insert name), and I'm so sorry." He would eventually walk away, sulking.

When that failed, he would remind me that back in 1981 he came by my office and met one of my young co-workers, Michael, who had just started to work for JOVELLE. He said that Michael warned him to be careful about me because I was a loose woman. Disbelievingly, I'd asked him how was it possible that a young white kid who met him for the first time, who barely knew me, would walk over to an older black man and have that conversation about me. Even though he did not have an answer for me, he explained that was the reason why he never trusted me throughout our relationship. As improbable as that conversation was, Charles maintained that it was true. When I told that story to my friend Simone, (who also worked with us at JOVELLE) she laughed at me and told me I must have misunderstood Charles. "Oh Victoria, you know how Charles is," was her response.

After years of not drinking, I began to bring a bottle home again when the arguments got especially intense. I went back to my old method of comfort: taking a drink and then going to sleep. As dangerous as that behavior is for anybody, it was particularly so for me considering the history of alcoholism in my family. I was very susceptible to becoming an alcoholic myself, but I was sure that I could handle it. I reasoned that it was only a matter of time before Chelsea was ready for college, and that's when I would finally leave him.

I was eventually promoted to manage a large office in company, after I had a banner year: over eighty listings sold! Jealousy once again reared its' ugly head.

"I'm the one responsible for your success in business," Charles would tell me. "I used to stay at home in the evenings with Chelsea while you were out selling real estate, so you owe your success to me."

He continued to whine that I thought I was better than he was because I made more money than he did. I argued back that throughout the years, ever since we met, I made more money than he did, but never said or did anything to make him feel inferior. I knew that he was trying to force me to quit my job again, even though I'm sure he knew that he no longer had that control over me. Nevertheless, the pressure was building and my resolve began to crumble. I once again found myself on a slippery slope.

I got a second DWI seven years later! I knew by then that if I didn't leave I would surely die, but I still held on for as long as I could. I also knew that I had a problem with alcohol, but I fooled myself into thinking that I could fix it once I left him. This time, my license was suspended for two years, and I was devastated. I continued to drive with a suspended license, but drove only back and forth to work. I was grateful that I no longer had to work with clients.

In 2006 Chelsea, graduated from high school and was accepted at several universities. We did the college tours as a family, but to her dismay, we opted for Brighton University, near our home, since she was awarded close to a full academic scholarship there. I compromised and allowed her to live on campus so she could feel as though she actually went away to school. Charles was very upset about my decision because he wanted her to commute. I knew Chelsea was grateful to be away from home, and so I told him that he would not be financially obligated to fund her room and board; I would pay for it all. During her junior year, when she wanted to study abroad in England, I again funded that trip because he thought that it was also a waste of money. I felt that she needed every opportunity to grow and blossom as a young woman. I also wanted to do something to make up for the years of arguing and discord that she endured in the home. I felt responsible for any unhappiness she was feeling because I chose to stay in a toxic relationship.

I was also drinking much more frequently then. I blamed Charles because I felt that he 'drove me to drink'. But deep down, I knew that he didn't put the bottle in my hand, I did. I had other options but chose not to take them. I stayed in an impossible marriage and pacified myself with the self-destructive poison. My problem was that I was getting so deep in the mire that I was incapable of making clear choices. I was now on a clear path to death and destruction, and by the time I realized it, I was powerless to help myself.

While Chelsea was away, I had to deal with another accusation. This time, I was having an affair with a senior officer of our church. My husband claimed that he saw the officer hold my hand in order to get my attention on a Sunday afternoon after the morning service. This took place in the lobby of our church while we were surrounded by hundreds of people. But the fact that he held my hand was enough evidence of an affair, as far as my husband was concerned. Charles had always been jealous of this officer and often commented that he was more of a Bible scholar than this man was. He ranted and raved all week about the innocent act that had occurred on Sunday. I tried to ignore him, hoping that he would eventually tire of that argument, but that was not to be. His anger eventually became directed at me. He began recounting a time when he claimed he saw something between the officer and me, which confirmed his suspicion. I decided to make a bed for myself in our family room again. I couldn't bear the thought of being with my husband anymore. It was much too painful and too humiliating.

A couple of weeks later he accosted the officer on a Sunday morning and accused him of inappropriate behavior. I was not in church that day and so when he came home and told me what he did, I could have died from embarrassment. I immediately wrote a letter of resignation to the pastor of the church, explained why I felt leaving was the best option, and confessing to some of the indignities I had endured throughout my marriage. The pastor requested that we both meet with him one evening after work and discuss what had happened and why. The meeting did not go well for Charles. It was very painful for me to watch my husband squirm and attempt to rationalize why he felt the way he did. I imagined that while he spoke, and while he listened to what I had to say, he must have felt very embarrassed as well. In the end, Charles was asked by the church leadership to resign from the deacon board.

He left the church in anger and began attending another nearby church. Naturally, I received the brunt of his anger. Still convinced that I was carrying on this affair, he did not let up in his constant chastisement.

I only had one response. I told him that I was leaving because I had finally had enough. He did not believe me, but now there were no children at home to keep me there, and I needed to save myself from certain death. At that time, my sister Sonia and her two daughters were still living in the home with us, but she understood that I had to leave. She gave me her blessing and I promised to help her financially to get a place of her own as soon as possible. After almost 30 years, I was free.

BOOK 5

Exodus

CHAPTER 27

Within the week, I went looking at apartments in the nearby town of Mayfair. I wanted to be near Brighton University so that I could see Chelsea often, but I did not want to stay in Parkington. I found a two bedroom townhouse that was perfect for my needs. The second bedroom would be Chelsea's. I made arrangements to move in June 2009. I told Charles that same day that I had found an apartment, but after almost thirty years of taking his abuse, he thought that I would never leave. But I did. On the fifteenth of the month, I arranged for movers to come in while he was at work, and we moved Chelsea's baby grand piano, her old bedroom set, and my personal items. I also took a desk and a piece of abstract art my former boss, Miranda, had given to me. I left everything else in the home, including pieces of furniture I owned before I met Charles and everything else I had purchased during our marriage. My goal was to save my life, not to devastate him.

The following day, I went to a local furniture store and purchased a bed for myself. With that, I was finally content. Each day, as I walked into my apartment, I thanked God that I escaped with my life. At times, tears would flow when I opened my front door and it felt as though the weight of the world had been lifted off my shoulders. I began to attend an AA meeting near my job, and I knew deep down that my life would now have new meaning and direction; the dark cloud that had formed above my head was slowly dissipating.

As soon as the word got out that I was separated, friends began to call and congratulate me for finally making the move. Nothing happens before its time, they commiserated; this is now your time to heal. They offered their help if I needed it and some were even bold enough to tell me that they always wondered what I saw in Charles in the first place. One friend asked if I had started to sleep in the middle of the bed and I laughed, realizing that I still slept on my side of the bed, but it felt good. I did miss Charles, and even when I wanted to call him to find out how he was, I did not. It was too soon, and I knew he was probably still very angry with me for leaving. Eventually, though, his calls began to come in.

"Do you want a divorce?" he would sometimes ask. I responded that he could do whatever he wanted.

"Why did you leave me?" was another frequent question. "The Bible says…"

On and on it went. His calls alternated between guilt-ridden and accusatory. I eventually helped my sister to move, and finally, he was alone. After a while the calls and emails became more conciliatory, but I told him I needed time. I told him that we both needed to get counseling before I would even consider reconciliation. Those were my conditions, and I was very firm.

I thought it was hilarious when men began to call. It was interesting to me that there were a few married men who called to assure me that they were there for me. I was still a married woman, and beyond that, the last thing I would consider at that point in my life was a relationship with another man. I had proven in the past that I was really bad at it, and so I was kind but firm in communicating that I was not interested. A couple of years after Charles and I separated, I actually met someone whom I thought was a decent man, but something he said or did reminded me of Charles, and that confirmed to me that I was not ready to get involved in another relationship. I quickly broke it off and never looked back. I took solace in my family, work, and rekindled friendships.

I was fortunate enough to purchase a few pieces of furniture from a friend who was moving to California, and she donated a few other pieces that I needed. Chelsea had returned from her year in England by then, and decided to commute her senior year at Brighton. In the beginning, she would spend a week at my place and then a week at her dad's. As time went on, she was spending less and less time with him and more time with me. I was happy, but sometimes at night it was very lonely and I still grieved

192

the demise of my marriage. It was a bad marriage, I consoled myself, but in times of mourning I couldn't help but remember the good times—and there were good times, but there was so much more pain.

My relationship with Charles vacillated between awkwardly friendly and downright hostile. At one point, when we were civil, he complained that he was unable to pay the mortgage and the house was up for sheriff's sale. He said he knew that it would be an embarrassment to me because I was in the real estate business. He was apologetic that he had refinanced so many times. Now that we were experiencing a down turn in the real estate market, our home was worth far less than we owed on the mortgage. A while back I had refused to refinance the house with him, and so the mortgage was now in his name only, but the deed remained in both our names.

He was now being threatened with foreclosure, and so he asked me to give him a Quit Claim deed so that he could try to work out a compromise with any mortgage company that was willing to negotiate with him. My giving him the Quit Claim deed would allow him to do this freely without involving me in every step of the way. I thought about what he said, and even though I felt that it wouldn't be a wise move on my part to do so, I began to seriously consider it. He had shown me copies of his mortgage statement showing that he owed more than half million dollars on the home that we paid less than one hundred thousand dollars for in 1984. By my estimation, and knowing the condition of the home, I analyzed that the home would be worth between three hundred and three hundred and fifty thousand dollars in the current real estate market. I also knew that if they foreclosed on the home I'd be responsible for paying half of the delinquent amount because it was our marital home.

In spite of this period of financial duress, Charles decided that he would become legal guardian of Sadie's third child. At the time, Sadie, his daughter, was unable to care for her and she had been placed in a foster home. So in addition to the predicament with the mortgage, he began pestering me to come home because he needed someone to help him care for the child. I did not feel that was a valid reason for me to get back into a toxic relationship, so I ignored his pleas. Being as persuasive as he was, Charles began a campaign to wear me down. The more he called or emailed me, the more I began to drink again, and I felt my life spinning out of control once again. I was riddled with guilt because of my past failures and the alcohol only amplified my growing depression.

We eventually called a truce, but he continued to pursue me on and off. On two separate occasions he accompanied me to Michigan and we spent a few days with Shelby, my daughter, and her family. He was on his best behavior during those trips. On one of the trips, he brought his granddaughter with him, and I managed to spend a lot of time with her. He, on the other hand, spent most of the time doing odd jobs and landscaping on their home. It was during these times that I began to weaken and consider reconciliation. He confessed that his financial situation had gotten much worse, plus I felt that the child needed a woman in the home to care for her properly. He did not bring adequate clothing for her; she was very clingy and displayed severe anti-social behavior. I decided then to give him the Quit Claim deed so that he could get the refinancing of the house in order. I knew that if the bank foreclosed on the home, I would have been forced to have him move in with me, and I was not ready for that. Despite my act of kindness, my terms remained firm: he needed to get counseling before I would consider living with him again.

In addition to traveling together, Charles invited himself over to my place for dinner often. I didn't mind much, because he would help to repair things that were broken in my home. He began to come over for holiday dinners as well, and I made him feel welcome. I still felt badly that he was living alone with a two year old, and I pitied the child as well.. He mentioned that he was still having trouble sleeping at nights, and I imagined those were the times when his anger and embarrassment at my leaving began to fester even more. There were times when I would get a particularly vitriolic email or phone call from him, and I knew he was having a bad episode. Even with two parents at home, caring for a two year old is difficult, so I could imagine the toll it was taking on him. I believe he felt that the child would soften my heart and I would return home, but each time I refused, I would become his whipping post again, and the calls would escalate in frequency and intensity.

I was also aware of the fact that he had several very short-term relationships during the period that we were separated, but they usually ended abruptly for unknown reasons. I also discovered that the times when those relationships ended were the times that he would be particularly angry with me, but I was still pretty wounded, regardless of any influence by outsides factors. Twenty-seven years of verbal and emotional abuse does not disappear immediately because of a change in geography. I, too, needed counseling for my emotional state and my alcohol abuse.

Because I went for long periods without drinking, I fooled myself into thinking that I was in control. I began to drink again, mostly to help me sleep at nights. During one of our conversations, Charles surprised me by saying that he was seeing a therapist and he had been going regularly for a while. He told me that he was in a much better place, emotionally.

"When are you coming home?" he would ask. I told him, soon. I was not planning to break my lease because I would be responsible to pay the rent to the end of the lease or until the apartment was rented. I still resolved to meet with him and his therapist together.

I celebrated my fifty-eighth birthday in September of 2011 and my resolve to stay away from Charles was weakening more every day. He and I were now beyond our middle age, living in two separate residences. His grand-daughter still appeared mal-adjusted. She was usually unkempt when he brought her to my place, and neither of them appeared particularly happy with their situation. I was also growing increasingly agitated with the constant phone calls. I thought about our nine grandchildren and felt that it might be possible for us to finally settle into a comfortable life together. He never stopped trying to convince me to come home, though some of his attempts were less than favorable. Our children were dead set against our getting back together, but I decided to stop by the house unannounced, early one Friday morning. I still had my key, but I rang the doorbell and Charles came downstairs to let me in. We held hands and walked upstairs together. I stayed with him for five days.

During those five days, we went back to my place and I got a few things for my stay. We went to church and counseling together. He asked me if I was seeing anyone during the time that we were apart. I decided to be honest and told him that I did see someone very briefly, but I had decided to end it because I was not ready. He told me that he had dinner twice with someone recently, but he was not in a relationship. Thus we both established the fact that we were free. Charles then asked me to renew our vows and move back to our home immediately. I was optimistic, but hesitant. I told him that I wanted us to continue counseling for a while first.

I preferred to wait until Thanksgiving to renew our vows. He disagreed and was adamant that we do it immediately, but I refused to give in. We discussed it during our counseling session and the therapist agreed with me, but Charles and I were again at an impasse. I felt that if we couldn't agree on this, then we still had major issues that needed to be resolved.

During the five days that I was with him, he showed me another pyramid scheme that he was involved in. He had sent them several thousand dollars recently, and he was sure that this would be 'the one'. Unsurprisingly, he was unable to explain how the process worked, so he asked me to review their website and give him my opinion. I half-heartedly complied and soon learned that it involved real estate. Alarm bells went off in my head once more, and I sensed that the timing for us to reconcile was not right. I returned home because I was not ready to handle another get-rich-quick scheme, or all of the drama that would inevitably come along with it.

Over the next couple of nights, we argued incessantly over the phone. I still held firmly to my position to wait until we'd had a few more therapy sessions together. He, on the other hand, held on to his position that I move in immediately. Eventually our discussions morphed into a rehashing of the pain inflicted throughout our marriage, and it became ugly.

A few days later, his daughter Sadie came to my apartment and told me that her father had a girlfriend. I was shocked at that revelation since we were on the phone with each other almost nightly, usually discussing future plans. Not to mention the fact that I was just at the house with him less than a week before. She called her now three-year-old daughter over and asked her to tell me who was at home with her and grandpa. The child looked at me and smiled, and told me that she had "a new grandma".

"And where does your new grandma sleep?' Sadie prompted her daughter.

"She sleeps in Grandpa's room," she replied succinctly. I was floored. I was hurt, and now it was my turn to be embarrassed.

Sadie immediately added, "She is white, and a teacher at his school."

I waited a few days until I called Charles.

"How could you do this?" I demanded. I was still in a very fragile state, having once again become emotionally involved with him. I was hurt that he brought another woman into the bed that he and I had slept in just a few days before. He brushed me off with excuses and hung up the phone.

I sent him an email requesting that we meet. I told him that he had hurt me by bringing another woman in our home during our discussion about reconciling and that we needed to talk. I had hoped that he would meet with me so that we could make a decision about our home, and if necessary, make plans to divorce. At that point, I wanted definite closure of our now thirty-year marriage.

He responded with a curt, business-like response telling me that he appreciated everything I did for him throughout our marriage. He said it was now time to move on and wished me the best. He then blind copied all of our children with his response and forwarded them a copy of the email that I sent to him. I could not believe it. I went to the house a few days later, but they were not there. I went up to the bedroom and gathered up the woman's toiletries, housedresses, and sensible shoes into a large bag, drove to a supermarket near my apartment, and dumped them in the garbage. I then left him a note to 'get that woman out of my house'. It was even more embarrassing to me that the same sheets were on the bed that I had slept on the week before.

He called me later that evening and asked why I threw her stuff away. I responded that if he needed to ask me that question, he ought to have his head examined. He filed a police report against me the next day. He discovered that I could be charged with burglary if the things I threw out were valued at more than two thousand dollars, so he lied to the police about what was actually thrown out. He claimed that I took four or five gold rings that belonged to him, and shoes and clothing from his mistress with an exact value of two thousand dollars. Charles owned two gold rings, one was his wedding band and the other he wears on his middle finger at all times.

At that point, it would have been wise to move on, but I couldn't. The years of abuse and pain flooded my being and I was paralyzed. I did not want Charles back, but the shame and hurt were unbearable. I also wondered what woman would move in with another woman's husband, in another woman's bed and home, filled with all of her furnishings. I chose not to focus on the woman, since she would not have moved in if he did not invite her.

No, my problem was with Charles, not his paramour. He did not call again and even ignored the messages I communicated through Sadie that I needed some things I had left at the house. By that point, I had lost all sense of reason. The more upset I became, the more I drank. I began operating in a daze and the only emotion I felt was pain—sometimes even physical pain. That December, a few days before Christmas, the sheriff brought the divorce petition to my house, and I could feel my thin veneer of resilience begin to crumble at this most undignified conclusion to our disastrous marriage. Thirty years of being strong had finally taken its toll, and I could no longer cultivate a rational thought.

On New Year's Eve, the anniversary of our first date all those years before, I drank a half pint of vodka and headed over to the house. I had pretty much given up on Victoria and who she was supposed to be by this point. I wanted to hurt Charles where it mattered. He was incapable of truly loving someone unless there was something in it for him, but he loved our house.

I let myself in and broke most of the windows in the house except the ones in my daughter and granddaughter's rooms. I am sure I did much more damage because I was operating on auto-pilot, fueled by alcohol. When I left the house, I noticed that my hands were bleeding, possibly from the broken window glass. I later discovered that a neighbor heard the glass shattering and called the police. They pulled me over about half a mile from the house and I was again arrested for DWI and questioned about the damage to the house. A friend bailed me out later that night. The police impounded my car because they wanted to ascertain that the blood in my car matched the blood that was found in the home.

That night resulted in me being charged with burglary and criminal mischief.

I was not informed of those charges until I went to court about a month later. My bail was set at five thousand dollars. I was informed that I could pay a ten percent fee and be released, but I would be subpoenaed to go to court at a later date to answer to the charges. If I did not show up in court, I would be required to pay the total amount of five thousand dollars and I would also be jailed. I was advised to hire an attorney to defend me and so I did.

My children decided that was enough and had me taken to the hospital for observation. I was admitted to Morristown Psychiatric hospital for a week until I met with psychiatrists and psychologists. They determined that I was suffering from Post Traumatic Stress Disorder, an illness previously only associated with soldiers returning from battle. After a few days, I was allowed to resume my normal activities but required to continue attending an out-patient program. They said I should continue to speak with a professional because the damage that was done through my marriage was still affecting me. I enrolled in the Bradley Clinic Intensive Out-Patient Program for eight weeks, but it did not help much. I knew that I had to let my feelings run their course, but I was impatient with the slow-moving process of recovery.

I was a master at hiding my feelings in the past, but I could not lock them away anymore. I was hurting and nothing seemed to be able to stop the pain. Not the alcohol, not the outpouring of love that my children showed me, not the support from my friends. Death seemed to be the only solution, but deep down, I knew that I did not want to leave my family.

Just before the end of February, I received a letter in the mail from Charles. It was our final divorce papers. An addendum to the document read that our property would be sold in a timely manner and I would be awarded fifty percent of the net proceeds. Net proceeds, indeed. There was no profit to be made from the sale of the house. By this point, he owed almost three hundred thousand dollars more than the property was worth! What that paper solidified was that I would also be responsible for fifty percent of the delinquency when the property was either sold or foreclosed on. He had not filed the Quit Claim deed and so I still had a fifty percent ownership in the property.

The Ides Of March

CHAPTER 28

I once read that the former Cleveland Cavaliers coach Bill Fitch said after a particularly long losing streak, "Sometimes, you wake up in the morning and wish your parents had never met." When I saw this, I wondered how deeply sad and hopeless one must feel to utter such a statement.

On March 1, 2012, I finally understood the sentiment in Mr. Fitch's statement. I was scheduled to go to court to answer to the charges stemming from the two incidents on January 1st. I was certain that I would be incarcerated, and I was scared to death. No matter how I twisted and turned it around in my head, it just did not make sense. To the best of my knowledge, no one in my family had ever been in jail. I never knew anyone personally who had been in jail, and here I was, making plans to do just that.

And I did actually make plans. I resigned from my job a few days before, and I made my final will and testament. Dark thoughts continued to plague me, and eventually I came to a difficult decision. In my mind, I reasoned that I could not go to jail and I also could not bear to live anymore. Each night, as I lay in bed, I rehearsed my death scene. Finally, on the morning of my court date, I decided that instead of going to court, I would do what I always did when I needed to feel free: I would go for a ride—someplace far, far away.

My son Christian came to my home to accompany me to court. Just minutes before we were scheduled to leave, I announced that I was not going. He stared at me in disbelief and told me that I had no choice, to which I argued that I did. I had placed my will in a spot where it would be easily discovered, and with it were all my account numbers and life insurance information. Ignoring his protests, I left the house and went for a drive. As I was making my way through the Watchung Mountains, I remembered that Charles did not return the Quit Claim deed that I had given to him several months ago. I wanted it to be in my children's hands so they could consult with an attorney about releasing my estate from any encumbrances or liens on the property. Copies of my mother's legal documents were still at the house in Parkington and a couple of my coats and suits were still there. I had no intention of leaving those things there after I was gone. Charles' paramour was living in my house and the thought that she would probably be wearing my clothes irritated me to no end.

Since it was still early in the afternoon and I knew that they would still be at work, I drove to the house. Just as I suspected, there were no cars in the driveway. Because of the incident on January 1st, I decided to park on the next block so that the neighbors would not see and potentially recognize my car. It would only take a few minutes to grab the coats from the closet, the suits from Chelsea's room, and the documents from Charles' office. I walked up to the door and rang the bell to make sure no one was home. After a few seconds I pulled the latch down and found that it was unlocked.

I walked in and quickly retrieved my two coats from the downstairs closet, laying them on my couch in the living room. Then, going up the stairs to Chelsea's room, I took my suits from her closet and laid them on the bed. I was rummaging through the closet, looking for more of my things when I heard footsteps above me. I figured that Charles must have come home early, so I stood by the door, waiting for the inevitable confrontation.

What I didn't know then was that his girlfriend had a doctor's appointment that day and did not go to work. She later stated that she was given some form of medication for pain and anxiety and so she was upstairs in my bed, asleep. I was very surprised when I saw her approaching the door leading to my daughter's room, and I could see the same surprise mirrored on her face.

"Victoria, what are you doing in my house?" she demanded, adding indignantly, "We changed the locks!"

"*Your* house?" I countered. "What are *you* doing in *my* house? How can you consider yourself a Christian and move into the home of a married man?"

"Why don't you speak to your ex-husband about that?"

"There is no need for me to speak to him. You both have tainted the memories of this home that my children and I held. Good luck to you both, but especially to you."

I wished her luck because I knew the devil she was living with, even though I was certain he would have still been on his best behavior with her—by my calculations, it was still too early in their relationship for him to have shown her his true colors. I walked out of the room and back downstairs. As soon as I got down to the living room, I realized that in my anger, I had left my jacket and the things I had taken from the closet on Chelsea's bed. I considered leaving my clothes, but the March afternoon was still pretty cold and I couldn't go without my jacket. I walked back upstairs to retrieve my things, but the woman was still by my daughter's door.

I noticed that she had a phone at her ear and began to interrupt her conversation. I wanted to repeat to her what Charles's ex-wife meant to tell me many years before. In the conversation that he had recorded, she said, "I want to tell that woman what kind of a man you are..." It felt fitting to try and pass on the information I wish I had received all those years ago.

Before I could finish speaking, she suddenly screamed, "Don't touch me!" and pushed me back against the wall. I was so startled at her sudden outburst and physical force that I slipped and began to topple down the stairs. I grabbed on to her, bringing her down with me. When we landed, there was a brief struggle as we both tried to stand, and then I felt a blow to my head. I grabbed her hand to stop her from hitting me again, noticing that she was holding on to something large and heavy. In the confusion I could not get a clear glimpse of what it was. All the while, she continued screaming at the top of her lungs for me to get out, but was simultaneously blocking my path, preventing me from leaving.

Finally, I was able to get away from her. I was forced to take a roundabout way through the kitchen, as she was blocking the entrance to the front door. I tripped on the kick plate that led from the living room to the kitchen. It had been broken in two pieces for several years– one of

Charles' many attempts to re-tile our kitchen floor that had gone awry. I fell down again, and as she lifted what I later realized was a huge wrench, I held up a piece of the kick plate to shield myself. The force of her blow broke it into several pieces. She attempted to hit me again but this time, I deflected it with my elbow. The wrench fell, and we both lunged after it, colliding with a table that was by the wall next to the stairs.

Once again I managed to extricate myself from her, wondering if she had been preventing me from leaving because Charles was on his way home. As I moved toward the front door again, she hit me once on the back of my shoulder with the wrench. I looked back at the crazed woman standing in my living room, brandishing that enormous weapon. She took an uncertain step backward, and I walked out of the door and headed for my car.

Once I was inside my car, I put my head in my hands and began to sob uncontrollably. I just could not believe what had just happened. There were bloodstains on my white shirt and I began to inspect myself, looking for the source of the bleeding. I was wounded on my arms and my side, and my elbows had sustained bloody injuries during the struggle when we fell. I gingerly touched the back of my shoulder where she hit me as I was walking out the door. I realized also that I still did not have the clothes I had come to the house for. I couldn't begin to imagine the eventual fallout from what had just transpired. It really didn't matter, anyway, because I had plans for later that evening. Starting my car, I left my old neighborhood and just drove for hours, like I had originally planned to do.

I stayed at a hotel in South Jersey that night because I was bruised and aching everywhere. I sat on the bed for hours and thought about my plan. I wrote a letter to my kids telling them that they should go to the house and demand that he give them the things that belonged to me—things I had tried and failed to retrieve that day. I hoped Charles would, at the very least, do the right thing by them. I felt the need to pray. Not for me, but for my children and grandchildren. Each time I tried, I couldn't say much beyond, "Oh my God, Oh my God!"

I called home the following morning and my daughter sounded relieved to hear from me. She began to tell me something about Charles' girlfriend but I cut her off. I was sure Charles had told her about the altercation, and I wasn't interested in hearing his second-hand account of it. I told her that

I loved her and that I had to go, despite her bewildered protests. That was supposed to be my final goodbye.

I checked out of the hotel and drove around all day. By early evening, I ended up somewhere in Pennsylvania. I was still in pain all over, so I decided to rent another room for the night at a Day's Inn Motel. The friendly clerk at the desk commented on the now enormous bump on my head and I told him that I fell. He recommended that I use a warm cloth to massage it and the lump would go away. I smiled wryly and thanked him.

Up in my room, I tried to write another letter to my family, but the letter seemed garbled and made little sense. I then wrote a note to the hotel staff telling them the make and model of my car and my address in New Jersey, but when I imagined how devastated my children would be to get the news that I had committed suicide, I ripped up that letter as well.

I thought about the years I suffered under Charles's abuse and felt that I was doing this for my kids' benefit. I thought about where I was at that very moment in my life and convinced myself that all of my previous decisions were flawed. My children were never better off by my staying in a hopeless marriage. If I died now, they would grieve: of this I was sure. But eventually, I hoped, they would remember the good I tried to do. On the other hand, if I were to go to jail, they would be obligated to come see me and their friends and family would find out what a failure I was. I managed to convince myself that death was the preferable option.

I filled the tub with warm water and took the razor blades that I had purchased a week before out of my purse. I sat in the tub, opened the wrapper, and carefully assessed the veins on my wrist. I scraped the blade slowly and shallowly over my skin, tears streaming down my face blinding me but I just could not do it.

"Stop praying for me!" I began screaming to no one in particular. I couldn't shake the feeling that somewhere, someone was praying for me, rendering me unable to take my own life. I stayed in the tub, telling myself that I just needed to concentrate. I tried it again and again, but to no avail. I eventually got out of the tub, got dressed, went down to the lobby, and asked the clerk at the desk to direct me to the nearest pharmacy and he gave me directions to a Rite Aid about a mile away. I went there and purchased about a dozen bottles of Extra-Strength Tylenol, a few of their strongest brands of over the counter sleeping pills, and a bottle of soda. By the time

I made it back to my room, I was drained. Lying on the bed, I closed my eyes and had vivid nightmares of running away from hideous monsters, sometimes falling from a cliff. I awoke several times throughout the night, terrified, but sleep would eventually engulf me.

The following morning I began to feel a bit shaky, which was not surprising, as I had not eaten for more than two days. This had become a completely normal occurrence: I was rarely hungry and had lost about forty pounds in the course of three months. I turned the television on and watched mindlessly, uncaring and unaware of what I watched. I knew that today had to be the day.

I opened the bottles of pills and tried to swallow a small handful from each, but immediately gagged after tasting the soda. I placed the rest carefully on the dresser. Frustrated, I began to look around the room for something to crush the pills. Finding nothing appropriate, I wrapped a handful of them in my shirt and pounded them with the heel of my shoe. Again, my efforts were unsuccessful.

I thought that dissolving them in warm water might work, so I began rinsing one of the glasses that was provided, a habit I have always had since watching a documentary on the cleanliness of hotel rooms. I had been disgusted to learn that many hotel maids did not clean the glasses that were provided for the guests. I chuckled at the absurdity of my fussiness at a time like this—was I truly afraid of a few germs resting in a glass from which I was intending to drink my poison?

Once the glass was 'clean', I realized that it was much too small to hold all of the pills that I had purchased. I split the remaining soda between the two glasses, poured all of the pills into the now empty bottle, added warm water from the tap and waited. And waited.

Some of the pills seemed to dissolve eventually, but I wasn't sure if the warm water had actually done the trick or if I was just seeing the ones that I had crushed. I picked up the bottle, closed my eyes, and drank. This time, there were no tears. I started to walk back to the bed to lie down, but a new wave of nausea hit me, and I made it to the bathroom just in time to expel everything that was in my stomach.

I slowly staggered to the bed, holding on to the wall for support. I lay on my stomach and I wept. "Stop praying for me," I protested once more. I cried for the lost little girl who searched for her daddy all her life. I cried for the young woman I was before I met Charles, so full of life and hope. I could have done anything I wanted with my life. I had intended to make my life worthwhile. I couldn't stop seeing my children's faces, which is what pained me the most. They were crying for me, for my selfishness. I could see the accusation in their eyes. I had never felt so weak.

When I regained enough strength to stand, I checked out and decided to go home. That was my plan, but my resolve began to waver as I neared the New Jersey border. I pulled over to a convenience store and plugged in a random address in my navigator: 123 West Fifth Street. I figured that every town had a West Fifth, and that it would be in a distressed neighborhood. I was right. I drove around for about an hour until I spotted three young men hanging out on a front porch, laughing. I pulled up and beckoned to one of them, waiting patiently as he sauntered lazily over to me.

"Do you know where I could purchase a gun?" I asked. He looked at me incredulously and then smiled.

"Why do you need a gun?" he inquired curiously.

I smiled at him and told him that I was not the police; I just needed it for protection. He looked at me seriously, shook his head and told me, "No, I don't."

I thanked him and left quickly. I thought that since I was unsuccessful with other methods, it might have been easier to end my life in a split second with a bullet, but apparently that was not to be either. I stayed at another hotel that night.

On my way home the following day, I stopped at a gas station and purchased a dozen red roses, placing them on the seat next to me. I eventually pulled up in my complex and parked in the rear, then I entered my townhouse from the basement and began to make my way slowly upstairs. Chelsea was on the phone in the living room. It sounded like she was crying and from what I heard of her conversation I knew that she was talking about me. I had been gone for more than four days by then, and had shut off my cell phone so no one could reach me. I waited until I heard her footsteps travel up the stairs, and then I opened the door slowly and placed the flowers on the floor by the front door. I went back downstairs, got in my car, and drove out of the complex. My plan was to drive to the police station and give myself up because I did not show up for court.

As soon as I pulled out onto the main road, I saw the flashing lights behind me and a second later, I heard the siren. Heart pounding, I pulled over and watched the officer get out of his car and walk over to me. He asked me for the customary license, registration and insurance documents, which I handed to him without a word. I was thinking that because I had not shown up in court, I would be arrested on the spot. I watched him nervously as he went back to his vehicle and sat there for what seemed to be forever. It felt like the beginning of the end.

I looked down at the armrest in my car and saw the pack of left over razor blades that I had opened at the motel. Checking my rearview mirror, I saw that the officer was still in his car, so I opened one of the packets, closed my eyes tightly, and slit my right wrist in three places. Just to be sure that I finished the job, I took the blade in my other hand and slit my left wrist a couple of times. I gripped the blade with a shaking hand and slid it once more across my neck. The job finally finished, I put the blade down, closed my eyes, and waited for death.

The Day The Earth Stood Still

CHAPTER 29

I opened my eyes again and peered at the clock across the room. 2:48 am.

"This is a very long night," I said out loud to myself, my voice breaking the silence of my room. Each minute felt like an hour. Each hour felt like a lifetime.

A few minutes passed, and it was still unbelievable to me that it still wasn't time to get up. I went over to my bedroom window and peered through the blinds. The darkness was only broken by the streetlight that illuminated the intersection two units away from my house. It was no use; I knew that sleep would never come.

I grabbed a book that Shelby had loaned me some years before: Nelson Mandela's *Long Road to Freedom,* and tried to concentrate on the chapter where I had left off. I kept reading the same sentence over and over, and soon gave up trying to read and began to pray silently. I guess I did fall asleep eventually, because somewhere in the distance I heard the incessant chime of my doorbell, the cacophonous chimes of London's Big Ben, echoing on and on for what seemed like forever. Boy, did I *hate* the sound of that doorbell! With a bizarre sense of relief, I walked downstairs slowly. Every joint in my body ached. When I opened the front door, my son Martin was standing there.

"Good morning, Mom." He stepped inside, brandishing Dunkin Donuts. "I picked up a cup of coffee and a sandwich for you." I gave the greasy bag a baleful glance. Normally, I would have loved the sandwich, but this morning my mouth tasted like sand.

"Thank you," I whispered. I turned to go back upstairs, followed by Martin. He sat next to me on the bed as I took a hesitant sip of my coffee.

"What time will the movers be here?"

"At seven. Are you okay, Mom?"

"Yeah, I'm okay." I stood up and looked around the bedroom. "We'll probably need four more boxes to pack the rest of the stuff." Martin nodded, following my gaze silently. I knew I was being avoidant, but it helped to focus on logistics, on meaningless details. "And don't forget to tell the movers they should place Chelsea's bedroom set at the front of the unit. Sonia will be picking it up in a few weeks when she moves."

"Mom, I got it. Everything is under control," Martin said patiently. I nodded and fell silent, lost in thought. A few minutes later, Christian met us upstairs with a second cup of coffee and another sandwich for me. I was thankful that he hadn't rung the doorbell because he knew how much I hated it, and even though I would usually leave the door unlocked for him, he would ring the bell just to get on my nerves—a standing joke, though not today.

I smiled, "Thanks, Christian, you can put it next to the breakfast Martin brought me.

We all chuckled. As we puttered around halfheartedly, continuing to pack the items and clothes strewn about the floor, the doorbell rang again. This time it was Sonia and her daughter Kelly, closely followed by the movers. Martin met with the movers to give them instructions while Christian and Kelly went down to the basement to finish packing the odds and ends. I wandered around in a daze. I sat next to Sonia eventually, reminding her to take all the spices and food stuff from the cupboards and refrigerator. All too soon it was time to get ready. I went back upstairs, showered, and dressed in record time.

"Kelly, please come back for the final clean-up after the movers are done, okay? I'll give Christian a hundred dollars to give to you for your trouble, and thanks again for taking the day off from work to help."

"Don't worry, Aunt Victoria, I'll be back. And I don't want any money for helping you."

"Thanks, Kelly," the tears were finally threatening to spill.

"Victoria, you didn't eat a thing," Sonia fretted. "Will you be coming back after you are done, or..." her voice faltered. She left the rest of the question unsaid, and I swallowed.

"I don't know for sure. Christian will let you know, okay?" The tears began to flow freely.

"If anything happens," Sonia told me resolutely, "Find out if I can send you food sometimes." I smiled and nodded between the tears. My baby sister was taking care of me now, it did not escape my notice that not once did she say the word 'jail'.

"Sonia, do you have all the receipts for my coats, my insurance...?"

"Yes, yes, I have everything."

"Mom," Christian interrupted apologetically, putting his arms around me. "We have to leave now."

I picked up my purse and took one final look at the place that I had called home for the past three years. Today was April 5th. By the end of the day, I would be in jail. Martin and Kelly both came over and hugged me so tight that I felt that I couldn't breathe. My sister stood apart from me, her eyes also brimming with tears. I walked over to her and we hugged.

"I love you," I whispered to her. "I will be back sooner than you can imagine."

"I know," she reassured me.

Christian and I exited the house and went to the car. I looked back as I reached out to open the passenger side door and saw Sonia standing by my front door, sobbing as she waved to me. I could barely see through all of the tears. It felt like my heart was breaking.

So many things had occurred between that day and March 1st - the day when I decided not to go to court. As my son drove me to the courthouse, I thought back on the events that occurred that afternoon when I got pulled over outside my development. The officer had finally sauntered back to my car and asked me to step out of the vehicle. As soon as I stood up, he noticed the blood dripping down my sleeve and the line of blood across my neck. He immediately yelled out to his partner to call an ambulance and told me to sit down. I refused. I stood next to my car, shivering, and within a few minutes I heard the wailing sirens approaching. Two uniformed paramedics asked me kindly to lie on the stretcher, but again I refused. I just wanted to be left alone.

Ignoring my feeble protests, of the paramedics helped me into the ambulance. The older of the two men examined my arms and neck and worked on cleaning the blood away. He then bandaged both arms to stop the bleeding and began to speak to me compassionately. He tried to assure me that nothing could be as bad as the way I felt right now. He was very encouraging and solicitous throughout the fifteen minute drive to the hospital, and I began to feel at peace.

I was transported to Seminole Hospital and given a bed in the corridor because all of the booths in the emergency room were full. I was immediately seen by a nurse practitioner who informed me that my wounds needed sutures: five in my left wrist and two in my right. The wound on my neck was superficial and all I needed was some topical ointment. The young detective whom I had met on January 1st when I had first gone to court showed up to inform me that there was a massive manhunt organized for me—not because I did not show up for court like I thought, but based on my ex-husband and his girlfriend's accusations. I now had additional charges against me: attempted murder, aggravated assault, possession of weapon for unlawful purpose, unlawful possession of a weapon and first and second degree burglary.

I gave the officer a bewildered frown, which I am sure he understood, because he immediately handed me some paperwork—as if that would be sufficient proof for me to believe that Charles would be party to this travesty. As much as I could read and understand, the document confirmed everything he had just said to me. I was officially living a nightmare, and no amount of pinching me would make this go away.

For months after my third DWI arrest, I was paralyzed with worry about the fact that I would be jailed, and that was the reason why I did not show up in court that morning. I would have preferred to die rather than go to jail. The new accusations against me made my old worries seem like child's play. I read the paper over and over, and it still said the same thing.

"Does this mean that I am going to prison?" I asked the detective. He said something about an attorney, which I didn't pay much attention to. "How long will I go to prison for?" He repeated that I should consult with an attorney.

All I could think was that I needed to have my children call Charles; these charges had to be a terrible misunderstanding. My mind was completely scrambled; I had no idea what to say or do. When the detective announced that he was leaving, I figured that I would be released from the hospital to go home, but I was wrong, again. A female officer showed up to replace him, and when I asked her how long they were planning on keeping me at the hospital, she only stared at me silently before reaching for something on her belt. To my alarm, she removed a pair of handcuffs and shackled my ankle to the bedpost.

"Why are you doing that?" I asked, trying to hold back anguished tears. The metal was cold and made my skin crawl where it touched me.

"Procedure," she replied shortly. I wanted to tell her that the detective before her had not done that, but then I realized that he was probably just being kind to me. This woman clearly did not share his sympathies. I covered the shackles with the thin sheet that they gave me and said nothing more to her.

After a few hours, she was relieved by another police officer; so it went on for two whole days they kept me in the hospital hallway, shackled to the bed. Some of the officers were kind and did not shackle me; some made small talk; others just sat nearby and ignored me. I was sure that the hospital patrons and staff must have thought that I was a dangerous criminal because of the officers guarding me, even though they could not see the cuffs on my ankle. I remembered then that the document the detective gave me confirmed that I was a dangerous criminal. I asked for an additional sheet which I used to cover my face just in case someone I knew happened to walk by and recognize me.

I barely ate anything for those two days. I was dying to see my children, but I didn't want them to see me like this. However, I knew they had to be worried sick about me by this point, so when the kind detective returned I asked him if my children knew where I was. He said that they did, but were not allowed to see me.

Hearing this was the last straw. I began to open up to him: I told him that I was 'a regular person' and that the craziness that was going on was all a huge mistake. I kept rambling, telling him all sorts of things about my life and what I had gone through, and surprisingly, he listened. He even told me some things about himself. I felt that I built up some rapport with him, because when he was replaced the second time, he returned shortly afterwards with another piece of paper. He told me that he had spoken to a judge who agreed to release me on my own recognizance. I wasn't sure what that meant, exactly, but I thanked him profusely. He also said that I should stay away from the house, and that the judge had recommended that I go to an inpatient facility for evaluation. Those conditions barely mattered: I was free!

I was discharged and transported to a nearby hospital for a couple of days. Finally, my children were allowed to visit me. They were stunned when I showed them the charges that were levied against me. But I tried to assure them that the charges were dropped, and I showed them the document I had received from the detective. Neither the kids nor I had ever been involved in any criminal cases, and although I tried to assure them that everything was fine, deep down I was still scared to death. I began to wonder if the term "released on one's own recognizance" might mean something other than "charges dropped".

My son did some research on nearby mental health facilities and found that the Potomac House was highly recommended for treating depression and substance abuse. We submitted an application and I was soon admitted into the program. I was again transported by ambulance to the facility in Potomac where I was surprised to see many 'normal' people, like myself, trying to cope with varied issues, from drug or alcohol dependency to various types of anxiety or depression.

I began to learn the slow process of forgiving myself, something I thought I could never do. It was a very difficult and painful lesson. The most difficult aspect, by far, was the fact that I had to release Charles, a lesson I am still working on, to this day. It didn't matter if I understood him, agreed or disagreed with him; I must forgive him for what he did to me and forgive myself for allowing it to happen. There were so many 'aha' moments that I was constantly writing notes to remind myself of all these positive stimuli for when I got home. Isolating myself was one of the most damaging and self-destructive things that I did. The woman who was 'there' for everyone else was too proud to allow anyone to be 'there' for her.

Six days later I was discharged, suddenly faced with an uncertain world. A brand new life was awaiting, and I wasn't sure how to deal with it, much less conquer it. I was scared—terrified, rather—but the familiar refrain, 'one day at a time', kept playing in my head. There was nothing to immediately do but wait for my court date to roll around.

On the morning of April 5th I was sentenced to six months in the county jail, but upon my attorney's request, the judge agreed that I would spend ninety days there and the other ninety days at a rehabilitation facility. When he banged his gavel, I looked back at my son sitting behind me, his eyes glistening with tears. I nodded to him; I will be OK, I tried to convey. The bailiff led me through a side door toward the back of the courtroom. I asked him if I could give my purse to my son, but he told me that he would arrange for me to see him before they took me to the jail. I followed him numbly, feeling like I was sleepwalking.

"One day at a time," I whispered to myself, "One day at a time."

My memory of the events that followed is very hazy, as I kept a safe mental distance from all of the things happening to and around me. They took mug shots and fingerprints and I signed papers that contained statements that made little sense to me at the time.

I remember sitting on a very uncomfortable metal stool in a twelve-by-twelve open space that had several handcuffs attached to the wall. I occupied one stool and four or five other prisoners were similarly seated, looking forlorn. One young man, Ray, introduced himself to me in very broken English. He was dressed in a bright olive green sweatshirt and an ill-fitting pair of green denim slacks. I also noticed that he was wearing white sweat socks and a rather unattractive pair of brown plastic slippers, so I assumed that he was homeless.

As he talked, I found that I was beginning to exhibit all the classical symptoms of tension. My pulse was racing, my jaws were tightly clenched, and I felt the beginning of a pounding headache. I listened half-heartedly as Ray explained that he was a mechanic who had been test-driving a car that he was repairing for his customer, and somehow got pulled over and arrested for car theft. He was a bit concerned because he was from Mexico and did not have a Green Card. After about an hour, a man who I presumed was Ray's attorney showed up with an interpreter and a very heated conversation ensued.

Finally, the officer brought Christian to see me. We did not say much to each other—after all, what was there to really say? I gave him my purse, and he bent down and hugged me just as the officer told him that he had to leave. Another two hours elapsed before I was unshackled from the wall. The officer then re-cuffed me with his own handcuffs that he removed from his belt, ordered me to stand, and turned me towards an exit. I must have made an interesting picture: dressed in a designer business suit and four inch heels, trying to climb up the steps to get in the police van with my hands cuffed behind me.

"These cuffs are too tight," I complained.

"They were not meant to be comfortable, ma'am," the stone-faced officer replied shortly. "If you run off, I would lose my job. I have a mortgage to pay."

I simply looked at him and the second officer walking just behind us. I couldn't decide if he was just being cruel or if he actually thought that an almost sixty-year-old woman might out-run two thirty-something year old trained police officers brandishing pistols. I stood still after my first failed attempt to climb the steps, and the other officer walked over and helped me up into the back of the black and white van.

Jailhouse Rock

CHAPTER 30

Ray and I were then driven to the county jail. He was seated on the other side of a four-foot high solid metal divider with a thick plexi-glass top that went all the way up to the roof of the van. We both rode in silence. We were not friends, and we would never be friends, even though we were apparently headed to the same destination. The date was April 5th 2012 and it was the first day of the next ninety days of my life. I looked forward to July 3rd, when I'd be free, but in the meantime, I was certain that this torture would critically, cataclysmically affect me for the rest of my life. That was as far as I allowed my thoughts to wander. I had already blocked out my children's faces, especially Christian's, when I handed him my purse.

"What's your name?" the correction officer behind the desk barked at me when we arrived at our destination. "You been here before?" "Go sit down over there 'till we call you!"

It is a known fact that anticipation is usually worse than the actual event, but definitely not in this case. The person who propagated that farce must never have been sent to jail.

The strip search was next and by then, I was a walking zombie. I learned later that they look for cigarettes, drugs, and other contraband in the most unlikely places on your anatomy. The female officer who attended to me must have noticed the stark fear and embarrassment in my eyes and spared me the 'full-blown' search. I will be forever grateful to her. Everything I wore was confiscated, including my bra, because it had an underwire. I was given a receipt for the clothing that I discarded and they gave me my new set of clothing - two pairs of green slacks, two bright green sweaters, a pair of ugly brown plastic slippers, two pairs of white sweat socks, new bras and underwear, a small tube of toothpaste, and a new tooth brush. I immediately thought of Ray, the 'homeless man'—he and I were now similarly dressed. I also received two sheets, a pillow-case, and a drab olive green blanket. Once I changed into my new uniform, I was photographed and given a plastic band that was strapped onto my arm with my new identification, inmate #89517. Then I followed the officer to my new home, holding my worldly belongings in a heap in front of me.

We were buzzed through several locked doors and slowly made our way through an overwhelming maze of passageways. We arrived at the medical unit, where I was asked to wait until I was called. I watched fellow inmates come and go freely once they were buzzed in, while the officers seemed to be having a good time discussing sports or whatever interesting tidbits they shared among themselves. I eventually saw a nurse who asked some general medical questions. (Was I pregnant? What was my drug of choice? Was I on any medications?)

I was then given a shot in my wrist, which I later found out was a mandatory test for tuberculosis. The friendly correction officer (C.O.) who had performed the strip search later returned to escort me 'home', through two more locked doors that led to a small reception area. I was asked to display my wrist band. Eyes averted, I raised my left wrist, trying to obscure the ugly scars that had healed but were still clearly visible. We were buzzed through yet another door where I saw eight or ten women who were all dressed like me. They were either laughing and playing cards or watching a small television set that was attached to the wall. The officer opened a small cell door, nodded to me, and waited until I walked in before slamming the cell door behind me.

The small cell contained a bunk bed, a metal desk with a stool attached, and a commode. I looked behind me at the metal door from which I had just entered. There was a plexi-glass window approximately twelve inches long and six inches wide. Below the window was what appeared to be a trap door (twelve inches by twelve inches) but it was tightly closed.

I placed my belongings on the bed and walked back to the window, wondering why I was locked in while the other women were allowed to wander around freely, seemingly doing their own thing. For lack of something to do, I made my bed and placed my things in an empty milk crate that was sitting next to it. These tasks completed, I sat on my bed and simply looked around me, struggling to process what my life had become. I still felt too numb for tears at this point.

Some time later, there was a loud clanging sound from outside the door. I jumped up and stared at it nervously, wondering what the sound signified. The trap door opened and an inmate pushed a tray toward me. I slowly walked over and looked at what was supposed to be my dinner for the evening. There was baked chicken, rice, string beans, and an unidentified brown lump on a heavy plastic tray, divided into sections. There was a small plastic spork (combination spoon and fork) provided as well. I peered through the window and saw that the other women were now seated at a long table, enjoying their meal together. Again, I wondered why I was not allowed outside with them. Then again, it didn't matter much, because I had no intention of socializing. I shrugged, sniffed my dinner, and placed the full tray on the desk. Some minutes later, an inmate opened the trapdoor once again and retrieved the untouched tray.

Sleep eluded me most of that night. It didn't help that every fifteen minutes; someone flashed an extremely bright light on me, visible even through my tightly closed eyes. I tried to keep my eyes closed as much as I could so that I didn't have to look at the walls. I wasn't very successful. After a while, they seemed to be moving in around me and I began to worry that there wasn't enough air in the room. Time and space seemed irrelevant; there was no clock in my cell, which was limited to the fifteen or so steps from one end to the other. The only means available to maintain my sanity was my ability to think, but even my thoughts betrayed me at times.

I thought about Charles and his paramour sleeping comfortably in my bed, and immediately closed my eyes even tighter to get that image out of my head. I tried to look up to the heavens through another smeared plexi-glass window in the back of the cell, but I couldn't see much. The glass was smeared with paint; I suppose that being in jail meant that one should not expect to see daylight for quite some time.

And so I did what I had been avoiding for a very long time. I tried to pray. I tried to speak to the one who knew everything that I had done and everything that was done to me. I tried to ask, "Why?" But there were simply too many "whys" and I didn't know where to begin. At some point during the night, I was startled by a loud BANG, and my door opened. I kept my eyes closed, but I knew that I had gotten a roommate. Maybe the fact that another person was in the room with me allowed me to finally surrender to sleep. My dreams were more vivid than I have ever remembered. I even jumped up suddenly at one point because I dreamt that I was in jail.

I learned quite a bit from my roommate, Jen, the following day. She was in her mid-thirties and was what was generally referred to as a frequent flyer. This was her third time in county jail, and she had done the 'world tour' (been to several other jails), she proudly informed me. She showed me the 'library' - a milk crate with several books, which I quickly devoured over the next few days. She explained that we would be locked in our cells for twenty-two hours each day for the next three days, or until they determined that we did not have tuberculosis. Until then, we were not allowed to be with the other women who had already completed their 'intake' process. The section in which we were being kept was commonly referred to as "seg" (segregated unit).

Women were placed in seg if they had mental or physical issues or were "kickin". I had no idea what "kickin" meant and was afraid to ask and appear dumb. I did not have any mental or physical disabilities and so I wondered why I was housed in seg. I later found out that because I had attempted suicide prior to my arrest, the jail officials were alerted that I might be a suicide risk and had to be monitored every fifteen minutes. This explained why the bright lights were shone in my cell at regular intervals. I found out later that women who were "kickin" were detoxing, or being weaned from drug or alcohol dependency. They displayed several symptoms including intense worry, nausea or vomiting, shakiness and/or sweating. More severe withdrawal symptoms included being extremely confused jumpy, or upset; or feeling, seeing, or hearing things on your body that are not there. I heard that in some instances, people died while "kickin". During my stay in seg, I saw several women who were experiencing some or most of these symptoms, but to the best of my knowledge, no one died.

My knowledge of seg did not make my stay any easier. Just like that first night, the walls would often appear to close in, and I would have great difficulty breathing. In order to alleviate the tightness in my throat and chest, I would jump up, and walk around, and press my face against the window. Sometimes it helped, but there were times that even closing my eyes and covering my head with a pillow made no difference at all.

Jen would talk me through during those times. She would begin to ask me random questions about my children and grandchildren in order to distract me from my surroundings, and eventually I would begin to breathe normally again. I dreaded those attacks and began to anticipate them. I would immediately go to the window and stay there until the feeling dissipated.

After three days, it was determined that I did not have tuberculosis, and I was finally permitted to be out of my cell for six to eight hours daily with the other women. I was very grateful for the respite because of the panic attacks from being locked into such a small space for so many hours. About a week after that, the psychiatrist determined that I was not a threat to myself, and I was moved to the general population.

We Are The World

Once again, I traveled with my bed linen and clothes through the locked doors in seg, but this time I was on my way to the general population. I had three different roommates in seg and found each to be quite personable and 'normal' despite the legal (and sometimes medical) issues they were facing. Each was there because they were involved in shoplifting (or boosting), a drug bust and/or boyfriend issue. I listened to their stories, but I would usually get lost at some point because of their foul language or because we lived in different worlds and I could not identify with some of the stories. I certainly did not want to appear different, because I had seen movies about prison, and even though I discovered that there was a difference between prison and jail, I wanted to appear 'hip.' (I dared not say this out loud to anyone—my daughter Chelsea made me promise not to ever use the word 'hip'.)

Even though I had kept to myself, rarely eating and staying very quiet during mealtimes, they all waved goodbye to me when I left seg. No one other than my roommates had asked me why I was in jail, which I found to be quite odd, since I was very curious as to each of their specific charges. And my roommates discussed it only because I volunteered the information, always anxious to assure them that I was 'normal'. I followed their cue and did not ask, and so I guess I pretty much fit in with the crowd.

A few weeks passed before I was able to make phone calls. The people I wanted to speak to, my children and my sister, each had to set up accounts with the company contracted to handle phone calls from inmates.

Calls were limited to twenty minutes. Each time I called, three dollars was deducted from their respective accounts. My first call was made to Christian, who had sent me a letter explaining that he had set up his account. Since my other children were living outside New Jersey, it was less expensive to call him. During our first call, we spent the first few minutes crying on the phone. He then explained quickly that he had set up an account for me to purchase snacks and toiletries from the commissary when I needed them. He had also contacted my social worker and asked about a rehab facility for me, because that was the requirement if I wanted to get out of jail in ninety days.

He shared information about the visiting rules: after thirty days, I was allowed to have visitors, but I needed to complete a visitor's request form in order to receive them at any given time. Visiting days were Tuesdays and Thursdays for half an hour, but each inmate was limited to one visit per week. At first I told him that I did not want visitors because I was ashamed for anyone, even my children, to see me in my new uniform. But he dismissed all my protestations, and as soon as it was permitted, he visited me almost every week that I was incarcerated. I derived much comfort from those visits, even though we were only allowed to see each other through a television monitor. The only contact visits I was allowed were with my attorneys, and later, my pastor and my best friend, Amanda, who was now a pastor in Maryland.

The children and I agreed that since Christian was local in New Jersey, I would call him every day to let him know how I was doing and he would communicate with everyone else. The long-distance cost of speaking to everyone else daily was prohibitive so I spoke to them on a weekly or biweekly basis and that gave me a little comfort. There were days that I had no communication with the outside world because the jail was locked down or the lines waiting for the phones were too long, because one, two or even all four of the public phones were out of order.

My new roommate (or, as we called them, bunkie) in general population was a very attractive and brilliant young woman. She was a Brighton University graduate and was in jail because of a VOP (violation of probation). I found her to be smart, witty, and funny, and we got along very well. She took me under her wing and taught me many survival skills in jail. For instance, since our sheets were substantially inferior to twelve hundred count Egyptian cotton, my sheet was always sliding off the two-inch thin plastic covered mattress. She taught me the trick of tying the ends of the sheet under the mattress to keep it secure (fitted sheets were a luxury of the past). Although I could feel the knot under my head and by my feet through the thin mattress, it was a lot more comfortable than waking up several times during the night to remake my bed. She was the first person I felt comfortable enough with to share my angst and fears. There were no judgments on her part; in fact, she often seemed wise beyond her years. She watched out for me during the time we were room-mates and made sure I had a seat at her table for each meal. Each meal was announced by a C.O. yelling "TRAYS!" and everyone rushed to line up as though they had not eaten in days. I remained aloof and did not make any other friends during that time.

It was at dinnertime while we waited on line that I noticed an Asian woman sitting at a table in the middle of the dayroom. She stood out because she was the only non-black, non-white, non-Latina woman there. My curiosity was truly piqued when I noticed that instead of the red armband that we all wore, hers was yellow.

"Why is she wearing a yellow armband?" I whispered to my bunkie.

"She murdered her husband," she answered disparagingly, giving me the details of the crime of which the woman was accused. "You must have seen her on television. She's in the news every time she goes to court."

"No, I never have," I replied truthfully, trying not to stare.

Later that day, when we lined up for our evening meal, I saw her again in the back of the line, standing apart from everyone. She held up both hands in front of her, and swayed her hips in a circle as though she was balancing a hula-hoop. I thought she might have been dancing to a tune in her head, or perhaps she might have been disturbed. I tried to look elsewhere, but my eyes were inexorably drawn to her; I was fascinated. A week later, I noticed that she began to jog in place while waiting on line, still seeming in her own private world; it finally dawned on me then that she was exercising. By then, she had been in jail for almost two years, awaiting her trial.

A few weeks later, another inmate arrived wearing a yellow band. Rumor had it that she was previously convicted of murder and spent several years in prison. After her release, she allegedly attacked her boyfriend, and was now charged with attempted murder and was awaiting trial.

Books were my best friends. I tried not to look anyone in the eye because I did not wish to engage in conversation with these people. I was certainly not one of them. We were allowed go to the large dayroom to watch television or play cards most days. It sometimes got very tense with several women disagreeing on which shows to watch. The crowd favorite was *The Maury Show, Lockup, Bounty Hunter,* or some other show about prisons. I had a difficult time understanding why anyone in jail would watch shows about people in jail when we were living it each day.

One day I was summoned by a C.O. and told that I should move my things to the dorm. It was a large, open space that contained fourteen bunk beds and had windows all around, overlooking the day room. There were painted plexi-glass windows on one side that faced a paved yard. I was skeptical at first, because I felt that living in a room with twenty-eight other women seemed like torture. However, an important lesson that I learned in jail is that it is better to obey, whether you like the orders or not so I packed everything and said goodbye to my friend.

The dorm was noisy! The characters ranged from funny to crazy to quiet and even sullen. I did not fit in. I hated being so close to all these women and I craved my alone time, even though I had hated the confinement of the cell. I liked the fact that there was no locked door to the dorm, but I hated that there was absolutely no privacy. I was learning that there was no upside to jail: there were things that you hated, and other things that you *really* hated. Even in this crowd I felt more alone than ever. The day that I moved in, a couple of the women came over to help me unpack my one milk crate. I politely thanked them and told them that I did not need their help. My sarcasm was not lost on them, and they left me alone. For the first few days, I felt numb—only getting out of bed when I needed bathroom breaks or when it was time to eat.

One afternoon, as I lay in bed reading, I heard a cell door slam. It was not an unusual sound, but something about it awoke something in me that ripped through my very heart and soul. At first I shed silent tears, but before I could hold back, I was weeping in my pillow. My pain, my shame and my loneliness were now open to the public. I turned my back to everyone and as I lay on my side, loud, gut-wrenching sobs ripped through my body. I did not care anymore. God had abandoned me, and the only people who knew where I was were my children and my sister. All I could think to myself was that Charles had won. He and his woman were in my house, and I was here, in jail.

I heard a voice in the background, but I tried to shut it out. When it became more persistent, I realized that the person was praying. I began to listen and then I slowly turned around. That's when I saw a group of women surrounding my bed. One woman was praying earnestly with her eyes closed while the others held hands and surrounded my bed. The Lord touched my soul at that moment, and I saw myself in every single woman around me. I could no longer see them as "them" with the disdain I had felt since I arrived. From that point, it became "us".

When Shirley finished praying, they all came over and hugged me— the woman who felt that they were beneath her—and each one said an encouraging word to me. I was convinced that God had spoken to my heart through these women. I had long since stopped praying because I felt that God had deserted me. I had heard over and over throughout my life that God does not give you more than you can bear, but I felt like I was way beyond my limit, and for that reason I had become very bitter. I knew what the word 'hate' truly meant, because I had nothing but time to think, and the only person that I hated more than my ex-husband was myself.

On that day, the women that I had previously scorned became my sisters. I listened to their stories and I cried with and for them. We began to pray each night before lights out. Each person said a prayer, and then one designated person prayed at the end. Although it was normal for the language to be atrocious before and after prayer, each one shared a reverence for our collective prayer time. We had parties for birthdays or whenever someone left. The few of us who had commissary accounts would purchase supplies to share with everyone in the dorm.

The most popular meal item was the "hook-up". No matter how hard they tried to entice me, I never became a fan. They used the rice from the meal earlier in the day, plus packaged cheese and some kind of packaged meat purchased from the commissary. They then wrapped it in plastic that was "borrowed" from supplies (we were not allowed to have plastic wrap in our possession). Finally, the three ingredients were tightly wrapped in a sweatshirt to 'cook' for an hour or more. I refused to eat anything cooked in a sweatshirt, I joked, but they did not seem to understand how I could refuse this tasty treat. Another crowd favorite was sweet buns. Chocolate bars were melted with hot water, poured it on the buns, and then topped with crushed Doritos. We also saved oranges and apples to add to our 'sangria' made from a powdered drink mix. My only comfort food was *Duplex Cookies* which I purchased faithfully each week.

I eventually told one of the more popular C.O.s that I wanted a job. A few of the inmates worked and were called "trustees." The positions available were in the areas of food service, laundry, or cleaners for the bathrooms or dayroom. I was given the job of cleaning the large bathroom each day. Quite distasteful, but we were provided with heavy duty gloves and cleaning equipment. My salary was a whopping two dollars per week that was deposited in my commissary account. We were not allowed to have cash at any time.

One of my favorite people there was Joan, my petite Italian friend, who was also in jail for DWI. We called ourselves Thelma & Louise, even though I was never quite sure whether I was Thelma or Louise. The other was my young friend Sandii, with her angelic voice and long dreadlocks. She was riot when we played Spades together. I became her mentor after we had a minor altercation in the bathroom that I was hired to clean. Joan and I were in the dorm together and she introduced me to ASAP (Adult Substance Abuse Program). It was through this group that I slowly began to learn to love and forgive myself again. We all shared our stories at the meetings, and listened to each other share how and why we ended up in jail. It was in ASAP that I began to realize that most of the women who were incarcerated were there directly or indirectly because of a man.

Everyone, including most of the C.O.s, addressed me as Miss Hale or Mom, while all other inmates were referred to by their first or last names. I told everyone that I hated to be called Hale; I preferred to be called Victoria or Miss Hale. I did not mind that many of them referred to me as Mom, because I knew that it was done out of respect. After months in jail my prayers eventually changed from "Lord, why me? How could you allow this to happen to me? I am a good person!" to "Lord, give me a word of encouragement for someone who needs it today." Even though I was slowly adjusting to this new life of mine, I still looked forward eagerly to the day that I would say goodbye.

During my incarceration I saw many of my new friends leave. Some went home, and several more than I would have liked went on to the women's prison in Clinton after their respective trials. It hit me the hardest when my two friends Shirley and Joan left. The one thing that kept me going after Joan left was that I was scheduled to leave a week later, and we had been accepted at the same rehab facility. We threw a big party for Joan because she was very popular in the jail. Rather than celebrating among ourselves in the dorm, I hosted her party in the dayroom and invited many of the inmates who were friendly with her. The next day, she and I cried as we hugged and she reminded me to stay strong, I would be out in just a matter of days.

Things went smoothly over the next few days, and the word got out that I would be leaving soon. Everyone gave me good wishes, but I was growing more anxious by the minute. What would I say to everyone on the outside when I was released? I had a status conference scheduled for the charges that my ex-husband had levied against me, but I was not that concerned. After all, I was released on my own recognizance before, and I believed that Charles would do the right thing and speak to the prosecutor, urging him to drop the phony charges. On July 5th my attorney and I both received documentation confirming my acceptance in the rehab facility where Joan was housed: I was one step closer to leaving. On July 6th, the day I was scheduled to leave, my attorney informed me that I needed to get the approval of the Superior Court judge presiding over my case before I could leave. We were scheduled for a status conference on the 7th anyway, so I needed to be patient for just a little while longer.

I was awakened very early on the morning of the 7th to prepare for court. Six other women and I were escorted to the R&D (Receiving and Discharge) area where we met several officers from the sheriff department. We were then searched and handcuffed together, as was the custom. However, as they were cuffing me, the tears began to flow again. It was extremely humiliating and demoralizing, and I tried to accept my shame silently, but at times it was simply too overwhelming. We, and a group of men who were also scheduled for court, were led to the van waiting to transport us. The van had no windows and we were packed tightly, seven on each side.

The smell was unbelievably bad in the back of the van and the conversation was atrocious. I never got accustomed to the foul language from most of the inmates and even the officers as well. The ride to New Brunswick seemed to take forever but we finally made it, after who knows how many interminable minutes of sliding and rolling against each other. We walked in a line, cuffed together, down several flights of stairs to the basement, where the men and women were separated into several "bull pens". The bull pens were large cages with a commode on one side and one long wooden bench on the other side. It was freezing in the basement and extremely noisy. The men made cat calls at the women and everyone yelled to or at each other from one pen to the next. Every now and then, an officer would step out of his office and scream profanities at the men, urging them to be quiet. It never worked.

I was eventually escorted to the courtroom in the early afternoon by an officer who re-cuffed my hands, shackled my legs, and led me to the elevator. I was told to wait by the side until the doors opened, and when they did, I was instructed to walk in and face the back of the elevator. I was not allowed to turn around until we got to our floor. When the elevator came to a stop, the two officers escorted me to the courtroom. It was there that I first heard Charles' new wife's account (via the prosecutor) of what happened on March 1st. I sat there, transfixed, because I could not believe that she and I were both describing the same events that transpired on that day.

I listened as the prosecutor spoke about 'a woman' (me) who broke into a house and brutally attacked another woman with a wrench, beating her repeatedly over the head, almost killing her. I was informed that I was formally indicted by a grand jury and was scheduled to stand trial at some point in the future. The prosecutor asked that my bail be set at two hundred and fifty thousand dollars. My attorney argued that I was not a flight risk and had had no previous criminal record, so he felt that that bail was excessive and recommended that my bail be set at a lower amount. The bail was lowered, but it was still more than I could afford because there was no ten percent option allowed. That meant in order to be released I had to pay the whole amount. I did not have access to all that cash and so I knew that I would not be able to post bail for myself. It now meant I would not be going to the rehab facility until the charges were dropped.

I forced myself not to think anymore. I had been praying day and night, and I just did not understand why God was closing all the doors just when I thought things were getting better.

———————

On the ride back to jail I stared dispassionately at my wrist trying my best to ignore the pungent odor that threatened to make me gag. I tried to cover the scars with the sleeves of my green sweatshirt but the hand was cuffed to my neighbor next to me. If only I could hold my breath for the next twenty minutes, I'd be fine, I could not blot out the noise around me but I could certainly close my eyes and pretend that I was somewhere else...anywhere. The police van jolted as it hit a pothole and we all swayed in unison as if our movements were choreographed. I kept my eyes tightly shut, resisting the impulse to look at anyone around me.

Less than three months ago I was the vice-president of a major corporation, managing a team of almost fifty people, today, my St. John suit is substituted by a pair of drab green denim slacks and a green sweatshirt...jail attire. I know now for sure that my hair is completely grey; I have not been to the beauty parlor in as many months. Over and over I again I ask myself, "How did I get here?" The county prosecutor's words kept ringing in my ears like the lyrics of a popular song; "Victoria Hale is formally charged with attempted murder, aggravated assault, possession of a weapon for unlawful purpose, unlawful possession of a weapon and first & second degree burglary. If found guilty, the penalty for all these charges could be more than forty years in prison." When did the wheels fall off my bus? Nothing in my life prepared me for this.

Once I got back to the jail, totally broken, I was told that I had to move back to the seg unit and that I had been scheduled to see a psychologist immediately. Unfortunately, he had already left for the day, and so I was forced to spend the night once again in the same cell that I was in when I got there ninety days before. I was devastated. Everyone wanted to know what happened, but I was not able to speak at all. I moved my things as ordered but refused to unpack because I did not want to be there. I also refused to eat and did not sleep a wink that night. The old familiar light was flashed in my face every fifteen minutes throughout the night.

The following day I met with the psychologist and he explained that the court had notified them of my change in status. They were advised of my indictment and wanted make sure that I was not a suicide risk again, hence my return to the isolation unit. I used as much bravado as I could muster and assured him that I was fine, and that I was sure that my attorney would be able to get the charges dropped. I suppose he believed me, because I was moved back to the general population, but not before I was escorted to R&D to document my status change.

When I got there my red armband was removed and replaced with a new yellow one, which now signified that I was a dangerous inmate with restricted privileges. I could no longer have a job, and I was moved from the large dorm and told that I would be assigned to a cell. I was not allowed to go to ASAP meetings nor was I permitted to go to church. I now joined the two other women in the jail wearing a yellow band, and we stood out among our fellow inmates. It was a badge of dubious distinction that none of us wanted.

I was sent to cell number 12, and my new bunkie was the Asian woman I saw when I first moved to the general population. I was very upset that I was assigned to room with her. She had been alone in her cell ever since I got there. Rumor was that she was a very difficult inmate, and after a few days of bunking with her, all her previous cellmates had requested to be moved. She was attacked by several of them due to disputes that erupted between them.

"Why am I assigned to her cell?" I asked the C.O. plaintively.

"Because of everyone here, you might be the only one who can get along with her."

In the past I had only exchanged a cursory nod with her. She kept to herself at all times, which suited me just fine. I was more concerned that I would be closed up in a cell once more and I would miss the camaraderie of the women in the dorm with whom I had grown very close. Chang and I became as close as she would allow anyone in jail. She did not speak to me about her charges, but she told me about her child, whom she missed very much. Since we were both professionals, she was a chemist, we had some things in common and eventually settled into an easy friendship. The C.O.s were pleased that she finally found a bunkie with whom she got along. I later learned that Chang was eventually convicted of murder and sentenced to life in prison with a possibility of parole in sixty-two years.

In the meantime, my depression was worsening. My sister and my children were devastated and began a campaign to speak to Charles to let him know what was going on. What they and I did not know then, was that he and his wife were the ones who had instigated the charges and that they were doing everything they could to keep me in jail. As long as I was locked away, they would be able to live comfortably in my house as long as they wanted.

My family was now having a difficult time hiding the fact that I was in jail. As far as my friends and relatives were concerned, I had dropped from the face of the earth three months ago and no one knew where I was. My sister decided to tell close relatives that I was in rehab for alcohol abuse.

My trial would be coming up soon, and my attorney told me that I could do nothing but wait. In the meantime I had learned to pray again— not so much for me, because I did not know how to pray for myself. I was afraid that if I prayed for myself and God did not give me the answer I desired, I would become bitter and turn my back on Him again. Instead, I prayed for the other women in jail with me. I prayed for and with Cathy, a young girl who was glad to be in jail because she had finally gotten away from her pimp. I listened to her amazing story of being abandoned by her mother as an infant, and the subsequent abuse from her aunt and other family members. I prayed for Chrystal, a twenty-one year old who had just given birth to her second baby in jail and was awaiting sentencing on several counts of armed robbery she allegedly committed with her boyfriend. I prayed for the women there who had gotten caught up in various crimes because they had unwittingly followed their boyfriends' leads, and I prayed mostly for my family.

I learned to play spades, but could never master it. I smiled sometimes when I remembered how I initially looked down on these same women who played cards as an outlet to combat the boredom and monotony of the days that dragged by. I decided to take over library duties since the books in the small credenza were always in disarray. It was not a paid position, but because I loved books, I wanted to be in charge of selecting the books that were available from the main library. Several times daily I filed and organized the books and requested new ones on a weekly basis. The 'hood' books (steamy urban paperbacks) were the undisputed favorites, but every now and then I would be asked to recommend a book, and so I eagerly promoted the more uplifting ones.

I read and wrote every single day. I learned to make crafts with the few things provided, and remade new ones when they were confiscated during our regular shakedowns. I learned the difference between a shakedown and a lockdown. A lockdown was when we were locked in our cells at nights or sometimes days at a time because of an infraction that someone committed, or for reasons completely unknown to us. Shakedowns, on the other hand, were terrifying. If the officers suspected that someone was hiding drugs or any other contraband, inmates were ordered out of the cells while they ripped our belongings apart, leaving them strewn all over the cell floors. I also learned to run to the nearest cell whenever the 'goon squad' charged in to break up fights or impending fights among the women.

The goon squad was a group of ten or more very large, male correction officers. Whenever they were approaching, you would hear an alarm buzzing from a distance, and within seconds, the thundering of boots and the rattling of the keys on their belts. It felt like a war zone. I was scared to death during those raids - from the women screaming and scattering to safety, and from the men yelling profanity at us on the top of their lungs. There was always the danger of being run over by these officers if you were in their way when they came charging in. Fights were regular occurrences, and although it was human nature to watch the event and pray that no one got seriously injured, I learned that it was better to watch from the safety of a cell.

When the weather was good, all inmates, with the exception of those housed in the seg unit and the ones confined to solitary lock-up, were allowed to have 'outside recreation'. We were let out of the unit into a small yard that was partially paved and had a volleyball court. There was a high concrete fence surrounding the yard with coiled barb wire at the top. We all looked forward to this each day, and many of us chose to walk around the perimeter of the fence for exercise while others played volleyball or just sat on a ledge and enjoyed the sunshine and our false sense of freedom for two hours each day. On rainy days, or when the weather was cold, we were sometimes allowed to have inside recreation in the large gymnasium.

One evening just as a C.O. yelled "Lock it down!" for the night, I spotted a young inmate running toward my table. I saw her grab my new room-mate from behind and began to pummel her on the back. I thought that they were horsing around, but based on the reaction from the crowd (who knew that there was going to be a fight), I quickly realized that this meant trouble. I immediately jumped up, tried to pull them apart, and began to yell at them to stop. I heard many of the women screaming, "Miss Hale, get away from them," but I suppose I reacted on instinct rather than common sense. Within seconds I heard footsteps charging toward us like a herd of cattle and realized that the goon squad was fast approaching. I immediately grabbed my book, ran upstairs to my cell just as my eyes began to tear, and I started to cough uncontrollably.

"What is happening?" I asked the women in the cell next to me. My throat felt like it was on fire.

"It's pepper spray," they explained. I saw about a dozen of the biggest and fiercest male guards I had ever seen forcibly hold the two women down on the ground. One guard had his boot on my roommate's neck. I heard her scream *"I didn't do anything!"* over and over again.

The guards eventually handcuffed both women and led them out of the pod. Tears streamed down my face as I watched their cruelty toward these young women. No matter how many times I witnessed an event like that, it broke my heart when I saw how the women are being treated like wild animals.

An hour or so later, one of the female guards came to my cell and asked if my roommate had retaliated. I explained that she did not, and that she was attacked from behind. Tania was not placed in 'lock' that night, but when she returned to our cell I saw this tough young woman break down in tears as she hugged me and repeated "I want to go home, I want to go home."

She and I talked for a long time that night. I became her new 'mom' and she started a letter writing campaign to my daughter, Chelsea, introducing herself as an adopted sister. She never tired of hearing stories about my children. She told me that she too wanted to live in Europe like my daughter and that when she was a child she wanted to be a hairdresser or a judge. I giggled, and she laughed as well, and so we began a campaign to help her to get her GED. Eventually, I worked with many of the women who expressed an interest in getting their diploma, and I continued to pray that my time there would benefit the women who craved a better life.

―――――⊱⋅◈⋅⊰―――――

We held Bible studies in the day-room regularly. Since I was no longer allowed to attend any church services, many of the women met with me privately to share what they learned in the classes. My nights were torturous; I dreamt of Charles almost every night and I still hoped and believed that he would do the right thing by me. Each morning before I opened my eyes, I reached over to my left to touch the rough wall next to me, which confirmed that I was still in jail. I would slowly open my eyes and look at the pictures of my family that I taped to the bottom of the bunk bed above me.

Some days were more difficult than others. There were days that I did not want to step outside the cell, but my friends would not allow me to isolate myself. Sometimes I would hear a voice yelling, "Miss Hale, Miss Hale," and I would respond, "What do you want?" pretending that I was annoyed. "Come on down here," would be the answer. I would walk slowly down the steps, and one or another of my adopted daughters would give me a hug and put her head on my shoulder. "That's all I wanted," they would say, and my heart was full. Most times I sat in the day room and watched everyone go about their business. Invariably, someone would sit with me and we would chat until mealtime or time for lockdown.

Among the many stranger aspects of jail was the fact that more than fifty percent of the population was on some form of medication. Three times daily the medication cart would roll around. The women all anxiously waited to hear the familiar "Medication!" call and would rush to line up for their dosages. I often wondered why everyone always seemed to be in such a hurry but I suppose there was not much else to do. Once the pills were dispensed, each individual had to swallow them in front of the nurse and the attending C.O. After swallowing, the inmate had to open her mouth to show that she had indeed swallowed. On a few occasions some inmates tried to hide the meds under their tongue, and were caught. They were immediately placed in lock down. I learned that the ones who were successful in concealing their meds would later trade them for commissary. The most popular items on the commissary list for those with a drug addiction were coffee, sour balls and hard candy.

Some inmates managed to run a 'store'. Should you need an item, and if your credit was good, you were expected to return double when you received your own commissary. Even though it was illegal to trade or run a store, everyone, including the C.O.s, knew the responsible parties and chose to pretend that it was not happening. From time to time, I would trade items with my friends, but I never required them to pay me back double, so many inmates began to come to me for the occasional coffee or candy. Many times I would give my commissary away to inmates who had no money. I was grateful that none of the 'merchants' bothered me when I took their business away from them, because they know that I was not doing it for profit. For the most part, people were diligent in returning the borrowed goods, because they wanted to be sure that they could borrow again at a future date.

One of incidents that stuck in my mind was the first major lockdown that occurred. We had days designated for different activities: there were hair days, house cleaning days, library days and even a day when we received razors to shave. We were required to go directly to the C.O. and place our names on a list before we were given a razor or shears to trim our hair (no scissors). Once we were done, we had to return the razor with blade intact to the CO who inspected it before we were dismissed. The razors were immediately placed into a secure container to be disposed of later.

One morning my friend, Debra, accidentally dropped her razor in the toilet and flushed it. She immediately reported it to the C.O., and even though the C.O. believed her, she was required to report it to her superiors. The goon squad charged in a few minutes later, locked us all down, placed Debra in solitary confinement, and then we were each searched and made to march down to the auditorium. We were instructed to sit on the floor and wait while all our personal belongings were thoroughly ransacked. When we returned several hours later, our belongings were scattered across the floor and anything that they deemed to be contraband was confiscated. Contraband is described as anything that we were using for a purpose other than what it was intended. I was usually guilty of having contraband even though I was never punished.

Shakedowns were very common in jail. One of the more serious ones occurred when someone smuggled drugs into the jail. One woman actually overdosed, began screaming uncontrollably at the top of her lungs and rolling around on the floor. The C.O.s suspected a woman who bunked next to me in the dorm, was one of the suspects. She was yanked from her bed in the middle of the night, and her belongings were thoroughly ransacked. From my bed I watched the officers ransack her things, and when he looked over and noticed me looking at him, he barked at me and asked if I wanted him to go through my things as well. I immediately turned my back, held my breath, and hoped he would not do as he threatened. Several women were put in lock that night because they either found drugs in their belongings or they were known to be friends of the woman who had overdosed. These women were tested for drugs and the ones with positive results were placed in solitary confinement.

Profanity was very commonplace. After I got to know an inmate better I would pull her to the side, compliment her on how beautiful she was, and then explain to her that cursing distorted her face. At first she would be taken aback at my boldness, but eventually whenever a curse slipped out, the offender would look at me and apologize, "Sorry, Miss Hale." After a while, I did not have to repeat my line to newcomers, the girls made sure that everyone around me knew that they were not allowed to curse when I was nearby. At one point, I told them that I was changing my name to "Sorry Miss Hale" because I heard the phrase used so often. Once, when I came back to the jail after a day in court, a young woman reported to me, "Miss Hale, we cussed today! Everyone cussed because we knew you were away, but now we will all behave." Even I found it very funny and we all laughed together.

Necessity is the mother of invention, and so because we had very few luxuries in jail, we became very adept at making the things we were accustomed to on the outside. I was the official pen maker because I wrote constantly. I was unable to write with the pen that we were given, and so I made my own. I was informed that just about anything could be forged into a weapon, and so we were given only the flexible inside of a ballpoint pen. I used strips of paper from magazines to wrap the 'pen', and then used masking tape to secure the paper together. I became very skilled at making pens, and eventually most of the women would bring me the pen that they were given, paper, and tape, and I would make them a 'real' pen. Sometimes I personalized it by writing their names on it in calligraphy. Unfortunately, during shakedowns my supply of pens would be inevitably confiscated, but I would eventually make more for myself and my friends.

Pen making was not the only enterprise I headed in jail. I made liquid soap for bathing and for laundry from the bar soap purchased from the commissary. It was a simple reminder of the things I was accustomed to on the outside. I also chose not to have my laundry done with everyone else's, so at first I washed my clothes by hand and hung them to dry in my cell. After a while, the girls on laundry duty would to sneak up to my cell, collect my laundry and wash them separately in the machine for me. Of course, I offered to repay them with commissary items, but most would refuse my gifts and did it for nothing. One of the girls made me flowers from toilet paper and colored it with M&Ms, and so I made vases from empty plastic shampoo bottles wrapped in colored magazine pages. I also used old *Traditional Homes* magazine covers from the 1990's to wrap my milk crates so that they looked like 'real' furniture. I even joked with the girls that all I needed was a portable room divider to separate the commode from the rest of the cell, and some curtains for my windows.

Sanitary pads that were distributed were indispensable. I peeled the tape off and attached them to the bottom of my sneakers and made my own version of a "Swiffer" cleaning pad. Some of the women made tampons using the inside cotton from the pads. Necessity, I found, was not the only mother of invention: sometimes, it was simply boredom. Very few things were wasted; hoop earrings were made from white circular plastic rings from discarded bras, while rolled up candy wrappers were used to make nob earrings. I would use colorful magazine pages to wrap empty saltine cracker boxes to use as garbage containers or shower caddies. Plastic perm cups were very hot items; they would be used as coffee or juice cups after they were thoroughly cleaned. I also used my empty toilet paper rolls as eyeglass holders. After breaking a few pairs of eyeglasses, I decided to tape the cardboard roll to the wall next to my bed or at the bottom of the bunk above for easy access to my glasses when I read or wrote in bed at night.

Many of the women who had no money to purchase commissary items used butter as a substitute for hair grease and/or hand and body lotion, a practice I found to be quite disgusting. Women were constantly 'borrowing' hair grease and lotion, and so one soon learned to keep those items hidden in a safe place. One of the funniest innovations was the conversion of the county provided underwear into a sports bra by cutting out the crotch—with a pencil, of course, no scissors allowed. Not only were we all very inventive, but everyone put their various talents to good use. Everyone braided hair (even the white inmates) and everyone was an expert barber. Since I kept my hair very short, I learned that I had to ascertain whether or not my barber was upset with anyone before she decided to give me a haircut. An upset barber can usually get very creative with your hair.

Since we were never given needles or thread, I used a pencil or the staples from the county provided pamphlet to carefully remove one row of thread from my slacks. I used the thread for sewing (the staple was used as a needle). I also supplied the girls with thread to be used for eyebrow threading. Sadly, no one volunteered their eyebrows to allow me to practice this new skill.

Free At Last

CHAPTER 32

I spent my fifty-ninth birthday in jail. That morning I received dozens of cards and letters from my fellow inmates and I cried as I read each and every one of them. The cards from my sister and my children were very comforting and I thought back to my fiftieth birthday when Charles gave me a surprise birthday party at the Marriot Hotel in Somerset. My family, friends and co-workers were all in attendance and I could feel the love from everyone. I wondered where I would spend my sixtieth birthday, but I didn't dare to dwell on it too much.

I was beginning to lose hope that Charles would do anything to help me. Nonetheless, I couldn't help but think back to his years of abuse and infidelity and remember that most of the time he eventually came to his senses and begged for forgiveness. I thought about the fact that when he was forced to come face-to-face with his mistakes, he would ask me to help him, and I would do so while he cried. So, again, I waited for him to come to his senses. He *had* to know that this was tearing our family apart. He and I had chosen to live apart, but our children and grand-children were still a part of our legacy. I continued to hope that he would do the right thing, not for me, but for them. I hoped that he would, at the very least, speak to me to hear my side of what happened on that fateful day.

I knew that Charles had no money, no credit, and no assets to speak of. All he had was the house. He had started on a project to get the bank to forgive all the loans he had foolishly borrowed over the years. I was slowly beginning to realize that he needed this woman, because if he were unable to hold on to our home, he would be saved from homelessness by virtue of the fact that she had a small house in Plainfield. She told a friend that when she started her affair with him, he was living in the house with his grand-daughter and there was no electricity in the home. She decided just like I had all those years ago, to pay his bills in order to get him back on his feet.

Each time my children visited or called I asked them for an update, but their news grew increasingly depressing. They simply could not reason with their father. Christian told me that he swallowed his pride and decided to *beg* his father to stop this madness. He went to his father's school, because he refused to enter the home where he had spent most of his childhood that was now become irreversibly tainted. He prayed that he would not see Samuels, because she was also a teacher there. His father's response was that I deserved to be in prison for twenty years. Up until this point, I had never thought of my ex-husband as a deliberately cruel and vindictive person. I knew he was weak and insecure and that was why he hurt people. But now it seemed that he had evolved into someone that I did not know, someone that was inherently evil.

Our children kept reminding me that Dad had mental issues and may never come around, but from where I sat, I just could not afford to give up hope. They reminded me of his long periods of depression followed by periods of extreme happiness and exhilaration, and those memories saddened me even more. It was usually easier for me to remind myself of the happy times. Even though they had decreased over the years, I now focused on those memories to carry me through the abyss. In spite of my surroundings, I worked hard not to lose myself again to that deep, dark place.

Letters of encouragement came very frequently from my sister. She joined the charge to speak to Charles as well and begged him to end the madness. He promised her that he would. He told her that he would write a letter to the judge explaining what happened, and that he would also speak to the prosecutor and see that the matter was resolved. When she called him to see whether he had kept all of these promises, he pretended that they never had that conversation before. As a last resort, she called Charles' pastor to tell him who this man really was, this man who prayed louder and longer than everyone, who could quote scriptures better than everyone else, who always had a word of Biblical advice for other people's problems.

She said that even though she knew that he could not help, she thanked him for listening to her and told him that he would eventually learn the truth about Charles when the mask disappeared. Finally, she convinced me to call Susan, my cousin, and her husband Jake, who were both highly successful attorneys in Georgia and I promised her that I would. All of the hope that I had harbored for Charles and his wife to do the right thing had finally faded. I had to become more proactive in pursuing my freedom.

Some time later, I was told that there had been a Hale family gathering where Charles showed up with Samuels. To the family's surprise, he introduced her as his wife. Many were confused since he had called them a few weeks before and asked them to pray for us because we were in the process of reconciling. It quickly became apparent that was no longer the case when he started to vilify me at the family gathering, mainly by announcing to all who would listen, that I was in jail. Once again, the calls to our children escalated, everyone clamoring to find out if he were telling the truth. I told my children to tell them what happened and to give my address to the family members who wanted to write to me. Many of them did. Every single letter expressed pure disbelief that I was in jail while Charles and his new wife were living in my home. Everyone wanted to know what they could do to help and I simply responded that I needed their prayers. I did not want anyone, other than my children, to visit me.

The arrival of Thanksgiving signified that I had been in jail for nearly seven months. I knew we could not continue to lie about my whereabouts for much longer to my side of the family, and frankly, by that point I was too tired to care anymore. Sonia volunteered to host the family's Thanksgiving that year—in the past the gathering was always at my home. I knew that she was not looking forward to the questions about me nor the hurt feelings that would inevitably occur when everyone discovered that they had been kept in the dark for so long. I also decided not to wait until then to call Susan and Jake. It was now painfully obvious that as far as Charles was concerned, they could keep me in jail forever. I needed as much help as I could get.

Jake, Susan and I spent more than an hour on the phone the day that I finally called. They were understandably shocked and hurt that I did not call them immediately. I was instructed to let my attorney know that they want to be involved in my defense as lead attorneys. I made the necessary calls, introductions were made, and my defense team began to work on a strategy to get me out of jail as soon as possible. Sonia was delighted and relieved when I told her that Jake and Susan were on board. After all, we had known each other all of our lives, and my cousins had known Charles for more than thirty years as well.

I was beginning to get more concerned about my mother and how the news that I was in jail would affect her. We could not keep it from her much longer now that the rest of the family would soon find out, and there was a real risk that I could go to prison. She demanded of Sonia repeatedly if she had heard from me, and somehow Sonia was able to avoid the question or lie that she did not know where I was. I spoke to Sonia almost every day; she kept me abreast of how things were going, offered me constant encouragement, and even managed to make me laugh in spite of all my worries. My sister was my rock, and I couldn't imagine how much more difficult life in jail would have been if not for her.

A few days before the holiday, I tried to call Sonia and could not reach her, which was highly unusual. I tried calling her in the morning and then again late in the evening, but it seemed her phone was either dead or shut off. Two days before Thanksgiving, Christian and Chelsea paid me an unscheduled visit. From the look on their faces, I knew that they had bad news to deliver.

"What is it?" I almost screamed in the phone at them. They told me that my sister was in the hospital. She had battled with illness for most of her life, and her condition had dramatically declined in the past few days. She was now in a coma, they said, and the doctors were not optimistic.

I broke down completely. *Not my baby sister*, I begged God. *I am the one who wanted to die, I am the one who deserved to die*, I cried. *This is not the natural order of things; I should go before she does.* The Lord did not hear my prayer. On the morning of December 19th, I was summoned to the social worker's office. I knew immediately in my spirit what she was going to tell me; my sister passed away the day before.

She began by saying that she had just received a call from my son. After giving me the details, she tried to comfort me by saying that I could sit with her as long as I needed to, but I shook my head, dried my eyes and left. When I returned to the pod, all the inmates were staring at me, many with tears in their eyes. They knew that my sister was critically ill, and from the look on my face they guessed that she had passed. I went directly to my cell and my usually aloof cellmate hugged me and tried to comfort me. The C.O.s relaxed their rules that morning and allowed many of the inmates to come to my cell and offer me their condolences. I was blessed by the many hand-drawn cards and notes they gave me. With the C.O.s permission, they brought food up to my cell—food that I barely touched all day. The next day I went downstairs and was very appreciative of the kindness I received from these women. I knew that death was no stranger to them, and they truly understood my pain.

If there was anyone who had not already found out that I was jail, it would become obvious when I was unable to attend her funeral. My attorneys' petition to allow me to attend the funeral was denied due to the seriousness of my charges, but I had mixed feelings when I was told that I would not be attending. If they had allowed me to go, I would be escorted by several police officers and in handcuffs the entire time. I did not want my mother and children to see me like that. I tried to resign myself to the fact that I would never see my sister's face again, and that my mother would have to deal with the news of the death of one child and the incarceration of her other child simultaneously. My grief in those days seemed depthless, fathomless. I read and re-read the cards and letters that my sister had sent to me in the months I was in jail and did my best to draw strength from them.

After the funeral, my cousin and her husband came to the jail to meet with me. During each visit, I tried to maintain the "Strong Black Woman" façade that everyone thought me to be, but my tears eventually betrayed me. Amanda also visited me and I bragged to her about my accomplishments in jail and about the women who had become my friends. I proudly showed her the pens that I made and described what each day was like, and we laughed. Just like the good old days, we managed to find humor in everything. After the laughter, Amanda prayed. She prayed for me like I never heard her pray before and I once again hoped against hope that God was preparing a way for me. She told me that God had a special purpose for me in that place, but in due course He would open the doors and set me free.

Amanda called Charles after she met with me, because like me, she felt that she knew him well enough to reason with him. She later confessed to me that she ended the conversation feeling that he was even more unstable. He told her a story that took place around twenty-five years ago, when against his wishes, I chose to meet alone with some old friends during our trip to Jamaica. He said that he had no other option but to leave the island immediately, because I would not take him with me. He felt that I must have been meeting with an old boyfriend; even though that was the first time I had been back to Jamaica in many years. The purpose of that trip was to bring food and clothing to my family and friends who were adversely affected by Hurricane Gilbert. Despite the many years that had elapsed since that trip, he was still very upset about it.

Understandably, she was completely confused as to the correlation between what happened then and what was happening now. More to the point, he told her that his wife did not want him to speak to the prosecutor because she was afraid that he was beginning to feel sorry for me and that he and I could possibly end up together again if I were released from jail. He seemed very distracted, she continued, and he even asked her to pray for him because he was suffering from some kind of physical ailment.

"Forget about Charles," she advised me. "He will never lift a finger to help you."

Unbeknownst to me, my attorney had continued to battle with the jail officials to allow me to see my sister. My nieces informed me earlier that her body was to be cremated at some point after the funeral services. On the morning after her funeral, I was awakened around five o'clock and told to get dressed and report to R&D. I dressed in my better 'greens' and was met by two officers from the sheriff's department. They told me that they were taking me to the funeral home to see my sister's body. While my tears flowed, my arms were handcuffed, my legs were shackled, and then they did something that they had never done before: they wrapped a heavy chain around my waist and then secured my handcuffed arms to it so that I could barely move my hands. The female officer looked up at me and said softly, "I am so very sorry. I am required to do this." I nodded in understanding, grateful despite my shame and embarrassment. I focused only on the fact that I was going to see my sister one more time. I silently began to waver about whether or not I really wanted to see her as she was now, or if I preferred to remember her standing on my front porch waving to me that morning of April 5th, right before I went to court. Breaking my reverie, the female officer held my arm and led me to a waiting sheriff's car, not the windowless van, thankfully. Throughout the long drive to the funeral home in Westfield, tears spilled down my cheeks that I was unable to wipe away. How was it possible that my sister was gone? I would have given my life in her stead in a heartbeat. I couldn't help but think, over and over, that God must not even want me.

There was no one at the funeral home when we arrived. We waited for half an hour and I began to worry that they were going to take me back without seeing Sonia. The officers were very kind, however, and didn't show any signs of impatience. The proprietor eventually arrived and they led me to the back of the building. We walked through a passageway past several coffins and I was shown to one coffin that was set aside from all the others. I shuffled over slowly and looked down at her.

Neither of us knew on that morning almost a year ago that was to be the very last time we would ever see each other face to face. How could we? But had we known, I know that we would have hugged a bit longer. We would have said "I love you" at least one more time. Instead, we just waved and said so long.

She looked very peaceful, but very alone. The red suit she wore looked very smart, I thought, but I wondered why she wore gloves on her hands. My sister never wore gloves. It was much easier to focus on the meaningless details at that moment. I touched her and she was cold and stiff. I closed my eyes and thanked God for the time we shared as children and also for the fun we had as adults. I reminded her about the lump I received that day during my altercation with Megan when I tried to defend her honor. I thanked her for praying for me, and also for all her cards and letters of encouragement that she sent to me. I told her that things were going really well and I thought that I would be out of jail before Christmas. In my mind's eye, I saw her smile and say, "I told you we should have called Susan and Jake a long time ago." I leaned over and spent a few more moments straightening her blouse and jacket, not because it needed to be straightened, but because I wanted to do something for her one last time. When it was time to leave, I kissed her lightly on her forehead and left some

245

of my teardrops on her face. I walked out slowly without looking back. I wanted to remember Sonia laughing and relating a funny story about Douglas, our brother, or some crazy thing that our mother did. I didn't want to remember her cold and still in her coffin.

I was later told that while my sister was on her deathbed she confided to a mutual friend and pastor that Charles tried to court her. Prior to his marriage to Samuels, he tried to convince Sonia that it was biblical for her to be with him since I was no longer in the picture. She did not want me to know this because she knew that I would have been hurt and embarrassed, but she wanted someone to know how disturbed Charles was. He desperately wanted someone to help him to raise his grand-daughter and so he figured that she would have been a good candidate. I could not believe that Charles would consider hurting me by seducing my sister. I thought that she, of all people, would have been off limits. After expressing my disbelief, I discovered that Charles's ex-wife April had not been his first choice for a wife. He had been seriously dating her older sister, but when he met her, he dropped her sister and began dating her. That confirmed to me that he felt there was nothing wrong in spreading his amorous advances within a family.

This detestable behavior was not limited to sisters; he had confessed to me a while back that he made a pass at his former mother-in-law one day while massaging her arm. Apparently, she suffered from painful arthritis, and both Charles and her daughter gave her massages from time to time to alleviate the pain. One day he decided to become a bit more familiar with his hands, not unlike what he tried to do to me on the day that we met. His mother-in-law, appalled by his actions, immediately complained to her distraught daughter. Much like I did, April eventually forgave him, but he faced no real consequences for his reprehensible behavior. In the end, he was always able to talk himself out of any bad situation.

I know that Samuels will eventually see the true Charles behind the man that April and I fell in love with. But at that point, if they were successful in sending me to prison, she might feel that she rescued him from me, the crazy wife. I still could not wrap my brain around the fact that she lied and continued to lie. I was told that neither she nor Charles could or would change their story now without admitting that they had lied to the police, and so I was trapped.

My next court appearance was just as disheartening as the others before. I could do nothing but listen to them talk about this evil woman who had committed these awful crimes. At the status hearing, I sat quietly and listened again to the maximum jail time that each charge carried. When my attorney tried to assure me that in the worst case scenario, I would 'probably' not be sentenced to the maximum time, I did not find it very comforting. The only thing I heard, and could focus on, was that I would spend time in prison. As far as I was concerned, my life was over.

My attorney was able to convince the court that since I was part owner of the home, the burglary charges should be dropped. After much arguing, the court agreed to drop one of the two burglary charges. Each time I went to court I was shackled and cuffed, and I always looked to see if Charles and his wife were there, but they never showed up. Once I saw a middle aged white woman looking at me nervously, and I guessed that it might have been Samuels, but I wasn't sure. My sons always came, and eventually all my cousins came to give me their support. Even though I was happy to see them, something inside me died every time they saw me chained and shackled like a wild animal.

Not very much happened over the next few months. The days dragged into weeks, then months. I was eventually told that my trial date was scheduled for March of 2013. Although I was looking forward to it, I was still afraid that I could be found guilty and be sent to prison for the rest of my life. I thought about all of the people in the news who were wrongfully incarcerated and I was afraid, very afraid. I knew that Charles and Samuels would be at the trial and wondered if they would be able to look me in the eye.

Susan and Jake met with me in an open conference area in the basement of the courthouse one day. She loaned me her lipstick and blush to add some color to my face as we discussed our strategy going forward. She complimented me on what I had accomplished thus far and reminded me that I was a strong woman, never averse to taking chances. She then explained what to expect during the trial, because there were several options facing us.

Since I had been locked up for almost a year, she and Jake wanted to try to make a deal with the prosecutor in order to avoid a trial. If he agreed,

I would probably only serve another year or so, but I would be transferred to the women's prison in Clinton. Our second option was a plea bargain, which would mean that I would go to prison for five years. Compared to prison for forty years, a compromise seemed like the most prudent choice to make. The prosecutor, of course, would have to agree with that plea.

My third option, of course, was to throw myself on the mercy of the court at a full trial. They reminded me also that because there were several open charges, there was that possibility that I could be found not guilty on most of the charges, but found guilty on one or two of the other ones. Should I be found guilty on any of the charges, I could still be sent to prison, possibly for five years. The first order of business, she told me, would be the jury selection, but there were some housekeeping issues that needed to be attended first.

Finally the day of the trial arrived, and on my way to the courtroom, one of the police officers held on to my arm and tried to guide me briskly through the hallway. Because I was dressed in street clothes, my high heels kept getting caught in the shackles around my ankles. I asked the officer to slow down, afraid that I would trip and fall. He ignored me completely, but his partner looked at me pityingly. I was so upset that I pulled my arm from his grasp. He immediately stopped and glared at me with pure hatred in his eyes. He then grabbed my arm and squeezed it tightly, put his face just inches away from mine, and dared me to pull it away again. My heart began to pound. At that moment, I thought that if I dared to do it again he would have shot me right there and then in the hallway. I complied and kept up with his pace as best I could as we approached the courtroom. As soon as we got close to the door, he slowed down and relaxed his grip. Once I entered the room and sat down, he came over to me, smiled solicitously, and asked if I were comfortable. I glared at him and looked away without answering.

When the proceedings began, Jake once again filed a motion to dismiss all the charges. Based on the discussion among the judge, the prosecutor, and my attorneys, it seemed that they were at a stalemate. After much discussion, the prosecutor agreed to a lesser charge on the condition that he needed to speak with Samuels first, she was not in court. He left the courtroom and called her, but she informed him that she needed to speak to her husband and would not be able to do so until later that evening.

Court was then adjourned until the following day. Once I was returned to the jail, I spent the night staring up at the ceiling. Should I go through with the trial or should I take the plea if it was offered? I begged God to give me an answer, but I honestly was not sure He was responding, since neither option seemed very appealing to me.

The next day I was again awakened very early and transported to court in the usual fashion. I sat in my now regular spot, only able to pay the barest amount of attention to the arguments. I did pick up on the fact that the plea was no longer on the table, either because the original charges were too severe, or perhaps Charles and his wife did not agree to the plea, or both. Jake did not give up. He again argued on the motions that he had prepared, specifically on the most serious charges of attempted murder and aggravated assault, each of which carried a sentence of ten years. Finally, the prosecutor acknowledged that the state did not have enough evidence to prove the attempted murder charge. He moved that that charge should be dropped. The judge agreed, and I finally began to believe that our prayers were being answered.

Jake then proposed that since the most serious charge was dropped, the judge should dismiss the bail as well. He reminded the judge that I had already been incarcerated for the past fourteen months. The judge agreed to lower my bail. Court was dismissed and we were told that a new trial date was set for September 23rd. I was escorted back to the bull pen, all the while wondering what it meant now that my bail was reduced. Dare I even consider freedom? Before I could process what had just happened, Susan came down to the bull pen and told me she and Jake had just paid my bail and I would be leaving soon. I asked her to repeat that once more, because I was not quite sure what that meant or when I would be able to leave.

I began to make a mental note of the things I planned to give away to my friends. I also wanted to finish a conversation I had started with a woman who was back in jail for the seventh time. She and I had begun to discuss steps that she needed to take to prevent an eighth stint for her. I wanted to hug Ayana and Kadee and promise them that I would write. There were some C.O.s I liked and I wanted to give them a hug. More than anything, I wanted to hear a C.O. yell, "Miss Hale, pack it up!" I had heard that for the past fourteen months, and watched my friends leave, only to see many of them return later. I dreamed of hearing my name attached to the now familiar phrase. There were so many things I needed to get done; I could not yet fully process the reality that I might be leaving that very day.

As it turned out, when I returned to the jail later in the evening I was ordered to sit in a holding room and was told that someone would get back to me. Eventually, an officer came in and told me that I was leaving and my things would be brought to me.

"But I have to go in and say goodbye," I responded foolishly.

"No," he responded dismissively. "You are not permitted to go back in the pod."

I continued trying to convince him that I must say goodbye to my friends but he simply ignored me. I was very nervous when they asked me to sign the dotted line, my receipt for the clothes they held for me. I stood very still as an officer cut the shameful yellow band from my left arm. I accepted the hanger with my clothes, still hoping that I could walk the long passageway and through the locked doors for the last time so that I could say my proper goodbyes. But that was not to be. I was unceremoniously directed through an unfamiliar door and then shown to a reception area next to the parking lot. There were two women seated there who were in the jail with me and who were now also waiting for their ride home.

"Miss Hale, are you leaving?"

"Yes!" I responded incredulously, still not believing that my day had taken such a drastic change for the better. I hesitantly walked outside, just to test this new theory of freedom, and sure enough, the door opened and I stood next to the cars and just breathed. I walked around the parking lot for a few minutes before I went back inside and called my son from the phone booth in the lobby.

"I heard the good news," Christian said as soon as he heard my voice, "I am almost there."

By this time I had lost all sense of propriety. I was beginning to jump up and down from excitement. Fewer than five minutes later I spotted his car pulling into the lot and I ran out once again to see Christian and his partner Kourtney alighting from the car. Another car pulled up next to them and I saw Chelsea and Martin running toward me. Tears flowed again as we all hugged in total relief that the day had finally arrived.

"Mom is free!"

It was several minutes before we got back in the cars and headed away from the jail. My daughter Shelby and my granddaughters arrived the following day and the celebration began once more.

Swan Song

CHAPTER 33

Rose Kennedy once said, "It has been said, 'time heals all wounds.' I do not agree. The wounds remain. In time, the mind, protecting its sanity, covers them with scar tissue and the pain lessens. But it is never gone."

I will never forget those months that I spent in jail. Some of the memories are good, because I met many amazing and talented women there. Nonetheless, with those memories comes a pain so deep and unfathomable that sometimes it seems impossible not to hate. But I made a solemn vow that this man who tried his best to ruin me will no longer have control over my life and actions. I have taken my life back. In addition to my writing, I spent many hours perusing the writings of great minds that are no longer with us. I also found that many of my contemporaries who have lived through pain and heartache have a wealth of knowledge and encouragement to convey. When I wonder why corrupt and evil individuals seem to thrive and prosper, I remember that Mahatma Gandhi once wrote, "When I despair, I remember that all through history the way of truth and love have always won. There have been tyrants and murderers, and for a time, they can seem invincible, but in the end, they always fall. Think of it—always."

Less than a year after I left jail, the world celebrated the life of a true hero who had just passed. He had been unjustly imprisoned for twenty-seven years, but when Nelson Mandela was finally released, he chose to forgive. I have tried to follow his example, and I earnestly pray to God for the strength to do so—even though there are times when I reflect on my life and I find it very difficult to do.

As the days wound down to my trial, I chose to spend the time reconnecting with friends and family, rather than to allow my nervousness to incapacitate me. The camaraderie of loved ones was what I missed most of all in the fourteen months that I was jailed. It was also when I was locked-up that my reasons for writing my story became more palpable. Those were the times I felt most inspired to tell my story to the women that I had met in jail, and even more so, to the women on the outside who might be dealing with a similar tyrant and manipulator. I wrote to encourage them all, because even back then, when I was severely restricted, I was experiencing freedom in spirit. I wanted to tell them, "I have good news for you; you do not have to take it! You and your children will be much better off in the long run if you leave a bad marriage, because if you stay, a different piece of you—your soul, your confidence, your humanity, your ability to thrive—will die each and every day."

A few days before the trial, I began to peruse the discovery materials that my attorneys had sent to me. I was amazed when I saw all the discrepancies in the statements that Mildred Samuels gave to the police. She spoke to the police on three separate occasions, and each time her account of the events on March 1ˢᵗ grew increasingly worse. Susan was unable to make it to the trial due to a prior commitment, but Jake flew in a couple of days early and spent his time finalizing my defense and learning how to get around the New Brunswick area. Family members called for directions to the courthouse and information about the days and time they should be there to support me, while others assured me that they would be praying and fasting for me. The prosecutor informed us that that his witnesses needed about four days for their testimonies, while my attorneys said that we could wrap up in two days or less. I figured that the trial would run for just over a week. We had four character witnesses, and I was the only witness scheduled to testify on my own behalf.

On the day of the trial, I looked around the small courtroom and discovered that neither Charles nor his wife was present. I still could not remember what his wife looked like, but I felt that I would recognize her if she was with Charles. I also discovered that jury selection would last for almost two days. Since there was no court on Fridays, and we had no way of knowing how long the jury would deliberate, we now estimated that the trial would last approximately two weeks.

There were times that I desperately wished that the scene unfolding before my eyes was a television drama or a Grisham novel, but it was real. It was actually happening to me! I advised everyone that since jury selection would last for the first two days, there was no reason for them to be there during that time. Despite this news, Christian and Martin insisted on being there every day to support me. My youngest daughter, Chelsea, is a teacher in New York, so she could not be there every day; and Shelby, my middle child, has two young children and lives in Michigan so she could not be there either. Both girls were in constant communication with my sons to stay informed about what was going on. My nieces, cousins, and friends came by on the days that they could get off from work and their show of support helped me tremendously during those dark days.

By the middle of the first day, members of the jury pool began to file in. I watched them closely as they took their seats and murmured quietly to each other, thinking to myself that these people could not be considered my peers. Most seemed bored; many looked as though they were just stopping by to see what was going on. My nervousness grew when I looked out at the crowd. Because the courtroom could not accommodate all two hundred and twenty potential jurors at the same time, they were brought in in stages to begin the voir dire procedure. When they were told that the trial would probably last more than a week, I could actually hear the shuffling in the room. A few minutes later the tedious job of interviewing each one began.

Potential jurors with small children, vacation conflicts, or obligations to care for sick family members were excused immediately. Others were excused for work-related issues. The process continued until we were down to just under one hundred people. I was given earphones so that I could hear everything that transpired in the courtroom, specifically things that were said during sidebar, and so I listened to some of the excuses that people made to avoid being on the jury. One woman actually said that she did not want to be on the jury because she believed that I was guilty. She knew that she would be dismissed immediately because of that comment, and she was. I began to wonder how many members of the final jury might have pre-conceived ideas of my guilt or innocence even before they heard the testimonies.

The second day seemed to go by a bit faster, and at the end of the day, I was able to look at the thirteen people (including one alternate) who would have an incredible impact on my life from that day forward. I looked at each of them and wondered what they were thinking about me. I did my absolute best to look confident and alert, but all I wanted to do was to yell at the top of my lungs, "This is a horrible mistake! I should not be here!"

I began to learn a bit about each of them based on the answers they gave to the general questions that were asked. I discovered which ones had bumper stickers on their cars and what the bumper stickers said; I learned what they did for a living, and even who the occupants of their homes were. I learned whether or not they watched television and what some of their favorite programs were. After a while, I could not remember who said what, but in the end I felt that did not matter much. I watched them as they listened to all the charges brought against me, and I cringed just like I did each and every time I listened to them listed one after another. This is really happening; I kept reminding myself. Every now and then, I would look behind me and nod to my family and friends. I even managed a smile at times, just so they would know that I was all right.

Redemption Song

CHAPTER 34

At the end of voir dire, I sat in the courtroom and listened to Jake resume his argument about whether or not the burglary charge had any merit, since I entered my own property. The judge charged the attorneys to research prior cases for precedence on that matter, report their findings to him after lunch, and then he would make a decision. After each attorney argued their case in the afternoon, he decided that while the elements in the cases that he and the three attorneys found were somewhat similar, there were enough differences that he had no choice but to let the jury decide on my guilt or innocence. He would not drop the charge. Jake had several other arguments relating to the wrench that was used in the struggle, specifically, whether or not it should be classified as a deadly weapon. Again, the decision was left for the jury after they heard all of the testimonies.

All these arguments were made while the jury was sequestered. When it was determined that the attorneys were ready to proceed, they were brought back into the courtroom and both attorneys gave their opening statements. The prosecutor spoke first. He stated that several crimes were committed on March 1st of 2012, and he had testimonies from various sources to prove my guilt, "beyond a shadow of a doubt". He gave an eloquent rendition of what allegedly transpired on that day, being sure to touch on the fact that I had committed these crimes out of jealousy. He spoke for more than an hour. All I could do was watch him, listen to him, and wonder how he could speak with such authority when he was not there to know the facts. I couldn't help but feel that were I a juror, I would probably believe everything that he was saying. My attorneys, much more accustomed to courtroom drama than I, had warned me not to lose faith. I was finding their advice difficult to follow, and my heart sunk further and further as he continued enumerating my 'crimes'.

I could not wait for Jake to give his opening statement. I desperately wanted everyone to hear my side of the story. Until that point, I was never given an opportunity to speak in court. Since I was the one indicted on these charges, this would be the only time that my voice would be heard. Finally, Jake, who sat to my left, walked over to the jury and addressed them conversationally. He told them that the charges were all fabricated and that he was there to show them proof that he was right. There was no attack, he said, and in the next few days he was prepared to repudiate each and every charge brought against me. I watched the jury members closely as they listened to him and noticed that they hung on to his every word. It was then that I began to thank God silently that my sister had insisted that I call Susan and Jake to work on my defense. Jake had known Charles and me for more than thirty years, so he could speak with an authority that no other attorney could.

The first witnesses for the prosecution were several Parkington Township police officers. Each reported that a call was made by Mildred Samuels, who tearfully reported that she was attacked by Victoria Hale, her fiancé's ex-wife. They testified that upon arriving at my home, they found Samuels pacing in the street, brandishing a large wrench. She was bleeding from a wound on her head. They had a video tape recording of the scene when they arrived. She reported to the police that I broke into the home, hid in a bedroom closet, and attacked her when she came downstairs to investigate a noise she heard. She also told them that she tried to follow me but did not see what direction I took. Because she was bleeding from the head, the officer asked her if she was alright, and she replied that she was. He then asked her to release the weapon to him and suggested that she sit on the sidewalk while he called for an ambulance as a precaution.

Several other detectives arrived on the scene, and they walked around the perimeter of the house to ascertain where I had entered, assuming that I had broken in. They discovered broken glass under a picture window in the rear of the home, which confirmed their suspicion. Even though they were aware that the window was broken prior to March 1st, they claimed that the taped cardboard covering the broken window was lifted in one spot, and provided a painstaking explanation of how that proved I had used it as my way in. Because of the design of material from which the window was made, it was impossible to get fingerprints, they said, but a break-in had definitely occurred. They concluded with photographs showing that the dirt that was formed on the window-sill appeared to have been disturbed.

Upon cross examination, they quickly backed down from their assumption that I entered the property through the window when my defense attorney was able to prove that the window had been broken for quite some time, and the glass and debris beneath the window was undisturbed. The area where the cardboard was supposedly 'lifted' was more consistent with wear and tear from the weather, rather than from someone entering from that point. There was no broken glass or prints in the bedroom from that window. As shown in their photographs, the bedroom was filled with garbage that was strewn all over the floor, so the police had no evidence of entry from that point. They also did not have any finger print samples from the door knob or the railing leading upstairs to prove their theory. Clearly, they found none of my prints, and were embarrassed when they were forced to admit it in court. My attorney summarized that because they saw a broken window, they decided that must have been the point of entry and disregarded the fact that I actually entered through the front door. He reminded them that since it was my house, it was entirely possible that I actually had a key. Apparently, the police felt that they had a stronger case if their report claimed that I entered the house surreptitiously through the window in the back of the home.

Following that, the 911 tape from Samuels' call was played for the jury to hear, and then multiple photographs of the cut on her head, were blown up and shown from several angles on the large screen. They also showed pictures of her blood stained bra and her blouse, which were both numbered exhibits. After a few minutes, my attorney objected to the number of angles of each picture that depicted spots of blood on the floor, her clothing, and her head, because in actuality there was only one cut on her forehead. I was grateful that they had a six inch ruler next to the pictures, so one was able to correctly judge the size of the cut on her head, rather than rely on the menacing blown up exhibits that were on the screen.

There was one other prosecution witness scheduled. He had told the police on March 1ˢᵗ that he saw a well-dressed African American woman walking briskly across our neighbor's front lawn. He gave a brief description of the shirt I was wearing. I did not have a coat on because I left it in my daughter's bedroom. (Samuels had attacked me on the steps before I could retrieve it.) He said that he stopped to look because it was unusual to see someone walking in the neighborhood unless they were exercising. He also stated that he then saw a middle aged white woman on her phone speaking "gladly" to someone. His testimony was part of the discovery, but unfortunately, he passed away before the trial. It was important to us that the jury should hear that testimony, especially since the witness reported that Samuels was speaking "gladly" on the phone, evidently not as close to death's door as she later claimed. Through expert questioning, Jake was able to get the police to inadvertently reveal that there was another witness, and thus he was able to have the statement read to the jury.

Next, the wrench was dramatically unwrapped from a brown paper package and shown to the jury. They and I and everyone else in the courtroom were transfixed. The prosecutor called two expert witnesses who went through a lengthy discourse explaining that there was more than a ninety-nine percent chance that the blood on the wrench was Samuels'. After what seemed like hours of testimony, I looked over at the jury and noticed that a few of them were fighting to stay awake. I tried to follow both witnesses as they explained the tedious process used to prevent the evidence from being contaminated and the rigorous tests done to arrive at their final conclusion. All the while, I kept thinking that everyone, including the jury, had to be convinced that it was indeed Samuels' blood on the wrench. The police video showed her brandishing it when they arrived on the scene. I found the torturous testimony irrelevant, but I guessed it was necessary to make the prosecution's case appear more compelling. When it was finally over, we broke for the day and were adjourned until Monday, as there was no court on Friday.

On Monday morning, I arrived early as usual and sat on a bench with my children and friends outside the courtroom, waiting for the judge's arrival. Suddenly, there was a hush. I looked up and saw Charles and his wife walking past us. It was my first time seeing them together. Neither of them looked in our direction. I eventually looked away and pretended that I was unaffected. I knew that everyone was watching for my reaction and so I continued with my conversation as though it was the most natural thing in the world. Inwardly, I wondered what would happen in the courtroom when Charles was asked to testify. I still believed in my heart that he would never be able to swear on the Bible and lie about the events of that day, because despite his actions, he still professed a fear of God. However, he had surprised me before, and I couldn't rule out the possibility of him doing it again.

A few minutes later, the bailiff interrupted our conversation to let us know that the judge was on his way. We all filed in the courtroom and took our places. First, the jury arrived, closely followed by the judge. After we took our seats, the trial resumed.

The first witness of the day was Charles. The bailiff walked to the courtroom door and summoned him to enter. As he slowly walked in, I noticed in surprise that he was dressed in a suit that I had purchased for him a while back. He went directly to the podium as directed and sat down. All eyes were riveted on him. After swearing on the Bible, the prosecutor greeted him and asked him to identify himself. He did so very quietly. In fact, he responded to all of the attorney's questions barely above a whisper and had to be encouraged on several occasions to speak louder and into the microphone so that the jury could hear his testimony. When asked if he could identify Victoria Hale, Charles looked directly at me, and for the first time in a long time, our eyes met, if only for a split second. It felt like a shock had gone through me, but I did not flinch. For the benefit of the court, he was asked to point to me and describe what I was wearing, and so he pointed in my direction and acknowledged that I was wearing a blue jacket.

I immediately thought of defendants J.W. Milam and Roy Bryant from the 1955 Emmett Till murder trial. It was reported that when Till's great uncle, Moses Wright, was asked if he could identify the murderer, he pointed directly at Milam and said emphatically, "Thar he." It was still unbelievable to me that now I was the defendant on trial, deeply entrenched in the fight of my life, and my ex-husband had just pointed to me and said, "Thar she."

Charles' sworn testimony was that he had taken his girlfriend to have a procedure done earlier that morning. He went back to the doctor's office during his lunch hour to pick her up, since she was given medication and advised not to drive. When they returned home, she immediately went upstairs to sleep while he grabbed a sandwich and left for work. The next time he saw her was after she called to tell him that she was attacked, at which point he hurried home. By then, she was on the stretcher and on her way to the hospital. He confirmed that he went to the hospital later to be with her and she had gotten three staples in her head due to the cut that she received in the altercation. He explained to the court that he had told me that our relationship was over, but I kept calling him and trying to reconcile only after I discovered that he had been seeing someone new.

When it came time for the cross examination, my attorney decided to dig a bit deeper into events prior to what took place that day. He felt it was important to give the jury a clear picture of the relationship between the parties involved, why I had a right to be in the house, and reveal the truth of what really happened that day. Through his questioning, I learned that Charles wanted be able to stay in the house for as long as he lived, and my being around was a constant threat to him.

Jake began by briefly giving the jury a bit of the history of Charles' persona and his behavior in the past. In order to do that, true ownership of the home needed to be established because of the burglary charge, and motive for the lies and deceit needed to be uncovered.

When Charles was asked who paid for the home in 1984, he truthfully stated that I did. He also admitted that I spent an additional eighty-five thousand dollars of my own money to renovate the home in 1989. He further testified that we had problems in our marriage and asserted that I left because he refinanced the home more often than he should have, and that, coupled with the current real estate downturn, caused the house's value to turn upside down. He said that I threatened to leave him because of those financial issues, and he had pleaded with me to stay, saying that things would get better eventually. He also volunteered that he was recently successful in getting the bank to refinance the mortgage and forgive a debt of more than two hundred thousand dollars. He had been working with banks for the past three years to get it accomplished and during that time he did not make any mortgage payments. I was surprised to discover that he had been living in the home for more than three years and had not made any mortgage payments since I left.

I listened incredulously as Charles' lied about the reason that I left him. I saw him look in my direction for a brief second when he said that he pleaded with me not to leave. At that point, I desperately wanted to stand up and remind him that he was under oath. All I could do was shake my head sadly, wondering if he really believed what he was saying. All of my hopes about him telling the truth under oath were now out of the window. Jake also knew that he was lying, so he decided to continue the conversation by asking Charles more questions regarding our marriage.

"Let's talk about your relationship with your former wife. Were you jealous and insecure during your marriage?"

"Yes, I was insecure in the beginning, because Victoria was always the principal breadwinner in the family," he admitted.

"What about the incident involving the elder of your church? Were you jealous about that?"

At this point, Charles became more belligerent—gone were the hesitant, soft-spoken responses. In describing the incident with our elder, he completely broke from character, jumped out of the witness chair, and began to waltz across the courtroom with his right arm out and his left arm on his chest, showing how the elder and I had allegedly waltzed around the lobby of the church. I was, once again, horrified and embarrassed by his actions. I looked up at the jury to gauge their response, and their expressions ranged from questioning, to snickering, to complete shock at his impromptu performance.

He was immediately asked by one or both attorneys to sit down, but he held up his hand and barked, "Let me finish! She is MY wife and I was protecting her!" When he said this, I simply lowered my head as he continued his story. He went on to explain that he had approached the elder on a Sunday morning and told him that he thought that his actions were inappropriate. Probably not knowing what Charles was referring to, the elder, blindsided and dumbfounded by the allegations, apologized to Charles if he felt that he had disrespected him or me in any way. He told the jury that I wrote a letter to the pastor complaining about him, and after a meeting with the pastor and me, Charles was later asked to resign from the deacon board. He left the church in embarrassment.

The questioning then shifted to Samuels. When asked if they were engaged at the time of the incident, he responded that they were not, although Samuels had described herself to the police as his fiancée on March 1st. His explained that they had known each other for years because they both worked for the township school system. On September 1, 2011 he told her that he was looking for someone with whom to have a relationship and eventually marry because he was caring for his four year old granddaughter and needed help. On that same day they went to dinner down by the shore, he said, and while they were on their way there he received a phone call from me. He said he told me that he was in a relationship and that our relationship was over. Since I had rarely ever initiated a call to him during our separation, I wondered why he chose to lie about that. I also wondered, again, that if at any point during his testimony he remembered that he had sworn on the Bible to tell the truth.

At some point during his testimony he 'recalled' (after much prompting from my attorney) that he and I had attempted reconciliation in late October 2011 and that I had actually moved back to our home for five days. Less than a week later, on October 30th, Samuels spent the night with him and never left. It was his sworn testimony that he had filed for divorce from me months prior to her moving in. My attorney asked him several times if he was sure of the timeframe and encouraged him to think before he answered, but Charles insisted that the divorce was filed long before he moved his girlfriend into our home. Jake then produced a copy of our divorce papers, showing that he actually filed for divorce the end of November 2011 - after his girlfriend moved in. When confronted with this lie, he brushed it off, stating that he was an old man and he couldn't remember all the facts.

He must not have felt that he had the opportunity to express everything he wanted to say, because before exiting the stand, he managed to exclaim, "I know that she was attacked!" After he was dismissed, he left the stand looking like a broken old man, head down and shoulders drooped, never looking in my direction or at his children seated behind me. I could only stare at him, finally knowing that that there could never even be a friendship between me and the man with whom I shared a bed, a life, and a family.

Mildred Samuels took the stand the following day. She was calm, soft spoken, and appeared to be a credible person. But when she began her account of the events of March 1st, I again wondered at times if she too really believed what she was saying. There were some truths in her story, but enough omissions and downright lies that it became very obvious that she would be confused when the time came for her cross examination. She did testify that she was sleeping and then awoke suddenly because she thought she heard a noise. Yes, she must have, I thought sardonically, because I rang the doorbell before I entered through the front door. She claimed that when she went downstairs to check on the noise, she thought she saw someone in Chelsea's bedroom, which was one level below the master bedroom. She went back upstairs to get her glasses, and then went back to the bedroom where she thought she had seen someone, walked over to the closet, opened the door and found me hiding there.

Upon cross examination, she was asked if she thought a reasonable person, upon hearing a noise in one of the bedrooms downstairs, would go back upstairs, retrieve their glasses, walk in the room where they thought they saw someone, open the closet door and confront the would-be intruder if they were alone in the house. Even if she thought that her boyfriend had come home, why would he be in the closet? She also testified that when she confronted me, we exchanged words, and then I went downstairs toward the front door. At that point, she went back upstairs to get her phone to call her boyfriend and/or the police. She was on her way downstairs, she continued, and on the second or third step from the bottom, I suddenly appeared and hit her on the top of her head with a "weapon", causing blood to spurt everywhere. She claimed that she did not see me, even though she previously said that I was directly in front of her when I hit her.

In the police report, her story was different. She said then that I must have had the wrench hidden outside, and that I rushed out the front door, retrieved it, ran upstairs, and hit her on the head, unprovoked. That was the statement that led to my burglary charge. The police acknowledged that when I went to the house to get my belongings, I did not expect anyone to be there, since I went in the early afternoon when Charles and Samuels would have normally been at work. That meant that I did not go into the home with any intent of committing a crime. But because she told the police that I walked out the door and came back in with a weapon, it then became grounds for a burglary charge. She had clearly forgotten what she said to the police originally, because on the stand she told the truth; she said I did not leave the house, I went downstairs, and then I headed back upstairs.

She continued that as she was heading downstairs, I hit her on top of her head with a weapon from my vantage point at the bottom of the stairs in the living room. This blow caused blood to spurt all over the steps. She repeated that she did not see me coming. My attorney asked her to explain how was it possible for me to stand in front of her, at the bottom of the stairs, and hit her so hard that blood would "gush everywhere", when the police found absolutely no evidence of blood on the steps. Additionally, for her explanation to make sense, I would have to be at least seven feet tall.

Her police report also stated that she was hit two or four times with the wrench before she was able to forcibly get it from me. We then struggled and I wrestled it from her. At some point, I also attempted to assault her with a marble kick-plate that was between the living room and the kitchen. In the doctor's report that my attorney pulled from the discovery, Samuels originally claimed that she fell down the stairs but did not pass out. In her second interview with the police, she claimed she did not fall.

I admit that at first I did not understand the implication of her two conflicting stories. On cross examination, however, it was established that after she spoke to Charles that day at the hospital, they decided to change her story to say that she did not fall. In doing so, she could claim that the cut on her head was from the wrench and not the fall.

Her original claim that she was hit with the weapon two to four times became grossly exaggerated in court. She now claimed that she was hit six to eight times. When asked about the discrepancy, she said that when she got home from the hospital, she counted the bruises on her body, which is how she knew that she was hit six to eight times. According to her new story, the bruises were not caused from us falling down the stairs, but from the blows from the weapon. She also stated emphatically that she had her cell phone in her hand during the entire struggle. My attorney asked her several times how it was possible that she could have been in a struggle for her life, during which she was able to forcibly take an eighteen inch wrench from me several times, and manage to hit me with it, all while maintaining her grasp on her cell phone. She answered that she wasn't sure, but "That was what happened."

Samuels also admitted that she and Charles were not engaged at the time, even though she had referred to him as her fiancé when she spoke to the police.

"When did you get married?" my attorney asked.

"On March 7th, 2012," she replied softly.

"When did you and Mr. Hale *decide* to get married?"

"I'm not sure."

Jake handed her a copy of their marriage license and asked her to read the date that she and Charles applied to be married.

"March 2nd," she read, her voice nearly inaudible.

Jake looked around the courtroom and reminded everyone that the incident occurred on March 1st.

"Did you and Mr. Hale decide to get married immediately so that it would look worse for Victoria Hale?"

The room was hushed as we awaited her response. She did not answer, so Jake repeated his question.

"Did you and Mr. Hale decide to get married immediately so that it would look worse for Victoria Hale?"

"Yes."

The prosecutor rested after four days of presenting his case. As I listened to the testimonies, I realized that based on their lies, Charles and Mildred Samuels were completely determined to send me to prison for the rest of my life. I was very afraid. I wondered over and over whom the jury would believe. I knew that they were lying, and I felt that Jake was able to show the court that this was a conspiracy, but could the jury actually see it? I had never met Samuels before that day on March 1st, 2012. However, she claimed that she had met me in our old church when my youngest daughter was born, more than twenty years before. I had no idea about her honesty or character until I read the police report and heard her testimony. I was told that she claimed to be a devout Christian, so I was as surprised by her testimony as I was by her moving into my home while I was still married to Charles.

I couldn't help but wonder: after everything Charles had done to hurt me, would I turn my back on him if he ever needed my help? I knew beyond the shadow of a doubt that were he in trouble, I would help him. I could not imagine lying and conspiring to harm him. I would be there for him, not because I wanted or even believed that we could be friends, but because of the years we had together, and the fact that he is the father of our children. I truly believe that if I hurt him, I hurt my children as well. During the trial proceedings, a mutual friend of ours told me that he asked her if she thought he should try to help me, *merely* because we had been married for thirty years. At that point, she ended all communication with him. Even when I realized that he worked so hard to put me in prison, I had still hoped that in the end he would have told the truth.

My witnesses consisted of four people who knew both Charles and me for a long time, but were willing to be character witnesses for me. They were each asked how long they knew me and questioned about my character. "Does the fact that she is charged with these crimes change your opinion of her in any way?" Each of them answered, "No." They told the court about my character and the person they knew me to be. It felt good to hear what they had to say after days of listening to the police, Charles, and Samuels testifying that I was a monster. Amanda drove in from Maryland that afternoon to be questioned about my character for less than ten minutes. My former co-worker, whom I had mentored several years before, also volunteered as another witness on my behalf. Charles's niece, Skye, flew in from Atlanta on the day before her testimony, and then caught a flight back home a few hours later. My fourth witness was the senior pastor of our former church.

I was the last person to take the stand. I told my story as clearly and honestly as I could. Upon cross-examination, the prosecutor tried to get me angry, with no success. There was very little emotion left in me.

"Why did you try to reconcile when you did? You did it because you found out that he was seeing someone else, didn't you?"

Charles and I both knew that to be a lie. I tried to reconcile because Charles told me that he was finally seeing a therapist. He had appeared to be a kinder, gentler person to me at that time. I believed that the years of our separation had changed him. One day after babysitting with his granddaughter, I began to feel sympathy for her and decided to help him care for her. I had also just celebrated my fifty-eighth birthday and I had begun to weaken under his constant pressure to reconcile. We were older now—Charles would be sixty-two years old in a matter of months. I thought about our legacy, about our children and our grandchildren. Even though I knew that our children were adamant about us not getting back together, I wanted to try once more. I had ignored his pursuits for three years, but the fact that he was seeing a therapist convinced me to come to the decision to try once more.

The defense rested after I testified, and the jury was excused so that the judge could listen to any additional motions from the attorneys. My attorney moved again that the burglary charge be dismissed, because by Samuels' sworn testimony, she retracted her statement to the police and stated under oath that I did not leave the house to get the weapon. The judge and prosecutor agreed to dismiss that charge.

It was then established that her injury was neither severe nor was it ever life threatening. The judge decided to give the jury two options, should they not want to consider the "Assault with a Deadly Weapon" charge. Of the two additional assault charges that were added, one carried a lesser penalty, while the other was a misdemeanor. I listened to all this, believing that my attorneys were looking out for my best interests. I was too numb to even hope for any favorable outcome by then. I knew in my heart that I had an army of warriors praying for me because I did not have the strength to pray for myself.

My attorney gave his closing arguments in which he included thirty-one clear points why the charges were false. He reiterated the blatant lies that were told to the authorities and to the court, and he recounted the incident the way it actually happened. Next, the prosecutor spoke about Samuels' injury. He painted me as a jealous, angry woman because Charles was with someone else. At times, I looked back at my children and saw the tears in their eyes.

The judge then spent a long time explaining to the jury each individual charge as it related to the law. He explained what reasonable doubt was and what it was not, and then he gave the jury a written explanation of what he had just said. He cautioned them again not to discuss the case among themselves or with anyone else. Deliberation would begin the following morning.

As I left my son's home for court on that last day, I thought of myself just about a year and a half ago. I thought back even further to a much happier time, before I ever met Charles, and cried when I remembered the mistakes I made in trying to cope with his abuse. I wondered if this was the last time that I would ever see this home, or even the outside world. My children had pampered me during the months I stayed with them and I was very grateful. I never revealed how afraid I was and neither did any of them. They all tried to encourage me that justice would be served, and while I agreed outwardly, I was still very afraid. I thought of Chelsea and how this must be tearing her apart, as since she was the only offspring of Charles and myself. I thought of my daughter Shelby, her husband, and my two amazing granddaughters. I thought of my firstborn Martin, who never failed to tell me how much he loved me, and who I knew prayed for me every day. I thought of his children, my Norwegian grandchildren who I saw very rarely. And I could only imagine how my mother grieved during this time. We had gotten very close over the years and I realized how much I had inherited from her. I did have a lot to live for after all.

In the courtroom the following morning, I listened closely to the judge as he gave the final charge and looked at the people who would now determine my fate. Jake had told me the night before that he needed to fly back to Atlanta because of an emergency, but he could be reached by phone. My other attorney, sat next to me and would squeeze my hand from time to time, when he sensed that I might be coming unglued. Christian and Kourtney were the only ones with me today since we did not know how long the jury would deliberate.

We were eventually dismissed when the jury began their deliberation. We sat outside the courtroom and I watched my son send countless texts to the dozens of family and friends to whom he faithfully promised to keep informed every hour on the hour. It was then that I thought about my sister, because I knew that she was interceding for me in heaven.

We were called into the courtroom after an hour because the jury had a request. They wanted a map of the streets by my house. I had previously told the court that I parked my car on the next block when I went to the house that day to get my things, because I did not want the neighbors to tell Charles that I was at the house. I preferred that he did not know that I came by and got them since he refused all of my past requests to send them to me. However, the prosecutor had argued that I had unlawful intentions, which was why I "hid" my car. The jury wanted to get to the bottom of this issue by locating exactly where I had parked in relation to the house.

Unfortunately, their request was denied, because a map was not originally placed into evidence by the defense or prosecution. They filed out of the courtroom once again and continued their deliberation. We were called in once more when the jury had another request: they wanted transcripts of both my and Samuels' testimonies. They were brought back into the courtroom, and the judge explained that there were no written transcripts, but there were tapes of both our testimonies. He explained that the testimonies were probably over six hours long. The jury decided to take that under advisement and said they would make a decision after lunch if they needed the tapes. We broke for lunch, but soon we received word that they did not need them after all.

During the afternoon break, Christian and I went to a nearby coffee shop to get a cup of coffee. Even though I had not eaten anything all day, I still was not hungry. However, I was beginning to feel drained, as I had barely slept a wink since the trial started. As soon as I got my coffee, my attorney called me. I answered my phone with shaking hands.

"The jury is back."

"Do they have another question or do they have a verdict?" I asked nervously.

"They have a verdict."

I looked at Christian trembling, and told him what I had just heard. We headed slowly back upstairs to the courtroom to take our positions. He immediately texted as many people as he could to let them know that the jury had a verdict and that we were on our way back to the courtroom to hear it. Many of my friends and family had planned on coming to the court the following day; we did not expect such a quick decision. I tried to remember what I had read in the past—did a quick deliberation mean a decision of innocence or guilt? Was this even considered a quick deliberation? The past two weeks had been probably the longest of my life. I sat next to my attorney and waited until the officer announced that the jury was entering. Like we had done so many times before, we stood until they entered the courtroom and took their seats. I tried to read their faces as they settled into their seats. I had heard somewhere that if the jury smiled or looked the defendant in the eye, that usually signaled a 'not guilty' verdict. I was entirely too nervous to look at them for long, however, and simply bowed my head and waited for the judge to speak.

"Madam fore-person, do you have a verdict?"

The juror in the front row to the far left stood and replied, "Yes, Your Honor."

"And is the verdict unanimous?"

"Yes, Your Honor."

"On the charge of Aggravated Assault, how do you find the defendant?"

"Not guilty."

My hands began to tremble, and then my whole body began to shake uncontrollably. I dared to look up at the jury for the second time since they came into the courtroom.

I heard a far-away voice ask, "On the charge of possession of a deadly weapon, how do you find the defendant?"

"Not guilty."

"On the charge of assault with a deadly weapon, how do you find the defendant?"

"Not guilty."

I have no idea what the judge said afterward. I looked at the jury, most of who were smiling at me, and tearfully mouthed, "Thank you!" I hugged my attorney and bawled loud ugly tears, thanking him profusely. After I regained my composure, I walked out of the courtroom, and Christian and I hugged for a long time. He continued texting everyone while I started to tell the people milling around what God had just done for me. I was laughing and crying at the same time, and I just could not stop myself.

We eventually left the courthouse, and once we got to the end of the block, Christian asked me to put down my purse. I asked him why, but he just asked me again and this time I obeyed. He then hugged me and we both began crying on the street again, not caring what passersby thought.

I did not want to let him go. I was weak. We had all been to hell and back—through my struggles with alcohol, my attempted suicide, my fourteen months in jail—and now, my freedom. I finally felt safe. I was finally free. While we were still hugging, I felt someone tap me on the shoulder. I turned around and saw one of the jurors smiling at me. I smiled back at her through my tears and noticed that her eyes were also wet.

"I wish you all the best, Victoria," she said sincerely. "You've certainly been through a lot."

"Thank you," I whispered, and she hugged me as well. She patted my back and then released me, smiling at me before walking away. Christian and I slowly headed back to his car, laughing and crying all the way, thanking God that the nightmare was finally over. My phone kept buzzing in my pocket, alerting me to all of the text messages that were coming in, but I ignored them all, just for a little while. All I could hear were the iconic words of Dr. Martin Luther King ringing in my ears: *"Free at last, free at last, thank God Almighty, I'm free at last!"*

All truths are easy to understand once they are discovered; the point is to discover them.
Galileo